DREAM LOVER

Leander escaped farther into her fantasy world. A delightful warmth such as she had never experienced spread from the area of her heart. A faceless, black-haired man had come to take her away. He murmured in a midnight voice that he wanted her, needed her, would love her always. Mesmerized by the velvety words of the tall, olive-skinned man in her dream, she longed to draw closer to whatever was infusing her body with delicious heat, was bringing surcease to her aching, sorrowing heart . . .

Sometime in the dark of night, gentle lips bestowed kisses upon black curls, and as if to answer an unspoken demand, Leander turned her delicate face up toward the questing mouth.

"*Querida,*" Justin whispered. "You are mine now forever . . ."

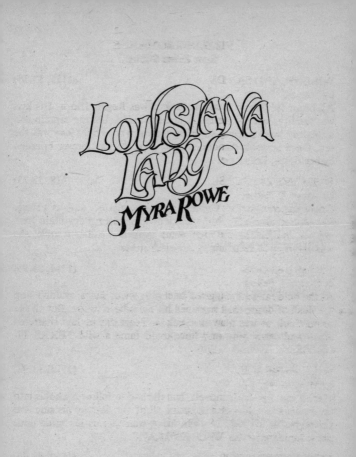

LOUISIANA LADY

MYRA ROWE

ZEBRA BOOKS
KENSINGTON PUBLISHING CORP.

ZEBRA BOOKS

are published by

Kensington Publishing Corp.
475 Park Avenue South
New York, NY 10016

First printing: November 1986

Printed in the United States of America

To the supreme, earthly influences in my life: my mother, who taught me to read, revere the written word, and believe all goals possible; my husband, who has been my romantic hero since high school days and who never falters in sharing my dreams; and our four children, who have led me to see that love, joy, and pain can be made visible, even viable.

Prologue

Her heartbeat thumping in her ears, Leander Ondine pressed her back closer against the inside of the
hollow tree and tried to make herself even smaller. She
did not try to identify the animal scent some nocturnal
visitor had left behind. Nor did she give thought to the
displaced soil beneath her feet or to the cobwebs
fingering her black braids there in the afternoon's eerie
shadows. In one hand, she clutched a roll of vellum; in
the other, a thin piece of charcoal.

The dead oak, standing among several others between Leander's home in the distance and the Mississippi River before her, had often served the lonely,
imaginative ten-year-old as the turret of a castle, the
hold of a pirate's ship, and the secret bower of a fairy
godmother. But today—October 1, 1769—the familiar
hiding place wore no airs of childhood fancies. It was a
true refuge. It prevented the Spanish soldiers of Louisiana from finding the only child of the Frenchman they
had sailed upriver from New Orleans to arrest.

"Leander Ondine!" called a deep voice so near the

7

tree that the hidden girl flinched and suffered a new attack of goosebumps. "Come on, men," it said after footsteps crunching upon fallen leaves paused close by.

From within the darkened hollow, Leander spied black boots with silver chains arching over the insteps and held her breath. Determined little teeth imprisoned her traitorous bottom lip and forbade its trembling. Through the soles of her shoes, her feet sought a firmer hold on the curiously soft earth carpeted with rotting leaves and debris. She tried to concentrate on the pungent smell of the rich soil beneath her and not on the sickening taste of fear in her mouth.

The alien boots tramped out of sight while the man's voice continued in ever-fading tones. "We've searched most of the afternoon, and there's not a trace of the imp. She must have wandered off into the woods to sketch, just as our friend Grinot told us she was prone to do. It is obvious that the slaves won't help us find her. The soldiers staying behind in the house can catch her when she gets hungry and wanders home. We need to be on our way before dark or Governor O'Reilly will have our heads along with that of the traitorous Etienne Ondine."

Another voice lifted to answer. "You're right, Lieutenant. Mayhap we should stop by that outlandish houseboat we passed downriver. The old one-eyed man might have seen her."

The men's conversation sifted back to Leander like something out of a nightmare. Surely the Grinot mentioned could not be Felix Grinot, overseer at Beaux Rives. Felix had left for New Orleans earlier in the week. But why would he be discussing anyone from the plantation with the despicable Spaniards? New fears attacked her, but she buried them. No, it couldn't have been Felix. Grinot was not an uncommon name among the Frenchmen living in Spanish Louisiana. Having come with Etienne and his bride to establish Beaux Rives thirteen years earlier, Felix was her father's friend as well as his overseer.

Other words haunted her then. Would they bully Dom, the ex-sailor tied up beside the southerly banks of Beaux Rives for the past month? When he had espied Leander and Fleur peeping at him from the woods, the old Britisher had invited them aboard his floating home. The man with the awesome black patch over one eye had delighted the giggling girls with stories of his days at sea. Leander had returned again and again, somehow drawn to the man old enough to be the grandfather she never had. Upon meeting Dom, even the cautious Jabbo had finally relented and approved his young mistress's new friend.

Leander recalled that earlier in the afternoon, she had heard Fleur, the slave Sheeva's granddaughter from a neighboring plantation, adding her timid calls to those of the Spaniards. But she hadn't answered her occasional playmate any quicker than she had the others.

More voices and footsteps, farther away. Leander's teeth released their hold on her bottom lip, but her heart still wrenched. She visualized the soldiers walking down the steep path to the landing pier that, until this day, had served Beaux Rives in grand manner ever since she could remember. For it to be receiving the farewell step of the founder and owner of the large plantation fronting the west bank of the Mississippi seemed absurd to his daughter, not at all in keeping with the natural order of things.

Since her mother's death from swamp fever over a year ago, Leander had tried to reach through the alcoholic haze her father seemed to prefer to reality. But Etienne Ondine had closed his eyes to the needs of the grief-stricken girl who so resembled his beautiful Violette and plunged down a road leading inevitably to disaster. No longer did he view his mansion and vast acreage as "beautiful dreams." No longer did his dark eyes sparkle when he talked of "tomorrow." It was as if he had no desire to inhabit a world minus the pansy-eyed bride who had traveled with him from France to Louisiana in 1755.

Echoing creaks and groans of the ship, mixed with the barked orders of the Spanish crew, told Leander there inside the tree that the vessel was moving downstream toward New Orleans. She tried not to imagine what her father must be thinking or feeling. The lump in her throat doubled. Did they have his hands bound? Was his handsome head lowered?

For a day which had started out in the finest way, Leander reflected, it had turned into one of terror. When she had crept from the two-story mansion that morning after breakfast, no one was stirring except Sheeva. The motherly slave had smiled to learn what her little mistress was planning for the autumn day. Uttering the usual cautions about snakes and alligators, she had added a hunk of cheese and a crust of bread to the excited girl's treasures: a roll of vellum with one clean side and some sharpened pieces of burned wood.

"I saw a snow goose on the bayou deep in the woods yesterday," Leander had confided as she prepared to leave Sheeva. "He must have gotten lost from his flock. I'm hoping he hasn't already joined them and flown up North so that I can sketch him."

"Don't you think you ought to wait to tell Jabbo what you're up to?" Sheeva had warned, her round face solemn. "He'll be coming from the quarters to eat soon." Dark eyes squinted toward the row of small houses set even farther from the mansion than the overseer's neat house.

"He'll know where I am," Leander had remarked, pursing her lips in annoyance. "I don't need him dogging my tracks every minute. I'm no longer a baby, Sheeva." Envisioning the giant black man whose assigned task since she could remember was to keep her from harm when she was outside, she frowned prettily. "Tell Jabbo he need not come blundering after me and scaring away the goose. If he wants to find me, he knows how to signal." And with those orders, she had rushed to find the snow goose.

That her father's warnings might come to pass that very day had never occurred to Leander. Only when she had wandered toward the house after her morning of glorious sketching and chasing orange butterflies had she glimpsed the ship. It was then that she had scooted into the hollow tree.

Afraid to venture from her hiding place until dark, Leander hunted for something to think of other than the recurring pictures of Etienne at that moment. She pulled up the memory of the last time she had seen him. He had called her into the library the previous night to tell her that soldiers might be coming to arrest him soon, and that if they did, Jabbo and she must keep out of sight. Though tempted for a brief moment to fling herself upon his chest and let her questions and fears pour forth, she had kept her stance before the cold fireplace and listened, her small face solemn, her intelligent eyes attentive. Over the past year, Etienne had rebuffed her attempts to cling to him so effectively that she sometimes felt older than the man lolling on the settee before her, tossing off brandy as though it were watered wine.

One part of her mind had noted when she entered the room that the tip of a roll of vellum peeped from the ornate umbrella stand of wrought iron near the door. Even Etienne's frequent states of inebriation since his wife's death had not stopped his habit of sticking discarded rolls of paper and vellum in the holder for his daughter's use. There had been a time, Leander reflected while waiting to learn the reason her father had sent for her, when he had shown as much pride in her ability to sketch as had her tutor and her mother. Back then, she had found goodly supplies of fresh paper to supplement the castoffs found in the flared cylinder. Etienne had stayed closer to home in those days and had left less of his business to the overseer Felix, thus finding more discards for his daughter's use.

Leander had forced her mind to concentrate on her father's ramblings, squelching the joyful thought that on the morrow, for the first time in weeks, she would be able to spend a day in the forest drawing. Only through practice over the past months had she learned to control her tendency to speak her thoughts the minute they flashed into mind. Such outbursts had displeased her father, though, and she wanted nothing so much as to find favor on that beloved, handsome face. She waited with an outward composure that almost any adult could have envied.

"The Spanish dogs will see that I die as a traitor," Etienne had announced in that mocking tone he often took when drinking heavily. "But Jabbo will look after you, Leander. He gave me his word when I bought him the year after you were born. Swore it on the soul of his heathen mother, the poor suffering devil did. I've never regretted putting my faith in him, and you should always do the same. And Beaux Rives will always be yours. King Louis signed the papers himself, and no Spanish bastard can ignore the wording, even if he tries. 'Forever to Etienne Durocque Ondine and his heirs' he wrote in his own royal hand. That carries weight with any who can read." A glimmer of some cast-off dream sparked dark eyes for a moment, then faded into bleakness.

To hold back unwanted tears, Leander had blinked hard and fast. Etienne's face looked like that of a wronged child, and she had clenched her fists to keep from running to throw her arms around him—and not for her own comfort. How could the Spaniards mistreat a man so obviously kind-hearted and sincere? Could he help it if he were a Frenchman through and through, one unable to accept the hated flag of the Spanish any more than he could accept the death of his beloved wife? Had he not told her a thousand times how unfair it was that colonists in Louisiana were told that they no longer were Frenchmen simply because of some blundering capitulation between European monarchs?

Europe's problems did not belong in New France, Etienne would proclaim to the big-eyed little girl when he chose to allow her in his presence on his infrequent stays at home. The fleur-de-lis had continued to fly over the Place d'Armes in the capital of New Orleans until two months ago, he had told her again and again that autumn. Wasn't that sign enough that even the yellow-livered Spanish Governor Ulloa had at first recognized as legitimate the colonists' demand to remain under French rule?

For the past two years, Etienne Ondine and his fellow disgruntled colonists had petitioned for the return of Louisiana to the French, had even sent the respected merchant Jean Milhet to Paris to bend the ear of the king. Reports of Milhet's failures were both unbelievable and unacceptable to Etienne and the other conspirators—and thus to Leander. Since the death of her mother, her father had become her world. What might merely annoy or irritate him sent her into paroxysms of agony.

"Ever since the hired soldier from Ireland marched ashore with two thousand armed soldiers in August and hoisted the despicable tri-color on the parade grounds in front of the St. Louis Cathedral, we true Frenchmen have had our days numbered. O'Reilly is worse than the first pitiful excuse for a governor— Ulloa. O'Reilly is no Spanish governor. He and his hired soldiers are thieves and will yet be murderers," Etienne raved in between great gulps. He raised his glass to inspect the remaining brandy in the candle-light before going on in gloating fashion. "Gladly I shall lay down my head as a true patriot. Never let anyone tell you that I begged for mercy." With great care, he straightened his shoulders and smiled crookedly at the little girl staring at him with open adoration. Dark eyes focusing on her critically, he asked in a new vein, "Why are you dressed like that?"

Leander looked down at the homespun pants and shirt, the type of garments she had worn for the past month. Etienne had been home for part of that time. Had he never before looked at her? With a careless flip of long braids designed to hide her hurt, she replied, "I outgrew my dresses and Sheeva made these for me from what she had on hand. She said she had asked you to bring a seamstress and some goods home from New Orleans but that you keep forgetting." When he continued to frown at her, she fidgeted where she stood on the brick hearth and went on. "I don't mind, Papa, really I don't. Ever since the tutor left in the spring, I spend so much time riding Thunder and exploring in the woods that skirts would just be a bother. Sheeva says you might not have enough money to—"

"What does an old black woman know? There is more than enough to replace your clothing with something suitable for the young heiress to a plantation of two thousand arpents," Etienne broke in harshly. "When I returned from New Orleans the other day, I instructed Jabbo to hide the gold from this year's harvest and sales of horses," he said in a low voice heavy with some emotion she did not understand. "I'll arrange for another tutor, and I'll contact a seamstress . . . soon. If your mother's brother in English Landing had not succumbed last year to the same fever as she, I would have sent you to study and grow up with Felicity. For your cousin to have to put up with that shrew of a stepmother is bad enough, but for you to share the ordeal seems to be no answer at all. That my precious Violette's image should be clothed as a slave's ragamuffin boy . . ." His chin sank upon his chest for an instant, his eyes hidden behind an opened palm, his mouth drawn down as though in pain. A shuddering sigh filled the dimly lighted room, pricking at the raw spots in Leander's young heart.

"I don't want to leave Beaux Rives, Papa," Leander assured the shabbily dressed man, taking a step toward him in spite of her resolve to keep her distance. "I wouldn't like living in a town, and I don't like the way Felicity always treats me like I'm a baby. I'm almost eleven, and I'm only two years behind her. Besides, I don't care for Aunt Maurine any more than you do." She was close enough to touch the bowed head but didn't. "I'm better off here with Jabbo and Sheeva . . . and you."

Averting his eyes from those troubled violet ones watching him from beneath thick black lashes, Etienne recovered, quaffed the contents of his glass, and rose, a new mood upon his face as he walked unsteadily toward a sparkling collection of crystal decanters and matching glasses on a nearby table. "You're not a baby, Leander. You're a bright girl, wise beyond your tender years," he said over his shoulder. "Someday you will be able to take what I have left you and show the world what it really means to be the daughter of Violette and Etienne Ondine, true French patriots. The dreams we sought here can become yours."

Leander heard the old lilt creep into Etienne's last words and half smiled. When he cocked his head as he was doing and smiled beyond her shoulder in that secretive way, she could almost imagine that her beautiful mother were yet alive and had entered the room. So seldom did he talk to her of anything but his hatred

16

of the Spanish that she could not fight down the little rush of warmth in her heart. Surely all that he had told her was no more than a new version of the usual, jumbled musings. Sheeva often consoled her with assurances that such unsettling talk came from the alcohol rather than the man. She sighed. There was so much to understand now that Papa kept insisting that she was no longer a child. But hadn't he just called her "bright" and "wise beyond her years?" She perked up.

Even as Leander took a light step toward him, Etienne's smile faded, dousing the spurt of hope lifting her spirit, freezing her in place.

All color and life vanished from the cultured tones as quickly as they had come, and he added almost in sotto voce, "There was something else I meant to tell you." The hand not holding the glass sawed at the air as if in frantic search. ". . . but it escapes me now. Mayhap I will remember it tomorrow." The hand, seemingly drained of purpose, moved to his forehead and pressed against its noble arch. "Tomorrow, yes, I'll take this up with you again on the morrow. Go to bed. I am weary of talk." Seemingly unaware that his only child did not vanish with his last slurred syllable, Etienne poured from a bulb-shaped decanter into his glass with little erratic scrapes and clangs of bell-like tones, never glancing her way again as she ran from the room.

Leander opened her eyes to reality there inside the tree. She stuck the charcoal and roll of vellum in a niche level with her shoulder and stooped to peer outside. Twilight had slipped up on her while she relived the last time with her father. A hush reigned. From the thick stand of trees downriver, she heard the demanding "Who-Who-o-o?" of an owl. Jabbo's black face came to mind, and she smiled. With caution, she darted from her hiding place and raced through the familiar forest. A second owl call guided her.

Chapter One

Almost four years after the slave Jabbo helped her elude the Spanish soldiers and seek refuge on Dom Wilding's dilapidated houseboat, Leander Ondine sat on its deck fishing. That spring morning of 1772 seemed full of promise — all sparkly and new-washed. She sucked in a noisy sniff of the familiar scents of river water, rotting damp wood, fish — both alive and dead — and let it out with the satisfaction of a fourteen-year-old free of duties. From the eastern bank of the Mississippi, where the boat had been moored since the night of escape, drifted a whiff of honeysuckle and yellow jasmine. And that time when the girl cocked back her head and breathed in, she smiled.

Black braids tucked up beneath a sailor's navy cap, thin legs and arms encased in boys' breeches and shirt, Leander angled her pole against the low guard rail and lay back upon the rough planks. A grimy, bare foot waved contentedly from where one leg rested on the propped-up knee of the other. Through graceful, slitted fingers, she peeped at the clouds sailing overhead in their sea of blue and let her mind skip and play. Lost in the war she watched overhead between herds of fluffy-maned horses and what had to be a fierce-looking Indian chief in flowing headdress, Leander didn't notice that the ship she had seen earlier was no longer out in the middle of the Mississippi. The slap of waves upon the sides of the log barge invaded her daydreams; the sudden rocking and rolling of the deck dislodged her fishing pole.

Leander jumped to her feet, doubly angered at what she saw. The ship threatening the houseboat kept heading toward her, and it was no ordinary ship. The Spanish tri-color flapped in the breeze.

"Keep away, you lousy Spaniards!" she yelled, shaking a small fist at the impendent vessel. She spread her legs to keep her balance on the rocking deck. "You have no right to be at English Landing. Stay on your own side of the river." When the ship's course didn't alter and the waves slapped high enough to splash her feet, she screamed, "Mangy Spanish dogs! I hate you! You'll swamp *The Lady*. Steer away!" Both fists then menaced the faces peering down from the tall prow aimed her way.

"That boy is ready to attack us, wouldn't you say?" asked Bernardo de Galvez from his lofty perch. The hat of a Spanish officer sat squarely upon his head. "What is he saying?" His face and voice showed amusement.

"Nothing we would want to hear, I'm sure," remarked his companion, Justin Salvador. Removing his hat, he leaned over to see if the large ship was going to pull away before smashing into the ramshackle houseboat. Bright sunlight fingered the tiny stripe of white streaking his jet hair from left side to crown. Eyes as black as his hair shone with obvious appreciation for the spunk of the youngster jumping up and down in furious dance and shaking angry fists at Bernardo and him. He cupped a hand to an ear and laughed. "We can't hear you," Justin called, his teeth flashing white when a smile lingered on. "Curse us a little louder!"

Leander glared at the grinning faces of the men. They were close enough now that she could see their dark-skinned features, could see that both wore the uniforms of despised Spanish soldiers. The one with the white streak in his hair infuriated her more than the other because he tried to answer her taunts. She stuck out her tongue, crossed her eyes. She poked thumbs in her ears and waggled her fingers. Just before common sense bade her turn to dash ashore for safety, she saw that the ship was slowing, was swerving back toward the main channel.

Now that the danger had passed, the two men seemed to be enjoying her antics even more, laughing so hard as to have to hold onto the rail. Bending over the bucket of fish entrails and scraps from the morning's cleaning, Leander scooped up handfuls and flung them as high as she could, hoping against hope that at least some of the bloody, smelly leavings would reach her targets. "Yellow-livered Spanish mongrels! Stay away from me!" Her eyes blazed her hatred.

"Have you ever seen such amazing eyes?" Justin asked, sidestepping a sailing fish head and grimacing at the odor. "I swear they look more violet than blue."

Chancing another look over the side, the tall Spaniard was rewarded with a loud splat from a tail fin on his smooth, olive cheek. He pulled a handkerchief from a pocket and wiped at the spot. A good-natured grin rode his handsome Castilian face. "The little devil has a man-sized temper, doesn't he? I suspect it's good that the lad seems to know how to be aggressive. One with lashes and eyes like that is bound to run into all kinds of bullies who'll be looking to smash such a pretty face."

"You're right," Bernardo replied with a low chuckle, also dodging fish entrails and leavings but having more success than his friend. "And despite his bad temper, he has a decided look of refinement about him." He craned his neck to look ahead then and saw that the ship was aiming for the center of the wide river. "I'm glad the captain missed both the sandbar downstream as well as the angry boy's home." Turning back to watch the houseboat bob and strain at its lines with lessening force, he sent his gaze to wander beyond to the small settlement on a high bank. "I have wondered if we Spanish might not yet pay dearly for having lost the east bank to the English colonies at that infernal Treaty of Paris. You can see how prosperous this settlement has become over the past several years."

Justin tore his eyes from the sight of the fiery youth still hurling refuse from a bucket and nodded agreement, saying, "I noticed the British fort just downriver at the spot called Baton Rouge seems well fortified and manned. I must confess I was a bit surprised to see redcoats so near New Orleans. Perhaps it's good timing that I'm being discharged right now." A deep, teasing laugh rolled from him. He returned his hat to his head

22

and laid a hand on his friend's arm. They were of like size and age. "Although I will be at your service if you need me, Bernardo. My leg wound from our fight with the Apaches in the West is almost well and will heal soon. I'll be good as new. We've been through too many battles together for—"

"Don't talk nonsense," Bernardo interrupted in a light tone. "You say you have no desire to seek advancement under the Crown as I do. You've earned your discharge and the plantation as well. Our army needs the kind of horses you will raise there, and you will be contributing in a grand way to our cause by supplying our troops with fine animals from those studs your father is sending over from Seville." With one more glance in the direction of English Landing and the swaying houseboat, he said, "We should be reaching your concession within a couple of hours. What name did you say the French traitor had given it before the Crown claimed it for nonpayment of assessments?"

Justin smiled. "He called it Terre Platte. On the map it is south of the plantation named Beaux Rives— 'beautiful dreams'—another belonging to one of the traitors." He, too, threw one more look at the houseboat dwindling in the distance before saying in a musing voice, "I like the fanciful names the French choose for their holdings. I think I will keep the name Terre Platte. 'Flat land' should be a perfect place to raise horses."

"And a family," Bernardo teased.

"First I will have to find a wife."

"You have much to offer, my friend. Remember

there are still others of great beauty back in Seville. Just because—"

"I can't explain it, Bernardo," Justin broke in to say, "but all at once I have a strange feeling that she is already here in Louisiana and that I will know her when I see her." When Bernardo made no comment, he went on. "What about you? You can never hope to follow in your father's shoes and become Viceroy of Mexico without a proper wife."

"Mayhap I will latch on to your 'strange feeling' and expect to find her in Louisiana," his friend replied with a chiding smile and a doubting look in his eyes.

Deep in conversation about their promising futures in Spanish Louisiana, the young men turned to go below.

Her body still tensed with loathing, Leander watched the Spanish ship move upriver through the muddy swirls and ripples. She hadn't been that close to a Spanish soldier since that afternoon she had hidden in the hollow tree at Beaux Rives. Sometimes Spanish ships did pull up at the docks of English Landing, but since *The Lady*'s home was in a cove around the bend, the girl had been spared close contact with their crews. She glanced ashore at the solitary building sitting on a sandy rise at the base of a steep hill. The simply lettered sign hanging from the second-floor porch said Josie's Inn.

Was Josie up and about yet? When it was time to go over for lessons, she would tell the pretty woman all about the near collision. Josie was the only woman with whom the girl had had regular contact since leaving home, and sometimes . . . Leander sighed. What could be keeping Dom and Jabbo this morning?

The coltish girl wandered to plop again upon the deck, her earlier mood dispelled. She seldom relived that awful night when she had hurried through the woods to follow Jabbo's owl calls. Without her willing them to, old memories surfaced and she was once again in the forest with Jabbo heading for Dom's houseboat tied up downriver.

"Come aboard," Dom had said that night in clipped British tones when Jabbo called for him to throw out the boarding plank. "I've been halfway expecting you ever since the bloody Spanish stopped before dark to ask had I seen either one of you. The blokes even rowed over and searched my place. Criminee! I was so hot that they wouldn't take an old salt's word." In the sputtering lantern light, he studied the drawn face of the little girl leaning her head against the giant slave's arm there on his desk. "Old Dom and Jabbo will keep you safe, Leander."

"I wanted to go home but I heard a soldier say that others were staying behind to catch me when I returned," Leander said. A sob tore at her throat. "They've taken my father to shoot him as a traitor. I guess they want to shoot me too."

"Nay, luv," denied Dom, putting on a cheerful face. "They wouldn't harm a child. Come eat the leftovers of that old channel catfish you watched me try to catch last week. I outsmarted the barmy fiend today."

Having been at sea some thirty-odd of his fifty years, and having seen more cruelty than he chose to remember, the one-eyed man confessed to holding a tender spot for the helpless. Ever since Leander had wandered down to where he had tied up *The Lady* and visited with him from the safety of the bank, he had thought more than once that had he married back in his younger days, he could have had a grandchild about her age. Dom had been the eldest in a family of five girls and a boy, and more times than he could recall, he had tended his little sisters in those years before the sea lured him away. When he would have returned to England to live out his final years, he learned that his parents had died and that the sisters had married and scattered. A vivid memory of visits to the port of New Orleans led him to make one more Atlantic crossing two years ago. Dominion Wilding had built his houseboat, bought himself one of the newfangled harmonicas, and become a river rat.

"What is going to happen to her, Jabbo?" Dom asked after Leander had crawled upon the bunk he had pointed out and closed her eyes. He peered up into the black face a full head-and-a-half higher than his own. Dom had his own ideas about slavery, but he had no wish to call attention to himself and ignored the practices of the settlers in Louisiana as best he could. He motioned for Jabbo to take the chair across from him.

"Nothing, if this black man can help it," Jabbo replied, hesitating before daring to sit with a white man, but finally easing upon the chair. He glanced at the apparently sleeping girl, his massive features softening. "Massa Ondine bought me from the block in Algiers fresh from Jamaica. I must'a been some sorry sight. Soon as he claimed me, he told me my lifetime job was to protect his wife and baby girl who wasn't yet a year old."

The old Britisher's one eye could size up a person as well as most people's two. The black man was nearer seven feet tall than six; his huge arms and chest bulged with muscles. Dom had never met Etienne Ondine, but it was his opinion that under ordinary circumstances, the Frenchman would have never assigned such a task to a man as young as Jabbo would have had to have been at the time of purchase. He figured the slave was not much over thirty now. To save time, Dom asked point-blank, "Why did he think you were the man for the job?"

Jabbo studied the weathered sailor in the same manner in which he himself had been scrutinized before answering. "My massa in Jamaica was a Frenchman who had strange ideas about the slaves on his sugar cane plantation. He taught us how to speak and act as he did, but he couldn't stay out of the quarters. When he took my woman, I attacked him and would have killed him if others hadn't pulled me off. He took away my manhood and sold me the next day to a slaver heading for New Orleans." Black eyes filled with remembered pain for a moment. "Massa Ondine learned what happened from the auctioneer and took me to a doctor in New Orleans before he ever brought me to Beaux Rives. I owe the Ondines my life . . . and my sanity. Both of them were mighty good to me. When I would have stepped in to help Massa this morning when the soldiers came, he ordered me to the woods to look after Missy, reminding me that she was my charge, not him. I guess she's stuck with old Jabbo, whether or not she likes it." Thick lips closed into a line of determination. Wide nostrils flared from the deep breath he took.

Leander opened her eyes there in the half-dark room on the houseboat. Before she could ask questions about the puzzling things she had heard Jabbo tell, both men had let out oaths and run outside to the deck.

"Is that a fire?" Leander asked when she joined them and stared in the direction claiming their startled eyes. When neither seemed to notice her presence, she gasped. "Is that Beaux Rives burning?"

Dom put an arm around her trembling shoulders then.

"That has to be the main house, missy," Jabbo answered her, his grieving voice almost too low to hear over the night sounds from the river and the forest. "Guess those soldiers must have given up waiting for you to return."

Within minutes, Dom and Jabbo reeled in the mooring lines and let *The Lady* drift into the tide of the river. Leander stood upon the deck and watched the fiery glow on the far side of the forest for as long as she could see it. Only a sliver of a moon gave off any light. Surely in the darkness it would be all right to give in to tears, she reasoned. Trembling hands slapped at the despised, scalding rivulets on her cheeks.

Jabbo's cheery whistle brought Leander back to the moment. By the time he walked the planks serving as walkways from the shore, she had pushed aside her troubling memories.

"Why were you so long delivering the fish to Josie this morning?" Leander asked when he reached the deck.

"Miss Josie had some chores about the inn for me to do. I chopped some wood and stacked it in the woodshed," Jabbo replied. "What caused the walkways to be so out of line? Why are the poles off the roof?" He motioned to where they lay in a disorderly pile.

Leander told him then, sparing no detail of her fit of anger at the near crash from the Spanish ship. An occasional salty term picked up from Dom spiced her story.

Jabbo calmed her by asking her to climb up on the roof and take the poles when he handed them up. He was going to have to talk with Miss Josie about weeding out from Leander's speech those crude words, he mused. Leander's hatred of anything Spanish had seemed natural at first, but lately he had feared she was letting it grow out of proportion. He might not be what was called literate, Jabbo concluded, but he had learned what havoc hate could cause if allowed to run rampant. Behind the passive face, his mind delved into the problem named Leander.

Josie, the owner of the inn upon the shore, always shared any news she picked up from what she called her "gentlemen callers," plus her views on how Leander should be reared. With advice coming from the "ladies" of her several second-floor rooms, as well as from the madam herself, both Jabbo and Dom sometimes despaired of ever turning the girl into what she was born to be—a Creole young lady destined to control a large river plantation.

The boy's clothing that she wore seemed to have released the hoyden in Leander over the past four years. After the evening meals, if playing games was ruled out, she delighted in listening to the men talk. Dom told dramatic tales from his years at sea and in foreign ports—and at least a dozen versions of how he lost his eye. Jabbo's accounts of life on tropical Jamaica always brought a dreamy look to her expressive face. On those nights when the three seemed to favor private moods, Dom brought out his harmonica, tapping it against the side of a withered thigh before bringing it up in cupped hands to his ready mouth. With his good eye shut and his balding head cocked to one side, he breathed in and out and worked his hands in gentle rhythm, calling up such haunting notes and melodies as to lull all into reverie or peaceful sleep soon afterward.

Dom's rollicking tunes and songs learned from sailors always sent Leander into fits of laughter, even when the bawdy messages escaped her. At such times, Jabbo grinned his own, quieter pleasure. The lilt of the melodies, the body gestures, and the little jig steps Dom used to spice up his act fascinated her. In secret during the daytime, she practiced and brought dropped jaws and shocked expressions to the faces of the men when she gave her own versions. The men exchanged horrified looks while trying to control twitching mouths. When Dom cautioned that such were not meant for the eyes and ears of young ladies, much less for their imitating, she nodded solemnly and mimicked in his words and accent: "For sure, luv. Only for the likes of two chaps such as yourselves would this lass strain her pipes. Criminee! Would ye be thinking I'm daft?"

On clear, balmy days, Leander climbed trees on the banks and hung from her heels, shouting for Dom and Jabbo to watch. She became expert at throwing rocks at designated targets and startled a number of lumbering turtles with volleys upon their shells. Once she stunned a bluejay and rushed to where it lay on the sand, not a whit more surprised than the momentarily helpless bird. When it struggled upright, staggered valiantly on reedy legs, and flew away, Leander sank upon the ground with relief.

Running became a favorite pastime, and always the energetic girl tried to outdo the previous day's performance. After one lesson from Jabbo, she delighted all three when she learned to whistle like a man through two fingers stuck between perfect little teeth. Seasonal nests of birds and squirrels in the trees, ducks and rabbits on the land, fish in the backwaters — all received almost daily visits from the soft-walking, eager-eyed girl. And when the young creatures appeared, she gave detailed reports to the men as to their growth and progress.

Before noon that spring morning of 1772, Dom returned from his trip up the steep hill to the markets in English Landing. In return for the day's fish, he had bargained for needed staples and supplies. Leander met him with her tale of woe, and the two men exchanged long looks of puzzlement. What would they ever do with their charge? What if the soldiers had been some who might have recalled seeing *The Lady* near Beaux Rives that fateful October afternoon and decided to investigate the youngster making such a spectacle?

Dom had allowed Leander the freedom of the wooded bank between Josie's Inn and the houseboat, but he had kept her away from the town beyond the crest of the hill. He never let Jabbo deliver fish in the town, for fear that his unusual size might cause someone to notice and remember him. So long as the old Britisher was unable to find out what action the Spanish officials might take if they located Ondine's daughter, he would continue to keep her and her doting slave from public view.

The next two years brought no more Spanish ships near the houseboat. Her seventeenth birthday coming up in December, her face and body delivering on that earlier promise of startling beauty, Leander no longer asked that summer for news about Beaux Rives. Her pranks became fewer and farther in between. The previous, boiling inner energy had apparently settled into a simmer. She seemed content to explore the red, sandy beach quietly, or to fish or read or loll about the deck when there were no chores for her. And when Dom would shoo her off to Josie in the mornings for tutoring in language, math, and etiquette, she didn't balk as she had at first. She seemed to thrive on the occasional visits with Josie's "ladies." Too often, she shocked Dom and Jabbo with tidbits of information she picked up.

"This morning some of the ladies came into Josie's sitting room so I could practice entertaining at a tea party. Lily told me that Josie doesn't believe that old story about a child's bones being found after the fire at Beaux Rives," Leander announced one night while they were eating. She chewed noisily and waved a piece of fried fish in her hand to emphasize her news. A recent lesson in etiquette from Josie nibbled at her conscience, and she closed her lips and laid the food on her plate.

"Lily might not should be telling what her boss lady says," Jabbo spoke up. More than once Dom or he had taken Josie aside and informed her when her ladies had been too talkative around Leander. Each time Josie had apparently taken action, but the turnover at her place was rather fast, and sometimes a new lady would not have gotten the word. Lily must be new.

"If that overseer Felix Grinot hadn't found them and thought they were yours, would he have buried them alongside . . . ?" Dom's voice dropped. God's blood! Why had he brought up graves? He fingered the ever-present black patch over his sightless eye.

"Oh," Leander said airily, "it doesn't bother me anymore to think of Mama and Papa being buried in the cemetery back home. Dom, I'm glad you told me about Felix's bringing Papa's body home from New Orleans after the bloody Spaniards shot him. I never much liked Felix until after I learned about that. He always seemed to be trying to find fault with Jabbo. But I realize that he must have cared a lot for Papa." Pursed, rosebud lips joined crinkled eyes to paint a picture of deep contemplation before she continued. "And if that had been me burned in the fire, I would have wanted to be lying between them. I never have believed there were any bones." She fixed candid eyes on first one shocked face and then the other. "I think that was what Felix wanted everyone to think so that the soldiers would stop looking for me."

"And why, pray tell, would you be thinking that?" Dom asked. Sometimes the depth and direction of her thoughts knocked him into a spin. For the most part, she laughed and joked like any high-spirited girl—and something nudged at him. Though Leander was still small in size, as she would likely always be, she hadn't been a girl for years now. Jolted at the revelation, Dom thought of the numerous times that summer when this girl-turned-into-young-woman had sat on the deck and stared out at the river for hours. Even when she held paper and charcoal, as often as not she made not a single mark. When he would question her about what she was dreaming about, she would always laugh and give some flippant answer. But he suspected her quick mind whirled with as many hidden thoughts as the muddy river roiled with unseen, treacherous currents.

"I've figured out that this new house Felix has built," she went on after dabbing at her pretty mouth with a napkin in that way Josie had showed her, "is really for me, though I hear it's not so grand as the first one. When I return all grown up at eighteen and can claim my inheritance—only a year-and-a-half away—he will have everything ready for me, and I can turn the house into another mansion. Lily says he must be the best overseer along the river, for she heard one of her gentlemen talking about the huge crops Felix has made the past two years. By the time I can come out of hiding, Beaux Rives will again be one of the finest plantations around here."

34

Having shed the required cap at the first hint of darkness, Leander flipped a thick, black braid behind a slender shoulder and smiled at her two fellow conspirators. Large, pansy-hued eyes within their black, curling frames seemed too wise in the delicate, oval face. Her beauty seemed exotic, out of place in the crude cabin.

"Are we going to play Brag tonight?" Leander asked, once they cleared the clutter from their meal. "I'll get the cards." Her eyes sparkled in the light from the lantern overhead. When neither man answered, she moved to a shelf, saying, "All right, then it'll be dice. We've not played Hazard in a while."

"Not tonight, luv," Dom replied in a voice sounding tired even to him. He heard the clack of her dropping the squared caribou bones with their carved-out dots back on the shelf, the same dice he had bought upon his first visit to a Far East port an age ago. For the first time since he had used his deck of cards and the worn dice to entertain her back during that difficult first winter, Dom wondered if it had been wrong to teach her games of chance. Not that they had ever wagered money — there was none, had he been tempted — but even the writing down and ciphering of scores to keep her knowledge of numbers sharp appeared to him in a tawdry light now. He headed for the deck. "I've too many blasted things to mull over tonight."

Most of the settlers living along the river south of Natchez traveled down its wide path to do their trading at New Orleans. A few of those from the plantations only an hour or so north of English Landing did put in at the small dock from time to time, though the majority chose to stop upriver at Point Thoms on the Spanish western bank. There they could glean nuggets of gossip about their fellow Creoles and learn what was going on in New Orleans. News at English Landing dealt more with King George and his colonists on the Atlantic, dull fare for most of the Louisianians. Cargo ships with their few passengers hitching rides from New Orleans made periodic stops on their way north to Natchez and settlements farther upriver. They sometimes stayed overnight to unload or take on goods, spilling a few bored passengers into the port's stores and bars — even fewer to Josie's Inn. Having just left New Orleans, most of the men had satisfied their lusts and were ready to return to their homes. Thus it was that over the past six years, Dom had been able to hide from knowing eyes the black man and the young woman disguised as a boy.

The majority of the men seeking what Josie's Inn offered came from the British fort a half-hour downriver at Baton Rouge, and they usually came on horses. After leaving them in the livery stable, they clambered down the steep hill path from the town to lose themselves in the delights of drink and flesh. And had a caller wished to tie up even a small craft near the inn, the shallow water and hovering trees of the alcove would have prevented his doing so. No one coveted the houseboat's claim to its spot. With equal indifference, the townspeople seemed to ignore the existence of both Josie's Inn and the strange little house on the raft in front of it.

The next day following Leander's unsettling announcement, Dom, after delivering fish up the hill, stopped to visit with Josie before returning to the houseboat. He had seen Lea—the name Josie, Jabbo, and he used for her in case some astute ear might be tuned that way—ambling from the inn into the trees with a book in her hand. Obviously the morning's lessons were over. Jabbo sat mending fishing nets on *The Lady*'s sunlit deck.

"Josie, I have a feeling our luck is about to run out," Dom said after he savored the first sip of wine from the glass she handed him. They always visited in her spacious, private quarters on the first floor. Opened windows caught the summer breezes from the river. He had learned soon after drifting there on that fateful night that Josie came from a respectable, educated family in Charleston. One of the local merchants had also come from Carolina, and it was he who had caused the handsome woman to build the inn and bring her ladies to the small settlement. Though Dom did not know exactly what their arrangement was, he suspected that it had something to do with mutual need and a special kind of love, or at least respect. At any rate, the buxom, dark-haired woman had been a Godsend to the trio out on the river. She was as smart as she was kindhearted. "Lea won't be able to pass for a boy much longer, even to people traveling out on the river."

Josie let out one of her throaty laughs. "So you've seen those little bumps pushing against her shirts, too." She tucked back a fall of hair striped with silver before pouring herself a measure of wine. Dom had noticed over the years that in the mornings when she met with Leander, Josie wore elegant yet quiet gowns, gowns resembling not at all those bold satin creations he had seen her wear at night in the role of madam. Today she wore a pink-striped cotton with modestly scooped neckline. "Surely you knew when I told you a couple of years back about her running to me to find out about the 'monthlies' that this was coming."

"Aye, but I'm still not ready for it. This summer she seems to be growing up right before my good eye. A beauty on our hands is what we've got, luv. To tell the truth, I don't know for sure I've done the right thing to keep her whereabouts secret from that overseer Grinot—or from that cousin of hers up over the hill. She told me the uncle had been her mother's brother and how she never could abide his second wife, the widow, and her grown son. But I feel right guilty to have kept her from sneaking in a visit with the cousin Felicity. She might need to be making contact with some other young females in her class about now, and that girl is only a couple of years older than Lea." He took several sips of wine and tugged at his eye patch. "Have you heard any more about the widow pushing for marriage between her son and Felicity?"

"That no-account Claude won't ever win that pretty blond stepsister of his. I shudder to think what Felicity's father would have done to him if he had lived to see the way that boy has repaid him for sending him down to New Orleans to be schooled. I never could see how Maurine tricked Arnaud Marchand into marrying her. Even if she hadn't had that half-grown boy from her first marriage, she didn't have much to offer. Talk was that he thought he was getting a mother for his little girl after hers died so young." Josie relaxed against the curved back of the settee and propped her feet on a stool. The room was tastefully furnished, a fitting backdrop for the obviously well-bred woman.

"And now that he's dead, too, this Maurine controls the store. Life deals some tough hands, doesn't it?" Dom didn't even expect an answer, and he didn't get one. Both drank their wine and enjoyed the companionable silence.

"Funny that you should have Felicity on your mind today," Josie said after a while. "I heard last week that one of the plantation owners up close to Beaux Rives stopped at English Landing week or so ago. It seems he spotted Felicity clerking in the store and made several inquiries about who she was. And now I hear he has already returned and called on her. Could be that someone like that might be coming to court her and get her away from Claude and Maurine."

"Do you ever go in their store?" Dom digested what she had told him, having learned over the years that what she reported usually turned out to be the truth. He had stopped being surprised at the way she knew everything about the citizens living above her in the village.

"Not unless I have to," she replied with a grimace. "Claude has been mad at me ever since I threw him out last year for mauling one of my ladies. I can't stand a man who beats up on women. I had just as soon face a coiled snake as look at him." Josie cut her eyes over at the old sailor. "Why?"

"I was just wondering if mayhap you might get a word with Felicity sometimes and hint that you know something about her cousin." At the frown upon the pretty, plump face, he added, "Unless you think that might be a bad idea."

"I'll give it some thought," she countered, picking up the bell from a side table and ringing it. "But it's my thinking that the fewer people who know a secret, the more likely it is to remain a secret."

"Yes'um?" the small young woman asked after she knocked and shuffled into the room, head down, mouth slack. Her face with its café-au-lait coloring wore a pleasant yet vacant look. "I heard the bell."

"Throw-away, please bring some more wine," Josie said.

"More wine?" she echoed. Eyes lifting shyly, she waited until her mistress repeated the request before leaving.

"I'll never know why you put up with that dim-witted Throw-away," Dom said in a low voice. He always felt uncomfortable around the young mulatto. That she still believed Lea to be a boy when signs to the contrary were now so obvious showed how simple she really was.

"You do know. I told you when you first came here how that terrible planter back home who fathered her on one of his slaves told the mother to throw her away. The mother wasn't much kinder by giving her that awful name, but the child never wanted me to change it, even after I took her in and raised her," Josie replied. Then, as if to ward off any talk about her having a kind heart, she pointed out. "Besides, she's good kitchen help. If she didn't earn her keep, I wouldn't still have her around."

Throw-away returned with a carafe of wine and a loaf of bread. She made a childlike curtsy and pre-

40

sented the bread to Dom, saying, "Miss Lily made bread today. This for you."

"Tell her I appreciate it," Dom replied. He was accustomed to having the ladies share the results of their occasional culinary efforts with those on *The Lady*, but he never took such favors for granted.

A partial smile lending life to her face then, Throwaway refilled the glasses and left.

Getting back to their conversation, Dom said, "As for the wisdom in telling Felicity about Lea's being alive and right here at English Landing, you need to be aware that I might not be around all the time. It could be that we'll need someone else to know the facts." A deep sigh followed.

They sipped from their glasses in silence. Both knew without saying that for Josie to be the only white person aware of Leander's existence could prove disastrous, what with her having no social rank or prestige. And no telling what might happen to Jabbo if folks were to learn a slave—neutered or not—had secreted away his beautiful young mistress since she was ten.

Even the last gulp of wine didn't chase away Dom's nagging worries, but he stood to be on his way, saying, "Think about what we might need to be doing over the next year and a half, Josie. Who knows what those Spaniards will do when she shows up and tells who she is? I'm pushing sixty and probably already living on borrowed time. From the way that girl's mind is keening up, she'll take over this game one day soon, and we might all be in trouble if we don't have some countermoves."

"Lea is not that hotheaded and you know it," Josie

chided while she walked with him to the porch. A doting smile on her face, she said, "She's shaping up nicely, Dom, in spite of the way Jabbo and you have spoiled her and let her run wild. I trust her judgment, and you should, too. She's just a budding beauty, full of vinegar and spit and wonder. When the time comes for Lea to take charge of her life, she will be ready."

Somewhat reassured, Dom went on then, the loaf of bread beneath his arm, delighted beyond reason when Lea spotted him and ran across the sand toward him. Not for the first time that summer, he noted that there was something of the grace of a dancer in the way Leander carried her tall slenderness, something both provocative yet innocent. Did she know that even the way she moved no longer suggested a boy?

Chapter Two

On a blustery night the following November, all the loose ends that Dom stewed over began to come together.

"I can't believe you're still alive," the pretty young woman said for the third time since arriving at Josie's kitchen door under cover of twilight. "Leander, you look exactly the way I remember Aunt Violette looked—so fragile, so lovely." She reached to hug her cousin close again before settling back on the chair in the small room, never letting her blue eyes stray from the exquisite face so near. The cousins had visited for nearly an hour, and what she had learned boggled her mind. "How could you have been so brave?"

"Felicity," replied a still shaken Leander, "you're the brave one to sneak down here this evening to see me. If Aunt Maurine or Claude were to—"

"Don't fret," Felicity interrupted with a saucy smile and a toss of golden curls. "They'll never guess that I'm not with Docie and her son trying to find chickens to cook for the dinner we're having tomorrow night.

Docie remembers you and was glad to lead me here, though I must confess she mumbled something fierce about my meeting you at Josie's Inn." She leaned forward, a secretive look about her finely chiseled features. "Maurine seemed pleased that I insisted on going along to help select choice chickens at the farmer's on the edge of town. My fiancé is coming to call and we want to have a grand meal ready for him."

"You're getting married?" Leander burst out. A giggle erupted, sending new dancing lights to her huge eyes. She made a lunge toward her cousin and hugged her again. "No wonder you look so radiant and beautiful! Who is he? Is he handsome? Tell me all about him." Seeing Felicity all grown up after remembering her the past six years as a girl had jolted her. When Dom had told her yesterday that Josie and he had arranged a meeting between the two, Leander had felt a happiness she had not experienced in a long time. At first, the poised young woman in the elegant gown had seemed a stranger. But after the first few words, the two had recaptured that old intimacy.

"He is no stranger to you," Felicity replied. She cocked her head and pursed her lips knowingly. "He owns the plantation north of Beaux Rives."

"Belle Terre?" Leander asked, her mind racing back into childhood. "You're marrying one of the Ferrand boys? Which one—Antoine or Philip? Antoine always seemed to think he was much too grown up to have anything to do with me, even before he left for school in Paris. But Philip isn't much older than you. I remember that I always loved to play with Philip while our parents—"

"No," her cousin broke in to say with an indulgent

smile. "Neither of the sons. I'm marrying Andre, their father."

Leander sank back against her chair in shock and did what she had been trying to break herself from doing. She blurted out the first thought in mind. "But he's old enough to be—"

"And he's rich enough to please Maurine and get me out of that wretched house," Felicity interrupted to point out with a venom Leander recognized. ". . . and away from that despicable son of hers." With suspicious brightness in the blue eyes and a tremble on her lips not so noticeable, she went on. "Leander, I would marry almost anyone to get away before my step-mother forces me to become Claude's wife. Andre is still a fine-looking man, and he is kind to me. He says he needs me, loves me—can you imagine how much I need to hear those words? I may not love him as a fiancée should, but I shall in time. I shall be faithful to him and make him a good wife." Her chin lifted then, and her lovely mouth took on a determined look. Blue eyes searched violet ones for understanding . . . and approval.

Leander made all the proper replies, but inwardly her heart ached. She skipped over the niggling little thought about how important it might be to any orphaned young woman to hear a handsome man say he needed and loved her. Long talks with Josie, plus readings of poetry and romances, had convinced her that she would never marry until she fell madly in love. And if she never met a man who could set her heart on fire, then she would remain single. Never would she resort to marrying for convenience.

Besides, Leander reflected as she half-listened to her

cousin's happy recital, her major goal did not center on marriage. She intended to claim Beaux Rives and turn it into a fitting tribute to her dead mother and father, one which would show the arrogant Spaniards that the French Creoles were the only true citizens of Louisiana. Once she was able to return home, the monies her father had squandered on the ill-fated Conspiracy would no longer flow into channels away from Beaux Rives. He had sought his way to beat the Spaniards . . . and failed. Not she. She would build the grandest mansion, produce the finest crops, obtain the respect of her fellow plantation owners, throw the most elaborate parties — and never, never allow a Spaniard on the sacred soil of Beaux Rives. Lately she had picked up the news that to trade with the English rather than the Spanish irked them, and she had already decided that Beaux Rives would offer no goods to the Spaniards. She did empathize with Felicity's plight, though, and forced a cheerfulness into their conversation about the upcoming marriage.

By the time Felicity had confided the myriad details of her past few years as well as of the approaching wedding, it was time for her to leave. "I must go before that thundercloud we hear crosses the river and dumps on us." She looked around the candlelit room and confided in a half-whisper, "I'm disappointed that Josie's rooms are so plain."

Leander laughed, saying, "The fancy rooms are upstairs. This is one of the servants' rooms behind the kitchen. If you could see Josie's apartment across on the other side of the inn, you would be impressed."

"Doesn't it bother you to have to braid your hair and wear those horrid boy's clothes? And not to be around anyone but . . ." Felicity's voice faltered.

"Not at all," responded Leander. "I've grown accustomed to the breeches and shirts. I'll probably not feel right in petticoats and a dress when the time comes to wear them. As for Josie and her ladies, everyone has been so nice to me that I have never felt I was alone in the world. Dom is sick right now, but Jabbo and he have looked after me well. He had hoped to feel up to coming to meet you." She caught her cousin's hands, dragging her thoughts away from the ailing old man. "How I wish I could be in your wedding next week, the way we always planned. I will be thinking of you and wishing you all kinds of happiness. In a few weeks, I'll be seventeen. And next December when I become eighteen, I'll be coming home. What fun we'll have! We'll be neighbors then. We can both be looking forward to that time, can't we?"

"Yes, oh, yes," Felicity declared, reaching to draw her shawl around her shoulders. The November night was far from warm, and distant thunder was approaching. "I promise never to let on you're alive, and I'll do my best to find out what the Spanish would do to you if you were to show up before you're of age. We'll be spending our honeymoon in New Orleans, and maybe I'll be meeting some of the officials. We don't plan to go to Belle Terre until right before Christmas. Promise me that you'll come to me there the minute you can. You'll be such a stunning beauty by then — not that you aren't already — that every young man in the area will be storming your doors, including my stepsons. Antoine has come home from Paris with a license to practice law, and Philip is their father's right hand about the plantation."

47

When her black-haired cousin tossed her small head and laughed a denial that any bachelors might be interested in her, Felicity gave her one more hug and kiss. She left Throw-away's room and went to join Docie waiting outside with her gangling, teen-aged son.

Leander tucked up her braids and donned the cap before leaving. Jabbo met her when she left the kitchen door soon afterward, his size and blackness blending with the fast-falling night.

"I brought word from Josie," he told her when they moved into the shadow of a tree. "She came over to check on Dom while you were visiting with your cousin, and she sent word for both of us to stay away from *The Lady* until Dom is better."

"Stay away?" Leander repeated, not believing her ears. "Where would we stay?" A roll of thunder from across the river seemed to echo her rising uneasiness.

"I'll sleep in the woodshed out here. Josie sent word that Throw-away is to stay with the other servants and give you her room."

"But why?" Her mind whirled. She had never spent a night off the houseboat since the night they had fled there. "What is wrong with Dom? We should have sent for a doctor. I want to help take care of him." She took a step away from the big man.

"No," Jabbo said, reaching for her arm and spinning her around to face him again. The usually placid black face wore a frightening sternness. "Josie says he now has the rash of the flux fever and that we'll be lucky if we don't catch it. She had it back when she was young and won't be getting it again. There is nothing we can do now but wait until she says it's safe to come aboard."

48

He struggled with some inner emotion, swallowing hard before going on. "We'll both do what she says." When she stared up at him and her mouth moved without sound, he said in a pleading voice, "Don't fight me on this, Missy. Please."

Leander knew then that what she had suspected over the past week was true. Dom had more than the slight fever he had told her about. He was seriously ill. He might die. A slump in both spirit and body forced her to let Jabbo lead her back inside the kitchen. At the big man's direction, Throw-away took Leander's arm then and led her back to the room where she had just had the joyful reunion with Felicity. When the simple-minded mulatto left her alone in the dark, the grief-stricken young woman threw herself facedown on the bed. She wept for the first time since she had watched her home burn that October night.

The only two passengers aboard *The Enterprise*, cargo ship on its way from New Orleans to Illinois, leaned into the wintry winds and climbed up the hill from the dock toward English Landing. Behind them came the slap of wind-driven waves and the sounds of sailors tying up for the night.

"My fiancée and her family aren't expecting me to arrive until the morning," Andre Ferrand told his companion as they neared the boardwalk of the single street. Slight of build but possessing regal posture, Andre would have passed for a man far younger than his fifty-two years. "But I feel sure that Mrs. Marchand will find room for the both of us. I've visited in her home several times this fall, and I know there are plenty of spare bedrooms."

"Isn't there an inn here?" Justin Salvador asked with unaccustomed sharpness, obviously not liking the idea of tagging along with the man to seek shelter from the approaching storm. "The ship's captain was a fool to think that by leaving port early, he could get ahead of this storm. Had he waited until the scheduled sailing time on the morrow, all of us would have been better off."

"You're probably right, Justin," replied the older man. "And if you're determined not to go with me to the Marchand house, you might ask at the bar up ahead about available rooms for rent. The only place that I know of is Josie's Inn below the hill — not exactly a hotel, if you know what I mean. I've heard, however, that it is a far grander place than you would expect to find in such a small port. And no doubt one could rent a room without a companion, if he were so inclined." He laughed then at the sidewise look his companion gave him and added, "Of course, a single man such as you might like to while away a stormy night with an armful to soothe him."

"I might just do that," Justin countered. "I'll be returning to the ship in the morning to go on home to Terre Platte. If you're staying on to visit with your fiancée, I'll likely not see you again until the wedding next week."

They reached the bar then, and Justin turned to shake hands with his friend and fellow plantation owner. He couldn't help but admire the springy steps the older man made as he continued on down the boardwalk. A little flare of jealousy nipped at the young man. He should have already found himself a bride by now and be hurrying to be with her. It had

50

been over four years since he had settled at Terre Platte. With each passing year, he was finding it harder to reconcile himself to the fact that the woman he could love had not been among the numerous ones he had met and socialized with. At first he had been so sure that she was close by and that he would recognize her the moment he met her. Now he wondered at those earlier, fanciful musings.

After a fourth or fifth shot of whiskey, Justin lost count. He entertained morbid thoughts there in the dim barroom. A few locals still nursed half-empty mugs, but the hour was growing late, and their number was dwindling rapidly. Apparently respecting the preoccupied look about the lean face of the stranger with the white streak in his black hair, no one had spoken to him. Not even the bartender had done more than respond to the handsome Spaniard's demands for more drink. Justin drained his glass and asked the way to Josie's Inn, not caring that the man behind the bar cut a sly look his way. What did it matter what others thought, he asked himself as he went out into the night. The rain had come while he was inside, and he entertained the thought that to have changed into his old boots and clothing had been wise. He welcomed the cold splash of drops on his face. A self-accusing smile lifting one side of his generous mouth, he confessed he was more than a little drunk. All he wanted at Josie's was a bed.

He wouldn't be feeling half so sorry for himself, Justin reasoned when he started down the muddy hill toward the lantern lights on the two-story inn, if he hadn't picked up a packet of mail from home while in New Orleans. His father had written from his horse farm just outside Seville that his older son Manuel had fathered a second boy.

At one time, Justin knew that his heart would have pained him to think of Serita's having given birth to a child by another man. But the wound left from his first love's having chosen his older brother over him had long healed. No, what pained him now was that he was already twenty-seven and had not even a bride in mind. His dreams of a life in Louisiana had always included a beautiful wife and children. True, he had met many who could claim the title of beautiful but none who set off more than a primitive spark of desire when he kissed their hands or held them in his arms upon the dance floor. Having once known the exhilaration of that first love, Justin had no wish to wed until he found something akin to it. Already he was finding that to own a plantation with profitable fields of cotton and pastures of fine-bred horses was not enough to fulfill him. He pulled his cloak closer and took another slippery step.

A small sound reached his ears. Was that a puppy whining somewhere close? Justin stopped and shielded slow-focusing eyes with his hands. Even through the pelting rain he saw a pale blur. His love of the small and helpless penetrated both his drunkenness and uncharacteristic mood of self-pity.

"Come here, fella," he called, not surprised to see the puppy creep toward him with head and tail down. Someone must have mistreated him and tossed him into the woods, Justin fumed, reaching to pat the wet little head and tuck the shivering animal inside his cloak.

For a moment, Justin forgot where he was and

where he was headed. But a sailor climbing up the trail at a brisk pace and mumbling a ribald greeting reminded him. Occasionally stumbling into the bushes beside the path but still clutching the puppy, he went on toward the lanterns below.

"Madam gone," the young woman mumbled when Justin pulled the bellcord on the porch and found the door opened for him. "Come in. Wait for one of the ladies."

Justin stepped inside with a noticeable unsteadiness. The puppy wriggled when the dark-skinned young woman helped him out of his cloak. He could see that, despite splotches of mud, the puppy's coat was white, the only marks being finger-width black tips on both floppy ears. Tender fingers traced the unique markings while the small pink tongue searched for something not found on the kind hands.

"Fetch some milk for my puppy," he directed.

Throw-away backed toward the kitchen, returning shortly with a bowl of milk and setting it down on the hearth before the blazing fire. Her eyes joined the gentleman's in watching the little dog lap up the offering.

"Don't bother waiting for anyone else," Justin told the vacantly staring servant. "I only want a room for my puppy and me to sleep in."

Throw-away turned toward the tall, handsome man. "Just to sleep?" Her eyes flicked away, not meeting his.

"Yes, yes," Justin replied impatiently. "Show me to a room with a bed. That's all I want." He fumbled in his pocket for a loose coin, finding one and laying it in her reluctant hand. The warmth of the room was making his head heavier, and he wondered if his eyes would stay open another second. "Isn't there any place I can lie down? I don't care where it is. Just find me a bed." He blinked and swayed, almost losing his footing. "Now, damn it! Can't you see I need to sleep right now?"

Throw-away trembled. Normally she had little contact with the gentlemen callers. But with Josie out on the houseboat tending to Dom . . . The stranger's deep voice and obviously drunken state frightened her. He seemed far more powerful than the usual gentlemen. And the streak of white in the black hair made her wonder if he might be a demon.

"Have one room," she began but seemed to lose her nerve. She looked at the gold coin in her hand.

"Take me to it," Justin ordered. "I must get to sleep."

And so Throw-away, with frightened looks up the deserted stairway and anxious ones toward Josie's empty quarters, led the insistent man through the kitchen to her own room.

"This room for sleeping," she said, bringing the coin up to test it with her teeth. "Already—"

"Fine. Glad it's ready," the handsome Spaniard broke in to say. He wanted no more talk. He didn't wait for her to open the door but did it himself.

". . . the boy Lea is sleeping there." Throw-away found herself finishing her sentence for a slammed door. Still admiring the coin, she returned to her favorite place behind the flour barrels in the pantry and stretched out on the quilt there.

Leander lay in drugged sleep in the darkened room. Earlier, as she lay tossing and turning in her search for release, Lily had come to offer her what she called a sleep elixir. Gratefully Leander had drunk it, sensing that to lie awake all night worrying over Dom would serve no good purpose. The tender-hearted Lily had also brought a satin sleeping gown of hers and stayed until the reluctant young woman had shed her breeches and shirt and put it on. Unbraiding the black hair and brushing it out for her, then pulling up the blankets over the sad-eyed young woman, Lily had put out the candle and left. So lost in a drugged dream world was Leander when the door opened and shut that she never moved.

Dropping his money pouch in a boot and dumping his clothing in a heap in the nearest corner, Justin laid the contented puppy upon the pile and staggered to the pale spot he hoped was the bed. So good. It felt so good to ease his miserable head down onto a pillow. The jagged thought that he had reached a long-sought haven slashed through his fuzzy brain, that he was, somehow, where he belonged.

As if it moved of its own volition, a leaden arm landed on something firm but soft, something Justin well remembered from the past week of amorous nights spent in New Orleans. His head spinning, he tried to lift it and focus his eyes. Tiny cracks around the ill-fitting door let in slices of light from the lantern in the hallway. No. He lowered his misbehaving head again. He must be drunker than even he had thought. That couldn't be a female form lying beside him. He had specifically told that dimwit he wanted only a bed — or had he? His fingers moved to test his suspicions. Yes, that was a firm breast beneath smooth satin. A devastating blackness cheated him of further knowledge.

Leander escaped farther into her fantasy world. A delightful warmth such as she had never experienced spread from the area of her heart. A faceless, black-haired man was telling her that he had been searching for her and had come to take her away. He murmured in a midnight voice that he wanted her, needed her, would love her forever. Mesmerized by the velvety words of the tall, olive-skinned man in her dream, she longed to draw closer to whatever was infusing her body with delicious heat, was bringing surcease to her aching, sorrowing heart. She was no longer alone, no longer an outcast from the mainstream of life. Some-one who loved her was touching her, making her feel ever so special.

Begging, delicate fingers reached out to track up the large ones touching her breast, then the broad supple hand, and on up the well-muscled arm. The satin of her gown whispered beneath the blanket as the sleeping Leander inched toward the source of that masculine limb. The arm slid up to allow the curved body to snuggle against the naked, hard planes of its owner. Next it fitted itself around the slender back and rounded buttocks when the smaller form turned on its side to nestle against the larger lying on its back. The small head found an inviting spot between the bulging shoulder bone and massive rib cage. The cloud of fragrant black hair claimed space upon that arm and the broad shoulder, spilling its silkiness over onto the furred chest and teasing at the strong jaw and chin, relaxed now in deep sleep.

Some time in the dark of night, gentle lips bestowed kisses upon black curls hiding the face so near. As if in answer to an unspoken demand, the delicate face turned toward the questing mouth. Soft lips of un-kissed satin met practiced ones of warm, knowing smoothness, surrendering their innocence with a throaty murmur of eagerness. The muscular body turned to face the silken curves resting in the embrace of one arm. The skilled fingers of the free hand moved slowly, wonderingly over the delightful shape and texture of the oval face, the fragile column of neck, on down to caress the tantalizing swell of an uptilted breast. A virgin nipple peaked beneath an inquisitive thumb. Half-sleeping hearts sped rivulets of exquisite flames throughout half-waking bodies.

Rapid breathing became another communicating experience in the listening darkness. An intangible current of undefined electricity permeated the room and reverberated from the ceiling and walls, combining into a maelstrom of emotion there on the bed. And all the while, the kisses lengthened in time, deepened in intensity, turned two heretofore separate entities into one tumultuous, clandestine partnership apparently intent on consuming itself. A long, well-muscled leg captured a small, feminine one, the sensuous movement drawing exquisitely shaped hips to lie even closer to hard, trim ones. In the same way that the two pairs of lips had explored blindly and clung in sweet concourse, the heated cores of shared pulsations touched tentatively at first, then pleadingly. Then demandingly.

Half in protest, Leander climbed from the heated, foggy world of dreams. Something warm and beautiful had become cold and frightening. Was that a puppy whining? What was happening to her? As if a sudden douse of river water had drenched her, segments of her mind leapt awake. How had she come to be in the arms of a man? She became aware of her swollen lips, engorged breasts, and heated loins. And what was he doing holding her so close and kissing her like that? Her alarmed mind refused to acknowledge that she had not been unwilling. A kind of satiny cloud sought to drug her sensibility, to imply that escape was undesirable, that to give in to that rising primeval, inchoate longing was what she should do. Leander rent the final curtains across her brain. She struggled to free herself, her pulse a resounding volley of drumbeats throughout her body, one she no longer recognized. The man mumbled something in a deep, gravelly voice and tried to pull her to him again.

"Querida, querida," he murmured more clearly in that same distinctive purr, reaching across for her with one hand, rubbing at his eyes with the other.

Leander gasped and spit out her disgust. "Criminee!" Her emotions no longer vied with her brain for mastery. Was this why Josie had insisted on teaching her Spanish, so that she would recognize the word for "darling"? She had been in the arms of a hated Spaniard! And somehow he had snuck into the room and taken advantage of her as she slept in a near stupor from Lily's elixir. The light edging the cracks of the door enabled her to see more than she cared to see. An impression of enormous shoulders and black hair with some peculiarity about it flashed across her consciousness. Without further thought, her eyes seething with loathing, she grabbed the pewter candlestick from the table beside the bed. Just as he rose up on an elbow and saw her glaring at him in the semidarkness, she struck him on the forehead. The candlestick rolled to the spot she had occupied. As quickly as the man had sat up, he fell back upon the pillow. Bloody, slimy bastard, she thought, words having been picked up from Dom falling easily into place. She hoped she had killed him.

Hopping from the bed, Leander spotted the blur of wriggling white on the floor. Was there no end to the night's surprises? That had truly been the whine of a puppy that had awakened her. If it had not been for its noise . . . When it licked her feet and wagged its tail, she pulled the small eager dog into her arms and whispered, "Thank you, little angel. You must be a fuzzy Gabriel."

Groping for a misplaced shoe, Leander watched the puppy go to the pile of clothing in the corner. Something shone in the dim light. She walked closer. Across the insteps of the boots were silver chains. She caught her breath. She well remembered where she had seen such decorated boots. Angered anew, she cast a furtive look at the inert form on the bed. So he was not only a Spaniard, he was also a soldier. Her fury blazed even higher. Was he the one who had passed so near her in the hollow tree that day her father had been taken away? She picked up a boot, longing to rip off the chain and hurl both at the man. A thud told her something had fallen to the floor, and she knelt to investigate a small leather pouch.

The puppy nudged at her legs, its tongue and little sounds telling her over and over that it liked her. She poured out the contents of the bag onto the clothing. Gold coins. Leander had never seen so many, and her mouth opened in awe. Perhaps with so much gold, Josie could then send to New Orleans to fetch a doctor for Dom as she had said earlier that she longed to do. Surely with this much gold . . . Hope displaced part of her anger.

Deciding that the despicable Spaniard owed her something for having helped get her father shot as well as for trying to seduce her, she counted out half of them and slipped them in her pocket. But then when she returned the pouch to the boot, she was aware that it weighed far less than originally. She had no wish to stir his suspicions while he was still at Josie's. What could she do to add weight? With a surge of power in her hands and decided relish, she jerked a chain off one boot, judging its weight to be close to those of the coins taken. Dumping out the remaining coins and dropping the chain in the bottom of the pouch, she laid the coins on top of it, pulled the drawstring, and dropped it back into the boot. The puppy nipped at her ankles with loving teeth and almost tripped her as she made her way to the door. Looking down into the pleading eyes, she patted the bulge of coins in the pocket of her breeches. The little head tilted in question.

A groan from the bed helped Leander decide. She scooped up the furry ball. With the puppy in one arm, she crept from the room, then dashed through the dark kitchen to the woodshed where Jabbo had told her he would sleep. Already a hint of dawn lightened the sky in the east.

Chapter Three

"Why does the captain want to sail so early? I don't want to leave here without talking to someone in charge," Justin Salvador grumped. He was addressing the sailor who had entered the room there at Josie's Inn to wake him and tell him that the ship's captain had sent him to fetch the passenger. "Surely there's someone who can make more sense than that girl who led you here. She sounds like the same wench who brought me here last night." When the sailor shook his head and mumbled something, Justin complained, "I've never seen a place where no one with any brains is around when you need information."

As he talked, Justin finished dressing and cursed inwardly at the storm of aches pounding his head from within and without. Taking two coins from his money pouch and dropping them on the washstand, he winced from their small pings. Holy Saints! His left eyebrow was killing him. He couldn't recall ever having one spot hurt so much more than another after a night of too much drinking. Nothing seemed right, though, and he

61

heeded the nervous sailor's warning that they had little time to make it to the ship. He considered staying on until another vessel headed upriver might put in at English Landing. But he knew that the architect working on the new house at Terre Platte was awaiting his return from New Orleans to begin the chimneys before the winter rains set in after Christmas.

Justin allowed the sailor to take his arm and help him up the hill, noticing that the sun was threatening to burst fully from behind a cloud bank and mark a new day. The way his head pained him, he felt he couldn't bear to look into the threatening bright light. Why did he have the feeling that he was leaving something of his behind, something important? Vaguely he had noticed that a chain was missing from one of his old army boots, and he tried to look for it beside the trail. No gleam of silver met his bleary eyes, though, and he dismissed the loss as unimportant. That wasn't it.

"Did you see a white puppy?" Justin paused to ask the sailor before they reached the top of the hill.

"A puppy, sir?" The young man remembered Justin as an honored lieutenant and showed respect in his manner toward his fellow Spaniard. But an amused smile hovered about his mouth. "No, sir. I saw no puppy."

"I think," Justin went on with careful enunciation, making no pretense that to do so was tedious, "that it had black tips on its ears." When his companion urged him onward and made no further comment, Justin gave up. It was plain that the sailor thought him barmy. Was the puppy also a figment of his blurry imagination? Even if there had been a puppy, he sensed that it was not what some part of him cried out for. His mind seemed an unwieldy, wet sponge.

The heavy-headed Justin was relieved to reach the ship, though the deck seemed to have taken on a new unsteadiness overnight. Not trying to make a lot of sense from any of the whirrings of his brain, he found an empty bunk in the passageway leading to the captain's quarters, fitted his long form into the narrow space, and slept.

The next thing Justin knew, the captain was telling him that they were nearing Terre Platte's dock.

"How did I get here? How long have I been asleep?" Justin asked groggily. The body he occupied must belong to somebody else. He couldn't make it move.

After the captain's sobering, lengthy answer, the young Spaniard tried to sit up, moaning and grabbing at his left eyebrow. Yes, the aching body was his— more's the pity.

"A nasty cut there," the captain remarked with a touch of concern, bending to give the little gash a look.

"Cut?" Justin's fingers went up to thick black brows to examine tentatively while his mind tried to call up images. So that was why he kept feeling stabs of pain from that area. He remembered that when he had tried to smooth his hair before leaving with the sailor, there had been no mirror in the room at the inn. "I must have fallen down after too much English whiskey. I can't seem to remember much of what happened last night." A self-mocking grin slanted his generous mouth.

But even as he spoke, Justin recalled that last instant there in the bed at Josie's Inn, the only one of the entire evening that seemed clear. The beautiful young woman—somehow, even in the darkened room, he knew she had been beautiful—with those strange eyes. Holy Mother! He must have been terribly drunk and unruly for her to have brought that candlestick holder down on his head with such obvious hatred streaming from those incredible eyes. Had they been blue or gray or—?

Surely not purple, he told himself, sitting up on the side of the bunk and rubbing at the grains of sand lining his eyelids. Nothing made sense, even now that he was sober and able to think of facing the bright sunshine reflecting from the hold just outside. And what could he have done to have brought such a look of loathing to those eyes, whatever their color? For the life of him, he couldn't recall actually making love to her, and yet there was the strangest feeling that he had, or he would have never left the coins on the washstand for her.

That same earlier touch of painful longing, that feeling that he had left behind something of inestimable value returned to haunt the handsome young Spaniard. He knew the missing bootchain had nothing to do with that feeling. He discarded a half-formed picture of a white puppy with black-tipped ears as ridiculous. Had it all been a part of a drunken dream? Little jabs of memories of satin lips and skin, of fragrant dark hair warred to surface but failed. Rising a bit unsteadily and taking careful steps on the uncooperative deck, Justin accepted the captain's offer to use his washbasin and prepared to leave the ship. When he returned the following week to attend Andre Ferrand's wedding, he would return to the inn and demand some answers. Up ahead he could see the dock belonging to his plantation, Terre Platte.

By the time *The Enterprise* had cast off from English Landing and headed up the Mississippi early that morning, Josie was walking wearily from the houseboat to where Jabbo had sat propped against a tree ever since midnight. The look on the madam's drawn face told him what he had not wanted to learn.

"Yes, Jabbo, he's gone," Josie said in a beaten whisper. "He never said much after midnight, but he ranted plenty before then. We must talk things over with Leander. His main concern was for the safety of you two."

Jabbo's big face contorted in a mammoth effort to hide his inner pain, and he gazed at the rickety houseboat which had served as home to the trio for the past six years. "Go on and find her," he told Josie. "I'll be along in a minute." At her frown, he assured, "No, I know better than to go aboard, but I want a few minutes to say farewell in my own way."

With understanding, Josie nodded and went on with leaden steps toward the inn to her quarters. Within a short time, she had washed in the hot water Throwaway had ready for her and dumped her clothing in the tub the minute she stepped out. Not much was known about the flux fever, but when she and others had suffered from it back in Carolina, the doctors had ordered that garments of those touching the contaminated be washed in harsh, lye soap or even burned. She recalled how even the mattresses upon which the ill had lain were often piled together and burned. And Dom had known how dangerous the horrible disease was, too.

Josie, already drained of tears, ducked her head and

hoped she could muster the strength to do what Dom had begged her to agree to in those final moments of lucidity. A harsh sound tore at her throat. The face staring at her in the mirror seemed to belong to another, so wan and tortured did it look. The hardest part had not yet been done.

Leander took the news better than Josie had feared, though her sobs tore at those who heard them. By the time Josie had told the young woman and then left her to a brief period of private grief there in her apartment, all of the ladies had gathered in the living room to await news they already knew.

"Once the rash appeared, Dom and I both knew how contagious his fever really was, that what we had begun to fear a day or two ago was true," Josie announced once the initial shock and tears had passed. "His biggest worry had to do with others. All last night he kept insisting that there was only one way to keep all of you safe and to prevent the good citizens of English Landing from coming down that hill and driving us into the river to protect themselves from the fever. I fought against his plan as long as I could, but I came to see that it was one typical of him and his concern for others. To get him to calm down and rest those last few hours, I finally agreed that he might be right. We'll wait until midnight and set fire to *The Lady* and—" The cultured voice faltered before going on. "Being hidden as we are beneath the hill and with most everyone asleep, no one will likely see the fire until it's too late to try to save the boat. We'll have to hope that no ships will be docking overnight and have sailors on watch. I'll assign one of you the job of checking at the docks to see if any ships are expected to stay overnight. We might have to wait until tomorrow night—"

"No!" Leander screamed from where she had come to stand at the door to Josie's apartment. With a fresh river of tears flooding the delicate beauty of her face, she begged, "No, please, no, Josie. You can't mean to burn Dom on board. Please don't consider such a thing. That's inhuman." A hand flew to pale lips, as if to hold back further pleas. A cold blackness seemed to pervade the large receiving room and seep into her pores, snatching at her already burdened heart.

"More inhuman will be to handle his body and spread the disease to any who touch him," Josie countered in a firm voice. She hugged her arms across her generous bosom, as though to smother a pain inside. "I'm telling you that this was his last wish. How can you not honor it?" When Leander shrank back in horror and clung to the door frame, Josie went on. "Dom said that if we're lucky, everyone will assume all on the houseboat died in the fire and won't be poking around asking questions. He worked so hard the past six years to keep your presence secret—can't you see the logic of his thinking, Leander?"

Jabbo had stepped from the kitchen and joined the group as Josie talked, dark eyes fixed sorrowfully on the face of his young mistress. Josie turned to him and fired the same question. "What about you, Jabbo? Can't you see what Dom was trying to do? Are you going to fight me on this, too?"

The big black man nodded, his gaze still locked on the forlorn young woman with the tear-drenched purple eyes. She had grasped the door frame for support, her slender body seemingly having lost its bones. Jabbo replied in that deep, soft way, "If need be, I will.

Missy must be the one to say if we don't do as Dom asked."

Leander gave the matter thought all that morning, grateful that no one pressured her or attempted to keep her from wandering alone on the banks beneath the trees. She no longer marveled at the large grains of sand deposited by the Mississippi in its periodic sweeps upon the banks, no longer admired the myriad shades of earth tones beneath her feet. The bared limbs of the willows against the wintry sky made no impression, might as well have been viewed by one of less artistic eye than the bereft young woman. The faint trails she followed were those she had made over the past six years as she grew from pretty girl to beautiful young woman. The disturbing events taking place in Throwaway's room the previous night lay hidden in her mind, not worthy of thinking about now or of reporting to Josie in the hopes of finding the treacherous Spaniard and seeing that he received proper punishment. Dom was dead. Nothing else had meaning or substance.

The grieving young woman was unaware that the gold coins filched from the Spaniard weighed heavily against her thigh, for her every sense seemed focused on the pair of dice in the other pocket. A hand slipped inside to fondle the caribou bones, the only objects of Dom's she would ever again touch or possess outright. Taking in a shuddering breath, she wished now that she had also taken his harmonica.

When Leander had taken the dice with her one morning after the old Britisher had spent a near delirious night, she hadn't returned them to the shelf afterward. He hadn't noticed, nor had she. She had always liked carrying them around in her pocket, even though Dom would always make her return them to the shelf when he would find them gone. It had seemed the natural thing for her to keep them with her while she wandered about in a daze and gave in to Josie's demands to stay ashore and let her care for the sick man. Now her sensitive fingers gained a strange feeling of both pleasure and pain as they returned again and again to the smooth squares in her pocket.

Leander's eyes kept seeking out the peculiar shape of *The Lady* there in the shallow backwaters of the Mississippi, as if some answers might be written somewhere on her oddly angled walls of mismatched boards. Weathered into a blend of muted grays with mossed edges of green, the rough planks seemed as dear and familiar to Leander as her hands and fingers. She didn't allow herself to think that on board lay Dom's lifeless body. A passing raft, loaded with pelts and bearded men floating down to New Orleans to sell their wares and rafts before buying horses and riding back inland where they lived and trapped the numerous black bears, made no imprint on her troubled mind. Nor did two closely spaced ships fighting upstream against the roiling currents. To watch the traffic on the wide, muddy river and question Dom about what she saw had been a regular pastime until that morning.

Having lost her beloved mother, then her adored father, Leander came to terms with the realization that all of her tomorrows would be flavored more sweetly from having known and loved the kindly old sailor. With awesome pain, she finally convinced herself that for his last thoughts to have centered on helping others was too like him for her not to acquiesce. When had he ever made a move to do anything but look after her welfare? The time of tears was over. With a firm set of jaw and a slight dulling of those dark blue spots in her violet eyes which lent them their hue of deep purple, she rose from where she had knelt beside a tree and hugged its rough trunk. A determined look riding her countenance, she went inside to talk with Josie and Jabbo.

"Oh," Leander exclaimed when she entered Josie's rooms and saw Jabbo sitting beside the hearth fondling a white furry ball, "isn't he beautiful?" It was the first time she had even remembered that predawn dash to the darkened woodshed. When Jabbo had made no reply to her soft calls, she had assumed he was sleeping and had sunk upon a pile of empty potato sacks and rested alongside the puppy. Then later when she awoke and went to the kitchen, she had forgotten the still-sleeping animal. Before she had had time to make inquiries of anyone other than the unreliable Throwaway, Josie had returned with the sad news.

Jabbo looked down at the little dog, glad to see even a wan smile upon his mistress's face. "I found him in the woodshed a while ago. I can't imagine where he came from, but he seems to think he belongs here." When the puppy rushed to sniff at Leander's feet and whine with black-edged ears perked, he added, "He likes you, missy."

"He must have been looking for a home," Josie said, exchanging pleased looks with Jabbo at the little glow upon the lovely young face.

"And he has found one," Leander declared, stooping to pick up the wriggling animal and cuddle him. "Gabriel. That is a perfect name for him. An angel, that's what he is." The need to make further explanations died aborning. Far more important matters awaited her attention. She turned to say, "I'm ready to talk." The overpowering blackness washing over her upon learning of Dom's final request had dispersed into distant corners of her heart.

Josie then told Leander that Dom and she had discussed some alternative actions for Jabbo and her. With Gabriel nestling at her feet, the young woman sat and listened, that part of her mind detached from grief selecting options in the way both of her companions seemed to expect.

"Send someone to buy horses, then," Leander told Josie, brushing with an impatient hand at black curls escaping from her neglected braids. "We'll leave for Natchez tonight. I have plenty of gold." When both Josie and Jabbo stared at her, she lied without batting one of her incredibly sooty eyelashes. "My cousin brought it to me when she came to see me last evening." She had learned from Dom that to pass off little white lies was sometimes necessary and that to keep an impassive face was a must. During the countless card games aboard *The Lady*, she had studied Dom's mastery of the art and acquired skills of her own—to her teacher's delight. Both Josie and Jabbo watched in disbelief at the coins Leander pulled from her pocket. "She thought I might be needing it, and she didn't figure she would see me again before she marries."

"Good," Josie said, obviously relieved that one major problem seemed to have taken care of itself. She could have come up with some money, but not that much on such short notice without attracting attention up in English Landing. "I'll get the letter written for you to give to Frenchie Dumain. He's an old friend of mine from Carolina days, and his tavern will be easy to find. The biggest problem will be that you'll have to travel at night to keep from causing people to wonder why the two of you are together." Both listeners took in her words with unvoiced understanding.

Josie continued. "You might as well know that everyone tends to suspect a black traveling around not in the company of a white man could be a runaway slave. And I hear that those mountain men going back home from New Orleans sometimes use that old Indian trail you'll be following, so you'll need to keep out of their sight. They can be mean just as easily as they can be decent and helpful. I don't think it will take more than two nights to get there, three at the most. All you have to do is keep within sight of the river and the main trail."

"Felicity would help in any way that she could," Leander suggested, the finality of the conversation sinking in with jarring force.

"True, but we need as few as possible to know our plans," Josie replied. "I'm not telling all my ladies everything—only what I have to. We're lucky that no one seems to have paid much attention to what goes on below the hill." There was no rancor in her tone, merely acceptance. With a calmness none could have dared hope for earlier in the morning, the sad-voiced planning went on until all three felt the major obstacles could be managed.

One of the gentlemen up in the town may have thought his favorite lady's request that afternoon for two horses and saddles rather unusual, but he complied. Before nightfall, the animals were tethered upriver along the bank. After a brief rest, Josie put blankets and food staples inside packs to tie behind their saddles. Once he saw how Leander and Gabriel doted on each other, Jabbo made a sling from an old blanket to loop over a saddlehorn and hold the puppy while they traveled. A last-minute thought of Josie's was to find toilet articles and a dress for Leander to wear if the need arose before she could make purchases in Natchez.

Under cover of darkness, Josie readied the houseboat for quick burning with packets of kindling and old rags soaked in whale oil. No ships had put in for the night at English Landing. The time had come. Leander and Jabbo rushed toward their horses soon after they saw the flames licking at the old boards which had sheltered them for so long. Gall choked both, but neither let feelings show as they turned northward in the darkness without once looking back. Jabbo led the way up the old Indian trail.

The silent travelers stopped soon after dawn and found a stream deep in the forest beside the trail. Tethering the horses and snatching bites of biscuits from their packs for the puppy and themselves, the two wrapped in their blankets and stretched out beneath pine trees nearby. Gabriel settled in contentedly with his new mistress.

Despite the appearance of the sun, the day was cold, and even Jabbo kept on his jacket while he slept. Leander's coat, one left behind at Josie's by some careless gentleman, fell over her hands and hips, providing coverage for her feminine shape as well as offering good protection against the wintry winds. Nightfall found them once again on the move, neither having spent many words or thoughts on the other after waking in mid-afternoon. Their burdens seemed too heavy to warrant verbal expression. The second night on the trail went as well as the first.

But late the next afternoon when they were preparing to mount and ride back out to the path leading to Natchez, a group of travelers moved through the pine forest in their direction, apparently planning to camp that night beside the same stream where Jabbo and Leander had slept during the daylight hours. They had no time to confer before one of the men galloped ahead of the others and looked over the strange pair. Leander had just put the compliant Gabriel in his hammock looped over the saddlehorn and was standing beside the head of her horse, checking the bit.

"What we got here? A nigger and a pore excuse for a boy with him," the bearded rider asked and answered all at once in twangy English, English not at all like the clipped kind Dom had spoken and taught his companions. The stranger's eyes narrowed when they fixed on Leander's slight form in the enveloping coat and breeches. "Don't guess you be a slave lookin' to find freedom by holdin' your master's boy for reward."

Jabbo knotted the cords of muscles in his huge cheeks, then forced a grin. "Does this nigger look like a fool, man?" he asked, trying for a jovial, self-mocking tone. "This here's the son of a gentleman in New Orleans who paid me to take him to his uncle in Natchez. I'm a Free Man of Color earning a little extra money for a white man doing business with me at my blacksmith shop right outside New Orleans."

The rest of the party had ridden up by then. Hoping her cap was covering her braids well and peeking from beneath her lashes, Leander, from the far side of her horse, counted four more men and a woman. Her hand trembled where it lay along the horse's nose. Like a loose shutter in a windstorm, her heart banged in erratic patterns. Jabbo was a giant, but he was only one man. Though she had never seen one, Leander figured the red-skinned young woman with a band across her forehead had to be an Indian. She had heard stories of how some men kidnapped or bought Indian women to cook their meals and warm their blankets in the forests. Every instinct told her to motion for Jabbo and her to light out up the trail and not tarry. It would be dark soon and chances were that the travelers had ridden all day and would be more eager to stop to eat and rest than to pursue two sorry-looking strangers. But Jabbo seemed to be ignoring her.

"Why would your pa want some nigger to be takin' you to Natchez, boy?" one of the newcomers demanded, dismounting and starting toward Leander. The horse still shielded her from full view. "What's your pa's name, anyhow?"

"Don't do no good to talk to him," Jabbo spoke up, flapping the ends of his horse's reins against an opened palm in assumed careless fashion and walking to stand nearer Leander. His position there in the shady forest blocked her even more completely from the curious eyes. Frozen in place beside the head of her horse with its reins in one hand, she was still trying to find some answer and welcomed his intervention. "Lea here," he motioned toward the small figure in the huge coat, "just mostly stands around looking down and not talking. He's always been like that. Some folks might would've called him a 'throwaway.'" Accenting his last word, he shot a telling glance in her direction. When he saw that she had gotten his message and let her eyes and bottom lip drop, he let out a derisive chuckle loud enough for the men to hear. "But his papa is a God-fearing man. He tried to do what he could for him but decided the boy would fare better on an uncle's plantation near Natchez. Not so much trouble for him to get into up there, you see."

"Shore now, and what's the name of this plantation and the name of these men you're talkin' 'bout?" the first man demanded. He eyed the big black man with suspicion, sending a measuring gaze all the way up the huge frame and then back down it. "My name be Lije Rogers. We'uns come from the Cumberland River close to Hogan's Landin'. If I be tellin' 'bout me, looks like you oughta be tellin' 'bout you. And don't try no smart stuff with us just 'cause we ain't been to your part of the country before."

"Tower Wilding, sir," Jabbo lied with a courtly little nod of his head in the direction of Lije and the other men. To have learned that the motley group was unfamiliar with the area was giving him much-needed confidence. Their mean looks and swaggering ways still bothered him, but he fought to hide his uneasiness. The tension in the air made the skin on the back of his neck prickle. They seemed the kind to try first to draw blood and then, if there was no serious opposition, attack. He meant to prevent their drawing any blood if he could. From the corner of his eye he could see Leander assuming a posture much like those Throw-away took when she was lost in that dream world she seemed to inhabit most of the time. "We got nothing to hide. Lea's papa works for the government at the Cabildo, and his name is Jack Turrentine. The uncle is

Mr. Dominion Turrentine and his place is called Belle Terre. Maybe you know him or Mr. Dumain who owns The Cockatoo Tavern up at Natchez." Jabbo waited in relief with stilled breath to learn what his casting about of believable names and facts would bring to surface.

"Never heard tell of such. That place sounds like one of those Frenchmen's fancy plantations to me, like those we saw from the river when we come floatin' down on our raft," another man spoke up, one of his eyes revealing an inordinate show of white around a dark pupil while he stared at the big black and the small, seemingly addled white boy.

All of the men gathered in a huddle a short distance away then and talked in low but carrying voices, every once in a while sending inquisitive looks at the giant black and his slight companion on the far side of his horse. The Indian woman stayed with the men's horses, sending darting glances toward Leander and Jabbo. Both strained to hear every word, their fear mounting at each one floating their way with disturbing clarity. Jabbo gave in to the urge to rub the back of his neck, but the movement didn't soothe away the agitated hackles.

"He don't act like no slave," Lije said in a matter-of-fact twang to his four companions. "I ain't never seen no slave look a white man in the eye like he looks at us, have you, Fort?" He addressed the oldest in the group, the one with the grayed beard.

"Naw, can't say as I have," Fort replied, moving a wad of tobacco from one side of his mouth to the other and spitting noisily at an anthill. Wiping his bearded mouth with the back of his jacket sleeve, he went on when all seemed interested in what he might say, "I've heard tell of them Free Men of Color down in these parts. They ain't many of 'em back in Virginny where I come from, but I hear tell this part is all different 'cause it's been used by the French and the Spanish ever since it's been settled."

"We can't trust that giant enough to camp with 'em, can we?" asked the smallest of the five. A hand jerked up to his furry cap with black and white-striped tail hanging from its back, identical to those of the others, and pushed it up a bit from his eyes. He peered in the gathering twilight at the strange couple and cleared his throat noisily. "He's about the biggest gol-darned man I ever seen anywheres—black or white." A nervous smile twitched on his lips, revealing small front teeth curving out like those of some small, gnawing animal.

"Naw, Squirrel, we ain't that stupid as to turn our backs," Lije answered. "Don't start gettin' your knife handy, though. We done promised Daniel Boone we'd be returning to help him build on that road some more this spring. If'n we was to tangle with that buck, at least one of us is goin' to end up dead or close to it. I don't know 'bout the rest of you, but I kind'a think our word to Boone is worth somethin'. And we did promise him we'd not be bringin' a bad name to the mountain men from up Cumberland way." When his companions shifted booted feet, scratched at crotches and bellies, and spat upon the ground aimlessly, he added, "We got gold of our own. If the man's got any, it wouldn't be much. It ain't worth making a big hoot over. We got no right to be robbin' or we'll find ourselves, and any others who might come downriver, run out of New Orleans if'n any of us ever want to bring pelts down again. You gotta admit we got mighty good prices, better'n when we sell 'em back east to the British."

"Well, look at it this away," another called Soames chimed in. His voice was sharper than that of the others. "Boone ain't our master. We gotta right to think for ourselves."

"What Lije is sayin' might be right," Squirrel countered, shoving his coonskin cap back even farther. He rocked back on his heels and looked away from Soames' condemning stare. "We'uns don't need to be huntin' no trouble. We got lots of Injun territory to go through yet."

"Two Feathers is gonna help us out there, though," Soames pointed out, darting a glance over his shoulder to make sure the young Indian woman still held the reins of their horses. The cunning look of a wild animal claimed the beady eyes in his gaunt face when he went on, "That was a right smart idea to swap likker for a squaw to cook for us and act as interpreter on our way back—even if I was the one who had to think it up." Obviously expecting some kind of approval, he swiveled his head from one face to the other.

Nobody seemed interested in replying to Soames. The man with the strangely enlarged eye spoke up. "We ought'er show the nigger we know how to be friendly to strangers and then let 'em be gone. You kin see plain as day that they was breakin' camp and fixin' to head out when we come up."

"But, Lefty," Lije protested, "we need to get Two Feathers started on a fire and get that deer meat to roastin' or we'll not be eatin' before midnight. To hell with bein' friendly, is what I say. I don't know 'bout the rest of you, but my belly's growin' to my backbone right this minute. We've been ridin' hard ever since before dawn. Let's let 'em hightail it on outta here and leave us alone. Whatcha say?" He queried each man's bearded face separately with searching looks.

"Fine with me," said Squirrel, looking up into the faces of the others.

"Not fine with me," protested Soames. He ordered over his shoulder, "Two Feathers, get a fire built in that spot this nigger used and put on that deer meat." To his companions, he said in a lower voice, but one still carrying to Leander and Jabbo, "It's a shame the boy ain't a gal. We could use us another female on the trail. From here he looks like he might be pretty enough to serve —"

"Shut up, Soames," snapped Lije with obvious disgust. He took his time in harking and then spitting upon a pine cone atop a little mound of fallen straw. "We ain't gonna let you talk us into actin' like animals just 'cause you're about half polecat yourself." A work-roughened hand moved to rest just above a large hunting knife in a scabbard around his trim hips. Dead silence claimed all five for the few seconds that Lije and Soames glared at each other in assessing ways.

"Let's tie him up and take him back to work on the road with us then," the beady-eyed Soames retorted with a lift of heavy eyebrow to suggest that Lije did not frighten him. "We could have our own personal slave. Hell, we'd have two of 'em, countin' the boy. Would that be more to your likin'?"

"And try to feed that giant and that useless boy on the trail?" protested Lefty with a scornful guffaw, giving Soames full benefit of his cocked eye. "You must be as daft as you're ornery. Even if the nigger proved worth the trouble, what about the boy?" He cleared his throat with a harsh sound, then spit on the ground between his feet in obvious disapproval, bringing his hands to his hips and spreading leather-covered legs. His movements shifted his coat enough to reveal a scabbard and knife, much like the one Lije and the others wore.

"Show us your muscle, boy!" yelled Squirrel in a raucous voice, turning toward where Leander and Jabbo still stood beside their horses. "We're tryin' to decide if you're worth foolin' with takin' along. Take off that coat and show us what you got." He giggled in a girlish way until he caught the brunt of Lije's stare. "I wish to hell we hadn't already run outta corn likker. We hadn't ought'er give so much to them Indians for that squaw. We'd all be feeling a sight better by now if'n we had us some corn."

As though resigned to deal with the unruly bunch in some kind of conciliatory way, Lije held up a protesting arm and chided, "No need cryin' over not having nothin' to drink, Squirrel. We'll find some farther on up the trail." To all then, he said, "Listen, you'uns. How 'bout this? We'll tell Tower we want to shoot a little dice while our supper is gettin' fixed, and then we'll let 'em go on their way." He waited for his words to sink in. The tension eased a bit. Their expressions seemed to say that at least they weren't going to have to stand by and watch the strangers wander off without the odd couple's knowing that their freedom was a gift from the five mountain men.

"Fine with me," said Squirrel, showing his incisorlike teeth in a quick little smile and licking his lips.

"We need to get on our way or the boy's uncle will be flying down that trail hunting us," Jabbo told the oldest man Fort when Lije and he came over to relay the plans. "He's a powerfully important man in these parts." Neither Leander nor he had missed more than a few words of the men's conversation. Both their minds and hearts had raced throughout — but especially when the suggestion came that they be taken along as captives and that Lea shed the coat. Though Leander hadn't seen which man sounded the cruelest and made the lewd suggestion which she only halfway understood, Jabbo knew he was the one called Soames. Not that the one with the spooky eye looked much better, he conceded. And Squirrel was obviously eager to please whichever man happened to need an ally at the time. Jabbo never had trusted a man who had no convictions of his own to believe in and fight for. "Gentlemen, I appreciate the offer. I truly do. I'm not much of a gambling man, and I don't carry much gold on the trail. Pickings from me would be mighty slim, almost a waste of your time."

Within a few minutes, Lije and Fort explained that they merely wanted a bit of sport with new blood before bidding the two farewell. Their moods noticeably high, they went to get things in motion. It was plain that they were offering the black man no option. Jabbo knew when he was up against a brick wall. He hushed.

In the lengthening shadows, two of the men began to clear a goodly area on a flat spot of hard ground beneath a large pine tree, kicking up piles of pine needles and cones into little mounds, laughing and joking about how lucky they felt. Another found a large rock to serve as bumping surface and called for help in propping it up against the broad base of the tree trunk.

Jabbo and Leander took advantage of the men's moving away from them to confer in furtive whispers and for her to slip some objects from her pockets to his. He motioned to the black soil and then to her shining, clean face. Nodding in instant understanding, Leander stooped to pick up dirt and strew it across her face, not realizing until she had already streaked it all around that some old, half-dried horse leavings from previous campers had blended into the finely grained soil. Jabbo stared at her with repulsion when the odor hit his wide nostrils. But it was too late to rectify the mistake.

With a grimace, Leander wiped off the extra filth on the sleeves of her coat. A favorite expletive of Dom's seemed appropriate and she almost muttered aloud, "God's blood!" She smelled like the stable yard she remembered playing around when a child. Her hands reeked so badly that she held them out from her body, always remembering to look down, let her bottom lip hang loose, and keep all expression from her face.

"Guess we could stay till the sun goes behind the top of the trees over there," Jabbo remarked in a tone suggesting that he had a choice. At the most, that would be close to an hour. If the roller of the dice happened to be hot, lots of numbers could show up in that length of time and perhaps satisfy the men's obvious wish for a chance to best the black man.

"That sounds about right, my man," replied Lije, already checking to make sure the surface cleared was large and hard enough to make the dice roll when they fell from the rock bumping surface. "Gimme your bones, Fort. I'll check out the bumper." He knelt and eyed the large flat-sided rock propped against the tree, scooting over to straighten it to give the proper, straight-up-and-down angle.

"I lost 'em in a game in New Orleans," Fort mumbled.

"Use mine," insisted Soames, digging into his pocket and dropping them onto the cleared area.

"Yours are always loaded and you know it," shot back Lefty from where he had already knelt on one side of the cleaned-off spot to join in the fun. Darkness was creeping into the heavily forested area, though the sun hadn't quite reached the tops of the trees across the cleared area of the trail close by. "Anyone else got a pair that'll roll a fair number?"

"I do," Jabbo spoke up when no one else volunteered. To play with dice known to be uneven in weight could cause all kinds of problems. From his pocket, he pulled out Dom's perfectly weighted bones and displayed them in the large, pinkish palm. Leander's mind was spinning as she followed behind him. What was Jabbo up to? He was acting as if he knew that at last he had outsmarted the white men intent on intimidating him. They reached the group gathered around the cleared area then, though she followed at a slower pace, stopping to stand behind Jabbo. "Try these, sir." He handed them to Lije when the man moved to let the black one take a place in the semicircle facing the tree trunk.

Lije picked up each pale square with testing thumb and forefinger and admired it, then shook them around in his loosely cupped hand. "Where in hell did you come across these?"

Leander could hear the familiar sound of the dice nudging each other in the man's hand, thought she detected a note of admiration for Dom's Far East

84

treasures in his voice. Something in her recoiled to think of the ruffian's touching the bones. If Jabbo hadn't been aware of her penchant for carrying them around in her pocket over the years and asked specifically if she had them, she doubted she would have told him they hadn't burned in the fire on the houseboat — at least not for a while. They were her private link with Dom. She was vaguely aware that somewhere nearby the Indian woman had a fire smoking and beginning to crackle. A whiff of drifting woodsmoke offered momentary relief from the odious dirt smeared upon her face, hands, and coat sleeves.

"Met a sailor gentleman who gave them to me," Jabbo answered. His eyes met Lije's with seeming frankness.

"Never heard them two names put together afore, did you, fellas?" asked Squirrel. He stood directly across from Jabbo. When no one seemed eager to laugh at his attempted jibe at the sailors, the little man shuffled his feet in the pine straw and, through his curving, pointed teeth, spat behind him with a vulgar sound. Wiping with the back of his coat sleeve at the spittle clinging to his sparse beard, he turned back to the men, complaining, "What the devil is that I smell? Somebody shore better clean off his boots."

The furry coontails flopping upon their necks, all dutifully checked the soles of their dirty boots, none able to find the source of the foul odor all had begun to notice. Apparently accustomed to accepting such unpleasantries, each man then took a turn or two at testing the dice, bouncing them against the rock, watching the resulting numbers vary in acceptable proportion. Leander heard them call out numbers they wished to roll, heard them laugh when they appeared, heard them grunt when they didn't.

None could find fault with the way Dom's ancient dice of caribou bones met the straight surface with a solid sound and rolled to settle squarely onto the hard, dirt surface. All five nodded in agreement there in the dwindling light beneath the giant pine tree. The game was on. What would be the stakes?

Chapter Four

"Put up your money," Fort called, including Jabbo in the encompassing look all around. As the oldest, he seemed to be the one the others expected to serve as banker and overseer. He scratched the bridge of his nose with a grimy forefinger. "We'll roll low dice for shooter. Shooter wins iffen he rolls a seven first; loses iffen he rolls one before he finds his point. I'll handle side bets on new points. When the sun is done out of sight over yonder behind that line of trees, we bid our new friends be on their way. Agreed?" In the deep shadows, he turned a gray-bearded face in question toward those squatting in a half-circle around the cleared area beneath the low-branched tree. When all nodded their acceptances, he gave one of his own and intoned, "So be it." Seeing Lea standing behind the hunkered Jabbo with her eyes downcast, her lower lip hanging loosely, he said with a sly smile, "Jes' for fun, let's get the boy to try his hand."

Bass guffaws and grunts of consent to Fort's suggestion assailed Leander's ears, touched off a little flame of resentment in her mind to nudge at her fear. She was becoming a bit more accustomed to the awful smell of the horse droppings mixed with the dirt smudging her face and hands and soiling the sleeves of her coat—but the odor was still revolting. With effort she maintained her pose of simple-mindedness. For one thing, the smell wasn't as bad when she was still, plus she had no wish to make them suspicious that she was more than what she appeared. If they were to learn she was not a boy . . . If the odor didn't end up choking her, the lump in her throat surely would. Jabbo and she would need all the good luck in the world to get away. She had no idea where the Cumberland River was, but she knew she had no desire to go there . . . under any circumstances.

"And now the boy tries for low," Fort announced when all had rolled to see who would be handling the dice. "Hellfire!" he complained when Leander moved nearer and fell upon her knees to get into position for a good aim at the flat surface of the large rock. "Where 'bouts is that cussed horse dung? I'll swear, the stink is gettin' worse."

Having just made his own try and come up with a four, Jabbo handed the dice to Leander. With her eyes deliberately not meeting those of the jeering, watching men, she took them. Bringing both filthy hands together to cup and form a closed cage, she shut her eyes and shook the bones several times in that way Dom had taught her. Trying to ignore the stench, she brought her hands up close to her mouth and blew upon them three times. Settling the dice in her right hand and slitting her eyes enough to see, she shook them until they showed on their smooth tops the spots she sought. Tilting her head and taking careful aim, Leander flung them against the surface of the rock out in front of her, holding her breath until they settled. In the silence they bumped with a solid clack and fell back onto the ground, tumbling a time or two before stopping. Each top surface showed only one blackened indentation. Snake-eyes! Leander's blood raced hotly. She had won low to become the shooter.

"Phew!" exclaimed Soames with a suspicious look toward Leander there on her knees at the top of the semicircle. He rose and sidestepped away, settling nearer the tree trunk. "It's plain where the stink is comin' from. Let's give the boy plenty of room." With sniffs of obvious disgust, the others laughed, forming a tighter group and also moving farther from Leander. "Maybe his shootin' won't smell any better than he does, and we can lessen our black friend's load in a hurry."

"And then we can strip the boy and throw him in the crick," Squirrel threw in, all caught up in the mood of teasing one unable to defend himself, the lowly position he seemed to occupy more often than not.

"Are we talkin' gamblin', or are we talking' bathin'?" Lije interjected with a tone of annoyance. "Ain't none of you famous for smellin' a helluva lot better."

Leander and Jabbo breathed easier when Lije deflected the conversation back to the dice game. Both had felt relief when the men removed themselves from such close proximity. But the casual threat to strip Lea brought new stabs of fear . . . Only Leander and

Jabbo now remained at the top of the semicircle. The men were less likely to figure out she might not be a boy there in the gathering twilight if they were not all clustered around her.

Once the gold coins being wagered lay in the spots Fort had designated, Leander followed the same procedure as before. Gasps of astonishment came when the dice stopped with a four-three; and when the next roll turned out to be a five-two, more than one groaned and complained at the boy's uncanny luck at winning two consecutive throws. More! They wanted more. Their chance would surely be coming up next.

Glancing down at the growing pile of coins at her feet, Leander repeated her little ceremony of the hands, turning up an awesome four-four.

"The point is eight," Fort announced. He watched Leander reach for a thin limb on the ground behind her and begin to snap it into little pieces. "What in hell is that simpleton doin'?" he asked Jabbo. All watched her motions and waited for the answer.

"Lea is making sure everybody knows his point by sticking twigs in the ground," Jabbo replied, glad that Leander had remembered to mark the number sought in some way. He felt an extraordinary pride in her ingenuity and level-headedness under the uncertain circumstances. The hair on the back of his neck had quit standing on end, but he was far from relaxed. "He knows how to count."

Leander had complained often to Dom and Jabbo that she never truly understood why they insisted she always record the point in some way. She had accepted their explanation that such action could keep down possible arguments later. She figured this was one of those times to be extra cautious. It was obviously no time for any of the players to forget the point or try to insist it was different from what someone else thought, especially if the seven or the point didn't come up after several rolls of the bones. In the past, she had amazed her teachers more than a few times with her ability to throw many numbers before turning either a seven or the point needed. She hoped this might be one of those times when the dice seemed to heed her wishes. From surreptitious looks hidden behind lowered lashes, she noted that even while apparently contented, as now, the mountain men looked fierce. She had no wish to see how they might appear when riled.

"Thought you said the boy was simple," Lefty accused Jabbo, studying the small, smelly figure in the oversized coat, but keeping his distance.

"In most ways, he is. But gambling was one of the things his papa was trying to get him away from down there in New Orleans," Jabbo lied with a skill Leander hadn't known he possessed until the travelers had arrived. He must have been learning all along from Dom, even as she had. She almost forgot her role to dart him an admiring glance but didn't.

"I knew he wasn't handlin' those bones like a beginner," somebody muttered.

"Well, we know they're not loaded, so how can we raise too much stink?" asked Fort. "We'uns agreed to the rules, so let's get on with it. The sun'll be gone soon." He removed his coonskin cap and shot a look toward the west.

Then they made coarse, disparaging remarks about

the way Lea's odor created a big enough stink as to need nothing added. Ignoring the men's jibes and deciding that her "perfume" was offering protection, Leander rolled first an eight-one, then a pair of threes. Money kept moving to Fort to handle as new bets on the side. She threw the six-three, delighting those who had placed new bets on that first nine. Next came a three-two and more new bets. Excitement was bringing laughter and jokes among the men as coins changed hands. Jabbo entered in, encouraging the festive mood to heighten, placing secondary bets of his own. He reasoned that happy men wouldn't be so quick to keep his young mistress and him from getting away.

With some betting along with Lea, twanging strange words of encouragement, and others betting against her, countering with negative calls, she came up with three more combinations—all rewarding those having chosen those numbers. Time was rolling by, right along with the caribou bones. Fevered talk and good-natured cheers accompanied her next throw. Amidst roars of delight from those siding with her, the five-three settled before them there on the black earth to set the needed winning point in that session. She smiled—but only on the inside. Somehow she sensed that Dom's spirit was with her and was pleased.

All but two of the next several rolls went against Lea, and Jabbo's and her fast-growing pile shrunk back near its original size. When she laid the dice on the ground to indicate that she would pass to another shooter, hoots of protests led her to retrieve them. Picking them back up, she came out with a six-four—the new point was ten.

Even in the chilling November shadows, Leander felt perspiration forming beneath her arms and between her breasts. If the men chose to bet against her — which she counted on them to do after the recent bad throws — and won, what would Jabbo and she have to forfeit to satisfy the next pot? She figured the sun must be nearly behind the trees but dared not lift her eyes to look. She could hear birds twittering and calling in that plaintive way which signaled their search for night roosting perches. Surely this would be the last game. Could she coax the bones to give her what she needed before they turned up a seven? A new dread created a bitter taste in her mouth, sent feathery paths snaking up and down her spine.

Amidst a great rush of talk and throwing of coins toward Fort, the acting banker, the men talked of the possibilities that Lea might make the point the hard way — by throwing two fives. After all, they conceded aloud in gleeful tones, the boy had been missing what was aimed for over the past several tries. To cover the unanimous bets against Lea's being able to make the ten with two fives, Jabbo handed over the last of their coins to the banker.

While Jabbo and the gray-bearded Fort worked out the varying bets, Leander tensed up even more. From years of acting as the main shooter for the games of Hazard on *The Lady*, she well knew the odds were heavily against her throwing a ten at all, much less that she could make it with two fives. That time when she brought cupped palms holding the dice up to her face, she thought of the words she had heard Dom use sometimes when he was hard pressed to come up with a tough point. Not that they ever made much sense to her, but they had seemed to work. Instead of shutting her eyes as during earlier rituals, she forgot her role and flashed them upward in desperate pleading.

"Geez," Squirrel piped up from down near the tree trunk, "he's got the dangedest colored eyes I ever seed."

A hush fell while all turned to see those pansy-colored orbs for that brief second there in the fading light.

"He's damned near pretty 'nuff to be a gal," Soames declared, squinting for a clearer view of the small face, but apparently not willing to brave the shooter's strong odor to give more than a perfunctory examination. As if hoping to get a rise out of Jabbo or the boy, he jeered, "Even his mouth looks like a gal's."

"If we're going to get this bet moving, we'd better get on with it," Jabbo broke in to say, not liking the way the men were sizing up Leander in a new manner. If even one decided to move closer and noticed the dainty hands, the curling lashes—Things had been going far better than he had hoped. He had felt that fate was on their side when he learned earlier that the group had no whiskey. The men had been having a good time. They had won enough to be happy and hadn't seemed to mind that they had lost about as much to Jabbo and Lea as they had won from them. Surely their good luck could hold for a few minutes longer. If she missed and the men won, that should satisfy them. If she won and they wanted revenge—uh-oh! The prickles returned to the back of his neck. "I suspect this is going to be the last bet before that sun leaves us." He was relieved to note that as soon as Leander realized her mistake in opening her eyes so boldly, she had lowered them and trained them on her hands. Once more she was in the passive role of Throw-away.

"Hold-up," called Soames, sticking out an arm and lifting an opened palm to motion for Lea not to roll yet. "I think I'll change my bet to go with the boy. I got me a gut feelin' he'll make it."

Nobody protested. Fort made the necessary changes in the pot. Offering for others to make changes but receiving no takers, he signaled for the shooter to throw.

Leander could feel the intensity of the men's gazes upon her as she knelt there in the gathering darkness and fought down a giant shudder. With supreme effort, she repeated the ritual and brought cupped hands close to her mouth, no longer aware of the awful scent of horse droppings. Too much lay at stake to think of anything other than the bones and their blackened spots.

In a voice too low for anyone except Jabbo right beside her to hear, she breathed Dom's plea onto the small squares in her hands—"Be there, sweet Mama!"—and aimed for the bumper rock. To her, it seemed an eternity crept past before the tumbling dice lay still on the ground.

Silence. Then a jubilant yell from Soames, mixed with good-natured curses of disgust from those betting wrong. The bones lay there before them, each showing a five.

"A ten made the hard way, by God! I can't believe it," moaned Squirrel. He slapped his forehead with an open palm.

"That's the game," announced Fort after dispensing the clinking piles of winnings and laughing at the groaning losers. "The sun done hid behind the trees a few minutes ago." An assessing look upon his weathered face, he watched Jabbo pocket the dice and then pick up the goodly pile of coins in front of Lea. Even the huge hands couldn't take them all at once. "Iffen you ever decide to take up gamblin' for real, you oughter take Lea with you. I don't know iffen it was the dice or his hot hand, but they shore make a helluva team."

Soames tried to insist on a final high roll for one more big stake, but the others overruled him. They complained that they were getting hungry from the smell of roasting meat drifting their way from the nearby campfire.

"We do need to get on our way now," Jabbo told Lije, the obvious leader who was rising and moving toward him while the others headed in the direction of the Indian woman and the blazing fire. "But I'll do whatever you say, Mr. Rogers." He fought not to reveal his impatience to get Leander away.

"Naw, you go ahead now," Lije replied, walking beside Jabbo toward the waiting horses, ignoring the trailing Leander. "You're a good man, Tower Wilding. Why don't you drop that boy off and join up with us? Daniel Boone, the man headin' up a bunch to clear a road through the Cumberland Mountains for settlers to follow, is known to judge a man by what he seems to be, not what color he is. We'uns could use a strong man like you up there. And I can promise you that a share of land will be yours, all fair 'n square. All you'd

have to do is come with us. Boone would welcome you."
He shot a quizzical look at the small, smelly figure
following on the far side of the giant-sized black man
there in the gathering darkness. "You'll be rid of that
boy soon. Drop him off and follow on up this old
Indian trail and catch up to us, you hear?"

Barely able to wait for the white man to stop talking,
but knowing he must, Jabbo jumped in with his
response. "I appreciate your offer, Mr. Rogers, but I
already know what I aim to do for the rest of my life."
He cut a look toward the silent figure beside him and
said in a softer voice, "Come on, Lea. Let's get going.
We've a long way ahead of us before we can rest."

Lije stuck out his hand. After a brief hesitation, the
black one engulfed it firmly for a moment. The
mountain man turned toward the campfire to rejoin his
companions, calling over his shoulder, "Iffn you ever
change your mind, we'uns will be glad to see you
anytime."

Jabbo and Leander faded into the fast-falling night
toward their horses, still not daring to talk. Jabbo had
feared that if they walked away winners, there would be
arguments or threats, but the men seemed surprisingly
agreeable. All seemed to be living up to the kind of
reputation Lije had talked of wanting to gain for any
who might float down the Mississippi to trade goods at
New Orleans in the future. They might appear crude
or rough on the outside, but on the inside, both
Leander and Jabbo decided privately, they had proved
more honorable than not in matters that really
counted.

A weak-kneed Lea scrambled upon her horse and

followed Jabbo on out to the main trail toward Natchez. One hand fondled the awakened, whining Gabriel. Not for a moment had she doubted what Jabbo's answer to Lije's offer of freedom and land of his own would be, but she well knew that many slaves would have joined the mountain men without a second thought.

Even after they had covered several miles, Leander wondered if her heart would ever stop trying to leap from her chest — and if she would ever be able to get rid of the smell of horse dung.

Chapter Five

After leaving the mountain men, Leander and Jabbo reached Natchez way past the witching hour that night. Her original supply of gold from the Spaniard's money pouch had tripled.

Once or twice, the memory of the hated experience in Throw-away's room that last night at Josie's Inn dared her. Peering up ahead at Jabbo's broad back, Leander would wonder what he might think if he knew how she came to have the gold. Then she would dispel the recollection of awaking in the arms of the Spaniard, returning his kisses, and vow never to think upon the disturbing events of that night again. Never.

Josie had been right. The weary pair had no trouble spotting The Cockatoo Tavern on a corner near the riverfront beside a sputtering streetlamp. Leander admired the colorful parrot painted on the dimly lighted sign out front and admitted fatigue. Josie had assured both Jabbo and her that Frenchie ran a first-class tavern, with no ladies about the premises. Her stilted explanation about such places as hers being located beneath the high bluffs at Natchez, in a way similar to her own situation at English Landing, made Leander wonder if Josie were as happy with her life as she had always seemed. Within a short time, Jabbo had used a small coin from their winnings to convince the sleepy stableman out back that he had a personal message for his employer, Frenchie Dumain.

In the lantern light there in the tack room, Frenchie held the letter from Josie up close and read it a second time before saying, "Friends of Josie's are friends of mine. She and I go back a long way. I gather you both need some decent rest." Sleepily, he scratched a tousled head of gray-sprinkled hair while studying the mismatched pair.

Leander nodded her agreement and spoke, her voice low but firm. "I will pay for our keep. If you can get me to a room without anyone's seeing me dressed like this . . ." She looked down at the filthy breeches and shirt, the smelly coat, and wrinkled her nose. "And please, could I have some water for a bath? I will be ever grateful. After I get some rest, I can explain about this awful odor. I have a gown in my packet to wear tomorrow until I can make some purchases."

"As Mistress Ondine's slave and bodyguard, I'll need to sleep near her," Jabbo announced in a manner suggesting that he would brook no argument. He ignored the startled look Leander sent him, figuring it came from his use of the title a slave should be using when referring to his owner.

Both of the bedraggled travelers had already noticed that Frenchie was short, with a fat belly, a pleasant round face, and an obvious love of people showing in sleepy but lively eyes — just as Josie had said. An air of joviality seemed to hover about him, even when he wasn't smiling.

"No problem," Frenchie remarked, amused but relieved to learn that the young beauty poorly disguised as a boy knew that she didn't smell much like spring flowers. If he were any judge of character, and he knew from having spent years behind a bar that he was better than most, the account would be interesting. "I have a room upstairs for the young lady, and there's one right next to it for you to catch up on your sleep for the rest of this morning, Jabbo. Tonight, I'll have to move you out to the stable—you know how people might feel on seeing a black man in the halls of my tavern. I can assure you that your Mistress Ondine will be safe on my second floor."

"We'll see," remarked Jabbo, sending a measuring look at Frenchie. The older man seemed decent, even likable. Jabbo trusted Josie's judgment, but when it came to the welfare of his mistress, he always reserved the right to make some on his own as well. Mayhap Frenchie had his old friend Josie fooled and really did run a brothel; Jabbo was determined to find out for himself. After all, Leander was a beautiful young innocent, and Frenchie Dumain was a man.

"I'm just trying to be reasonable, Jabbo," the tavernkeeper said, aware that the black man could pick him up and break him in half if he so chose. Somehow, though, he doubted that if such actions were a normal part of Jabbo's nature, he would ever have warranted the praise Josie had given him in the letter. Her mention of the cruelties he had suffered in Jamaica bothered the soft-hearted man. And the reason both were in flight seemed doubly sad. He softened his directives with an understanding smile. "Josie indicates in her letter that the less attention you two cause, the better. All I want to do is help."

Wanting to believe Frenchie was as trustworthy as Josie seemed to think, the newcomers exchanged long looks before following the tavernkeeper into the back door and on up the stairs. All they could do now was put themselves into Frenchie Dumain's hands.

About midday, Leander awakened and looked around testingly. It seemed Frenchie was what Josie had promised. Nothing had disturbed her dreamless sleep. She felt refreshed and eager to don the gown Josie had packed. So that she could begin the next phase of her enforced new life, she wanted to investigate the stores and find some decent clothing. Not to dwell upon yesterday's sorrows was a philosophy that Dom had tried hard to sneak into her thinking. He achieved a success he would not have believed—in all matters, that is, except when it came to Leander's memories of her father's death and her hatred of the Spaniards. Before she had crawled into bed at the predawn hour, not only had she bathed in the tub Jabbo brought up to her room, but also she had washed her hair. She had vowed never to be around horse dung again.

Late-morning sunlight poked through lace curtains at the single window overlooking the Mississippi below the bluffs while Leander studied her image in the mirror over a chest. Yes, if she had to say so herself, the gown fit well, was even flattering to her slender figure. It was a soft pink with tatting edging the rounded, ruffled neckline and elbow-length sleeves. Never having seen the tops of her breasts revealed in

102

such manner, Leander tugged at the straining fabric with little effect. It felt strange to be showing those ample marks of womanhood when for so long she had sought to hide them.

While leaning forward to check if the mounds might escape, then straightening with relief when they merely moved closer together to form a tighter valley, Leander remembered the incident in Throw-away's bed back at the inn with disturbing clarity. A tremor from some mysterious source raced over her, and something caused her nipples to tingle and tighten. Firmly she put the memories of that faceless Spaniard back into the darkest corner of her mind. She had no intentions of disturbing them again, felt both puzzled and angered that they had surfaced just then. Damn the man! He was obviously some kind of regenerate with no business haunting her in her new life.

With an angry flip of hair and a muttered curse, Leander returned to the moment's examination of her appearance. She could do little with the long mass of black waves and curls. Using the brush found in the packet, she brushed it straight back from her face and left it to tumble around her shoulders and down her back. But each time she moved to complete her toilette, straying curls bounced over her face. For a moment, she was tempted to return to the daily parting and braiding. That she knew how to do.

Recalling having seen a piece of pink ribbon folded inside the dress, the solemn-faced young woman fetched it, then fought to secure it around a resisting handful of curls pulled back from her forehead. Who would have thought such a seemingly simple task could be so difficult, she fumed. But at last a rather crumpled pink bow perched near the crown of black hair. Satisfied to find the top section stayed off her forehead now, Leander pushed the masses still hanging in front to fall behind her shoulders. A sigh of relief mixed with aggravation sounded there in the nicely furnished room in the tavern. There was so much to learn.

Could she pass for a cultured young lady, she wondered. Not elegant enough to have an overskirt draped back from a fancy, revealed petticoat, the gown had a full skirt falling from a bodice veed in front and back. One petticoat was all that Josie had been able to get into the small packet. It did little to hold out the skirt, but Leander's waist was so small that the tightly gathered pink silk ballooned out over her hips on its own. She decided that she didn't look much different from Felicity that day she had come to call. The effect was less elegant, and she wondered if mayhap hers might not be one she had heard Josie refer to as a morning gown, the kind Josie had worn for their tutoring sessions. Until she could have some new clothing made, she could manage quite well.

When Leander opened the door, she saw Jabbo sitting on the floor beside it, leaning back against the wall. She motioned him inside, but he refused to do her bidding.

"What's wrong with you?" she demanded, glancing up and down the hallway and seeing no one else.

"It's not proper for me to come into my mistress's bedroom," Jabbo whispered. He hadn't realized she would look so grown-up in a gown and with her hair not braided. Her appearance awed him. She looked even more like her beautiful mother than he had realized.

"Criminee!" she burst out in exasperation, bringing dainty hands to the tiny waist. "You get some of the strangest notions." An inner voice told her he was right, though, and she let the matter drop, along with her hands. "I need to get to a shop and order some clothing made up. Josie told me I shouldn't be calling attention to myself by not being dressed properly."

Jabbo nodded his agreement. "I'll fetch some coffee and biscuits before we go."

Within a brief time, Jabbo returned with a tray and set it on a table near her door. They ate and drank silently in the deserted hallway before going downstairs.

Frenchie was friendly and helpful when they approached him where he stood behind a receiving cubicle in the lobby. Within a short time, he had borrowed a serving maid's black shawl for Leander to wear as protection against the brisk November wind. He then walked with them to the street and pointed up toward the shop he had recommended.

Leander let Jabbo convince her that he should walk at a discreet distance behind her and wait outside while she shopped. Josie had warned both of them on that last afternoon—had that really been only three days ago, Leander mused as she let her thoughts wander—that they would have to adapt their normally casual relationship to the socially acceptable one of young mistress and slave bodyguard. And already she was forgetting, she scolded herself as they walked up the boardwalk. For a minute, Leander was irritated that the black man was more apt to recall how they should act than she. She would have denied that she wished to appear flawless to the one who served, no matter how incongruously, as surrogate father—even had she realized such a relationship possible.

She half-turned to snap. "When I come out of that shop, Jabbo, I'll treat you like a slave if that's the way you want it." Her chin tilted at a saucy angle. Her eyes sprayed little purplish sparks at the impassive black face.

"I don't make the rules. But I do try to follow them," the big man replied in what sounded like martyred tones.

Before she looked ahead again with a disturbed black eyebrow and a forceful flip of long hair, Jabbo grinned. He was pleased to see the return of her natural spunk. Even as a young child, she had not liked having her mistakes pointed out. But she seldom repeated them, once he or whoever was in charge of her at the time voiced a serious criticism she could comprehend. Though he confessed that others weren't the only ones to spoil her, when he meant to make her take charge of herself and act right, all he ever had to do was tell her what she had done wrong. Her flares of temper were intense but brief, forgotten as quickly as they came.

Determined he wouldn't have the last word, Leander added over a stiff shoulder, "If we're going to be following silly rules, you had best not forget to treat me with the respect I deserve." She tried to stare him down before turning back to watch where she stepped on the board walkway. They had reached the shop.

"You do smell more like a young lady today," he replied laconically, moving to open the shop door for her.

Glimpsing the amusement in Jabbo's knowing eyes

just as they hid behind lowered lids, and recalling the miserable way she had smelled the previous night, Leander felt laughter bubbling up to float away her bad temper.

"If they sell whips in here," she hissed, a giggle riding her words and dancing in her eyes, "I'll buy one so I can beat you in public. That ought to prove to those 'proper people' Josie says we must please that you are my slave."

Even as she greeted the beautiful young woman entering her shop and invited her to look around, the shopkeeper eyed her askance. The pink morning gown was becoming and in good taste, but whoever had tied the hair ribbon obviously was no hairdresser. The older woman had to confess that the beauty of the radiant black curls was not diminished, but none of her regular clients would have been caught dead in a cemetery at midnight looking so windblown. The prospective customer must be a member of a Loyalist family moving to Natchez to escape the trouble brewing on the Atlantic between King George and his Colonies. Sometimes those new people had money, and sometimes. . . . But when she saw that the clumsily handled reticule bulged with what could only be gold coins, the shopkeeper became eager to help. Probably the young woman was unaccustomed to shopping alone and would need special assistance. She could certainly use a new purse.

"My name is Belle Monroe," she told her lone customer after a few minutes of allowing her to examine the varied bolts of fabric and trims. The young woman seemed interested in the few finished garments, as well as shoes, hats, and purses. "I understand that

107

many of the newcomers fleeing to Natchez arrive without their original belongings and wish to replenish their wardrobes right away. I know I've not seen you before, so I'm assuming you must be one of the new Loyalists."

Leander's ears tuned in the welcome news. She wouldn't have to concoct some believable lie as to how she came to be in Natchez under such strange circumstances. More than once, she had heard Josie and Dom talking about the trouble brewing between the English colonies and their mother country. The terms Loyalists, or Tories, and Patriots were familiar to her. She sent a dazzling smile at Mrs. Monroe. Already she had decided on a name to use.

Doing her best to ape Josie's cultured English, Leander responded, "How perceptive of you to be able to tell. My name is Lea Wilding. I've arrived ahead of my parents with only my bodyguard and practically no wardrobe at all. From what I've seen in your shop, you may well be the one to help me out. You have so many garments already made up. I was told such would be unavailable in your village."

Leander had been unprepared for what she found upon her first visit to a shop. Her eyes darted about, still seeking their fill of the glorious array before her. How was it that she had never realized such bounty awaited shoppers? The tantalizing smells of new goods tickled her nose, and she gave in to the urge to sneak in an extra sniff. Miniature poufs of luscious-colored silks hung from brass hooks at key spots about the small room, and she had already discerned that they were what permeated the air with spicy, sweet-smelling potpourri.

An old memory of the way her mother's clothing had smelled came rushing over Leander, reminding her of who she was and lending her courage. The textures and colors of the bolts of material she had already examined fascinated the artistic side of her—plush velvets of purple, red, and green; soft silks of pale blues, lavenders, pinks, and of flower-sprigged white; crisp taffetas of every shade in a rainbow; lustrous cottons of dazzling white and deep-hued colors, some bold, some muted. She took in a deep breath. Some part of her had been secretly starving for just such sustenance as the sight and smell of the lovely shop and its contents offered.

"That's true that most shops don't keep garments made up," Belle replied with a proud look. Whatever was bringing that glowing look of apparent appreciation to Miss Wilding's face as she looked around the shop could lead to goodly sales. "But we've had many like you to come to Natchez seeking protection under the British flag since that sneaky attack last December on our ships in Boston Harbor. The talk here is that more than tea may be lost before the Patriots give up their ridiculous claims. I try to keep a few basics partially made up. That way, my seamstress and I can alter to suit and finish the garments in a short time." Professional eyes traced the perfectly formed figure. "I have a gown of blue taffeta in your size that would be most attractive on you. Would you care to see it and try it on?"

In a short while, Leander was finding that the dark blue taffeta did fit. She liked the way it looked and felt—and it had a stylish overskirt caught back from an embroidered petticoat. If she could have had her way, she would not have chosen to wear the panniers tied at her waist to hold out the full skirt, but she accepted the contraption as necessary to achieve the stylish look she had seen Josie's ladies wear. There were two other gowns lacking only a few stitches and alterations before she could wear them. Her fingers moved lovingly across the sleeves, the necklines.

Leander bought a soft sleeping gown with matching negligee of tawny pongee. One lovely set of yellow satin lost its appeal when she ran her hands over the material. She withdrew them with an indrawn breath, as if she had come in contact with something loathsome. Goosebumps trailed up her spine.

The gown Lily had loaned her that night at the inn had felt like that. In that heart-stopping instant, Leander remembered with painful clarity the touch of the unknown Spaniard's warm hands caressing her satin-covered body — and the disturbing, rippling sensations they had created within her. Her face flamed. Irritated at the day's second reminder of an incident she was determined to forget, she shuddered and moved to select different fabrics for other gowns and negligees.

The black velvet cape made to go with the taffeta dress and lined with identical blue brought Leander's instant approval. A lacy shawl of natural-colored wool appealed to her, especially when she tried it on and felt how warm it was and saw how attractive the hand-tied tassels across its outer edges looked when she twirled before the full-length mirror. Finding gloves to fit in several colors was difficult because her hands were so small, but Belle came up with enough to do.

Stockings of white silk seemed much more elegant than cotton. Eyes twinkling with pleasure over the newly discovered game, Leander bought a dozen pair. And wonders of wonders! A pair of black kid slippers, with heels almost as high as her thumb was long, clung to her slender feet as though designed for them. As an afterthought, she bought some of bleached leather in a similar style. Leander wanted to wear a pair out of the shop but feared she might trip and fall. She planned to practice walking in them in her room that night. Wide-topped boots would serve well for riding. Embroidered satin slippers for wear in her bedroom seemed a must.

Leander left the shop, weighted down with packages. But not before assuring the elated shopkeeper that Jabbo awaited her outside and that she would return for further selections and fittings.

Inside, Belle Monroe counted the gold again, pleased with the afternoon's activities, then moved to draw the curtain over the front door to signal that the shop was closed. Obviously Miss Lea Wilding was a young beauty of considerable means. At first Belle had wondered at the quaintness of Leander's speech and mannerisms. While she seemed unusually intelligent, there was something about her suggesting a naïveté not usually seen in one so obviously willful. Someone had probably waited on her hand and foot and spoiled her dreadfully.

Still, the shopkeeper reflected as she straightened bolts of material, to hear such a lovely young woman let out a bawdy oath when Belle had pulled the laces too tightly on a proffered waist-cincher was unheard of. Despite the older woman's insistence that such under-garments were a "must," she had made no sale. It was at that moment that Belle's heart had swelled with sympathy for the natural charmer; within the next

111

several minutes, she fell quite in love with her.

Belle vowed that when Miss Wilding returned tomorrow, she would fill her in on how a proper young woman of obvious good breeding such as herself should dress, look, and act in local society. No doubt her father's plantation was far from Charleston, and she had led a sheltered life there. With a little guidance, the young woman could hold her own alongside any beauty Belle had ever served. That the young woman was already staying at the village's most respectable tavern was a positive note. Too many of the fleeing Loyalists spotted the disreputable places "beneath the hill" alongside the Mississippi and headed for them before investigating what might be available atop the bluffs in the village proper. Belle hummed a tune of anticipation while she tidied up her shop.

When the tired but satisfied Leander stepped outside with her purchases, a whistling lamplighter was torching the whale oil in upturned containers atop tall poles up and down the narrow street. From not too far away, playful barks floated toward her on the breeze from the river below the hill. And mixed in, as if children might be playing a game with the dogs, she could hear shrill shouts and bursts of laughter.

Leander's thoughts ran to Gabriel. She hoped that Frenchie had lived up to his promise when Jabbo and she had arrived to keep the puppy happy out in the livery stable. She had meant to visit her "angel" when she awoke, but she had slept far longer than expected and knew she must attend to the shopping. No one other than the lamplighter was in sight when Jabbo appeared from the shadows to take her purchases.

"You should have opened the door and motioned for

me," he mumbled good-naturedly. "I could have come in and picked up these things for you."

"I'll do that next time," she replied, moving toward The Cockatoo Tavern. "We'll shop for you tomorrow at the place Frenchie told us about, Jabbo," Leander said over her shoulder, exuberance lending notes of excitement to her voice. Why was it so important that he walk behind her? It was the deuces to try to talk to somebody behind. Especially one so tall.

"I don't need anything."

"The hell you don't!" she exclaimed.

"No Creole young lady uses such language," Jabbo reminded her after looking behind him to make sure no one had come out upon the street.

Ignoring the reprimand, but acknowledging inwardly that he was right and that she must rid her vocabulary of Dom's negative influence, Leander went on. "If you're going to follow me around as you seem bound to do, you'll need a whole new wardrobe. You won't recognize me when you see me in all the fancy clothes I've bought. You'll have to look as if you belong to a Creole lady of class."

Jabbo smiled, allowing a deep chuckle to roll out. She had him there. "Did you have plenty of money?"

Neither had had any idea what anything they would need to buy might cost, not having been allowed to go into English Landing while living on *The Lady*. Actually neither had ever had cause to go into a store and buy anything in their entire lives. Having realized that, Josie had done her best to coach them on what to expect and how to act. Dom had made the few purchases needed over the past six years, and most of those he managed through bartering of their catches from the river. Josie had assured them that she thought the coins Leander had with her would be sufficient to purchase clothing and live on for a month or so at Frenchie's until Leander might could learn what her true status was with the Spanish government. And now that they had tripled that pile. . . .

"I could have bought out the store and had money left over to play with," Leander replied, sneaking another glance at him over her shoulder. "Money is the problem of the mistress, so you'd better get used to letting me handle it."

Somehow the buying had been made sweeter from her feeling that she had "earned" the gold coins . . . after a fashion. Certainly she had worked at rolling those dice, and certainly she. . . . The nagging memory of waking in the arms of the Spaniard with swollen lips and aching breasts pricked at her again. She upped her chin. Taking half of his money had been no crime. Look at what he had almost stolen from her! It seemed plain that he owed her something. Why couldn't she keep such thoughts buried, she agonized.

"I thought maybe you did buy out the place," Jabbo countered, the dry comment breaking into her self-recriminations. He looked down at the pile of packages filling his arms and hands. To have her accept management of money suited him fine, and he breathed a sigh of relief. He had never had any, had never done anything but depend on others to provide for him. If she didn't bring up the subject of money again, neither would he.

"Pooh! Just you wait, Jabbo, till we get you outfitted and I pick up the rest of the things I'll be needing. We've a busy week or so ahead of us. We'll have to buy

114

a trunk—or maybe two." She smiled there in the twilight, deliberately aiming her thoughts forward. The shopping today had stirred something to life which had lain dormant. Her future still seemed vague, but she felt that somehow she was one step closer to returning to her life among the French Creoles downriver.

The Cockatoo Tavern lay only a few steps away. Smells of delicious foods floated from the dining room and set their stomachs rumbling when Jabbo followed Leander inside the cozy lobby to deposit her purchases at her door. Though not put into words, slashing memories of the many savory meals shared with Dom attacked the veneer of their outward acceptance of the moment. And if thoughts surfaced of the vast differences in their present circumstances from those unnerving ones among the mountain men at the same time on the previous evening, neither dwelt upon them.

Chapter Six

At English Landing on the last day of November, Don Carlos Justin Salvador left the gala wedding reception at the spacious home of the bride's step-mother as soon as he decently could get away. He couldn't blame fellow-planter Andre Ferrand for being so smitten with Felicity Marchand, his lovely young bride. From what Andre had told him about his older son's disapproval of his father's taking a bride younger than his two sons, Justin thought it a shame that Antoine Ferrand had refused to attend the wedding. Had he seen the way the pretty blonde seemed to dote on her much older but still handsome groom, Antoine would have been as happy to welcome her into the family as his younger brother Philip had seemed to do. As planned, Justin turned his back on the postnuptial gaiety and hurried in another direction.

The handsome young Spaniard had chafed over the past week as he waited to go back downriver to attend his friend's wedding. Four years earlier when he had first arrived to claim Terre Platte, Justin had expected his fellow plantation owners to snub him. Talk in New Orleans had led him to believe that the French Creoles were as adamant in their refusal to accept Spaniards into their social circles as they had been during Governor O'Reilly's military-backed year as the representative of the Spanish Crown. Justin had therefore steeled himself to being ostracized and, during those initial years, had been obstinate in his decision to be the one doing the snubbing.

Somehow Andre Ferrand seemed to have sensed Justin's problem. With persistence, he gradually wore down the younger man's delusions that a major barrier still existed under the benevolent rule of Governor Unzaga. Each passing year tempered the original discord throughout Louisiana between the French landholders and the Spanish officials. Andre had been one of the first Creoles to make more than polite overtures toward his Spanish neighbor, and over the past year, they had become good friends. Justin had truly wished to be present for Andre's marriage and meet his bride Felicity.

But of far more importance was his plan to make a call at Josie's Inn. This time, he promised himself while searching for the barely remembered path leading down the steep hill from the edge of the village, he would insist upon seeing the madam and getting some answers. He hadn't slept well since returning to Terre Platte. Long legs in elegantly tailored black knee breeches above spotless, white silk hose ate up the distance down the clay hill to the inn beside the Mississippi.

Lifting the brass knocker on the impressive front door, Justin let it fall several times in rapid succession.

While awaiting someone to answer, he fingered the lapels of his black brocaded coat and turned to look at the wide river in the late afternoon light. A barely visible pile of burned rubble out in the shallows rocked in a rising wind, moving just a bit in the sucking currents. The way the river was swelling from recent upriver rains, Justin mused, the muddy water would soon claim whatever had burned and settled there in the backwaters and wash it on downstream. A vague memory sailed across part of his mind. Upon his arrival that morning by ship, hadn't he noticed that the old houseboat sitting there ever since he had first traveled upriver to claim his plantation was gone? And hadn't there been a boy cursing Bernardo and him that first day when their ship had almost swamped . . . But then he heard the doorknob move.

"Good evening," a lilting voice called in English when the door opened. "Welcome to Josie's Inn." An older woman stood aside to allow the tall, broad-shouldered gentleman to enter.

Not for an age, Josie was thinking, had she seen such a handsome collection of masculine features. The thin streak of white in the gleaming black hair was unlike anything she had ever seen, and she tried not to stare. A snowy cravat and gold-embroidered vest beneath the well-tailored coat accentuated the olive complexion and proved a perfect complement to gleaming teeth showing between noticeably sensuous lips. An air of confidence and power added extra charm to the somewhat boyish half-smile he was bestowing upon her—though he was far from being a boy. She judged him to be close to twenty-five. Too bad Lily had moved on after the hullabaloo of Dom's death and the departure of Leander and Jabbo. Lily had had a penchant for handsome, wealthy gentlemen such as the stranger seemed to be.

"Thank you," Justin responded with a polite nod of the well-formed head. Once inside, he glanced around the spacious receiving room. Yes, he thought he could remember that it was into this room that the simple-minded, young black woman had ushered him. "I would like to speak to Miss Josie." Sharp black eyes wandered in appreciation over the lush figure and plump, unlined face of the one studying him.

"Speak away, Mr. — ?" Josie responded, already curious as to why he would single her out. If he had ever been at the inn before, she would not have forgotten it. No woman with a drop of red blood, no matter what her age, could forget those laughing, searching eyes, those prominent, olive cheekbones, that promising, full mouth — not to mention the tall, manly physique. The sight of him was enough to take away the breath of almost any woman. She guessed he must be a Spanish don of considerable means, and perhaps of rank as well.

"Justin Salvador, at your service, Miss Josie," he said then, the deep voice taking on a note of new respect. "I hadn't expected to find you to be so young and beautiful." With a courtly bow, he brought her hand up to his lips to bestow the lightest of kisses before releasing it. He wasn't lying. Never before had he met a madam of such apparent good breeding and culture. Her voice was both musical and throaty, a rare but attractive combination, he realized.

Josie motioned for the stranger to follow her to a cluster of chairs and settees near the fireplace. She sat and patted a place beside her on a long, velvet-covered

119

settee. The rich red of the plush fabric flattered her faintly silvered, dark hair and wide, expressive eyes.

"You're as gallant as you are good-looking, Don Salvador," she said with sincerity, once he seated himself and turned toward her with something more than ordinary courtesy. There seemed to be an intensity in his face which she doubted had much to do with any mere physical gratifications he might be seeking at her inn. He seemed to be lost in puzzling thought, and she prodded, "May I ask why you've come? Not many Spaniards visit here. Do you wish to look over my ladies?"

The dark head moved from side to side while his eyes strayed across the attractive room toward the staircase, finally settling on the door leading toward what must be the kitchen. "Not really. I was here at your place last week, and I wanted to visit with the young lady I spent the night with. I'm ashamed to admit that I was more than three or four sheets in the wind and don't know her name."

"I wouldn't like to call a gentleman a liar, sir, but I think you are mistaken. I can't believe you have been here before or I would have remembered. I nearly always open the door myself and see to the needs of my guests." Josie was certain that she spoke the truth. There was no way she would have forgotten meeting or even seeing Don Justin Salvador. "Mayhap you have my place confused with another up at Natchez or down in New Orleans." Her melodious laugh rang out in the large, luxuriously furnished room. Not hiding the fact that she plainly enjoyed looking at him while he studied his surroundings, she leaned back against the cushion and offered, "But I'll be happy to serve you a drink while we discuss why you believe you were here. I well know how too many glasses of spirits can befuddle the mind. I may prove of some assistance in helping you figure out exactly where you spent what must have been a . . . pleasurable night."

It was then that the caller turned at an angle for her to glimpse a pinkish line extruding from the far edge of his left eyebrow almost a half-inch — not that the threadlike, apparently healing scar detracted from his looks in any way. Somehow, she sensed that a member of her own sex might have put it there. She had little doubt that her devilishly handsome caller was a bit of a rake. An appreciative, remembering smile for the ways of high-spirited, passionate young men and women made her face even prettier as she awaited his explanation.

"Oh," Justin assured her with a pursing of that mouth Josie was admiring with the eye of an expert, "it was here all right. I can remember that I arrived late that night in a pouring rain, and that it was not you who let me in." When he saw a frown mar the madam's forehead in quandary, he added, "It was a week ago this past Monday night, to be exact."

Josie dropped her eyes to the handsome ring of rubies and diamonds her lover up in English Landing had given her the past Christmas. To be able to collect her thoughts behind lowered lashes, she pretended concern with the center diamond. The night to which the mysterious young man was referring was the night she had spent with the dying Dom out on the houseboat. Painful memories tried to deter her from clear thinking, but she didn't allow them victory. An inner alarm went off. Evidently something had gone on that

121

Lily, the one she had left in charge, had not told her. From all accounts it had been an unusually busy night due to a cargo ship's having stopped overnight at English Landing, but no mention had been made of such a caller as the one sitting beside her.

"Mayhap if you can describe the young woman you seek, I will recognize her," Josie told the now solemn-faced young Spaniard. Once more she could allow her eyes to meet his. "I recall now that I was out of the inn that night, though I truly had forgotten it. As it so happens, the one left in charge has since left me for places unknown."

Justin had watched the play of emotions on Josie's face while she toyed with her ring, not understanding the ones indicating some great sorrow. "As I said, I was drunk and I can't remember much about the way she looked," he began, feeling like a fool to have to admit to being so lost in his cups and knowing that what he was telling made no sense. "There was a young black woman who let me in and took me to the room we shared. If I could speak with her, mayhap she could help—"

"No," Josie interrupted, sitting up straight and clasping her hands on her lap. "She would be no help at all. She is rather simple, actually no more than kitchen help. That night she must have found that no one was around to let you in and took on a duty she is normally forbidden to handle. I suspect that if we were to question her, she would be too afraid to admit she had let you in, even if she were to remember you. I feel very protective of her, and I assure you she would be unable to help, would, in fact, probably become hysterical were we to press her for answers of happenings over a week ago." Her fingers interlaced and tightened. What she was saying about Throw-away was true. "Tell me what you do recall about the young woman. There are only two here who could truly be called 'young,' but I'll try to be helpful." How could she not be, when the beautiful dark eyes seemed to hold genuine pain?

A bit shame-faced, Justin replied, "All I could vouch that I saw was a cloud of dark hair and . . ." He paused, wondering if he dared describe what he thought he had seen. "And purple eyes." He cleared his throat and switched the way he had his legs crossed.

During her years as a madam, Josie had mastered the art of lying down to a fine point. Even so, she was glad that Justin was engrossed in getting those handsome legs rearranged and couldn't see the shock which must have flared in her eyes at his words. Sweet Saints! He was describing her beloved Leander. Only the day before, a sailor had come to bring Frenchie's message that Jabbo and she had arrived safely and seemed to be faring well. Josie grappled with a part of her that wanted to jump up and scream obscenities at the caller, at the whole damned world. What in hell had been going on over at the inn while she was on *The Lady* with Dom? How could Leander have gotten into a bedroom with the Spaniard? And where had Jabbo been? Vaguely she recalled having noted the big black leaning against the cottonwood at the end of the walkway to the houseboat that night when she had stepped outside for a breath of air. At one point, she had meant to call out for him to go get some sleep, but Dom had moaned feverishly and . . .

Her composure in place by dint of supreme self-control, Josie said with what she hoped was an amused little chuckle, "My, but you were more than a little drunk, Mr. Salvador. I've seen few eyes of purple. I do have some ladies with long dark hair, but as for the eyes—I suspect you must have been lost in a hazy dream."

"No," Justin denied with a deepening of tone, "I can't be mistaken." Fingers with well-groomed nails lifted to smooth at the broad, agitated forehead, dipping to fondle the scar in his eyebrow. He seemed to be staring at something only he could see. "Ever since that night, those eyes have haunted me. They seem to beckon me. I have a feeling that I'll never rest peacefully until I see them again."

Josie dreaded making the next remark but knew she had no choice. "She must have pleasured you very much—whoever this young phantom creature was." She glanced down at her lap to see that the knuckles of her clenched hands were white. She forced them to relax, sending one to rearrange a ruffle on a sleeve. Inside she was fighting down the crazy urge to demand that he tell her what she had to know. She swallowed at hot gorge attacking her throat, trying to recall if Leander had seemed upset over anything that next morning other than Dom's death. But how could anyone have known? The entire day and night had been a ghastly hodgepodge of horrors.

"Actually, now that I've had the past week to mull it over, I realize we never did . . . never did truly make love," Justin admitted, surprised that he would tell such a thing, even to a madam with an astonishing look of keen interest on her face. Somehow, the need to impress the obviously compassionate Josie with his masculine prowess in bed bore no importance. It mattered not to him that she might think him a lesser man for such a confession. The most important thing was to find out had he dreamed the feel of that tantalizing, responsive body in his arms. And from what he was learning, he feared he might be forced to admit that he had imagined the majority of the happenings of that night. She had seemed so real. Half-shadowed memories assaulted him: The captive fragrance of dark curls against his face and bare shoulders, the touch of satin lips beneath his, untutored at first, and yet skillful at capturing the marrow of his very being. A thumb and forefinger tugged at an earlobe; a troubled look rearranged the laugh lines around his mouth, turning them into rueful indentations on the clean-shaven face.

"Are you married, Don Salvador?" Josie asked, another fact she felt she must know. Especially now that she was so relieved to learn that Leander had not been seduced or ravished. She felt within her bones that Justin had not lied. Such a suffering, vulnerable look rode his features while he made his confession that Josie had no cause to doubt his words. But her easement was less than complete. The last thing she wanted was for anyone—especially a young Spanish don of such apparent wealth and power—to become interested in tracking down Leander and bringing her to the attention of the Spanish officials before she became eighteen. Mayhap if the young man were married and came from down New Orleans way— Before he even seemed aware of her first question, she parried with another. "Do you live around here?"

"I live at Terre Platte, my plantation about two hours upriver. And no, I have never been married."

"Well," she said with a touch of forced levity, "it appears your imagination joined with the whiskey and played a trick on you that night." Upriver at Terre Platte? Josie's mind whirled. Wasn't that the plantation next to Leander's? She let the new worries rush on by for later fretting. "I'm sorry that you've been troubled over it, though. Sometimes dreams can seem so real that we—"

"I brought a white puppy with black-tipped ears with me," Justin interrupted in a rude manner totally unlike him. The thought had just occurred to him. As vividly as he recalled caressing the young woman and then lifting his head to see her eyes glaring at him before she brought down the candlestick on his forehead, he remembered the feel of the warm, furry little dog. And the smell of the wet fur—how could he have imagined that? Certainly the scar in his left eyebrow was real. "Is there such a puppy here?" Before returning to Josie's surprised face, black eyes darted toward the hearth, the very one where the little dog had lapped up the milk.

"No, we have no puppies or dogs here." Her heart turned a somersault. Why had Leander not told where the puppy came from? And the name she had called it right off—Gabriel. An angel, she had said, as if she already knew its name. Curiosity blended with concern and tore at Josie, but she worked to conceal more than polite interest from the perplexed-looking Spaniard. "May I offer you some wine before you leave?"

"No, thank you." Justin flicked at an imaginary spot on a spotless ruffle falling from his jacket sleeve. His mouth no longer suggested it might burst into a charming smile at the least provocation. "Would you permit me to talk with your . . . your, uh, ladies?"

126

Josie considered his request from all angles. If she didn't satisfy the young man's curiosity completely, he would no doubt return and try to seek out Leander again. And that time, she might not be present and able to direct the inquisition. She must quash his hopes to find her, must do all possible to convince him that he had dreamed her, that she had never existed. And later, she promised herself, she would yank Throw-away bald-headed, skinny braid by skinny braid, if she didn't tell her everything that went on that fateful night.

"To keep my ladies from knowing what we've been discussing, Mr. Salvador, I would ask you not to talk with them about this matter. Part of my job as madam is to keep them free from the cares of the outside world, you see. They're a nervous, twittery group, all six of them. I've found that such little interviews with strangers about anything but frivolities tend to bother them, and I know you wouldn't want to upset our lives here." Though nobody but Josie knew where Leander had gone, she had no intentions of permitting him to describe her and learn she had ever been at the inn. Justin was cocking his head and moving his mouth as though he might be going to make a harsh demand, but she soothed him with an airy wave of a pretty hand and said, "I'm going to help you all that I can, within reason. I have no objection to your seeing all of my ladies. They should be dressed for the evening now. I'll call up the stairs for them to join us to prove to you that I'm not forbidding any to come down. I must insist that you not do more than speak to them as though you're here to meet and admire them. You may look all you wish, but you must promise that you will not ask direct questions about this phantom beauty you've dreamed up." Taking in a deep breath and fixing a demanding look upon him, she asked, "May I count on your word as the gentleman you so obviously are to do as I ask?"

Justin saw nothing but compassion in the brown eyes meeting his with such apparent honesty. Josie seemed genuinely concerned over what he had told her, and he didn't care to cause her needless stress. He had had no idea that a madam's job was so complicated. What she had told him did seem to be logical reasoning, inasmuch as he had never before considered brothels as serious business enterprises with problems other than occasional, unruly gentlemen. What could he lose? Maybe the young woman was here and he had misjudged the color of her eyes in the semidarkness. He sensed he would know her, even if her eyes were not as he recalled. With the first truly pleasant look upon his handsome face since entering the room, he announced, "You have my word. I promise to do no more than fill my eyes with their beauty and exchange pleasantries."

"Who knows?" Josie asked as she rose to go to the bottom of the staircase across the large room. "You may find someone you like even better than the one that you dreamed up and wish to stay and—"

"No," Justin broke in with finality, then added with a noticeable huskiness, "I'll not tarry after I look them over, unless . . ." The deep voice faded away there in the lovely room. He couldn't complete the hopeful statement, not with the madam giving him such an open look of doubt.

Turning away, Josie climbed the first three steps and called up, "Ladies, can all of you come down for drinks? There is a friend of mine here whom I want you to meet."

Every inch the ladylike madam she prided herself on being, Josie came back down the stairs and walked to the sideboard holding decanters of sherry and small stems of crystal. "Won't you take a glass of sherry?" Her guest startled and returned his attention to her. "Sherry is one of my favorite imports from your home country."

Justin favored his hostess with a smile and nodded his acceptance. "Actually," he said, "the Jerez horses that I breed on my plantation descended from the same area as the wine comes. You may already know that the English — ancestors of yours, I presume from your speech — took such a liking to the sweet delicacy a couple of centuries back that they altered 'Jerez' to the current pronunciation."

"No. I knew only that sherry comes from Spain," Josie replied, liking far better the way his voice sounded now that it was not so laced with sadness. The black eyes pierced so intently, looked so intelligent, that she wondered if he believed all she had said as readily as he seemed to. Justin Salvador was not a man to underestimate, she warned herself. She would be wise not to let the conversation return to the matter of the night of Dom's death, even after the ladies came and went. "And you're right, my parents came from England to Charleston when I was an infant." She arranged the crystal glasses as she talked. "So you raise horses, do you? That sounds like a fine business to be in." A sidewise glance telling her that he was moving toward the sideboard with the manly poise of one accustomed to being in control, she poured the amber liquid in upturned stems.

"Yes, and I like working with them here in Louisiana. I grew up on my father's sizable horse farm near

Seville, so the work is not new to me. Right now, my chief market is the Spanish army, but I plan to seek buyers in the East and abroad within a few years when my herd exceeds the needs of the government." The lights in his eyes quickened as he talked and accepted the glass Josie handed him.

By the time Justin had taken one sip of the thick amber wine, Josie's six ladies were descending the staircase with practiced grace and coquettish looks. Amidst a flurry of introductions, pretty giggles, and open looks of admiration at Josie's handsome guest, they sipped at their sherry and talked gaily of the possible menu for dinner that night, the weather, and the latest fashions from New Orleans. If any one of them thought Justin's deliberate movement from one to the other for a private word of civility was odd, she didn't show it. Maybe deep down, each hoped that his almost stern appraisal would lead to his requesting that he be allowed to join her at dinner and then accompany her upstairs. But the hopeful look claiming the Spaniard's striking, olive face when they had first come downstairs faded a bit more after each individual interview. When all sherry glasses were empty and once again on the sideboard, Josie sent all six away with a private signal. Like a mockery, their perfume lingered on.

Justin watched the last silken skirt brush against the top stair step before he turned to Josie and said in a tone suggesting deep grief, "Thank you for giving me the opportunity to set my mind at ease. You were right, Josie. She isn't here, but I had to see for myself. I confess now that I must have been dreaming, that somehow I've confused fact with fancy, something new for me and something I'll have to deal with in my own way." A part of his heart stretched and strained in what seemed futile protest.

An air of defeat about his broad shoulders, Justin turned to lay a gold coin on a courtesy tray beside the sherry decanter. There seemed no point in bringing up the matter of the coins stolen from his money pouch— or of the deliberately placed boot chain beneath the remaining ones to postpone discovery of the theft. No doubt the young black woman was simple-minded only in matters not having to do with money. The sum taken was a goodly one, but he was blessed in that its loss had presented no problems. There was little chance that it would be returned, even if he could prove anything. And to pursue the bit about the blow to his head from the candlestick holder seemed as futile as his original quest. He had no wish to stir up problems for the gracious madam. Nothing could bring to life the young woman of his dreams.

"No, please," Josie urged, placing her hand on his to prevent his depositing the money. Somehow she had known from Justin's having kissed her hand upon arrival that his own would be warm, pulsating with that masculine sureness she had sensed to be a vital part of him. How was it that Leander had come to be near him and captivate his heart so completely? Obviously he had done more than get a brief glimpse of her. The young man was plainly besotted. "I've enjoyed meeting you and talking with you. It's my pleasure to have had you share a drink with us. I hope you'll want to return—and without a sottish head next time."

Josie removed her hand from his and walked beside him to the door. The smile she gave him that time was as genuine as he had imagined all those earlier ones to be. It struck her that she truly liked the handsome Spaniard, and that her liking had nothing to do with the fact that he held a reverence — no, it was something far more, her heart told her — for the young woman as dear to her as a daughter would have been. If only Leander were older, already established as heiress at Beaux Rives . . . She sighed for all that might have been.

Justin left then to catch the ship back home, his heart heavy from a mysterious sadness. But for the present, his mind seemed satisfied. Logic insisted there had been no young woman with purple eyes at Josie's Inn whose lips and body had set him on fire that night, had seared his very soul. To one whose steps on the way down had been light and eager, climbing back up the hill in the wintry twilight seemed particularly tedious. Only the naturally uptilted corners of the generous mouth kept the brooding, handsome face from appearing totally dejected.

Chapter Seven

Never would Leander have thought that shopping for the wardrobes Jabbo and she needed could turn out to be such a time-consuming task. When the right moment came for them to go downriver to Beaux Rives, she intended that they should make good appearances. Exactly how or when such a return would be made possible still eluded her, but she spent much time giving it consideration. Their safety in the English settlement of Natchez was vital until she could learn what the Spanish might do to her if she showed up before she was of legal age.

When December came the week after their arrival at the tavern, Leander realized that by then, Felicity was honeymooning in New Orleans with Andre Ferrand. Zinging little hopes downriver that her cousin was finding happiness as a bride, she began counting the days until she would be seventeen. She had no wish to wait an entire year to go home, but she knew she must

133

not let her heart rule her head. Some bit of good luck would turn up and show her a way. She depended on it.

"Why do I need to get measured for a suit?" Jabbo asked on the day Leander decided to get his wardrobe in order. "Where am I going to be wearing fancy clothes?" He sensed she was pretending not to hear him, and he added, "Tell me why, missy."

Walking ahead on the lightly peopled banquette, Leander said over her shoulder, "It's ridiculous for you to look like a ragamuffin tagging along after me, now that I'm beginning to look like that 'Creole young lady' you keep reminding me I'm supposed to be." Up ahead she could see the store Frenchie had told her was the town's finest for menswear.

Reluctantly, Jabbo opened the door she stopped before and, at her bidding, followed her into the ladies' parlor at the side of the store.

With eyes bugging from Leander's orders and the size of her slave, the tailor ushered the giant black to the back room to take his measurements while a clerk displayed samples to Miss Lea Wilding, the cultured-talking slave's professed, and obvious, owner. Leander chose a silky black wool to make Jabbo's dress suit. In spite of the clerk's raised eyebrows, she selected heavy black satin to form the lapels and cuffs. And nothing would please her for the vest other than a black-and-white striped satin. As though she knew what she was doing, she ordered shirts be made of finest linen, two with ruffled cravat and cuffs, the others with simple, looped cravats and tailored cuffs. For Jabbo to wear on regular days, she ordered plainer cut black suits of a durable fabric. Shoes and boots selected were to be made of finest leather.

Leander did know what she was doing. From her growing friendship with Belle Monroe during her frequent visits to the ladies' shop and her admiration for the trim, older woman's sense of fashion, she had learned the manner in which many of the wealthiest planters in the area dressed their majordomos. Belle's favorite young client confided to the inquisitive but caring shopkeeper that her father would be installing Jabbo in that position as head of household . . . as soon as he and her mother arrived from Charleston and found a property in the vicinity to their liking.

Jabbo gave up trying to have a say about what his young mistress chose to buy him those long days of shopping. He had encouraged her — no, pushed her, he confessed when he gave it serious thought — to take on her rightful role as mistress. By the time December rolled around, he was wondering if, unknowingly, he had unleashed a pansy-eyed monster with a soft, silken-clad voice cleverly concealing tempered steel.

Leander wore her elegant new gowns with the air of one never having worn any other kind of garment. She had mastered the art of walking in the high-heeled shoes without relinquishing any of that natural dancer's grace which had always characterized her movements. But when Jabbo and she had time for private talk, such as when she came to the livery stable to play with Gabriel, Leander still confided almost every thought to Jabbo — at least those she deemed proper to voice. She had already learned over the past six years to keep back those which might puzzle or cause undue concern to the two men who had served as surrogate family. And

135

now Jabbo was all that she had left.

Never would she confide aloud to anyone, man or woman, how often the memory of the night in the arms of the Spaniard haunted her, Leander promised herself again and again. In fact, she more often as not refused to admit that she thought of the man at all. But in the nights when she might awake to see moonlight fingering through her window curtains to tease her from dreams, Leander would pull a pillow to tingling breasts and relive the overwhelming feeling of quiescence she had felt in the stranger's arms — before she had awakened and acknowledged that it was no longer an acceptable kind of peace which was washing over her. It had never occurred to the orphan how seldom she had been held close or touched lovingly since the death of her mother over seven years ago. If it had, she would have hooted at the idea that subconsciously she longed for such, would have insisted that all she needed for complete happiness was to return to Beaux Rives as mistress.

On those restless nights, Leander chafed at the realization that a latent desire she had not known she possessed seemed to have tried to spirit away her comfortable innocence there in Throw-away's bedroom. And it was that disturbing acknowledgment which appalled her. Josie had done a thorough job of explaining to the inquisitive, adolescent Leander that casual sex such as was offered at her inn was not what a respectable young woman such as herself should settle for. There in her bed at Frenchie's tavern, the restless black-haired beauty would cogitate and toss at the thought that some secret passion within could have

136

affected her so strongly, could have come so close to leading her to surrender what Josie and her own instinct told her was to be reserved for the one who would love her, need her, make her his wife. And that such a debilitating emotion had been stirred to life by a hated Spaniard was a thought which she abhorred to an even greater degree. Guilt mixed with anger mocked her. Sleep eluded her.

During the numerous sessions of fittings and alterations at Belle's shop, Leander grew fond of the shopkeeper. Josie's frequent talk of her earlier years in Charleston had provided Leander with enough information to sound fairly knowledgeable about it. When the doting older woman might have pushed to know details which the fibbing younger one couldn't know, Leander would bring her hand up to her forehead and sigh.

"Please," she would insist in one of those tremulous voices she had sometimes used when putting on a show for Dom and Jabbo in order to get her way about some trifle, "I can't stand to talk another minute about my home back in Carolina, or I'll just die of homesickness. I can feel the tears fairly knocking at my eyelids this very minute. Can't we talk of something else?"

At such times, the widowed, childless Belle would console Leander with talk of her niece Roseanne and how the young woman was still suffering from homesickness at a boarding school in Mobile. Homesickness was a sign that one came from a good home, she would insist, scolding herself for having almost upset the young woman she adored.

Leander's effervescent charm and vulnerability still

held Belle's enthralled, though more and more she was feeling sorry for her. With tact she had offered to teach Leander how to arrange her lovely hair when they would be in the back fitting room, explaining that she could understand why, without her personal maid sent to accompany her, the poor dear had been unable to manage on her own. Belle would sigh when she thought of the delayed arrival of Leander's parents. She couldn't bear to think of the possibility that something may have happened to them, like a storm at sea or, perhaps, capture by some misguided patriots. The young beauty was so alone. Except for the big black bodyguard, who so obviously lived up to his name. He had become almost a permanent fixture on the bench beside her shop.

"I hope you'll come visit at my home when Roseanne arrives for Christmas with her family," Belle said one afternoon. At Leander's second visit to her shop a week or two ago, the shopkeeper had insisted that the young woman call her by her first name as did her other patrons. Theirs had become a comfortable relationship—except when Belle persisted in trying to learn of life back in Charleston. In the back room, two seamstresses worked on Leander's wardrobe. In an alcove of the shop itself, Belle sat bent over, hemming one of Leander's silken negligees while the young woman sipped at a cup of lukewarm tea. Leander's abhorrence of using satin for her nightwear puzzled Belle, but once she saw that her young client was adamant, almost vehement, on the subject of allowing satin to touch her skin, the astute businesswoman dropped the subject. "There will be parties for the young people, and I know

Roseanne will love you and want to have you meet her friends and attend some of the galas."

"I'm not sure of my plans, Belle," Leander demurred. She replaced the rose-patterned cup on its saucer. Criminee! She was sick of lukewarm tea. Both Josie and Dom had taught her not only to make it hot but also to serve it hot. But then she felt remorse at having let something so trite cause her to criticize the warm-hearted Belle who had shown her so many kindnesses—and accepted without question every lie Leander had told.

Leander wasn't at all sure that she would be able to fool the niece who had apparently been studying for a number of years at Miss Julia Shepherd's School for Young Ladies in Mobile. Daily she was seeing that she had huge gaps in her knowledge about ordinary happenings. Just in case she were to be forced into Roseanne's company during the upcoming holidays, she asked questions about the niece's letters to her aunt, hoping to learn what normal young women might have been experiencing over the past six years. Belle always complied. She loved to hear Leander's delightful laughter spilling out into the shop when she would recall Roseanne's accounts of pranks at the obviously fashionable school. And there were many to tell. On more than one afternoon, Leander had left the shop with laughter's tears still sparkling on curly black lashes over enjoyment of Belle's latest tale about Roseanne's life at Miss Julia Shepherd's School for Young Ladies.

It was while Leander was waiting several days later in the ladies' parlor of the men's shop for Jabbo to have the final fittings that she first felt someone was watching her. She had just given the attendant an order for extra white gloves and stockings for Jabbo's dress attire. Over the shoulder of the young clerk, who was earnestly taking down that order and others for practical and plainer white vests for everyday wear, Leander glanced toward the small glass in the door opening into the main room of the men's shop. She saw no one, though she suspected a shadow flitted out of sight just as she looked up. Had some gentleman customer, the only kind allowed in the big outer room, happened to pass by the door leading into the ladies' parlor and sneaked a peek to see who might be shopping for the gentlemen members of her family? If so, she had the odd feeling that he had done more than send her a cursory glance. Uneasiness washed over her. Why would anyone be looking at her in secret?

An outward calm reigned while Leander waited to view Jabbo in his new garments. But every once in a while, long after the tailor and Jabbo came out and gained her approval, she darted a look back at the glass opening. Sighing and blaming her discomfort on being overly tired, she made herself forget the incident. There was the need to choose a sturdy, coarser fabric for riding pants, as well as a warm winter coat for the big man to wear outdoors in bad weather. With an impatient toss of black curls falling from beneath a fashionable hat perched atop her head, she attended to the matter at hand. Since her hair was no longer confined into braids, she had begun singling out a long curl to finger when deep in thought. A forefinger twirled itself now in a wispy, ebony curl falling across her shoulder.

Leander sensed prying eyes after that first time, but could never locate their source, no matter how slyly she turned her head or pretended interest in a shop window to check on strolling passersby. She had become accustomed to the flirty looks of admiration sent her way from young men that she encountered under ordinary circumstances, though at first she had not recognized them for what they were. But she had noticed that such young men made no pretense of their interest in her, some even going out of their way to try to make her eyes meet theirs, despite the ever-present, glaring black man.

If someone were watching her as Jabbo and she moved above the village, he was not one wanting to be seen, she mused. And there was always the possibility that she was wrong, that she was being overly sensitive now that she was exposed for the first time in the real world. She almost confided her suspicions to Jabbo when they were playing one Sunday afternoon with Gabriel in the yard beside the livery stable but decided such would only bother him. If there really was someone following and watching her over the past few days, Jabbo or she would have already spotted him.

At the end of their trying days of shopping—and there were many—neither Leander nor Jabbo had problems falling asleep early. After the first twenty-four hours, Jabbo had accepted Frenchie's word that his young mistress was indeed safe on the second floor of the tavern. He settled into a spare room on the far side of the tack room in the livery stable, making a bed for Gabriel in its corner. Because she found Jabbo a good conversationalist and not interested in fondling breasts reserved for another, a young slave woman took his meals to him there after the rush of the diners inside died down. Besides, she doted on the growing, frisky puppy.

Frenchie nightly invited Leander to dine with him in the tavern's popular dining room, but she was too weary to accept, opting instead for having a tray sent up to her room after the customary tub of hot water for her treasured bath. She had no wish for either Frenchie or Jabbo to know how poorly she had slept since leaving English Landing. Thoughts of the insidious Spaniard refused to go away for longer than one night at a time; even those were scarce.

The new phase in the lives of Leander and Jabbo began to seem normal and be moving in a smooth pattern as her seventeenth birthday approached. There were times during the nights, though, when she managed to keep the memories of the Spaniard at abeyance and let her thoughts move in other, more promising directions. Then she would lie awake wondering at the feeling that all the preparations she was making were only a first step toward something major. She felt she was waiting on a threshold before entering the door into the rest of her life. And then she would smile in the darkness and realize that it was all true—her future could not begin until she returned to Beaux Rives as mistress.

On the afternoon of Leander's seventeenth birthday, Jabbo and she walked on an open strip atop the hill holding The Cockatoo Tavern and the rest of Natchez high above the Mississippi River. Gabriel frolicked and played around them there in the December wind, reveling in freedom and the attention both were giving him.

Glad to note that no Spanish flags flew from the masts of the several ships anchored beneath the crest upon which they strolled, Leander hugged her shawl closer and smiled. The river smells always made her remember the good times spent aboard *The Lady*.

"I wish Dom were here so I could tell him how good it feels to reach seventeen, Jabbo," she said over her shoulder. She had come to accept that he must keep a discreet distance behind his mistress, but she still hated it. Feeling the need to let out some of her pent-up emotion, she spread her shawl wide like butterfly wings and ran to meet a gust of wind. Along with the cloud of black curls, her delighted laughter floated behind her. When she slowed and turned back to watch the big man continue walking after her, she burst out, "I had wondered if this day would ever come."

"I wouldn't be so impatient to mark off years, missy," he replied, though the look on his face showed that he remembered how some twenty-five years earlier he had felt some of what she seemed to be feeling. He threw back his head and sniffed at the moisture-laden air, grateful that the weeks at The Cockatoo Tavern had proved peaceful. The sun lay hidden behind clouds, yet it was a fine afternoon. "And I've a suspicion that Dom knows."

"The most important birthday still has to come," she replied, thinking of that eighteenth. They had come to a clump of bare-limbed cottonwoods, and she stuck two fingers in her mouth to whistle for Gabriel to return,

143

unaware that the unladylike action hardly went with her appearance. It would soon be time for tea before the fireplace at the tavern.

"I made you a little present," Jabbo announced when she turned to start back down the crest toward the tavern. Without looking at her, he handed over something small, something hard, covered with a crumpled piece of newsprint.

"What is it?" Leander asked, a pleased little high note riding her voice. Dom and Jabbo had never failed to come up with some little offering on her birthdays. She yanked off the wrapping and let it drift with the breeze. A small, square wooden box with miniature designs of fleurs-de-lis and leaves carved in the fragrant cedar lay in the palm of her hand. "Oh, Jabbo," she exclaimed with undisguised surprise and delight, "I never knew you were this good at woodcarving. It's beautiful." She brought the tiny box up to her face, noisily sniffing at the spicy cedar fragrance, her eyes closed in ecstasy. "Um-m, I love it!" When she lowered it and removed the tightly fitting top, she asked with awe, "Where did you find this luscious purple velvet to line it with?" She tested the plush interior with an inquisitive forefinger, hooking eyes of similar hue toward him.

Jabbo grinned with open pleasure. "Miss Belle gave me a little scrap from the riding outfit she's making for you." He hadn't expected to please her quite so much, and he was glad Belle had encouraged him to use the velvet to line the little box when he told her about it. Had Leander figured out what it was to be used for, he wondered, not wanting to rush her. He had learned long ago that anticipation could be a special part of almost any joy worth having.

Leander inspected the small box with its intricate designs, a dazzling wash of comprehension flooding her eyes and spreading wider the smile gracing her face. "You made this to hold Dom's dice, didn't you? What a thoughtful thing for you to do, Jabbo. I will treasure it always. Thank you." She loved the way the big man dropped his eyes and scuffed at the dead grass with the toe of one shoe. Who would have thought that those giant fingers could wield a carving knife with such skill? A muscle jumped in an ebony cheek before he allowed a flash of white teeth to relieve the blackness of his face.

"You're welcome, missy." He turned then to whistle sharply for the puppy still investigating something in the clump of low trees. "Come on, Gabriel. It's time for us to be getting back to the livery stable."

With only one or two more playful starts at a teasing tomcat perching in one of the willows, the puppy gave up and followed his young mistress and her bodyguard back down the walkway toward The Cockatoo Inn. When his fast-growing, wobbly legs would cause him almost to fall in his attempts to leap ahead of his admirers in bounds large enough to clear the dried weeds, their laughter merely urged him to try more ridiculous feats. Gabriel was apparently going to be a very large dog one day. Already he was responding to Jabbo's efforts to teach him to be protective of Leander.

Frenchie motioned to Leander the minute she entered the tavern's vestibule, which opened onto the business lobby on the left and the parlor leading toward

145

the dining room on the right. A quick glance toward the blazing fireplace in the parlor showed her the back view of a dark-haired young man. There was something familiar about the turn of his head as he sat reading in near profile beside a candelabra on a nearby table. Her heart thundered. If he had heard her come in, he made no sign of it.

"Leander," Frenchie said in a low voice when she went to stand before him at the registration desk. "The gentleman before the fireplace came in here soon after Jabbo and you left to go walking, insisting that he must see you, that he knows you. I was shocked. When I tried to deny that anyone was registered here under the name of Leander Ondine, he merely shrugged and told me he had been in town a few days and knew for certain who you are and that you're staying here." A hand brushed at his grayed temple with annoyance. "I talked myself blue in the face, but the man described the clothing you wear. He even referred to Jabbo by name. If he's lying, he must have done some tall asking around in the shops to know so much." A worried frown rode the normally relaxed forehead.

"Did he give his name?" Leander asked, her fear breaking through and lending a quaver to her voice. What young man could know who she was, or that she was in Natchez? She had no doubt that neither Josie nor Lily would give out information — at least not knowingly. Had there actually been someone spying on her the past few days? "Is he Spanish?" For some reason, the hazy image of the man in Throw-away's bed crept into mind and grew into staggering proportions. She swallowed hard, awaiting her new friend's answer, recalling how something about the quick view of the partial profile of the man across in the parlor had rung a faint tone of recollection. Her heartbeat went berserk.

God's blood! What if the Spaniard had traced her here and was preparing to accuse her of thievery in Josie's brothel? The thought that she still had more than enough coins remaining to return his money brought little comfort. Somewhere from within a secret corner in her heart, she sensed that her reluctance in facing the unknown Spaniard again had less to do with being branded a thief than with attaching importance to the caresses and embraces she had endured—yes, "endured," she assured some tacky inner voice which tried to substitute the word "shared."

"Why would you suspect he might be Spanish? Don't look so worried and upset, little one. I doubt he is, though some of them can speak French and English as well as you or I," Frenchie replied in that same conspiratorial voice. "And he flatly refused to give me his name, saying he would wait and give it to you when you returned. He acted as if he knew you would be coming back soon."

"What do you think I should do?" Now she was wishing she had confided her suspicions to Frenchie about those feelings that someone had been following Jabbo and her over the past few days. If she had, the naturally glib-tongued tavernkeeper could have had some tale ready for such an occasion. He must have been taken by surprise and unable to come up with plausible denials. Not waiting for Frenchie to offer advice, she ground out, "I guess I have no choice but to go on in there and face him." Her feet felt rooted to the oak floor.

"From the man's mood, I gather you're right. He vowed he'd not leave till he saw and spoke with you." Coming from behind the desk, Frenchie offered a pudgy arm, saying, "At least let me escort you in so he can see that you're not at his mercy."

Not at his mercy? Irony washed over Leander. What a cruel joke. If the persistent caller were to be that abominable Spanish soldier whose bootchain she had removed and stuffed into the bottom of his money pouch . . .

Mustering an air of bravery to a proudly lifted head, an air not felt in a single cell, she took Frenchie's proffered arm and walked with him into the parlor. This time, the man must have heard their footsteps, because he laid the book on the table and seemed to be straightening his cravat and coat before rising. Yes, she thought with the panic of an inexperienced thief about to be questioned, there was definitely something familiar about him. It was not the first time she had seen the dark-haired young man. He rose then and faced her, his handsome face breaking into a huge smile.

"Leander Ondine," he said, stepping to greet her with both hands extended in friendship. "Surely you remember me?" he asked in a way which indicated her reply would be positive. The smile on his rather long face danced on up into dark eyes beneath heavy brows. "How marvelous to find you in Natchez."

Leander's hand tightened on Frenchie's tensed arm for just a moment. Shock and surprise combined to leave her speechless as the young man's fashionably clad legs closed the distance between them. Remember him? Of course she did.

Staring up with wonder into the tall young man's face, she exclaimed, "Antoine Ferrand! How in the world did you happen to find me here in Natchez?" Removing the hold on Frenchie's rigid arm, she held out both hands. The elder son from the plantation neighboring Beaux Rives on the north took them in his own. "Antoine, I can't believe it's really you."

"Dear little Leander," Antoine was saying as he ducked to place a light kiss on first one flushed cheek and then the other, "the surprise is all mine. Everyone thought you had died in the fire at Beaux Rives years ago when—"

"Well, it's easy to see that what everyone believed was wrong, isn't it?" she broke in to ask, not even noticing that he still held both her hands in his while she leaned back to get a better look up into his face. A warmth at seeing a familiar face from her childhood did more to chase the chill she had felt upon entering the room than the heat radiating from the fireplace. Had the caller been that Spaniard—she wouldn't allow herself to dwell upon it. "You haven't changed all that much since you left to study in Paris back when I was—what, all of eight or nine years old?"

"Something like that, I guess," Antoine responded, never removing his devouring looks from the lovely face and eyes lifted in obvious joy.

Leander took hold of herself then and introduced the two men. Permitting keen interest to temper his suspicions, Frenchie heeded her suggestion that he order tea for them. He didn't return.

"God, but you're even more beautiful than I remember your mother's being," Antoine said. He escorted her to a high-backed chair angled next to the one in which he had been sitting and reading. "I heard she died the year after I left. I was most grieved to hear it. To a young man in his teens, she represented the epitome of what he might dare dream of finding for himself someday. And then when Father wrote the following year to tell of the deaths of your esteemed father and of his lovely, precocious child, you—you can imagine how shocked I was to see you in a shop the other day. I felt I had seen a ghost and did quite a bit of checking to make sure that vision was truly you—Leander Ondine, alias Lea Wilding."

Antoine couldn't imagine what caused the obvious look of relief racing across her face at his last statement. The softness of her parted lips as she gazed at him with those incredible purple eyes and drank in the tributes to her parents charmed him all over again. He had not exaggerated. Truly, she was more beautiful than Violette Ondine had been. Never had he seen such long black lashes curling to perfection or such flawless fair skin or such alluring lips. He was a man ready now to settle down and practice law in Louisiana, a man a bit jaded from nine indulgent years in both the high and low societies in Paris. Such a gem as sat before him, regarding him with something which seemed close to adoration, was all that he lacked to make his life perfect. She had everything he desired, needed.

"How old are you now?" he questioned in a teasing tone. "Over tea you must tell me all about what you've been doing to cause everyone downriver to believe you perished in that awful fire."

Leander laughed, floating on a high such as she hadn't known in ages. She felt like pinching herself to make sure she wasn't dreaming. "I'm seventeen today, Antoine. And I believe seeing you must be a surprise present." The way he was gazing at her, as if he might be planning to taste her like some delicacy, sent all kinds of excitement tearing through her veins. She wasn't sure she liked all of the invitations in those dark brown eyes, but she confessed they were heady. Back when she was a child, Antoine, a lofty nine years her senior, had endured the presence of his younger brother Philip and her with undisguised boredom and annoyance. But now he was treating her as someone grown-up and very special.

A serving girl brought the tea tray then and set it on a low table before them. Their eyes continued a tête-à-tête while the young woman made sure everything was in order and then retreated to leave them alone once more. Edgy, but unable to figure out why, Frenchie had gone on back to the lobby, once he realized the stranger hadn't lied about knowing Leander and that she seemed pleased to see him. Except that the young man appeared too eager to let the initial kisses on her cheeks evolve into longer ones on her lips, he had to assume that Leander was able to take care of herself— especially since he was near enough to hear any call for help she might make.

"And so Jabbo followed your father's instructions and traveled in secret with you to that school in Mobile?" Antoine asked after Leander had plied him with what seemed to her the only reasonable explanation she could come up with on such short notice. He returned his cup to the tray with only the briefest of pauses in his attention there in the candlelight to her hair, face, breasts, and dainty hands.

Josie had warned Leander that to tell anyone where she had actually been since the day of her father's capture might cause some raised eyebrows and damage her reputation in the demanding Creole society she would be reentering. They hadn't had time that last afternoon to think up something logical, and so Leander had had to draw on her own imagination.

Thank God for Belle's incessant chatter about her niece Roseanne. Although Leander felt half-inclined to confide in the son of her parents' neighbor and friend Andre — now the husband of her cousin Felicity, she added mentally — she put the thought away. Pouring more tea into the handsome Antoine's near-empty cup, she smiled that her necessary deception was working. Once she had added the part about Jabbo's having worked in the stables at the school while she studied over the past six years, he apparently thought her entire story logical and seemed to lose interest.

"Yes, the years at school kept me busy," Leander replied after handing him the cup, wondering if the way his fingers brushed hers when he took it was accidental. That brief contact set off some kind of quivery feeling, but she was not certain that she cared for it. His intense scrutiny of her face and bosom bothered her more than she would have liked. Josie had told her over the past year that men often used such methods to let a woman know of their interest without having to put such admiration into words, that she should accept it as flattery when it came her way. Somehow, though, she decided she would have preferred spoken praise to the dark, assessing looks. Antoine's knowing eyes had a way of making her feel he knew what she looked like without a stitch on. If she was supposed to take that as a compliment, she confessed that she didn't. "I've been at Miss Julia Shepherd's School for Young Ladies until the past few weeks. I haven't dared come this close to home before now, as I have no idea what the Spanish might would do to me before I am eighteen and can claim my inheritance. I've no wish to become a ward of the Spanish. If I'm to be branded as the daughter of a traitor—no matter how falsely—then I can't be too careful, can I?"

"That's absurd, dear one," Antoine retorted with an amused smile. Young women could come up with some of the most outlandish ideas. She was as naive as he had assumed—and counted on. "What could they possibly do to you? Granted, they may be a trifle surprised to see that you are indeed still alive, just as I was, but as for being able to take action against you legally, there is nothing they can do—"

"Antoine, are you sure?" she broke in, placing her cup on its saucer with a little clatter. The brilliance of her smile dazzled him anew. "Do you mean that I may return to Beaux Rives at any time?" The thought sent her blood racing far more than any heated gaze he had been sending her had done. Her eyes blazed purple happiness. The oval face flushed becomingly. A little pulse in her neck fluttered. She leaned her head back against the upholstered back of the chair, clasping her hands and bringing them up to rest beneath her chin in prayerful-like pose. "I can't believe this! I'm so glad that you showed up, that you're a lawyer, and that you know such things. Thank you for clearing up this hateful matter — what a lovely birthday gift!" She reached again for her cup, not even caring that time when his eyes sought to race down her cleavage. If that was the way young men were going to act, she might as well get used to it, she told that protesting part of herself. She could go home! That seemed the only thing that mattered.

They sipped in companionable silence, each apparently caught up in private thoughts. The dancing flames in the fireplace sent out a welcome glow of heat and light on the wintry afternoon. The patina of mahogany wainscoting beneath walls covered with framed panels of olive green and centered with prints of English landscapes reflected the warmth of the blaze. Beneath her feet, Leander could feel the plush weave of the ornate Persian rug defining their sitting area. Other guests began to enter and find places about the large room to gather for tea, their murmured conversations and the soft clinks of porcelain cups and saucers making the room an even cozier place to the contented Leander.

"Tell me about Felicity's and Andre's wedding, Antoine," she urged, ready to get back to present matters. "Are they still on their honeymoon in New Orleans?"

"I didn't attend." His words shot out in sullen manner. "I don't know if they've returned home or not."

"Didn't attend your own father's wedding?" Leander

was aghast. What was causing the face she had thought so handsome to appear petulant, not nearly so attractive? "Why ever not?"

"Personal reasons." Antoine noted the disapproval in her voice. Placatingly he explained. "I was overly attached to my mother, and I suppose I just couldn't bear the sight of someone's taking her place beside my father." He watched through half-lowered lashes to see her reaction.

"You said earlier that you aren't married," Leander said after a moment's brooding. This time her eyes did the raking over the nearby face. "Is Philip?"

"No. He's quite the contented planter and seems blind to the charms of all those who would snap him up."

"Did he go to the wedding?"

"Yes," Antoine admitted with reluctance.

"Yours hardly sounds like a reasonable excuse for a grown man whose mother has been dead even longer than mine. Philip is five years younger than you, and yet he could accept another woman alongside Andre. I can't help but be hurt for your family—but especially for my cousin." Leander knew there was a scolding tone in her denouncement, but she didn't care. In her view, he was acting like a child. Brushing at the short, wispy curls ever falling forward upon her forehead and temples, she sent him a measuring gaze which found him lacking.

Antoine recognized the look his lovely companion was shooting his way. Other young women had sent them over the years. If he intended to woo the lovely young heiress, impress her, ever get her into his arms, he would have to make amends in a hurry.

"Hearing you say it aloud, Leander, makes me see how foolish I've been," he murmured in what he hoped was a contrite tone. "I've been in Natchez brooding over something I can't alter, shouldn't try to change. Mayhap a huge wedding gift and an apology to the couple will permit me to fall once more within their — and your — good graces." She appeared to be receptive, her full lips setting in pensive mood there in the glow from the candelabra on the table between them. The way her hair fell across one shoulder and trailed shining ebony across the top of one swelling, pearlescent breast created a fascinating picture of temptation. He couldn't remember being so eager to hold a young beauty in his arms with the intensity he was longing to pull Leander close. There was an innocent sensuality about her which captivated him, churned up all kinds of desires. First, he had to regain her earlier smiles and approval. "What do you suggest? I truly want to make amends. I need your advice."

Leander wanted to believe Antoine, wanted to believe that at last her world was about to settle into a desirable pattern. Over a fresh pot of tea, they planned a shopping trip on the morrow to seek grand wedding gifts from each of them. Now that she no longer needed to remain hidden, she could accompany him to Belle Terre for the holidays. When Antoine insisted that he wanted to wait for her to go up and dress for dinner so as to treat her to a birthday supper there at the tavern, she gave in to the practiced, charming smile, the ardent looks. To share a birthday meal with someone from those lovely days of her early childhood seemed a perfect ending for the special day.

Later, though, after she had slipped into bed and tried to find sleep, she wondered at the seeming discrepancies in Antoine's actions and his words. Dinner that evening had not been the happy occasion she had envisioned. Something seemed not right. Just when he would be too obviously ogling the tops of her fashionably exposed breasts in an unromantic way during dinner, he would come out with lilting phrases of compliments on her hair, her gown, her beauty. Each time she tried to ask about what Felix was accomplishing as overseer at Beaux Rives, he would answer her in meaningless replies, saying he had been home less than a year, that he actually knew little about what went on — as if she were a mere female too simple to understand serious answers. And the touch of his hand atop hers once as it lay upon the table sent no sizzling thrills racing through her veins as had those of the Spaniard back at —

"No!" Leander denied in a haunted whisper resounding in the dark bedroom. The wind moaned outside in eerie echo. She must not let herself keep thinking of the way she had responded to that stranger in the darkness. That had been wrong, hadn't been anything but forbidden passion aroused by the practiced seducer of innocent young women. The caresses and compliments from a Creole gentleman would not have to set up a similar torrent of fire inside to indicate that he might make an acceptable suitor . . . or husband, she reasoned.

With deliberation, the tormented young woman directed her thoughts away from taunting memories. A

Frenchman, especially a true Creole, one born in Louisiana of French parents, would have more gentlemanly ways of pleasing a young woman than some dastardly Spaniard of questionable heritage. She would have to give Antoine more than one evening before she could truly say she couldn't find him a possible suitor. To rush into the business of considering marriage was not a major priority.

Had Antoine not shown up that afternoon and exercised his charms on her, Leander reflected, she probably would not be lying awake thinking such thoughts. It was just that she was so uncertain, so inexperienced. She sighed along with a gust of wind tapping at the windowpane. There was so much to learn about being grown-up. And she seemed to have gotten the lessons all out of sequence.

Chapter Eight

"We'll miss you and Jabbo," Frenchie said a few days later when Leander came downstairs dressed in a warm but fashionable traveling costume of navy worsted. Almost a month had passed since the motley couple had ousted him from his bed to give them refuge. Their transformation into a believable, rich young mistress and devoted slave protector boggled his mind, when he let himself think about it. He wished he felt better about their leaving. Christmas was less than a week away. "And the livery stable will never be the same without Gabriel."

"You've been most kind to us, Frenchie," Leander said, stepping to plant a quick kiss on his plump cheek. She turned to watch Jabbo bring her enormous trunk down the stairs with ease. "I've already said good-bye to Belle. We'll miss The Cockatoo and you. Everyone in Natchez has been gracious."

"You're sure that it's time for you to return home and that to sail on the same ship with Antoine Ferrand is the right thing to do," the half-frowning tavernkeeper

159

remarked in a questioning way. For one who hardly ever met a man he didn't like, he had fought to keep down the feeling of mistrust he had felt about Antoine ever since their first meeting.

"Oh, yes," Leander replied with enthusiasm, sending a hand to check the sassy hat married to a top cluster of jet curls by a determined, ornate hat pin. "Antoine assures me that my cousin Felicity and her groom will be back from their honeymoon by now. Jabbo and I will spend Christmas with the Ferrands at Belle Terre before going on to Beaux Rives." Her eyes sparkled with new happiness at the prospect of returning to familiar places and being around beloved people. "I'll never forget your kindness. And if you ever come downriver, please stop by and see us. Promise you will—and that you'll let Josie know I've gone home. She warned me never to write her directly."

"I promise," he answered, hoping against hope that his feelings about Antoine were misguided.

The cart outside screeched to a halt. While Leander pulled on leather gloves and sent one more farewell look around the lobby, Frenchie watched Jabbo pile their belongings high and signal for the driver to take them away. The two men said their farewells then, one so huge yet trim, the other shorter and run to comfortable fat. The tavernkeeper watched the gawky Gabriel follow the giant black man and his beautiful young mistress until they disappeared over the hill, knowing that once out of sight, they would start down the wooden steps leading to the docks.

Frenchie was relieved that Antoine was to meet the couple on board ship and that he wouldn't have to see the smug-faced young man again. He went inside to write a letter to Josie. Not sure how he could describe the way Antoine Ferrand had shown up a few days ago and seemed to take over Leander without showing his prejudice against the Creole, he picked up a quill, dipped it in the inkwell, and began. To hell with it. He would tell it the way he saw it. It seemed plain to him that Antoine wasn't worth Leander's little finger, much less the hand in marriage he was obviously seeking. The normally jovial tavernkeeper didn't smile much that day.

The ship had barely moved away toward midstream before one of the young slaves idling about to watch the river traffic had dashed up to the two-storied mansion to report that some people had arrived at Belle Terre's dock. What seemed to Leander like a small army rushed to welcome Antoine, Jabbo, and her. And of course the one she was happiest to see was Felicity. They hugged, kissed, cried, then started the process all over again.

Andre seemed no older or grayer than Leander recalled, though she admitted that now that he was married to Felicity and she was seeing him through wiser eyes, he somehow appeared younger and more handsome. He was quicker to laugh and joke than she had remembered—but what child younger than ten or twelve was ever allowed to be around visiting adults for more than a brief time? As soon as she saw the newlywed couple hurrying down hand-in-hand to welcome the arrivals, Leander had sensed that theirs must be a good marriage.

Leander wasn't sure she would have recognized Philip had she run into him as she had Antoine. Since she had seen him, Philip had changed from pretty-faced boy into dashingly handsome young man. The remembered trembly voice was now unerringly deep yet soft bass. Pale brown curls still tumbled across his forehead, and he hadn't given up at trying to push them back. His smile still showed a dimple in one cheek, but for the most part, he was like a stranger to her. She had never believed he would be so tall as his older brother, yet there he was, his head on a level with Antoine's. And how could she have forgotten that his eyes were a mysterious gray bordered with black lashes, nigh as thick and curly as her own?

Not long after all had wandered up the long, tree-lined path to the pillared veranda, Felicity announced that she believed it best for Leander to retire to her bedroom for an afternoon of rest. The slaves had long taken in the piles of trunks and packages and shown Jabbo to a room behind the kitchen next to Toby's, Belle Terre's majordomo. Gabriel was allowed a corner in Jabbo's room, but only because Leander insisted and no one wished to upset her.

The three Ferrand men agreed with Felicity's suggestion that Leander be given some time to herself, for all could tell from the confusion in the lovely purple eyes that the slender young beauty was overwrought. Coming this close to home after her six years' absence had indeed drained her emotions. And Christmas, sure to be a holiday tough on any orphan, was only four days away. Admitting to a strange kind of fatigue, Leander consented to meet all in the main receiving room before dinner.

On the way to the second-floor bedroom, the two cousins held a whispered conversation. They compared notes and got their stories straight, though Felicity giggled in that way Leander recalled from their childhood years, once the lie about studying at Miss Julia Shepherd's School for Young Ladies fell from her cousin's lips. Leander was delighted to note an aura of happiness about the new Mrs. Ferrand and told her so. Married life seemed to be agreeing with the pretty blonde.

Leander waited until Chloe, the slave assigned as her personal maid during her visit, finished unpacking her trunk before giving in to her desire to slip between the sheets on the canopied bed and sleep. Her dreams were shot through with disturbing memories and half-remembered incidents from her childhood. Even so, she didn't awaken until the soft-walking Chloe called to her that she had a tub of warm water ready for her bath in the dressing alcove just off the large room.

"Thank you, Chloe, for helping me into my gown," Leander told the young black woman after she stood before the full-length mirror and pirouetted prettily before it. She had accepted Chloe's choice of the blue taffeta, the first gown she had purchased from Belle. "And I believe you have a magic touch with hair." She admired the shining curls caught up high at her crown before spiraling down in jet splendor across her back and bared shoulders.

Chloe smiled and said, "To make one so pretty as you look stylish, Miss Leander, is no trick at all."

Noticing that it was already dark out on the grounds sloping toward the river, Leander left to go downstairs to rejoin her hosts. She was refreshed and ready to face an evening of gaiety. Being once more in the familiar mansion had brought back pleasant memories, and she felt almost at home. When she entered the receiving room, she heard spatters of conversation which piqued her curiosity. She knew she wanted to follow up on them, once the initial greetings were over.

A fluted stem of sherry in her hand, Felicity came to hug her cousin and exclaim over the loveliness of her gown. Before Leander could do more than return the compliment, Philip had appeared with a crystal stem of the amber wine for her. And then Antoine ended the conversation with his father to wander in their direction, leaving Andre to follow unless he wished to be left alone. Leander felt the warmth of the Ferrands' welcome and relaxed.

Once the small talk died down, Leander asked, "What was that I overheard when I came in? Something about Terre Platte no longer belonging to the Turrentines?" Her eyes turned inquisitively from one to the other.

"That's right, my dear," Antoine replied, his dark gaze raking over her in that way she couldn't seem to like. "You may as well know that Jacques was arrested the same day as your father, though he was imprisoned rather than shot." When Andre and Philip shot him disapproving looks for his bluntness, he shrugged elegantly clad shoulders and said, "Leander is quite a grown-up young woman now and I see no point in painting false pictures for her." He turned back to address the poised young woman in blue taffeta. "But his wife had no money to pay the increased assessment placed on all of the properties of the Conspirators, and so the Spanish government took over his plantation."

Leander raised delicate black eyebrows in protest, saying with strong feeling, "The bloody Spaniards

164

seem determined to inflict punishment upon the Creoles, even after they have satisfied their thirst for blood by shooting five of the so-called traitors—my own father among them. I'm distressed for Mrs. Turrentine. What has become of her?" The only good to have come from the news was to learn that Antoine was no longer treating her like a ninny, incapable of facing matters of a serious nature. Did that mean he had changed his mind about her intellect, or did it mean that he had deliberately withheld information about what was going on at Beaux Rives? To mask her thoughts, she drew on a fragile, willed composure threatening to slip aside at any moment.

"She was able to keep her personal slave and lives now in New Orleans with an aunt and uncle." Andre spoke up, his solemn face and tone belying his seemingly casual report. A hand smoothed at grayed temples. "I suppose the fact that Jacques and she never had any children turned out to be a blessing, as she would have found providing for them trying. Jacques is still in prison not far outside the walls of the capital, but she is allowed to visit him quite often, I gather. He should be freed by this time next year."

"All of this is unseemly conversation for my cousin's first night back with us," Felicity chided, flipping her blond tresses in agitation, and sending her new husband a stern look of vexation.

"Not at all," Leander insisted. "I asked because I overheard something about it when I came in. If I'm to live on the river again, I do need to know my neighbors. Who is now owner of Terre Platte?"

"A prince of a fellow," Philip replied. "A Lieutenant Salvador, a pensioned hero from the Spanish army, from what we heard when he first arrived four years ago. He started out to snub all of us Creoles, but something seems to have brought him around this fall. At least now he admits that we other planters exist and have quite a bit in common, despite our different heritages. He even attended Felicity and Father's wedding at English Landing. Although I've been around him several times over the past year, I can't say as how I've ever been able to get him to talk about how he was wounded while fighting the Apaches out in the Tejas country. It's my guess the fellow could be damned interesting if he chose to be. He came to Terre Platte to raise horses and has some of the finest I've ever seen, don't you agree, Father?"

"I do," Andre said. "I think you'll like Don Salvador, Leander. We were talking just before you came in if perhaps to invite him to share Christmas might not—"

"No!" exclaimed Leander, almost throwing her empty sherry glass at the lot of them, surprising the four no more than she surprised herself at the near loss of control. "No! I will never have anything to do with a despicable old Spanish don, no matter that his land borders mine. Please don't ever ask me to again. I never want to hear his or his family's name mentioned in my presence. Is that too much to ask to honor my father?" Pain made rags of her normally cultured voice. She sent scathing looks at all three dumbfounded men. "So what if he left the army as an old army 'hero' and gained our unfortunate neighbor's land through some dastardly bit of politics? I find it a cruel mark of injustice. I can't believe that you, Andre, would be so quick to forget that he is one of those responsible for the death of my father, the burning of my home—"

Tears rose unbidden in the violet depths and coursed down her face. Only then did she turn toward Felicity, unable to continue.

Felicity moved close, offered her handkerchief, and whispered words of comfort, waiting until Leander had recovered her poise before saying to her, "You have the man all wrong, Leander. You're jumping to false conclusions. Actually he is not—"

"I do not have him all wrong if he's a Spaniard," Leander broke in loudly, rudely. A haunted, desperate look replaced the still lingering tears in her eyes before she could regain a degree of composure. Swallowing the bitter taste of hatred and allowing deeply felt contrition to soften her face and voice, she included all with her next low-pitched remark: "Please forgive my loss of temper and good manners. But please spare me any further talk about the man."

Felicity nodded her head in acquiescence, letting her mind race to find a way to have Leander meet her neighbor socially and see for herself that he was no old pensioner, no ogre. She wanted nothing more than for Leander to realize that her obvious dislike for the Spanish was no longer the general consensus of opinion among the planters up and down the Mississippi. The passing of six years under moderate Spanish officials had done much to lay to rest old wrongs, both imagined and real.

Only Leander seemed unaware that after the shooting of the five Conspirators as an example of their intent to rule, the Spaniards had allowed, even encouraged, life in the colony of Louisiana to resume its customary, leisurely pace. Felicity empathized that because one of those shot was her cousin's father, it might be natural for Leander to have such a violent reaction upon first returning to the area. Still, certain facts needed to be acknowledged and sooner or later would need to be trotted out for the pansy-eyed beauty to face. That Etienne Ondine had openly, tauntingly railed against officials at his trial and seemed to seek death from the firing squad was common knowledge — except to his daughter, of course. Felicity quickly forgave Leander and awarded her mind free play in seeking an answer to soothe away the obvious misinterpretation of present circumstances. She promised herself that she would come up with something.

With a gleam of anticipation in her blue eyes from a hazy, half-formed plan, Felicity turned to the men. "I would like to ask that you honor Leander's request and that during her visit here for the holidays, no more mention be made of the Spaniard living on the other side of Beaux Rives. Let's postpone social activities for her first weeks here. Would that be too much to do for her after she has been through so much anguish?"

"Why, no, my dear," Andre answered his bride, his lined forehead showing his concern for having unwittingly upset their guest. "I apologize, Leander. It may be too soon for you to have to face up to the bad memories you've stored up. Perhaps in time your feelings against the Spaniards will temper and be less painful. We'll cooperate with you in making the many adjustments necessary to returning to live among us here on the river. This season will be a quiet one here at Belle Terre, a time for all of us to get better acquainted." He included his bride and his two sons in his look, a pleased look about his mouth. "I assure you that we'll honor your request. Please accept my apologies for having upset you."

"And mine," Philip added, giving a courtly bow and sending her a devastating smile. It showed the dimple in his right cheek to advantage.

Leander read more than friendship in those flirty eyes and startled. Mayhap Philip was going to be the one to sweep her off her feet in that way she had heard so much about, couldn't help but long for in secret, despite her avowal that marriage might not be a major goal yet. Her gaze took in the way his attractive mouth curved in the form of an elongated heart shape over gleaming teeth. The blue of his satin dinner jacket warmed the gray of his eyes into a dreamy blue. Yes, he was far handsomer than his older brother, almost beautiful — and, she sensed in an intuitive way, far less threatening. She gave no credence to the half-formed memory of the Spaniard who had proved to her that all threats might not come from without her own body. A quick lowering of sooty lashes served to conceal her upsetting thought — and deepen Philip's unsuspecting smile.

"I too offer apologies," Antoine said, not missing the exchanged looks between Leander and his younger brother. He turned to fetch another glass of sherry from a marble-topped serving board. Allowing his fingers to caress hers as they seemingly performed a mere act of courtesy, he removed the empty glass from her hand and replaced it with a full one. "Belle Terre is honored to have you with us, and we need no others to make our Christmas complete."

"Hear! Hear!" echoed both Andre and Philip, their glasses lifted in amiable toasts.

Felicity gave Leander a kiss upon her cheek. Within

seconds, the Ferrands' animated conversation about happenings among friends and acquaintances in New Orleans society filled the handsomely appointed room. Leander felt surprise that she recognized a few names. By the time all crossed the wide hall to the dining room, she was once more delighted to be back among her own kind of people. They were the finest in all of Louisiana, she exulted—warm, caring, cultured, and eager to help others. She mentally repeated the promise she had made herself again and again as she sat dreaming aboard *The Lady*. Once she was able to return to her home, the hopeful orphan would vow, she would never associate with the Spaniards, only with that group to which she belonged—French Creoles.

The Christmas holidays at Belle Terre served Leander as a time of becoming reacquainted with Felicity, sleeping late and being pampered, catching up on major happenings in the area over the past six years, of learning to accept the fact that she was an attractive young woman—at least to the two handsome Ferrand bachelors. She begged for more time before having to meet again the other planters in the area, luxuriating in settling into the comfortable patterns of family life in winter at a river plantation replete with numerous slaves and well-stocked pantries. Neither the newly-weds nor the groom's sons appeared to give second thoughts to turning down invitations to seasonal parties in the area. The five seemed content to remove themselves for a little while from the mainstream of life.

On sunny days, they rode horses across brown-stubbled pastures, through bare-leafed woods bordering open fields lying fallow. Looking resplendent in her purple velvet riding costume, Leander became reacquainted with the sidesaddle and blooded horseflesh. On rainy days and at night after sumptuous dinners, they played all manner of card games, most of them new and strangely drawn-out to one taught the simpler ones of chance by a wily old sailor. Sometimes the players numbered two or three. At other times all five in the luxurious house asked for dealt hands and joined in the merriment and relaxed conversations. As often as not, Antoine and Philip competed for Leander's attention in good-natured, open rivalry.

Antoine never passed up an opportunity, even seemed to create some on his own, to touch or caress her in socially acceptable yet knowing ways. Philip offered a more blatant flirtation, one she found far more pleasing. His mysterious gray eyes charmed her by watching her every move with obvious fascination and delight. His handsome face would soften and come close to beaming when she would laugh at his teasing jokes, or respond warmly to his attempts to learn more about the grown-up Leander. Whereas Antoine's intense scrutiny made her feel somewhat defensive about being of the opposite sex, Philip's open adoration made her feel desirable, proud of those feminine charms on which both seemed to dote. Antoine seemed a threat; Philip, a promise.

After a few weeks, though, the young heiress could no longer deny her half-dreaded, half-anticipated desire to return to Beaux Rives. She announced one afternoon to her hosts that she would leave as soon as arrangements could be made. The three were chatting in Andre's study over afternoon coffee.

"Promise you'll come back within a month for a visit

171

and attend our Mardi Gras party," Felicity begged when she could not persuade Leander to wait until the rainy season subsided. Sitting beside her on a leather settee, she studied the pensive oval face and tried to imagine how awful it must be for her cousin to be going back alone to a home and a situation which would be totally new, alien. She wanted nothing more than to ease Leander's burdens, take some of the awkwardness out of her assuming her place among the Mississippi planters. If things were to go Felicity's way . . . Her eyes twinkled.

"We'll be devastated if you refuse," Andre added from his chair near the fireplace. "I would deem it a great privilege to introduce the lovely, grown-up Leander to our friends and neighbors right here at Belle Terre. I believe your parents would like that your arrival be announced in this way. Everyone will be delighted to see you're alive and to welcome you back home. By then, the word will have spread all up and down the river."

"You'll be a guest of honor at our very first entertainment as a married couple," Felicity added, not liking the look of hesitancy clouding her cousin's face. "I know you'll not wish to disappoint us. We'll send out invitations this week so that the guests will have plenty of time to put together costumes. We can get some musicians to come up from New Orleans—Oh, Leander, please say you will."

"I'm not sure I'm ready for such an affair," Leander demurred. What would she do if people cornered her about her whereabouts over the past six years? What if some young woman present had actually been in Mobile at Miss Julia Shepherd's School for Young

Ladies? She tried to ignore the pleading in Felicity's blue eyes. And she had less luck in ignoring the Ferrands' hospitality of the past three weeks. "All right," she agreed, fighting back a sigh. "I'll come, but I've no idea what kind of costume to wear."

Felicity laughed, all warm on the inside at the thought that her scheme was working. "Wear a face mask and come dressed as your wildest dream—a princess or queen or whatever. What fun we'll have pretending to be fantasy characters until the stroke of midnight. It'll be a night to remember—just you wait and see!" Positive that she spoke the truth, she leaned over on the couch to hug Leander.

After Andre's announcement of the party to Antoine and Philip at dinner that night, talk among the Ferrands livened and centered on guest lists and possible costumes to have made up. Leander couldn't muster enthusiasm, though she did manage to keep a pleasant look on her face and appear interested. Later, both Antoine and Philip, in private asides, assured her that they would be calling upon her at Beaux Rives in the meantime—just to make certain all was going well and to see that she was settling into her new role of mistress of the large plantation. She couldn't keep from laughing to herself in private that each seemed to have rehearsed the same speech—though with far different undertones in their words.

Leander became too eager to return to Beaux Rives to wait for the muddy ruts to dry and allow a Ferrand carriage to travel the crude road following the riverbanks. The flag had flown only two days from Belle Terre's dock before a ship headed downriver pulled over to answer the call. The chill of the January afternoon had done little to diminish the great rush of warmth filling her heart as the familiar woods and fields of her childhood neared. And now the vessel was getting underway again, after having let off the passengers traveling such a short way.

"Oh, Jabbo," Leander wailed in a voice of anguish. Gabriel whined and looked up at her questioningly. A gust of cold wind whipped her skirts against her legs, tried to pry her hat from her head, did manage to set Jabbo's hat at an angle before he grabbed at it and jammed it down more firmly. They still stood upon the dock, looking through the rising, sparsely wooded area leading to the former Ondine mansion. "I can't believe Felix would have built such a plain little house on the crest where . . ." Her voice rode off with the wind.

"It doesn't look that bad, missy," Jabbo consoled. Having adopted, along with Leander, Dom's oft-spoken theory that little white lies were sometimes more palatable than stark truth, Jabbo agreed with her privately. It seemed to him that if the overseer couldn't have re-created some kind of house more in keeping with the grandeur of the former mansion, he should have chosen another site. "Mayhap times have been harder for Mr. Grinot than you've been hearing down at Miss Josie's."

Jabbo lifted her trunk then and hefted it to his shoulder. Talking about it wasn't going to change things and dark would fall soon, both thought, though neither spoke. Leander stepped from the dock, solemnly eyed the big hollow tree off to the side where she had hidden that fateful October afternoon when her father had last walked upon the worn pier, and started up the path. Only then did Gabriel decide to go along.

Wild cries of jubilation met them when they reached the front verandah of the rather square two-story house of red brick. First Sheeva rushed outside, almost joyfully hysterical in both manner and speech. Then came her daughter Cara to throw her arms about both newcomers. Tears and laughter mingled and hampered coherent speech.

"Praise the Lord!" kept ringing from first one mouth and then the other as the two slaves begged for explanations, all the while leading their young mistress inside. Jabbo stepped around them, once he could free himself, and set down the heavy trunk in the foyer. Not daring break into the feminine melee, he returned to the pier for another load, the obviously frustrated Gabriel at his heels.

"What is all this caterwauling about, damn you!" yelled a slurred but threatening male voice from a room off the entry hall. When his words seemed to have been swallowed up in the continuing female sounds, Felix Grinot walked to the doorway of the study, a glass of whiskey in his hand.

Whatever it was the gaunt overseer meant to yell next died aborning. His normally beady eyes bulged. His prominent Adam's apple slid up, shot back down, then made a return journey with a noticeable gulp slipping from his gaping mouth. He almost dropped his glass. Some inner voice consoled him with the fact that he had polished off only one earlier drink; he was not drunk. His free hand gripped the door facing. But if he weren't drunk, he thought in desperation, how could he be staring at the only woman he had ever loved, the one he still dreamed of, despite the fact that she had died over eight years earlier? God! Only last night while on his way back to his bedroom from the quarters, he had wandered in a drunken stupor to kneel at her grave in the plantation's fenced-in cemetery and pour out his grief at never having held her in his arms. "Violette," Felix muttered back in his paining throat.

"Felix," Leander said, turning from the suddenly silent women and taking a step toward him across the polished wood floor. "What a lovely compliment to call me by my mother's name." She held out her hand, unsure as to what was bringing such a horrified look upon the overseer's face. For some reason, she had never truly liked the man, had accepted him only because her parents did. Then it dawned on her. "Oh Felix," she exclaimed with a note of apology, "what a terrible fright I must have given you. You must have believed, as did almost everyone else, that I died in the fire."

"Leander," the slight man croaked, releasing the door frame to take the hand she was proffering. "Leander, I thought you were dead," he added in what he knew was a foolish tone and choice of words. She was alive and standing before him, looking exactly as Violette had looked the first time he had seen her on the ship over from France — so vibrantly beautiful and radiant that he felt himself almost whisked back some twenty years into the past. Her gloved hand was warm and small inside his own. Leander was real. "My God, girl, where have you been these six years?"

"I'm hardly a girl anymore, Felix," Leander retorted, a bit stung at his choice of the belittling term after his first instance of addressing her as her mother, former mistress of Beaux Rives. Whatever was wrong with the obviously befuddled man? Removing her hand from his limp grasp, she drew herself up to full height and lifted her chin. "I'm seventeen now and I've come home. I'd heard you had rebuilt Beaux Rives, but I must admit I was surprised at . . . what awaited me." With obvious disapproval she glanced about the plain foyer, the boxed stairway leading unceremoniously to the second floor. Seeing his eyes return to their remembered, smaller size and his always-lean lips set into a grim, straight line, she realized she was sounding too critical and added, "Of course to have found any kind of home to return to is welcome, and I'm sure you've done the best you could . . . under the circumstances."

"Under the circumstances," Felix repeated through gray lips, like one demented. "Yes, well that's true . . . Leander." He caught himself before repeating the word "girl," the one he had often used for her in the past. She was right. She was no longer a girl. Though at first she had seemed the spitting image of her mother, she bore an air of her father back in those early days, an air of aloof yet unabiding control. But those eyes, that exquisite face . . . He drew in a noisy breath and forced himself to let it out slowly. He had to get a hold on himself. Where in hell had she been? What child's bones had been found in the fire and lay now in the plantation's cemetery? But more important, how much did she know or suspect?

Jabbo came through the front door with his own trunk then, his appearance creating no happier expression upon Felix's shocked face. Gabriel bounded to Leander's side and lifted testing, disapproving eyes to the grim-faced overseer. His mouth grimaced enough to reveal sharp teeth. Absently patting the puppy's inquiring nose pushing at her skirts, Leander turned away from Felix and took over. She sent Sheeva and Cara to prepare the largest bedroom upstairs for her, turning then to Felix to ask what manner of rooms existed on the ground floor.

"The study and office is here," Felix replied, gesturing toward the room behind him. He eyed the half-grown dog with a distaste equal to that he was receiving from it. "Next to it right down the hall at the foot of the stairway is a bedroom, then there's the living room across from us there." He indicated the area behind closed, double doors. "Beyond it is the dining room, with the kitchen separated by a whistle walk. Out behind the kitchen are two slave rooms for the house nig—"

"Fine," Leander interrupted before he could use the term her parents had forbidden to be used to refer to their slaves, a practice she intended to emulate. She turned to the silent, waiting black man. "Jabbo, you can move into the bedroom next to the study." When he seemed reluctant to follow her as she stepped toward where Felix had indicated it was, she looked over her shoulder to see why he hadn't stirred. The overseer was glaring up at the giant, a snarl curling his lips.

"Whatever is wrong with you, Felix?" she demanded.

"Why would you put a . . . ?" Felix caught himself, recalling how she had cut him off from using the term "nigger" earlier. He sipped from his glass before going on. She aimed to be as bullheaded as her parents about the "dignity" of the slaves. Ha! What did she know about how hard it was to get work out of them, how like savages they could be? "Why would you put Jabbo in the main house? That seems a mighty foolish decision."

178

"Foolish or not," she replied in a deadly, calm voice, "it's my decision to make, is it not?" When he refused to meet her demanding eyes and took a long drink from his glass but made no reply, she went on. "Let's get this straight right now. I am the owner of Beaux Rives; you are its overseer. Isn't that right?"

He wasn't ready to meet her eyes, but he did. Until he knew more about where she had been and what-all she had heard or learned, he had best play along. He would get a letter off to his friends in the Cabildo first thing tomorrow. "That's right, Miss Ondine."

"Felix, I'm not trying to stand on ceremony. Of course you may call me Leander," she said, not truly liking the idea but figuring that she was suffering from the pain of old memories and a touch of anger at his questioning her decision. She would view it differently later. He was probably feeling as awkward as she at the sudden change in their status. "But don't forget again that my decisions are to be honored unless I seek your advice. Do I make myself clear?"

Beneath the skin of his ashen face, Felix could feel anger heating, but he nodded and assumed an air of unconcern. "Quite clear."

Leander flipped her hair then with a touch of her father's arrogance, which she would have denied possessing in any degree, and led the way to the doorway down the hall, motioning for Jabbo to follow. Their steps rang loudly on the bare floor.

"What is all this?" she asked, once she entered the room followed by Jabbo and a slow-walking Felix. She gestured accusingly at the personal belongings lying about. "Is someone already staying in this bedroom?" Violet eyes flashed in the pretwilight darkness as she questioned the overseer just then appearing in the doorway.

"I am." Felix tried to meet those penetrating eyes but couldn't. He had no wish for her to see how upset she had him. Damn her for being alive! Damn her for being an Ondine! Her showing up unannounced like this was punishment from the devil. In one more year, if the Spaniards lived up to their part of the bargain, he would have obtained full ownership of the coveted plantation. Fear stirred his innards.

"You mean you *were* staying here." Fury underlined her words. How dare he? She had seen the overseer's house on her walk up from the river, still standing in good shape some distance from the main house, still adequate for his needs. The frightening thought that the man must think he held some claim to Beaux Rives wormed its way into her mind. But how could he, a mere overseer, have expected to become entrenched here as owner? How foolish for her to have dreamed that he had built a new house for her, had expected her to return. Through concentrated effort, she said nothing of her wild thoughts, let none of them show on her countenance.

"That's right. Jabbo can move my things out to the overseer's house. I was staying here because it was close to the office and all those records I've been keeping over the past six years," he replied, gaining some much-needed dignity by reminding her that he had been responsible for keeping the place running and building a house — even if she did seem to think it not good enough for her. He could see plainly now that she had far more fiery Ondine in her than genteel Marchand. The uncanny resemblance to her mother was purely physical. "Get busy, Jabbo."

"Send for someone else to do it," Leander ordered in a careless way. Taking in the flushed face and shocked eyes, she added with weighted candor, "You may recall that it has alway been the policy here at Beaux Rives that Jabbo doesn't take orders from anyone except an Ondine. Right now I have plenty for Jabbo to do in helping me get my trunk upstairs."

By then Leander had noticed that the two men refused to let their eyes meet. To see Jabbo apparently cowed for the first time since they had escaped that night pained her. Memories of the way the overseer had often talked roughly to the big slave during her father's frequent absences those final years came rushing to tear at her fragile composure.

She turned toward the still-faced giant and said, "Come on, Jabbo. Let's get started on moving my things upstairs. Sheeva and Cara probably have my room ready by now." Her head high, she waited at the doorway for Jabbo to walk on through it before saying in that voice he had termed "silken-clad steel" back in Natchez, "I hope you'll forgive me if I don't invite you to eat with me tonight, Felix." She turned to leave but halted to peer over her shoulder in the dim light. Looking older than she had expected, scrawny, not very tall, and very, very still, Felix reminded her of one of the countless, gray pieces of driftwood washed upon the banks of the Mississippi. He seemed all used up. She announced in a somewhat kinder tone, "I'm too weary to talk business. Plan to meet me in the study sometime before noon tomorrow. I suspect we have much to discuss." And with those words, the young mistress of the plantation left.

All the way up the unfamiliar stairs, Leander agonized at the difference in the way she had envisioned her homecoming would be and the way it truly was. Except for that plaguing, haunting memory of finding herself in intimate embrace with the passionate young man that night in Throw-away's room, wasn't she the same person who had escaped that October night six years ago? A bit larger, a grown-up now, yes—but on the inside, wasn't she still Leander, only child of Etienne and Violette Ondine, a true Creole by virtue of having been born to French parents in Louisiana? She begged that inner tyrant set on punishing her to promise, now that she was at home, that the disturbing, debilitating recollection of the hated Spaniard's effects upon her mind and body that night at Josie's Inn would disappear forever. Never before had she so desperately needed respite from that cruel memory. For the trying days ahead, she sensed that she would need all of her strength and wits about her.

Leander marshaled her thoughts to her surroundings. She examined the attractive bedroom to be hers, then breathed a sigh of longing for something unrecognized, something painfully elusive. The candle sputtered then, as if it might have the answer. The young mistress of the plantation sighed with enough force to set the flame to dancing. Beaux Rives was not living up to its lovely name. No "beautiful dreams" seemed to be awaiting her here. If there were to be any realized, she would have to search out new ones.

Chapter Nine

"That's right, Mr. Justin," Ona was telling her master one morning a week or so later at Terre Platte, the plantation downriver from Beaux Rives where Leander's disappointing homecoming had taken place. The soft-voiced woman was adding more coffee to his cup as he sat in the detached kitchen finishing up his breakfast and making little comments about her latest bit of news.

From outside came the clunks of split wood being piled in the woodbox beneath the covered walkway leading to the main house, the one referred to on most plantations as the whistle walk. The name fascinated Ona because she couldn't imagine Justin Salvador insisting that his slaves carrying in the dishes of food to the dining room be made to whistle all the way to insure they weren't snitching bites. Liking the continuing sounds of a mighty armload of wood being deposited, she let out a little breath of gratitude; Tobe had

183

remembered to send a boy from the stables to lighten his mother's load. With Tobe being her only living child, Ona couldn't help but be proud to see that he was shaping up into a nice young man.

Sometimes her young Spanish master seemed interested in the stories about his neighbors that Ona picked up through the slave grapevine, and at others he might as well have been listening to the crops grow. This morning he appeared more than normally amused at what she was telling. He was cocking his handsome head her way, revealing the tiny, silvery streak in the black hair, the one that, to those unknowing slaves from other plantations, she vehemently denied could suggest in any way that he might be a demon or a partner with the devil. Her insistence that he was fair and kind met with about as much belief. A half-smile played about Justin Salvador's full lips now as his amused, black eyes watched Ona go about her kitchen chores.

Jumping back in while she had his full attention, Ona went on, often repeating what she had already told at least once. "They say Miss Ondine just swooshed right in and swooshed Mr. Felix right back out to the overseer's place, quick as a wink. Tucked that big giant black they say her pa bought to look after her when she was a baby right inside the main house. No never mind that everybody knows he ain't never been what you exactly call a 'real man' since her pa bought him, but he's a slave, just the same as me. Can't see why he ought to be sleepin' in the bedroom at the foot of those stairs over there in that red brick box." Ona rolled her eyes and sniffed in disapproval before shuffling in a pair of Justin's cast-off slippers to set the coffeepot back on the iron monster of a stove with unneeded force. With balled fists on wide hips, she turned to add in a conspiratorial tone, "If you asks me, she gonna be sorry she crossed Mr. Felix, no matter how snippety she acts and dresses. Whoo-ee! She sounds like somethin' else, she do for a fact." In Ona's vocabulary, "something else" used in that way was far from complimentary. She picked up Justin's empty plate and went over to her work table.

"Maybe Miss Ondine feels the need for protection," the audience of one offered, sipping at the thick brew and grinning at his cook's love of the dramatic.

Upon first sight and brief exchange, Justin had bought Ona and her teen-aged son from a fellow Spaniard down near New Orleans right after he came to claim Terre Platte. The short, squat black woman had lived up to the man's brags of her being a good cook and housekeeper. The boy Tobe had turned out to be a natural with horses. Justin, refusing to consider buying one without the other, suspected that the way Ona ran her mouth might have been why her previous owner's wife had been willing to give up her growing boy and her. As for him, he could listen or not, reply or not, as he chose.

The pleasant-faced woman seemed not to mind if her master remained silent. Her moods were generally sunny, even when a few clouds hovered on the horizon. Actually, he reflected as he watched Ona return to the batch of bread dough resting on a board and knead it lovingly with the pinkish heels of her hands, her chatter often kept him from getting too caught up in his own thoughts at those solitary breakfasts not taken in the dining room in the main house. And her tales were nearly always proven true, a fact which amazed him, even after four years. Wondering what answer she might come up with, he asked, "If this overseer is not her friend, why doesn't the so-elegant Miss Ondine send him packing?

"The way I hear it," Ona said, cutting dark eyes his way with self-importance, "is that he done told her the day after she come back that he was her legal guardian till she be eighteen this comin' December, that she can like it or lump it, but he aims to stay there and oversee that place till she turns eighteen or finds herself a husband. He got the right, he told her." Deft hands lifted the mound of dough and flipped it over, letting it drop back to the board with a little round sound. The kneading continued then, the dough turning into a tighter, smoother mass at each firm movement. "Miss Ondine must've thought she was comin' back to be some kind of grand lady, like they say her mama was. But they ain't much over there at Beaux Rives still like it used to be, or so them's that knows tells. That must've been some showplace — not that ours ain't goin' to be as grand, if you ever get it finished!"

"Then this Miss Ondine will likely not stay around long enough for me to have to go call on her," Justin remarked, ducking her hint for him to tell her more about the new home he had been building over the past two years up the hill from where this smaller, simpler one built by the previous owners sat. "And that will suit me just fine."

"You might meet her at that dress-up party you got the invite to," Ona suggested. When he sent her a keen look but made no reply, she said, "You know, the one from the new Mrs. Ferrand up at Belle Terre." Justin studied the contents of his cup. "I heard you tellin' Mr. Lemange you might get word to your soldier friend Captain Galvez in New Orleans to pick out some kind'a outfit and send it on the next ship comin' this away." The extra sparkle in her dark eyes suggested that she liked the idea of her handsome young master going to a party. And such a fine one too, her manner hinted. "There's boun' to be all kinds of pretty ladies there. I ain't never seen you get an invite to one of them Creole Mardi Gras balls before."

Justin let out a deep breath. "You're right, Ona. I guess for the new mistress of Belle Terre to make me an honored guest at her first big party is quite a compliment to one not having lived among the Creoles any longer than I have. Looks as if I'll have to go — if for no other reason, to prove I've mastered their French now." His eyes met her questioning ones then, and he admitted with a little laugh, "And, yes, I sent off a message to my friend Galvez last week when the ship stopped to pick up some other packets. If he gets a costume up to me in time for the party, I suppose I'll have no choice but to attend."

Ona beamed then. "That's nigh onto two weeks away. For sure he'll send one before then. What kind of outfit did you tell him to get?" She was smiling still, shaking her head from side to side with pleasure, in rhythm with her kneading.

"I left the choice up to him. As for me, I couldn't care less."

"Um-umm!" the black woman grunted with a roll of eyes and a pursing of lips in real anticipation. "You're gonna be the most handsome man there, I can tell you that. And I'll bet that Miss Ondine, comin' back to river country all fancied up from that ladies' school in Mobile, is gonna think so too." Justin frowned and cocked his head in consternation at her conclusions. With cocksureness, Ona added, "She's sure to be there, 'cause I've heard the new Mrs. Ferrand is her cousin."

More than a little annoyed at Andre's bride for having placed him in a position of appearing a lout if he refused to show up as a guest of honor, Justin let a deep, bass "humph!" escape into the kitchen. "I feel I've been backed into a corner. I can't say as how I'm looking forward to going to the ball any more than I'm looking forward to meeting the illustrious Miss Ondine."

From what Ona had been telling about the returned heiress, Justin had put together a picture of the kind of young women he had met again and again on the river plantations over the past four years when he felt forced to accept a few invitations—beautiful on the outside, maybe, but too arrogant, spoiled, and vain to warrant a second thought as a possible wife. He let out a sigh. The weird fantasy he had experienced at Josie's Inn that night back in November still haunted his dreams, hindered his sleep—and here it was already past the middle of January.

Justin Salvador's rational, daytime self had accepted, after that visit with Josie, that the young woman had not existed except in his drunken dream. But his illogical nighttime self rebelled and kicked up all kinds of fuss. Surely, it would tell him, he had kissed real lips, caressed soft curves, smelled fragrant hair . . . About the only way he could come to any kind of terms with the puzzle was to take the dream as a generic sign that there was such a young woman somewhere waiting for him. But where? And how could he go about completing the interior of the mansion without having even met the one he had sensed from the beginning that he was building it for?

Generous mouth pursed, Justin patted his pocket for one of his thin cigars, glad in a way that one wasn't there. Ona would rant about his smelling up her kitchen so early in the morning. He asked in doubting tones, "How does the exalted Ondine heiress explain her mysterious absence of all those years? It seems strange to me that if some child's bones were actually in the remains of the burned mansion, somebody wouldn't have reported a child missing." His olive forehead wrinkled. A forefinger and thumb worried an earlobe. The affair did sound mysterious.

Ona pinched off giant globs of elastic dough and shaped them, slapping them into the greased bread pans lined up on her work table, saying as she worked, "There's some strange talk about that, Mr. Justin, but it sounds too much like gossip to put much store in it." She sliced a look at her master to see if he wanted her to repeat it anyway. He merely watched her hands smoothing the dough into the pans while letting his interest show on his face. The way he was tugging at his ear told her he was in deep thought. "Some says that there was a little slave girl named Fleur who used to come from down here at Terre Platte to visit her granny Sheeva up at Beaux Rives. And they says that Fleur ain't never been seen since that night." She clamped thick lips shut tightly over the final words and shot him a so-what-do-you-think-about-that look.

"Why would no one have reported her absence? Did her mother leave with Mrs. Turrentine when she left

189

Terre Platte and went to live in New Orleans? Would she have pretended she didn't notice her child was missing?" Justin rocked the straight chair back then on its hind legs and rested his elbows on the table for balance. He flung a hand in the air toward her in disbelief and disapproval, a scolding mien about the handsome face. "That does sound like gossip, Ona."

"Don't it, though?" She noticed his cup was empty then and wiped off her floury hands with a cloth. Lifting the heavy coffeepot with a hand protected by the same cloth, she came with little slapping sounds of the slippers to the table to pour him another splash or so. Over the years, she had learned what he liked. Both watched the fragrant, hot liquid meet the leavings in his cup and mix. "It 'pears to me that Mrs. Turrentine must of took the mother with her, 'cause she ain't around these parts no more. The part which puzzles ole Ona is the talk about the little girl's daddy being that overseer, Mr. Felix Grinot."

Ona remained beside the table, obviously intent upon making sure Justin wanted her to continue her tale involving the possible wrongdoing of a white man. His chair still cocked on its hind two legs, he held himself in place with only one elbow on the table and picked up his cup with his free hand, blowing gently before savoring those final few sips of the hot brew. Black eyes squinted in puzzlement at Ona's tale.

Taking his silence as consent, Ona continued in an ominous voice. "Some says he fathered that Fleur on Sheeva's daughter there at Beaux Rives and that Massa Ondine and his missus got all furious about it. Next thing anybody knows, from what I hear, the mama and baby done got sold to the Turrentines right here at

Terre Platte." The black woman shuffled on back to the stove to set down the pot again. Unfolding the floury cloth used as a make-do potholder, she turned back to add, "And these same folks says that Mr. Felix couldn't stand the sight of that child, wouldn't even look at her when she come to visit her granny or to play with Miss Ondine. The little girls was about the same age, you see, and was kind'a friends, though I heard Fleur wasn't 'zactly right in the head."

Justin rose then, his half cup of coffee finished, his face heavy with thought. The turn of the tale was bordering on the lurid. "Mayhap the mother was afraid to make a fuss about her child. Felix could have jumped to false conclusions about the bones belonging to the Ondine girl, and the slaves could have been too frightened to contest his announcement that she was the one who died."

Justin had heard stories from others than his own slaves that Felix Grinot was a devious, cruel man. Once in New Orleans, one of his soldier friends in his cups had confided knowingly that Etienne Ondine would have been Justin's neighbor had it not been for his overseer's fingering him as one of the main leaders in the Conspiracy of '68. When Justin showed his disbelief, the man had said that the talk among Spanish officers was that Felix had killed Etienne as surely as though he had fired the shots felling him and the other four traitors. The talk had been too flavored with whiskey to merit serious attention. But Felix might be too cruel, mayhap, for slaves to come forth with a story not to his liking, for fear of reprisals. From what Ona had told, the man evidently tried to pretend his illegitimate daughter did not exist; perhaps he therefore would not have cared to admit that she had died. Justin had met the man a time or two when they would be checking fences between the two plantations, and he had not found him pleasant.

When the young Spaniard had come to claim Terre Platte, he had learned that the relationship between slaves and their owners varied from plantation to plantation. Not all resembled the casual one of mutual need which he fostered at Terre Platte. Quite logically, Justin had reasoned it out soon after arriving at his property, once he faced up to the fact that no hired help would be available to him in Louisiana as it would have been in Spain. The blacks had already been kidnapped from their tribes, or sold by fellow tribal members, and shipped to be sold on the auction block at Algiers across the river from New Orleans. They were unfortunate humans who needed food, shelter, clothing, and decent treatment. As a plantation owner, Justin had to have laborers and was willing to expend money to obtain their services.

For Justin, the system worked at Terre Platte. He provided for the needs of his slaves, and, in return, they gave him the work required to raise crops and horses. He well knew that a major reason that things ran smoothly on his place was his good luck in luring over from his father's horse ranch in Spain the capable, fair-minded Petra Solo to act as overseer. Already a widower in his forties when Justin sent for him that year he settled in Louisiana, Petra seemed to have no problem in getting things done in an orderly way. And Justin would have staked his life on his belief that no one could accuse Petra of being cruel.

That many of the other planters pursued different

methods of handling their slaves seemed none of Justin's business. He had learned that white men often carried on secret liaisons with unwilling blacks in their slave quarters, a practice he found repugnant from all angles. Pale or bright-skinned children, such as the little girl Fleur must have been, could be seen around a number of the plantations up and down the river. Seeking not to judge, Justin preferred to avoid discussions about such matters. Let each man find his own path of right and wrong.

"Ona, I'm going up to the building site to speak with Pierre," he said, bending his tall frame to squint out through the window at the overcast skies. "For an architect, he's quite a working man. He told me last night at dinner that he would be sanding on the mantels for the fireplaces today if it gets too bad to carry on work outside. The way the rains have set in, it looks as if any work is to get done, it will have to be inside. Those bayous across the back of the place are already filled to their tops. We may be in for some flooding across the back areas as bad as that three years back."

"Yes, sir," the all-knowing cook and housekeeper replied. "I heard Tobe talkin' about gettin' some sandbags filled before the river covers up all its bars and first banks." Justin's having talked with her and listened to her would brighten her whole day, no matter what the weather outside. "Mr. Pierre came down this morning like always and had an early breakfast before goin' on up to the new house. After these two years of bein' around nearabouts all the time, he seems like he might nigh belongs here now. If he ever gets through buildin' our new house and goes back to New Orleans,

193

we's goin' to miss him." She paused before adding a stick of wood to the stove, not hiding the obvious hope that Justin would yet tell her more about when Pierre Lemange and his work crew might finish the mansion. "On the outside, it looks like they just about got it all done." The stick of wood remained in her hand, suspended in midair, as if it too hoped to hear some news.

With a lopsided grin of indulgence for the lovable but nosy Ona and a cheery wave of his hand, Justin pulled on his coat and left the capable woman to her tasks. Dark mumblings and the thumping sound of a stick of wood being thrown forcefully onto the iron stove grates followed him out onto the bricked whistle-walk. The naturally upturned corners of his mouth performing the job they did often and masterfully, Ona's young master smiled, his black eyes sparkling with inherent mischief. He figured she was probably scowling and muttering at her failure to get him to tell one thing that entire morning about the new house.

Upriver at Beaux Rives, its owner was beginning to find the unfamiliar becoming familiar. Those first weeks back home had taxed Leander to the fullest. She had deliberately put off having the heart-to-heart talk with Felix which she knew was inevitable. At the end of her third week back, she sent for him one rainy morning to meet with her in the study. Earlier talks between them had centered on the business of establishing their new relationship, running the plantation, examining past records, and making plans for the upcoming planting season. She had pored over every sheet of journals, had made notations of her own, and had talked at length with Jabbo about what he could remember of the activities during those earlier years. To her delight, Jabbo was extremely knowledgeable and helpful.

"Glad you had some coffee ready, Leander," Felix remarked when he came in and took the chair in front of her. He licked his lips and shot her a pleased look. With a bony, dirt-grimed hand, he lifted the porcelain pot from the tray there on the desk between them and poured himself some of the brew up to what must have been an imaginary line on the inside of the cup — for he had to pour two more short spurts before he was satisfied. Noisily he added brown sugar crystals.

The busyness of Felix's never-changing ritual of getting his coffee ready to drink always set off feelings of disgust in Leander. She couldn't remember ever having noticed how Dom or Jabbo or anyone, for that matter, went about fixing his coffee. But something about Felix's habits drew her attention, and she could barely keep herself from staring, or worse, saying something to him about his strange, uncouth habits. Even the way he brought the nearly overflowing cup to his mouth seemed repugnant. His inelegant head jerked downward as if some inner cord snatched at it. His thin lips pursed in greedy anticipation, the moment his hand began lifting, then made a crude, slurping sound when they met their goal. After three weeks of watching him drink coffee at those several times when they would be discussing business or at the two times when she had invited him to dine with her, she had hoped that she would have gotten used to it by now. But she hadn't. She always felt she was watching a glutton getting ready to feast on something rare, something he feared was likely to disappear if primitive haste weren't employed.

"Did your suitor go back home?" Felix asked, settled now to lean back against the chair. Half his coffee was already gone. He held onto the saucer and toyed with the spoon, as if forcing himself to wait before draining the cup.

"Philip left this morning, yes," Leander retorted. When Antoine had come to visit over the past weekend, Felix had asked the same question when he left. "I think it best that you not call every young man who calls here my 'suitor.' Both the Ferrands are my friends, not necessarily my suitors."

"Since I'm your legal guardian until you marry or turn eighteen, I guess I've a right to know what's going on with my ward," he shot back, not the least daunted at her disapproval. He had already received a letter from his friend in the Cabildo in New Orleans. Not everything was lost . . . yet. "I'm thinking that neither one of them has the money you're going to need to keep this place running."

Leander dropped her eyes to her hands clasped in her lap before looking across at the gray-faced man to say, "I realize we need to go over the holdings in the bank at New Orleans and this year's tax assessment, but I'm not ready to discuss those matters yet. Today I want to talk about what happened here the night the house burned. You told me last week you would be willing to discuss it later. We need to get everything out in the open. I think it's time now."

"What's to discuss? You got your mind made up that the burned bones belonged to some little slave sneaking around upstairs in your bedroom where she had no business." He gave in to the urge to empty his cup, all in one lengthy guzzle. With a smack of satisfied lips, he set the cup and saucer back on the tray. "Have you learned anything new? You know you can't believe half what them nig—uh, slaves, tell you. That's why I just put it out of mind. Nobody will ever know what happened for sure."

"I think you're wrong. I believe that from what I've learned, that it happened as I surmised. You were in New Orleans then, right?" She narrowed her eyes a bit at the changed color of his face. Somehow, it seemed to have faded to an even paler, more unbecoming gray. A forefinger twirled at a black curl falling across the shoulder of her morning gown of green wool while she awaited the overseer's answer.

"That's right. I was down there selling the last of the year's crops. And before I could return, the Spaniards had sailed down with your papa to hold his trial. When I learned about all that, I hung around to see if I might could help him any way." Felix's voice was brittle, a mite higher in tone than normal. The words came rushing out, as if they had been rehearsed. His hands fidgeted with the buttons on his work jacket. When the pansy eyes kept their unblinking gaze on him, he continued. "And then . . . afterward . . . I brought his body back to bury it beside your mother. I hadn't heard about the fire until then. I was as shocked as anyone to see nothing standing but the chimneys."

"And you assumed that the bones were mine?"

"Why wouldn't I?" he asked defensively. "You weren't anywhere around and every last slave swore he didn't know a thing about you or that giant. Nobody ever told me that your papa gave Jabbo orders to light out with

197

you to kinfolks in Mobile if something bad happened. Until you told me where you went, I didn't even know there were any kinfolks this side of France, outside of Felicity, of course."

That Felix knew so much about her parents' families surprised Leander, but she didn't show it. She went on with the despised task. "Now I've learned that Fleur was here all that last day, and I think I recall hearing her call to me while I was hiding from the soldiers in the woods. You know how—"

"Fleur?" Felix echoed, his Adam's apple jerking.

"Yes, Fleur—your daughter by Leone," Leander remarked with force. The memory of the painful sessions over the past days with Sheeva and Artemis, the housekeeper's husband and timekeeper for the field hands, tore at her, but she continued. "I know all about Leone's, the older daughter of Sheeva and Artemis, having to submit to you and bear your child. I never knew before why only their younger daughter Cara is still with them, how it was that Leone and the baby Fleur were sold to the Turrentines to get them away from you, yet keep them close enough to visit with family here."

"That's a pack of lies. You got no proof, just a bunch of crazy slaves trying to get an overseer in trouble," Felix shot back with false bravado. The uneasy truce instigated silently the second day after she returned and learned he was her guardian seemed in jeopardy. He worked hard not to give her a piece of his mind.

"All that I know didn't come from slaves. I learned most of this from Andre Ferrand when Felicity and he came for a visit one afternoon this week." She almost gagged at the thought that she would have to attend the

Mardi Gras party so soon. Next week, she realized. Both had seemed so excited and eager over the impending affair that she had again promised to be there. She was certainly in no mood for celebration.

"Nobody told me they came," Felix muttered, sending her an injured gaze. Even after three weeks of having Leander back, he could hardly look at her and not feel awed at her resemblance to Violette. More than once he had found himself torn between wanting to slap her and longing to kiss her. Each time he allowed himself to admit he hated her—as now—her beauty stunned him, brought him up short.

Leander ignored his martyred air and tone and went on. "Only when the three of us insisted did Sheeva support what Andre—and probably most of the neighbors—already knew. I don't believe I have to remind you that you will take no steps toward discussing any of this with the slaves, Felix." Leander's voice revealed the steel that time and gained the nervous little man's full attention. She had no trepidations about stomping on the unvoiced truce.

"Well," he countered, letting his eyes examine the familiar grime around and beneath his nails, "you're grown-up now and you might as well know that such things do happen . . . or did happen. I got no call to be talking it over with slaves. After your parents became upset about all of it and decided to send Leone and her baby away, we never had any more problems like that around here." One hand came up to stroke at the graying hair straggling back limply from a receding hairline. "It could have been that Leone was just a troublemaker. Some of them are like that, you see. I never did believe that child was mine, if you want to know—"

"I already know for certain that she was," Leander broke in coldly. "Her parentage is not the issue. The point here is that we now can identify the bones of the burned child, the child buried out between my mother and father. It was your daughter Fleur. I wish to have you correct the marker to show her name as Fleur Grinot, but leave her body where it is. My parents felt protective toward her in life; I'm sure they do in death as well."

Felix fidgeted and crossed his legs. To hell with the unspoken truce. He would face her head-on if need be. Anger swelled his throat and almost cut off his words. "Whatever you say, Leander." Sarcasm and the injustice of it all joined and came to his aid then. He spoke in a loud, testy voice. "As you pointed out that first night, you're the mistress here; I'm merely the overseer who stayed on and worked like the devil to keep the place operating . . . for you."

Leander rose and went to stand at the window behind her desk, thinking how appropriate that rain wept outside and fell in sad, erratic patterns down the window panes. She leaned her forehead against the cold glass and closed her eyes. "Don't you even want to know how Fleur happened to be in the house and burned to death?"

Felix squirmed on the chair and admitted with cutting honesty. "I don't much care about what happened to her." Then in plainly grieving tones, which sickened Leander, he went on. "But I loved that house as much as you did. All I know is that the soldiers said they were sampling from the wine cellar and must have left open the front doors. It wasn't cold that night and some of the windows were raised, but they had built a fire in the fireplace in the living room because they figured to wait up all night for you to come home and thought it might turn nippy. A wind must have come whistling through while they were out of the living room and sent some coals out onto the wooden floor. I expect you remember how the night winds from the river could whip out those long drapes. It wouldn't have taken much for the place to be blazing before a few soldiers lapping up Etienne's fine French wines down in the cellar would've noticed." Only the rain falling outside edged into the silence there in the study. Even the fire in the fireplace burned without sound. Clearing his throat, he went on with a noticeable quaver. "They swore they never meant to burn the house—that beautiful house that I watched go up, brick by brick, plank by plank."

Every word attacked Leander's heart, but not in the ways Felix might have believed. What was a house, any house, when compared to a human life? Doggedly, she turned from the gray February morning to face him. "Fleur often slept on the floor on a pallet in my bedroom upstairs when she visited her grandparents over here. Late that afternoon when Sheeva told her to return to Leone at Terra Platte, she must have slipped upstairs to my room to lie down and wait for me, as she had so often done. As you must have known, she wasn't as bright as most little girls. She must have dozed off and never knew the place was on fire until she was already being consumed by the flames tearing up the staircase. The slaves were terrified at being left with no one to look after them. Papa was gone, and so were you. It was late, and no one in the quarters noticed the flames until the noise became so loud." Tears of grief and pain lay within the purple depths but stayed in their beautiful prison. She too well remembered watching the eerie glow of the fire from the deck of Dom's boathouse as it floated off downstream in the darkness. "How can you say you don't care what happened to her?"

Felix's hard little eyes met the accusing, despising ones fixed on him and struggled vainly to escape. He could find no words for a long time. "Life gets hard," he finally managed to blurt past lifeless lips. So much for truces.

Leander had learned the whole nasty business, he groaned inwardly. It had never occurred to him six years ago that the child's bones weren't hers. And it had never seemed strange to him that none of the slaves had made any effort to touch the bones before his return. The way he saw it, they acted as they should have by waiting for the overseer to return and give orders. Now he wondered if some of them hadn't known all along who had died in the fire and had deliberately kept quiet when he announced it was Leander. The fools never had liked him and looked up to him as they had to Etienne. Had they known Jabbo and she had escaped and kept it from him all this time? He darted a look about the room to keep those accusing, Violette-like eyes from ferreting out his wild wish that it had truly been Leander that he had ordered be buried out in the Beaux Rives cemetery.

Possessing not a whit of sympathy for any other human than himself, Felix hadn't even wondered after Leander's return that no one had reported to him at the time of the fire that a child was missing. He recalled vividly how the blacks had moaned and cried and carried on for a week back then over the deaths of their master and what at least Felix had believed to be Etienne's daughter. No telling what the slaves had thought. The only person reported missing was Jabbo, and Felix had figured the big man had seen a chance to escape and taken it. What slave wouldn't, if he had the chance, was the way the cold-blooded overseer looked at it. That belief was one reason he kept such a tight rein on those under his control.

Only one slave, Tower, a huge young buck with a smart mouth and the idea that he had a claim on Cara, younger daughter of Sheeva and Artemis, had attempted to get away over the past six years. Felix had used the vicious cat-of-nine-tails, bought in New Orleans before he ever returned with Etienne's body, to show Tower and all others with similar ideas that Felix Grinot's authority was not to be questioned. The startling thought that it was not only being questioned by the young beauty sending him covert looks for the past three weeks, but was also being downright challenged, even overridden in subtle ways by that same person, raged through his troubled mind.

"If we don't learn to work together this year," Leander said in a thoughtful way, "life is going to get even harder. I suggest that we put away these painful memories and get on with the business of making good crops here on the place."

What else could she do, she agonized. The second day after her return, Felix had shown her the hated papers from Governor O'Reilly designating him as her legal guardian and caretaker of Beaux Rives until at least the coming December. When Antoine was visiting over the following weekend, she had asked him to examine them as a lawyer. Though it had obviously plagued him to admit it, he had told her they were, indeed, legal and binding. His seemingly careless rejoinder was for her to marry him on the morrow and allow him to boot the shiftless Felix on his way. As Leander had told the half-jesting Antoine with great seriousness, she had no intentions of making any hasty decisions about any matter—and especially marriage.

Just then, loud clumping noises in the hallway kept Felix from having to reply. After a hasty knock on the door, Sheeva stuck in her head to announce that Artemis needed an audience. She was hardly out of the way before her husband, his wet hat held against his chest with both hands, stood before their mistress and the overseer.

"Miss Ondine, Mr. Felix," Artemis addressed both, "the big bayous across the back of the plantation are about to overflow." His black face and troubled voice showed deep concern. "Every little stream tryin' to feed into them big ones is goin' to back up and flood all the fields iffen we don't get busy fillin' sandbags and start buildin' some levees about the place."

"Glad that you've told me," Felix said, eager to have an excuse to get away from Leander. He had meant to start the slaves to filling sandbags last week when he heard that the neighboring plantations were already taking such cautious steps. At least he had remembered to keep the older women busy each winter sewing up a supply of sacks for the flood season. "I've been noticing how the river is widening. We don't want a repeat of backwaters threatening the main buildings here on the rise like they did three years ago. Call out all able hands to the riverbanks with shovels and bags. Send some of the older ones on horseback to keep a close check on those little streams. We can't do much to control Frenchman's Bayou across the back, but if we can find the low spots beside the smaller ones, we might can contain the water until the big bayou can take it up. I'll be out to join you; we'll need every slave we can get. See if some of the young women and bigger children can help out. Getting started this early in the day, we ought to have plenty of sandbags by nightfall to start throwing up levees in the morning."

"Jabbo will want to help," Leander told Artemis when he seemed ready to rush from the room to get started. She hated to admit it, but Felix had sounded like a man with a head for planning and getting things done well. Was this the Felix her father had admired and respected? She had begun to wonder why the overseer had been kept on so long. But now . . . At least she could offer what little assistance she could by allowing Jabbo to work alongside the others. "You'll find him in the stables. Please tell him I sent you to ask for his help, Artemis. He can do the work of two without even trying."

After Artemis rushed off, Felix turned to give an assessing look at Leander standing there behind the imposing desk he had bought for himself. Again her startling beauty—no, it was Violette's beauty—over-whelmed him, stirred at dead fires. "You know," he said with a weak smile and a wild glitter in his narrowed eyes, "we might not make such a bad team after all." And with those strangely disturbing words, he, too, left.

Leander stared after the gray little man, her lips

parted in wonder at all that had gone on in the study that rainy morning in February. She could hear distant rumblings from far away. A new storm was approaching from the west before the present one wore itself out. For some reason she couldn't understand, she felt a new chill.

Chapter Ten

After the men hurried away, Sheeva served Leander a midday meal and asked leave to go early to slave quarters. She wanted to help with the children left behind while the able-bodied filled sandbags down on the banks of the rising Mississippi. Alone in the house, the young mistress wandered upstairs to her room. The day was still heavy with the threat of the approaching, second storm, but the rain had ceased.

Something nudged at Leander while she was standing at her window looking toward the river in the distance. Some bit of knowledge begged to be recognized. Her forefinger wrapping at a wisp of hair, she let it surface. The horses. The young horses were still on the back side of Frenchman's Bayou.

Within minutes, she was braiding her hair into the old pigtails, searching for the old pants and shirt she had worn on the flight from Josie's. For some reason, she hadn't been able to throw them away after

Frenchie's servant back at the tavern had laundered them.

Soon after Leander had returned to Beaux Rives, Jabbo and she had ridden over the plantation more than once. She had felt the need to see again those arpents she had known so well as a child. One afternoon two weeks ago, before the streams had risen to dangerous levels, they had come to Frenchman's Bayou, the big one running across the back of the plantation. The stream served as a kind of boundary between the concessions granted on the riverfront and those smaller pieces of land parceled out to settlers of less wealth or importance. Etienne Ondine had received a narrow strip of land on the far side of the meandering bayou, and it was there, on a site across Frenchman's Bayou, that he had built a hunting lodge for his cronies and him to escape to when they wished to hunt and get away from the confines of mansions and polite society.

Leander recalled all of that while she dashed about getting ready to go out to the stables. But what spurred her on was the memory of Jabbo's and her discovery two weeks ago. They had come upon an old pasture on the other side of the bayou near the lodge. Even in the midst of winter, it showed green there in its sheltering border of heavy forest. Having noted that the small group of young, unbroken horses pasturing on the side of the bayou toward the house and buildings were finding few sprigs of green to supplement occasional deposits of hay from the barn, she suggested to Jabbo that they drive the horses across Frenchman's Bayou to the better pasture.

Leander was keenly aware that Beaux Rives was

going to need the horses in good shape if her recent plan to build a large herd were to materialize. And before they returned at dark that night, Jabbo and she had succeeded in moving the horses to the choicer spot. The ride was long, and they had rushed to their separate dinners without taking time to mention to Tower, head stableman, or to Felix that they had moved the young horses. Later, Leander had become involved with the unpleasant business of Fleur's death and forgotten all about the changed location of the animals.

Dressed and ready for the lengthy ride, Leander hurried to the stables. When Gabriel didn't bound to meet her and lick her hands, she figured he must have followed Jabbo down to the riverbank. Only one saddlehorse remained. She recalled then that Felix had planned to send slaves out on horseback to assess conditions of the smaller streams. Talking to the aged Thunder who had served her well when she was a child, she slipped on his bridle and left him to search the tack room for gear. Only her sidesaddle was left. Having thought that to wear her breeches and use a regular saddle would lend her speed for her long journey, she grimaced and struggled to throw the cumbersome saddle onto Thunder. It took three tries and bruised palms before she succeeded.

Leander's face showed her amusement at the incongruity of being coiffed and dressed like a ragamuffin yet riding on a sidesaddle. She grabbed somebody's hat from a hook and poked her braids beneath it, glad she had remembered to bring her own leather gloves. Not until she brought them from her coat pocket to put them on did she notice that in her haste she had grabbed the pretty ones of blond leather. If she wanted to make the long ride, move the horses back across the bayou before it became impassable, and return before night, she wouldn't have time to go back for a more serviceable pair. She mounted and set out for Frenchman's Bayou.

The rain held off during the first hour of Leander's ride westward, though the rumbling clouds and streaks of lightning in the distance seemed almost low enough to touch the tops of the towering forest up ahead. She had half expected to run into some of the men out riding check on the swelling streams closer to the house and perhaps get someone to go with her, or at least tell Jabbo where she had gone. But when none appeared in the cold, gray afternoon and she realized how involved everyone was in preparing for what seemed imminent disaster from rising waters, she continued on her way. With good luck, she could be back home before complete darkness stopped outside activity and before anyone would even know she was gone. Somehow, she felt driven to pursue the path she was taking. To return the horses to the original pasture before streams rose higher seemed vital. Maybe it had something to do with her wish to be helpful, she reasoned when the rain again started falling and she couldn't force herself to turn back.

Leander urged Thunder onward when she saw Frenchman's Bayou up ahead through the forest. She had realized soon after leaving the stable why the old horse had been left behind. He was as cantankerous and slow as she had remembered from her childhood days of riding him. When they approached the swollen bayou and she saw the floating logs and debris in the muddy water, she almost turned back. The thunder and lightning were becoming louder, nearer. Thunder, not so brave as his name would indicate, shied and snorted as she contemplated good places to make him swim them across.

Compelled to go onward, Leander found the place where Jabbo and she had swum across on horseback the day they had driven the herd over to the pasture. Thunder responded to her soft urgings and went on into the rushing water. If a wayward log hadn't twisted in midstream to nudge at the nervous horse's rump, they probably would have made it across. They were almost to the other side when Thunder spooked at the attack on his rear and gave a great heave and snort. Leander, with only one stirrup to give her firm contact with the animal, found herself sailing into the bayou. Coming up with a furious curse at Thunder, she struck out swimming for the bank, dodging another floating log before she pulled herself onto the muddy earth. She turned her head to locate Thunder, calling out to him. He had stayed in the bayou and was swimming like mad on down its middle, his eyes showing whites and his whinnies of fear sounding in between nearing claps of thunder and lightning.

Leander muttered a whole string of curses then, pulling off her soaked gloves and feeling a chill seize her body. The stupid horse was going on downstream as if it knew where it was headed. Rain began to fall in torrents then and she turned to peer toward where she thought the hunting lodge would be. She thought she could make out a man-made structure through the darkening forest and headed that way. Streaks of lightning tore right above the tops of nearby trees as she ran toward what she hoped was the old hunting lodge.

Downstream a ways, another plantation owner was out in the storm checking on his livestock. Earlier that week, Justin Salvador had driven his herd of horses across Frenchman's Bayou to higher ground, but he had wanted to make one more inspection before the day's second storm made the back bayou impassable. A stray could have been left behind; though after a final look, he knew now that all were safe. He paused in the newest downpour to eye the threatening rise of the muddy waters before urging his horse on across to return home. From beneath a drenched, black felt hat, his eyes widened in shock. A clearly agitated horse was swimming around a curve from upstream. Its sidesaddle told him that some woman must have been thrown.

Justin directed Principe, his favorite mount, out into the water and managed to snag the reins of the wayward horse. Once he had the spooked horse back on the bank, the young Spaniard rode upstream, leading the animal, searching for some woman likely to be stranded and in trouble during the just-breaking, second storm of the day. On the far side of French- man's Bayou where he rode, few boundaries between Terre Platte and its neighbors were visible because the concessions reaching from the Mississippi had little depth beyond that stream. Justin knew that behind the big plantations fronting the river lay small farms to the west, but he had never ridden to locate them or their owners.

Once right after coming to Terre Platte, he had explored a short way through the forest and seen cleared fields and a farmer's house in the distance but hadn't gone any closer. Other planters had told him that those in that back area built their houses to front on an even more distant stream and used that waterway as their main travel route. Because none of the bayous or rivers in the area emptied into the Mississippi, those traveling other waterways seldom had cause to come into contact with the planters owning river property.

It was Justin's reasonable guess that the horse and its rider must have come from one of those smaller habitations located westward of his holdings. There was no reason to suspect that anyone from neighboring Beaux Rives would be so far from home in such weather. He was already entering an area of the forest bordering Frenchman's Bayou that he had never before explored. In the unnaturally early darkening of the stormy, February afternoon, Justin had no idea when he left his own land and when he reached that belonging to someone else.

Leander sprinted through the blinding rain toward the small porch of the lodge, praying that the door wouldn't be locked. It wasn't. She peered inside, barely able to see in the gathering darkness. Leaving the door open to gain more light, she walked for the first time into her father's hunting lodge. Except for the musty smell of a place long closed, the large room appeared inviting, even pleasant in a rustic kind of way. Shivering from the recurring chills shaking her body, she went to the fireplace to see if perhaps kindling and . . .

Within minutes, a grateful Leander was holding out her hands to the lovely warmth coming from the flames catching up in the large fireplace and shooting puffs of black smoke up the giant chimney. Even as she had worked to get the fire started, she noted that the fireplace was almost large enough for her to stand in its opening. The little pile of kindling seemed lost in it, but she had found a goodly stack of large logs in a generous brick niche beside the hearth. Now she began adding them one at a time, not believing her good luck in having found the lodge in the first place, and feeling doubly blessed to have found a supply of wood to last the night . . . or until someone found her. After having walked over it, she realized that the land on this side of the bayou was higher than that on the other and that the young horses would fare well in the temporary pasture. Besides, there was nothing she could do now about carrying out her plan to get them back across. She let out a sigh that her attempt to be helpful had failed. The flames licked at the logs, their hunger sending out welcome, crackling sounds along with waves of heavenly warmth.

When the shivering didn't cease even after the fire was well caught up, Leander realized that she needed to get out of her wet clothing. Gingerly she opened the two doors on either side of the fireplace and peeked around them. It seemed that the large combination kitchen-dining-sitting room being dominated by the fireplace claimed half of the lodge, with the other half being divided into two bedrooms. Squinting into the twilight and flinching from a nearby roll of thunder and crash of lightning, she saw several beds in both.

What caught the chilled young woman's eyes in the second bedroom were several men's robes hanging from hooks on the wall alongside hunting coats. Stripping to bare skin and leaving her sodden garments in a pile on the floor, she pulled a woolen robe about her freezing body and, after cuffing up the sleeves, tied its belt around her tiny waist to hold it together. The enveloping, wine-colored garment dragged the floor as she wandered about in search for something to put on her feet. Several pairs of soft slippers sat upon a low shelf in a shadowy corner, and she eased shriveling feet into the smallest pair. She took a hairbrush and a towel from a washstand, already feeling comforted from finding a dry covering for her chilled body. Like a child wearing a grown-up's shoes for the first time, she clumped awkwardly back to close the front door against the deafening storm. The towel around her shoulders and the hairbrush in the robe pocket, she then sank down upon the large bearskin rug in front of the fireplace and began unbraiding the sopping, black ropes.

That couldn't be a knock at the door, Leander thought with a mysterious shiver feathering up her backbone. Surely it had been only a new kind of thunder, maybe one forceful enough to rattle the lodge windows or even the door. It was too soon for anyone to have missed her back at Beaux Rives and come searching. The fire gave off an enormous glow of light there on the bearskin rug, but when she glanced toward the door and what she had suspected might be a knock, she could see nothing except a rectangular paleness centered with the vague form of a man. Then she had heard a knock, she reasoned. Later she might wonder at her complete absence of fear at what ordinarily should have been an unsettling sight. At the time, though, it seemed the most natural thing in the world to invite the man inside — it was almost as if she had been expecting him.

"Come in out of the storm," Leander called, pushing the nearly dried hair from her face and trying to make out the features of the one still standing in the doorway outside the circle of firelight. "You must be as drenched as I was when I came in here."

Justin Salvador couldn't move. The bright glow of the roaring blaze revealed each feature of the young woman sitting before the fireplace looking across at him. The soft French words of welcome tickled his ears, called upon some instinctive wisdom to reply in the same language, the one he had worked hard to master over the past four years among the French Creoles. What held him spellbound was more than the young woman's beauty — it was her eyes. They were the color of pansies. The storm raging overhead couldn't compare to the avalanche of emotion washing him into a private fantasia. He had found the beautiful young woman of his dreams. She was real. The glove he had glimpsed in the darkening woods not far from the bayou must be hers. When he had retrieved it and followed little muddy tracks, the path had led him to her. He might as well have run all the way, so labored was his heartbeat and breath.

"Thank you," Justin managed to say while closing the door. He guessed the noise of the storm had masked the sounds of his calls when he approached the lodge and went to unsaddle and house the horses in the neighboring stable. When he had seen the smoke fighting to rise from the chimney in the driving rainfall, he had somehow known that he had reached his destination for the night. Thank goodness he had told his overseer Petra that if he became stranded, he would seek shelter till morning and get out of the storm. It would be impossible to cross the treacherous bayou and return home before total darkness, even if the storm were to abate. And from the overhead sounds, the storm was not one to spend itself any time soon. "I apologize for intruding, but I seem to be lost and—"

"To get in out of the weather seems to be the most important thing," Leander broke in to say, watching the easy way the young man walked toward her, liking the swagger of his broad shoulders and the way his wet feet moved with sureness across the wooden floor. His French sounded quaint and she wondered if he might not have come from one of the farms behind Beaux Rives and its hunting lodge. She sent him a little smile because the look of inner happiness radiating from his face seemed to demand it. "You're welcome to share my fire. I was lucky to have found the lodge but even luckier to have found a great pile of dry logs."

"Then this place is new to you also?" he asked, reaching in his pocket for the glove and holding it out toward her. He sensed they were in a large, open room, but he couldn't see anything but the black-haired vision sitting in the glow of the fire. The very air seemed charged with a mysterious electricity akin to that being hurled outside by some determined Jupiter. "Is this glove yours?" He was at the edge of the rug now and could see more than her eyes. His heart nigh collapsed from its new pace. She was even lovelier than he had imagined she would be. Perfect teeth gleamed between the lovely, full lips smiling at him in the oval face tilting up toward him. A shimmering cloud of jet curls framed her face with alluring perfection.

"Why, yes," she said, her smile growing larger. "I

must have dropped it after my silly horse spooked in the bayou and forced me to scramble to the bank." The young man's face was the most handsome she had ever seen, and she couldn't seem to get enough of looking at the well-formed nose, the strong chin, the little uptilted corners of his generous mouth. The sparkling dark eyes and easy smile told her, along with his speech and gentlemanly manner, that he was one of her kind of people — a French Creole. Her heart skipped a beat at her good fortune in having been found by one so charming, one so obviously concerned for a stranger's welfare as to search for her after finding a runaway horse and a lost glove. She didn't notice that he returned the glove to his pocket.

"I found robes and slippers galore in that bedroom," Leander said, spying the puddles he was making on the floor and realizing he was as nearly drowned as she had been upon arrival. He had removed his soaked felt hat upon entering, and she saw then that its dye was running in little rivulets of black from his hair onto his forehead. She gestured toward the door and watched him follow her unspoken orders without comment of his own. What could have caused him to be out in such terrible weather?

While the young man was inside the bedroom, Leander got up from the rug and explored the contents of the kitchen area over in the far corner. First she searched for candles or whale oil for the lanterns sitting about but came up with nothing. Deciding that they would have no light except from that of the fireplace, she realized even at that distance that it was far more adequate than she would have believed. Before complete darkness fell, she wanted to see what kind of food and drink might have been left behind. She recalled that on the day Jabbo and she had ridden near the lodge, she had wondered aloud if the place had ever been used since her father's death. Jabbo had commented that Tower had told him of Felix's having had a hunting party there shortly before Christmas.

Leander's toes bumped into something solid beneath the edge of the cook table. She stooped to find a rack of wines with corkscrews hanging on hooks. Rising and setting a bottle and corkscrew on the table, she prowled through a closed cabinet nearby. When she opened a tall canister of tinplate sitting inside, she found biscuits of several shapes. And in a corner of the same shelf lay a fat round of cheese, still waxed over. Testingly, she sniffed at the salty covering, smiling to herself at the tempting aroma of a sharp cheese Sheeva must have preserved inside and packed for Felix to bring to the lodge. She wasn't surprised to find an abundance of glasses, plates, and cutlery filled other shelves.

After placing all that would be needed to provide a simple meal out on the dining table nearer the fireplace, a strangely contented Leander found napkins in a neat stack behind some cups. She found it easy to ignore the storm attacking from outside the cozy lodge. Already she had found a coffeepot and a tin of coffee and wondered where she might find drinking water. Only when she explored the other dark corner did she see an enormous, covered churn, and a pewter wash pan upon a squat stand. From nearby wooden pegs hung a gourd dipper and towels.

"I found a towel in the bedroom but I don't think I was able to get all the dye off my face," Justin called to Leander as he returned to the large room to stand before the blazing fire. Shivering just a bit when the warmth eased away some of the bone chill and jamming his hands into the robe's pockets, he let out a purely masculine growl of contentment all wrapped in bass sounds of "M-m-m-m." He turned his backside to the fire and peered from the circle of light toward her. "I could barely see into the little mirror in there. Ona is going to love having been right about how I shouldn't have worn that new felt hat out into the rainy afternoon. Even if my hair weren't already black, it would be now after the rain seeped through my hat."

Leander stood still, making herself ask, "Is Ona your wife?"

The stranger laughed back deep in his throat and replied, "No, she's my cook and housekeeper. I don't have a wife." The next question had to come from him, and he wished it didn't have to be given voice, but . . . "What about you? Is there some husband or father or someone already out searching for you?"

" 'No' to everything. I doubt anyone will notice my absence for quite some time yet." Her words came bubbling out, as if they sensed some attuned ear might be awaiting them.

Justin interlaced his fingers and bent them backward in an attempt to mask the need to let out a sudden burst of energy at the news. He wanted to jump up and down and shout. New happiness welled up inside to join that already making him feel younger and more excited than when he was a schoolboy. He could sight her, yet it was too dark over there for him to do more than determine that she stood near a table and was once more moving about. "What are you doing?"

"I've meddled about and found us something to eat,"

220

she replied from the far side of the dining table.

"Do you think whoever owns this lodge will mind that we've taken it over?" he asked, examining the large room with appreciation for its simple but adequate comforts.

"I'm sure the owner won't mind," she replied, glad that she was in shadow and that he couldn't see the amusement on her face. "With a storm carrying on like that one is now, nobody could deny shelter to those caught out in such."

Leander saw him nod in thoughtful agreement. In the bright light from the fireplace, his tall frame filled out the blue robe he wore in the way whoever designed and made it would have chosen, she decided. Had it been her father's, one he had had made at his tailor's in New Orleans? The soft fabric fell gracefully from broad shoulders and chest on past narrow waist and narrower hips into one blue wedge of manly shape. The slippers seemed made for his feet. She wondered if he knew how artfully shaped his ankles and the lower halves of his calves were. Of course he did. With men's styles calling for pants ending tightly below the knee, a man would have to know when he had legs and ankles so handsome as his. Probably all kinds of young women sent him flirtatious looks and let him know what a fine figure he cut.

That he seemed concerned with his still-wet hair and the smudges of dye around the hairline amused Leander. Was he perhaps a bit vain, or was he merely hoping to look his best for her? That last thought sent a rush of warmth to her face. Ever since having spent Christmas around the Ferrand brothers, she had learned much about the ways in which young men set

221

out to impress fancied young women. They seemed to place as much store on their appearance as any of her sex. She tried to pretend interest in arranging the ingredients for a meal. While he took up the brush she had left lying on the hearth and pulled it through obviously thick hair and shaped it back from his face with his hands, she sent little sliding, admiring looks his way. Even with the small traces of black dye touching his olive forehead, he was still the most devastatingly handsome man she had ever seen. Her heart sang.

"Don't you think that if we're going to share the lodge and a meal, we should introduce ourselves?" Justin asked, dying to know what her name was. How could it not be beautiful? All the while he had been shedding his clothing and getting into the warm robe, he had felt his pulses speeding up at the thought of getting to talk to her, ask about her, get to know her. She must be from one of the smaller farms behind Terre Platte and the other river plantations, or he would have already met her at some affair. Might she not feel a bit intimidated if she were to find out upon first meeting him that he owned such a large place? Such would have been the case back in Spain.

Leander shot thoughtful eyes his way before answering. His French accent was so different from any she had heard that she was surer than ever that he came from one of the smaller farms behind Beaux Rives. He might think, at this first meeting, that as the owner of such a large plantation, she would look down upon one from a place of less grand proportions. She met the starred, black gaze winging her way across the half-darkened room, acutely aware for the first time that she wore nothing beneath the voluminous robe. A disturbing sensitivity washed over every inch of her slender body. His presence in the circle of firelight dominated the room. An aura of magic seemed to surround him.

"My name is Lea," she said with a mysterious smile. The faultless solution had come to her. "I think second names are superfluous upon first meetings, don't you?"

Justin let out his suspended breath. Lea. It suited her with utmost perfection. A mental picture of a lovely field of green floated up—with her in its center, and him holding her in his arms upon a bed of flowers and—

"I do," he made himself break off his wild thoughts to reply before she might think him deaf . . . or daft. "My name is Justin." How perfectly her obvious love of the ridiculous suited his wish not to let her know right off that he was a Spanish don with a huge plantation. He might have known that the one of his dreams would be high-spirited and unique in every way. A warmth coming from someplace other than the fire behind him comforted him all over. Never again would he view a storm cloud as a bad omen.

"Well, Justin," Leander said, walking toward him clumsily in the oversized slippers, "I think we had better get our clothing on chairs near the fire so that they can begin to dry out, don't you?" She savored the sound of his name on her lips. Never before had she heard of anyone called Justin. The name sounded so . . . noble.

"You're right, Lea." Strange, he had never before thought the name suitable for a young woman. But what he had assumed he knew about young women before this moment seemed absurd, totally useless. He loved that she was practical as well as beautiful. "Let me move the chairs closer."

Within a few minutes, they had good-naturedly worked together and set up acceptable drying racks at both ends of the giant fireplace. Sidewise glances and high spirits made both of them light-headed, almost dizzy. Justin moved a chair holding her sodden garments on one side, another holding his to the other. Adequate space for the oversized bearskin rug remained directly in front of the roaring fire. He added logs to those she had put on before his arrival.

Leander stared in fascination at the way his muscles flexed and rippled beneath the close-fitting robe as he handled the firewood with apparent ease. She noticed his hands were also stained with the black dye from his bleeding hat. After he seemed satisfied with the way the logs were catching up, she ushered him to the churn of water in the ever-darkening corner. There they refreshed themselves with a bit of washing up. Once, their hands reached for the soap in the pan of water at the same time and touched. A streak of lightning outside could have gotten its spark from that first, innocent meeting of flesh there in the Ondine hunting lodge. Neither knew where to look but into the probing depths of the other's wondering eyes in the half-light.

"I saw a bottle of wine sitting out," Justin managed to say in what sounded like a stranger's voice. It was all he could do to tear away his gaze. He removed his hands and dried them. A trace of the tingle from her touch lingered in his fingertips. "Are you ready for me to open it?"

"Yes, please," Leander answered with what little breath she could find. The currents his touch had set off must have come from the charged air created by the lightning. Not since that night back at Josie's Inn when she had awakened in the arms of . . . She shook her head to clear it of that hateful memory, glad overhead thunder and heavy rain upon the roof helped her along.

Violet eyes darted to where a pursed-mouthed Justin now stood at the cook table with corkscrew in hand preparing to assault the cork of some dark wine, its label unreadable in the half-light. The young man with the elegant manners and arresting profile was here with her in her father's lodge, preparing to open a bottle of wine to share with her. He was far more handsome and exciting than that despicable, faceless Spaniard could ever have been. And there was not the least chance that Justin would attempt to force himself on her or whisper the hated *querida* in her ears. She was wasting thoughts on that night back in Throw-away's room, just as she had almost nightly since it came to pass. Now that she had met Justin and seen that the touch of a Creole young man could set off delicious tremblings inside, she could bury those haunting memories forever, she assured herself with a contented sigh. If she had never before believed in fate, she did now.

Leander's disappointment that flirty looks and touches from neither Antoine nor Philip had called forth such response from her as she had already learned smoldered within must have been a sign that the right Creole had not yet come on the scene. Was Justin the right one? An aura of good breeding and gentlemanly ways emanated from him as clearly as the

225

ready smile and sparkling eyes claimed his happy face. Endearments from him, if they were to come — and somehow Leander sensed within every cell that at some moment in her lifetime they would, and that she would welcome them — would be in the language she loved. Her heart expanded with anticipation.

"Shall I make a toast?" Justin asked. Without planning it, both had taken their glasses of wine and gravitated toward the welcoming, warming fire. He set the bottle of wine on the floor behind him and sank upon the bearskin rug, crossing his legs in tailor fashion before him, not seeming to notice that the robe slid upward and revealed his legs from knees downward.

"Please do," Leander murmured, trying not to pay attention to those muscular, naked limbs. When she had sunk down to sit on the rug, she had kept her legs together and let them angle out to one side. Intuitively she arranged them so that her body faced his and she could look directly into his face without having to turn her head. Curling, sooty lashes opened wide to reward her eyes with a full view of his face there in the golden light of the burning logs. Was it the dancing light, or did his skin truly have a touch of burnished gold about it? His cheeks looked so soft, yet terribly masculine with their touches of shadow signifying he hadn't shaved since earlier that day. And she had never seen such a strong chin, one sure to be a sign of great determination and ability to achieve goals.

Justin brought up his glass of deep red wine and held it toward her, admiring the way her smoldering eyes seemed to pick up mysterious, purplish lights from the wavering fire. When he nodded toward the glass she

226

held motionless in what had to be the daintiest, most gracefully formed hand he had ever seen, she seemed to startle and return to the moment. What he wouldn't give to know what was bringing that contented, secretive smile to those lovely lips. Another gesture from him, and Leander scooted closer, stopping just short of letting her robe-covered knees touch his bare calves. With such a brief space between them, she didn't have to lift her glass far until the two stems met with a melodious tinkle heard in spite of the storm raging outside.

"To strangers who met in a storm. May they look back upon that meeting as the most fortunate in their lives," Justin said in a voice heavy with feeling and promise . . . and hope. A little flicker of light deep in her dreamy eyes told him of her pleasure in his choice of words. They sipped solemnly, gazes still locked.

A log shifted and fell to the back of the fireplace just then, forcing their eyes to check its noisy, spark-filled path.

"You look like a princess," Justin remarked after he reached behind him for the bottle and replenished their wine.

Leander tossed her hair and lifted her face. Her throaty laughter filled in the small space between them. Looking up at him from behind half-lowered lashes, she chided, "I can tell you've never seen a princess."

"How can you tell?" Who would have ever thought that a partial view of those incredible eyes could be more captivating than a full one? He felt as if he were poised on the edge of a precipice, welcoming the impending fall.

"A princess would never be caught in such an

outrageous costume such as this . . . thing." She looked down with amusement at the wine robe hanging in great folds about her slim figure. Only then did she notice that the draped foldover had slipped aside a shade and was revealing a hint of cleavage. A rush of pink tinting her cheeks, she handed him her glass of wine and reached to tighten the belt and rearrange the garment at the neckline.

The sweep of long, black lashes against the blushing cheeks enthralled Justin almost as much as the glimpse of the valley between the twin mounds of firm flesh had done before she hid it. He returned her glass to her when she reached for it, not surprised that his fingers seemed determined to touch hers when she took it from him. That same spark which had startled them at that touch in the pan of water struck again.

"I feel like a frog," he commented dryly when her fingers slid away and brought the glass to her lips.

Leander giggled, having to remove her glass from her lips to keep from getting strangled. "Funny, I hadn't pictured you as resembling a frog in any way. You don't move like one. You don't talk like one. And you're far from being green or dark brown." Why were those black eyes drinking in her face in that lazy, consuming manner? And why did she not resent such blatant looks . . . as she had from others? The second glass of wine must be making her tipsy, she reflected. Her head seemed filled with air bubbles. And her heart was playing . . . leapfrog. She giggled again, this time at her warped inner musings. Talking with him was such fun. She expanded the thought — she had never had such fun in her life. She wanted to stop time, draw out these magical moments with the handsome Justin.

The way his black eyes caressed her face fanned blazes all inside, and she wondered if she looked as different as she felt. With mock solemnity she explained, "And Justin hardly seems a fitting name for a frog."

"I'm referring to the frog in the fairytale." The breathless little giggles charmed him, as did the dance of curls from a carelessly shrugged shoulder. He sipped at the wine, waiting for her to pick up on his thought. All at once the perfection of her nose fascinated him. It was small, yet bore a proud shape—probably the finest, most elegant little nose he had ever seen. His fingers itched to trace its form, to touch the tiny indentation running from the center of its nostrils to the full upper lip.

"I suspect you're closer to being a rake than a frog," Leander retorted in a teasing manner when she caught his meaning. Her cheeks burned again. He seemed determined to memorize her features. Each time she tried to do more than sneak a peek at his, he would be watching hers so intently that she would have to let her gaze skip away. "And anyhow, that story is for children. Nobody ever turned a frog into a prince by kissing him."

"Are you a gambler?" Those little darting glances of hers were tearing his composure to shreds. How much longer could he keep from touching her?

Leander dropped her eyes to study the red wine remaining in her glass, for fear that at such close range, those penetrating black ones could fathom how much of a gambler she truly was . . . or had been at one time on the trail to Natchez.

"More than you would probably guess," she replied, able to look at him by then. Devilment hovered about his full lips. What would he say next? Leander faced up to the fact that the handsome young man seemed to have cast a spell upon her.

"What would you bet that if you gave me a kiss, I would no longer feel I was a frog?" His laughter joined her sudden burst of feminine delight, his deep tones bouncing off the walls and blending with those higher tones of hers there in the cozy room. Neither heard the storm breaking with even noisier fury outside. Each time they seemed about to regain straight faces, one would set the other off into further gales of laughter at their shared, seemingly upside-down sense of humor. "Come on, now," Justin urged, once they both sobered at the same time and sat still again, her robe-covered knees and his bare calves within kissing distance. "What would you bet?"

"I don't have anything with me of value," she hedged, sending a hand to flip wayward, black curls from her face. She knew then that the wine must have her feeling high, though a second glass of wine had never before affected her in such a way. But nothing could truly be so funny as his bit about a kiss curing his feeling of being a frog had seemed at the moment. And when had her heartbeat ever acted so crazy? An unreasonable wave of expectancy accompanied another crash of thunder overhead, the first her ears had acknowledged since they had sat upon the rug. "You wouldn't have a wager without something to win or lose, would you?"

He cocked the well-shaped head and set handsome black brows into a straight line to suggest heavy thought. A thumb and forefinger slipped up to fondle an earlobe, while he shot her a playful look from behind half-lowered black lashes. "You're right, you know. We must make this a legitimate bet. What about your glove?"

"The one I have against the one you found?" she parried with the same mock seriousness of his own question. She pursed full lips in pouting consideration and sent a forefinger to twist inside a black curl falling across a breast. Pansy-hued eyes rolled upward, then from side to side, as if to view her answer from all angles before hiding what was discovered behind silky sweeps of sooty lashes.

"Yes," Justin replied. "Whoever wins gets the pair." The sparkle of mischievousness in her eyes before she lowered them charmed him all over again, as did her ability to play their little game of flirtation with such utter abandonment. From the minute he had opened the door and seen her sitting in the glow of the firelight in that great tent of a robe, he had sensed that she possessed an air of latent sensuality all covered over by pure innocence. And now he was certain of it, was so aware of it in every part of him that he felt breathless and humbled at the thought. The center of his world sat before him.

Leander held up a hand in protest, demanding in a playful tone of doubt, "How will I know if you no longer feel you're a frog—even if I do give you a kiss?" Black curls bounced and rearranged themselves in even prettier patterns of disarray when she tilted her head questioningly.

His mouth set into a dramatic, pompous line of truthfulness, Justin assured, "Because I promise I'll tell you, and my word is as good as gold."

As though sucked up the chimney, all play-acting

vanished. The two young faces moved across the brief space between them as if directed by some invisible force there in the circle of dancing firelight. Only their lips touched. They met in soft surrender, then moved to press more closely, his savoring the taste of hers and seeking to drink more fully than their separation allowed, hers accepting all that his offered . . . parting for more.

Controlling his urge to draw her into his arms and feel her body against his, Justin opened his eyes after that first instant of their kiss. His dreams of kissing her had omitted nothing of the actual thrill of doing so, he exulted with singing pulses. He watched her eyes flutter upward.

Leander's searched those black, starred depths so near. What she glimpsed there puzzled her as much as the thunder of her heart, as much as some hidden memory threatening to surface. Great flurries of fire charged through her veins. She drew back, ending the soul-shattering kiss.

"I'll never feel like a frog again, Lea," he told her in a tender, hushed bass when she seemed not to know where to look or what to do about her trembling lips. "You've turned me into a prince."

Seeing the rapid rise and fall of her breasts beneath the robe, Justin knew that his breathing pattern would match hers exactly. Her leaning forward to kiss him had again parted the neckline of the robe, and he could see the start of the delicious curves on either side of that earlier-glimpsed valley. With a yearning thumb and forefinger, he reached to tip up her drooping chin.

Justin was unprepared for the increased rate of heartbeat at that new contact. Eyes of purple flashed up to joust with his, an obvious sign that the upheaval of feelings was mutual. His bared calves touched her robe-covered knees, and even through the fabric, a current seemed to spark from the encounter. Everything inside Justin had turned all topsy-turvy during the kiss, and now he feared the condition was worsening, might even be becoming permanent. He had already discarded his empty glass just before the kiss, and now he eased hers from her fingers and laid it down on the furry rug. His hungry arms gathered her lithesome body and guided it to rest against his. This time, he promised himself, he meant to kiss her breathless.

Chapter Eleven

Once Leander accepted the shock jolting her when Justin pulled her close to him and again claimed her willing mouth, she gave in to the desire to return kiss for kiss. He tasted like wine and rain and . . . a delicious young man. That formerly hateful memory of what masculine arms and lips could arouse in her no longer taunted her. How else could she have known that greater joys lay in store for her? And this time, the kisses were welcome, the arms those of one accepted, even adored — after having met him only that afternoon. A wild abandonment of everything in her life before that moment freed her, and she welcomed each increasingly demanding kiss, leaned closer to exult more freely in the exciting touch of his body against her own.

Justin's lips moved over hers as though they already knew their pattern by heart, and something inside him rejoiced. An exploring tongue found the wondrous shape of her inner lip and committed it more firmly to reeling mind and senses. A violence of feeling akin to the force of the storm outside threatened to fuel his desire and seduce her into surrender, make telling demands before she could escape into that dream world of her former existence. But, his worshiping hands reassured him as they smoothed back tousled, silky curls from the lovely forehead and played in the textured cloud glossing over the finely shaped head, this young woman truly existed. She was his love, not one to coax into making choices about anything before she was willing. Lea was no fantasy. The mouth shaping itself to his . . . the tongue meeting his at first with hesitancy, then with daring . . . the warm breasts yielding against the muscles of his chest—all of them were real. And if he had succeeded in kissing her breathless, he hardly noticed, for he was so winded himself that rational thought eluded him, scampered to a distant corner.

"Lea," he whispered, his lips leaving hers to make their loving mark upon satin cheeks, the bridge of the perfect nose, the curve of a small ear. "I thought you would never come to me out of my dreamworld. I've loved you ever since I first met you there."

Leander startled. His words and breath right next to her ear sent titillating chills up and down her spine . . . and some kind of erotic message to the core of her being. Already addicted to the touch of his fingers and hands upon her, she accommodated his exploration of her face and ears by bending her neck in the graceful way of a flower upon its stem when a pleasant wind caresses.

"How can that be?" she made herself reply, not

wanting to break the enchantment his gentle hands were creating. The fire made little contented sounds, and she was tempted to join in. "I've never lived in a dreamworld."

"I can assure you that you have" was his unperturbed answer. He continued to work a spell, the faraway gleam in his black eyes suggesting that he might also be entranced.

Leander's hands cried out for a taste of touching on their own. She let them wander shyly over the manly pattern of his face, then gave them freedom to track the form of the lordly nose, and to trace with wonder the shape of the sensuous lips from one uptilted corner to the other. With a bass chuckle and a playful movement, Justin sent gleaming teeth to capture the small invading fingers with the lightest of pressure, pulling them inside to suck upon them gently. Her eyes widened in surprise at the intensity of feeling his movement triggered deep inside. Was every motion he made going to fan that stirring at the pit of her being?

"You have lived in my dreams, dear one, more than you could ever know," he went on after releasing her fingers and cradling her hand. Idly he opened his hand and fitted her small palm and fingers to his. "And how much more wonderful it is to have you now in my real world." Both glanced to note the enormous difference between the sizes of their paired hands, then exchanged looks of pleased admiration, looks having little to do with the size of anything. A flow of feeling from one hand to the other pulsated in rhythm with their quickened heartbeats. Discovery seemed to be the name of the game. "Have you any idea how long I've waited, how much I've needed you?" She seemed to be listening with her entire being, as if she had been waiting to hear what he was saying as long as he had been waiting to speak the words. Justin drank in the way the lambent flames in the fireplace lent a golden glow to the soft, fair skin, danced with abandonment in the shining fall of midnight tresses, highlighted the deep purple of the dazzling, black-fringed eyes. That such perfection as Leander's existed at all satisfied that part of him loving beauty for its own sake. That such loveliness lay within his arms stunned him. A stretch of silence filled with questing eyes and wondering looks seemed a part of the enchantment. Justin voiced a part of what he was feeling. "Ever since I entered the room, Lea, I've wanted to tell you how beautiful you are."

Overcome by Leander's little breathless "Thank you," and the enormity of what was happening there in the hunting lodge during the season's worst thunderstorm, Justin buried his face in the cloud of black curls on her shoulder, pulling her to him with fierce energy when his breath threatened to escape forever. The softness of her slender body stirred a longing to explore more than her face and hair.

From the dream, he remembered how his hands had stroked the warm, satiny skin with unbelieving, lazy discovery, how they had moved wonderingly, gently, reverently. Now those same hands set up frenzied patterns — where to begin, where to settle? He cautioned himself to move slowly, but his brain was barely in control. He caressed Leander's very real neck and shoulders of lustrous, silken texture, delighting in the tiny pulse leaping at the base of her throat. Kissing a path downward from that pulse, he slipped aside the half-opened robe to find the proud mounds of waiting, inviting flesh. Their saucy roundness filled his cupped hands in that way he had known they would, the awareness of that discovery setting him on fire in the way he had dreamed. His tingling palms retreated with a sensual slowness to allow sensitive thumbs and fore-fingers to tease the pebbled peaks into tight rosebuds perking up to be adored, kissed. The throaty, feminine purring he heard added to his happiness, for he longed to give pleasure as well as take it.

The play of Justin's hands upon her breasts called up that remembered, fiery burst of sensation in Leander's inner core. Moaning deep in her throat, she clutched at his head, her fingers already at home in the crisp, black hair at the back of his neck. A storm of heart-beats attacked her brain and sent it scurrying. She wanted nothing more than to bask in Justin's touch, to become even more caught up in overpowering feeling than she had once before. Already she could feel its churning deep inside.

Only this time, she assured her thundering heart and yearning body, she had no reason to deny, no reason to fight the maelstrom of passion flickered into life on that shameful night. With instinctive wisdom, she sensed that the revered young man whose mouth and tongue were turning her swelling breasts into twin volcanoes was a vital part of her destiny. Hadn't he told her he had dreamed of her, needed her . . . loved her? The magic words had crashed upon her starved heart like a tidal wave discovering a virgin beach. Only Justin's voice, Justin's touch could ever satisfy her. She knew it with certainty. And suddenly Leander wanted more than promise.

Love glowing in his eyes, Justin watched as though mesmerized when Leander leaned away and untied the belt of the oversized garment. With the careless grace of a dancer that seemed an inherent part of her loveliness, she stood and shrugged off the robe. Black hair framing the beautiful face and spilling across dainty shoulders, she stood before him there in the circle of firelight like some proud young nymph rewarding a worshipful god.

The perfection of Leander awed Justin anew. The beautiful oval face, the incredible purple eyes fixed on him with dewy expectation, the kiss-stung lips parted in the flushed wonder of discovery . . . the uptilted breasts, their rosy aureoles still damp from his kisses . . . the inward curve of the tiny waist . . . the boyishly flat belly with its ingrown button of a navel proving that she was of this earth, was not truly a nymph . . . the gently swelling hips, seemingly formed to fit the shape of his tingling hands . . . and the long, exquisitely molded legs, ending with ankles of finger-circling size and dainty feet — every feature of the one standing before him played murderous havoc all over again with his breath and his heartbeat. Miniature flashes, like zagging threads of lightning, had begun earlier deep in his groin and now were threatening to turn into man-sized bolts of destruction.

A hasty flip of Justin's trembling fingers and his belt was untied, his own robe thrown off to the side of the rug to cover hers in some kind of unnoticed symbolism. From where he sat entranced, he held out welcoming arms, his devastating smile and his adoring gaze adding their own invitations.

"Justin," Leander asked when she accepted and curled onto his lap, "what would have happened if we hadn't met tonight?" The manly fragrance of him and the way the mass of chest curls felt to her face when she nestled against him seemed peculiarly pleasing . . . and almost familiar. That she fit into his arms as though formed to do so came as no surprise, but the realization brought an overflow to her racing heart. She craned to look up into the handsome face. Her mouth was so close to his that she could feel his quick, warm breath upon her skin, could feel her own being bounced back. Puzzled eyes searched his probing ones. She sensed that something as extraordinary as the storm screaming outside was about to break loose inside the lodge, that nothing in her life would ever again be the same. The almost palpable air of expectancy and tension that had come in with him at the door a brief time ago could no longer be denied.

"I would have been destroyed," he replied. And just hearing the heartfelt words made him realize that he truly might have been, or at least would have wished to. "Only with you beside me will I be able to go on living. I think I may have loved you forever, Lea."

A flurry of warm, moist kisses washed away any wish to talk further. The communication being carried on by their bodies proved far more satisfying. Justin eased Leander to lie within his arms beside him, making sure that her body was the one nearer the golden flames watching over the unclothed lovers embracing in their circle of light. When he paused to admire the loveliness

240

he held, fingers of warmth from the fireplace bathed her countenance and melted the soft veneer of doubt attempting to surface. Sheer joy wreathed the exquisite, smiling face, shone from within thick, curling lashes, proffered heavy-lidded invitations of purple edged by sooty silk.

"Darling," Justin whispered, not sure that he had the strength to stop even if she bade him to. "Are you sure?" The walls seemed to move inward, as though to listen, as though to create a more private world for the lovers. Leander's joyous sigh of consent drifted out; the walls sent it back. She pulled his face down to kiss him with unrestrained passion. "My love," he said with tender hoarseness when she moved to nuzzle his throat. "My love," the walls floated back in even softer tones.

A memory of the way his hands had slipped down in that dream to measure the marvelous indentation of her waist sailed deep in his mind, like a promise long offered but never granted. Only now the reality was his. The tiny center of the hourglass of her shape truly did allow his thumbs to touch in front, his middle fingers to meet at the center of the slightly arched back. Justin had settled upon the imagined feel of her lips beneath his as a man's mere longing, his wishing for perfection. Now he was a mortal reeling from their nectar—but reeling inwardly. Outwardly, he gave free rein to his greedy mouth to nibble at, tease, tempt, sample from dainty corner to dainty corner, then crush with undisguised ardor those honeyed lips driving him into a welcome frenzy. His hands stroked and caressed their way all over the silkiness of her, as if repeating a path long remembered. Ah! he thought with exultation, reality was outranking fantasy. A storm of love for the responsive young woman in his arms railed throughout his every cell as he lifted his mouth to whisper, "Lea, my beautiful darling."

"Justin," she asked in a barely audible voice, "what's happening to us?" Joy had scampered into all the cavernous, secret places in Leander's heart at his kisses, caresses, and endearments. He had said he first knew her in a dreamworld. Was she in one now? To chase her fear that she might be, she leaned to nip at his lower lip with her teeth before letting the playful bite blend into another kiss.

Oh, yes, Justin was real. She could feel his manhood very near, almost touching her, knew instinctively that its throb was calling out to the one tantalizing her own center. Giving in to the swirl of feeling claiming her, she moved to press her hips closer against his as they lay on the soft bearskin. To feel their smooth bodies touching from head to toe created an avalanche in her heart, winged instant heat to her already swollen breasts and aching womanhood.

Wandering hands, both the large and the small, sought new curves, planes, and valleys to caress and mold into patches of pleasure. Murmured words of loving and sighs of ecstasy pleased the ears, served, along with the dancing flames of the burning logs, as a kind of musical accompaniment—beginning soft and low, becoming more audible as torrents of delight swept the lovers toward the brink of promising culmination, evolving at last into frenzied moans of racking rapture. The persistent warmth of Justin's arousal tossed Leander's emotions about as though they were mere feathers before a violent wind. It was a moment before she realized that a storm other than the one outside did exist, that their fevered kisses and embraces were setting it off. And that its fury could be abated in only one way.

Justin rose to make Leander his, to answer the challenge of the upheaval wreaking delicious chaos within their bodies. Captivating, incessant attacks upon her every sense flooded Leander, threatening to seep through what little self she had left and wash her out to some vast, unknown sea. No true spoondrift could have inundated her as completely as did the orb of divine sentiment exploding and spraying her every cell. Monstrous rolls of passion roared like thunder, and she heard them with more than her ears. Had she been a hidden cloud upon a night sky, she could not have felt more alive . . . more scintillating . . . more attuned with the universe . . . more filled with mysterious power than when Justin claimed her in the way a bolt of electricity gives light, form, and direction to a heretofore darkened collection of vapor. Does a cloud draw away from lightning, some dark side of the rapt Leander wondered as she struggled against blinding pain, one curiously blended with ecstasy? Or does the lightning split the cloud, then let it rush back together in splendid reverence? So the stab of hurt deep within seemed to Leander.

For her to have flinched and drawn back would have been a merely human act. No longer was she left on that level of response. Her arms tightened across heroic shoulders and back. She was the center of a compelling tempest. She desired nothing more than to follow its agonizing path. His kisses raining upon her face and pleading mouth, Justin branded her both inside and out with pent-up ardor. As if to anchor against the assault coming from without and within, Leander embraced the hard hips with her legs and clung, loving the feel of his moving inside her . . . loving the way something within flowered for him . . . fighting to stay abreast of pain, as sure of the cessation of its savage slashes as she was that a sun would rise on the morrow. Like a distant bell ringing in muffled cadence, an inner rhythm begged for her attention when the sharp ache eased. Heart pounding, she listened . . . flowed with it . . . found that Justin must be hearing the same music. Their movements synchronized in harmony.

The soul-shattering forces threatening to consume the lovers merged, became one for an instant . . . a velvet explosion . . . a sail into greater regions of bliss . . . a cruel desertion there at some intangible zenith . . . an enforced, shimmering float back to the nadir of coupled stillness. The storm had palliated.

Spent and shaken, Justin rested a moment before shifting his weight from his beloved. His face found refuge in the fragrant cloud of curls spilling across her shoulders and breasts. Would she despise him now that he had taken her innocence? Another horrendous thought occurred to him. How could he stand it if she were to turn away from him in disgust now that she had seen what power she had over him? Never had union with a young woman transported him to such paradise. He knew that never again could he find contentment on earth without Lea at his side. Fate had cruelly sent her first to his dreamworld; now fate had mercifully allowed him to find her in the real one. Once he viewed the direction for him to take in any walk of life, there was no turning back for the passionate young Spaniard called Justin Salvador. So it would be when it came to pursuing the one he loved.

"Beautiful Lea, I love you," he murmured, daring then to lift his head and view whatever her face revealed. "I've never felt about anyone the way I feel about you." A forefinger brushed across the delicate eyebrows of sable, then lazed down silken cheeks to outline the love-bruised mouth. Never had making love so aptly lived up to its name, he realized. Was that contentment he read on her features? He had not expected such fervent, unabandoned response from a virgin, albeit she had been far from unwilling—but then, he reasoned with what little mental powers he could summon, everything about her was perfect. Dared he ask her now to be his wife?

"Wonderful, handsome Justin," Leander replied in a voice yet husky with satiation. She unashamedly basked in the afterglow of love showing in the midnight eyes. That she had weathered the storm of their joining and found such bliss had left her with a spate of overwhelming feelings—awe, delight, a new awareness of self . . . and, most important of all, love for the young man showing her the full splendor of passion. But she felt too stunned to share everything in her still-quaking heart right then. "I've never felt about anyone the way I feel about you, either." Her pretty mouth formed a pouty little moue. A slice of jealousy edging into her words, she added, "Of course, I may not have had the opportunities that you've had to find out."

"You better not have," he threatened with mock severity, loving the purplish flash from her eyes and hoping that it might be a touch of jealousy. "I would kill anyone I thought had ever held you in his arms."

If Justin hadn't chosen that particular way to tell her how he loved her and wanted to call her his own, Leander might have felt ready to reveal her love for him. But his half-teasing remark brought guilt flooding over her, and she closed her eyes in defense. Had she responded any less ardently to the Spaniard there in Throw-away's bed that night a few months ago than she had to Justin? A part of her demanding honesty forced her to admit there was little difference. An uneasiness crept into her pores. Did that mean that she was a bit wanton, perhaps incapable of loving one man? How little she knew, at the very time when she should have been wise. Hadn't she vowed not to rush into any decisions, especially the one about love and marriage? She would have to bide her time and see how she felt tomorrow . . . or next week. Not that he had asked her to marry him, she reminded herself, but he had boldly declared he loved her and wanted her by his side. A butterfly kiss upon her eyelids led her back to the moment. What else counted? She could hear the overhead storm fading in the distance, could hear a log sputtering and jousting for position in the fireplace.

"I'll bet no one has ever been as hungry as I am," Leander declared, partially opening her eyes and reaching to stretch body and limbs like a satisfied kitten before a warm fire. With a sigh, she snuggled against the solidity of his shoulder and tucked her nose in the hollow above his collarbone. "Um-m-m, you smell good enough to eat. I'm tempted."

Justin smiled. When he had first kissed her, he had recognized the knowledge in those fascinating, purple depths that she felt something strongly for him, something that he felt sure was the awakening of a love akin to his for her. But she obviously wasn't ready to talk seriously. She was young and probably wanted to be courted. Well, he had waited this long, he decided magnanimously; he could wait a little longer. Courting such a vibrant beauty could be nothing but pure pleasure. Getting to know all about her would no doubt take a lifetime. His smile grew.

"Since I'm a prince now," he boasted, lazily sending his eyes to worship the lovely breasts, the curving hips, "I suppose it would be admirable of me to serve you something to eat." A hand idled across one tempting breast to the little swells spilling to the side. The feel of her head nestling so trustingly against him and of her breath fanning upon his skin touched at an inner core of tenderness he had not known he possessed.

"It would show that you've no reservations about mixing with the lower classes," she ventured in a teasing voice, almost purring from the contentment gained from being held so intimately against him. She moved to give him freedom to explore the other breast. "I've always admired that in a prince."

"Then consider it done, my lady."

Too soon to suit her, Justin rose and pulled the borrowed robe about the tall, well-muscled body she was admiring there in the firelight. A chill racing over her, Leander felt bereft and almost beckoned him to return to the bearskin so that she could feel again his

247

warmth. Before he went to the shadowy corner to wash up and explore what she had laid out on the table, he knelt to cover her with the robe she had discarded. He brushed back a curly lock from her forehead and kissed the tip of her nose with a noisy, satisfied smack. Reminding himself that the hunger already sprouting in his loins was not the priority of the moment, Justin headed for the kitchen area.

"When will I get to see you again?" Justin asked after they had munched on the cheese and biscuits with far less appetite than either had expected. As promised, he had brought the food to her there on the bearskin.

Her head cradled in her hand while she lay propped on an elbow, Leander held up her glass of wine. Seeing his handsome face through the wine brought little pangs of delight. She knew that she would be wanting to sketch those beloved features and committed them to memory. Half-closing her eyes and imagining how she might portray the broad forehead, she noticed the smudges of dye around his hairline and smiled.

"I'm not sure I'll recognize you next time unless you plan to let a felt hat bleed all over you again," she teased, tickled at his self-conscious swiping at his hairline. "On second thought, mayhap you should leave the smudges. I can't imagine your being better-looking without them."

"If that's what it takes," he replied with pretended hurt, "then that's what I'll have to do." Leaning across the small space separating them, he repeated, "When will I get to see you again?"

"I'm not sure." She took a sip of wine. The rising waters might create problems about the plantation over the next few days. She had no desire for Felix or Jabbo to learn of her meeting with Justin—or any young man. There was the sticky problem of telling Justin about who she really was, plus the one niggling at her about her feelings toward him. What she needed was time to think things through, to separate what she had felt in the stranger's arms from what she had felt in Justin's. Also there was the necessity to go to Belle Terre within a few days to Felicity's grand party. Stifling a groan, she let out a heartfelt sigh.

"What's the problem, Lea?" The troubled look claiming her smooth brow touched him. Was she afraid that for him to come courting might cause trouble? If so, with whom? She had said she had no parents, but surely she didn't live alone. Itching to know all about her but not wishing to move too fast, he said, "The storm is over, and it's likely that it'll be fair in the morning. Will you tell me your name and let me escort you home then? I must know all about you."

"Oh, no," Leander protested, sitting up at the startling thought of Justin's riding back home with her. "I think we should plan to go our separate ways in the morning and then meet again here . . . later." She sent a forefinger to play with a curl.

Justin groaned. "How much later?"

"At least a week—maybe ten days."

He tried to accept not seeing her for such a long time but failed. "I'll die if I have to wait so long to learn more about you, to see you."

"Surely you know that all about there's a flood threatening," she pointed out. "I can't believe that you'll not be needed about your place over the next few days.

Of course, I'm assuming you do come from these parts." The desire to know more about him almost overrode her feeling that revelations must wait until they met again. She peeked at the closed look about the normally relaxed face and suspected she might not be the only one to need time for reflection.

Justin sat up then, moving to put his arm around her, not surprised that her softness beneath the robe set his heart to racing again. He hadn't thought about what was going on anywhere outside the lodge, fought against doing so now. But what she had said made sense. Already he could imagine that Petra was awaiting his return to report on the latest rise in the small streams across the back of Terre Platte. Like a wayward horse not wanting to enter the barn with the herd, the thought that he was obligated to attend the blasted party at Belle Terre in a few days came straggling to mind. Damn! Of all times to have to go dance attendance on simpering Creole belles.

"You may be right," he conceded, ducking to nibble at her ear. "Mayhap it would be best for us to return here for our next meeting. I don't want to wait, but I can. You must promise me one thing." He set down their wineglasses and nudged at her chin with a thumb until the pansy eyes met his. "You must tell me everything about you then. Everything."

"Will you tell me everything about you?" The melting gaze upon her lips was sloughing her composure. His touch upon her chin tingled.

"Only if you promise that whatever I tell won't affect our relationship." Maybe having ten days to think over how to tell her that he owned such a large plantation and mansion might show him a way to do it without intimidating her. A cursory glance at the disreputable breeches and shirt drying across the chair had convinced him more than ever that she came from one of the small farms behind his place. Did she suspect who he was? He knew that their French was of different levels.

"You have to make the same promise to me, Justin." Leander had never been so serious. She opened her eyes wide to test the black depths so near. Did he suspect who she was? Her heart lurched at the thought.

"I promise."

"And so do I."

"I told you my word is as good as gold," he reminded her just before he gave in to the urge to kiss her.

"So is mine," she managed breathlessly when his mouth released hers. He lifted her hand and brought it up to reward its palm with a lingering kiss. Oh, she agonized, it's happening all over again. Her body was turning into warm jelly. Her pulses were singing a love ballad.

"Will you think of me?" he asked, his voice dropping to that deep huskiness which had thrilled her so while they were making love.

"Every minute." How could she not?

"Will you remember that I love you and want—?" Justin deliberately cut short the question before he asked her to marry him. If she wanted time, then he must give it to her. He feared that if he demanded an answer now, she might not give the one he must have. But he vowed that at the beginning of their next meeting, he would propose to her before he ever told

251

her one thing about himself. What difference could backgrounds and parentage make when two people felt as they did about each other? He slipped down her robe over her shoulders and kissed a trail down to her breasts. His heart hammering, he finished with, ". . . and want you beside me forever? The sight of you, the touch of you drives me insane."

Hardly able to hear the question, much less answer it, Leander closed her eyes in ecstasy at the rush of quivers emanating from his hands and mouth upon her breasts. Would she be able to live without seeing him for so long? Before she gave in to the pounding in her heart and ears and offered herself to him again, she promised herself that the first thing she would tell him upon that second meeting was that she was the Ondine heiress, that it mattered not to her where he came from or how he earned his livelihood. Such serious thoughts winged off into temporary oblivion. Her senses took over. She welcomed Justin's sensuous movements as he untied the belt of his own robe and then hers, once more gathering her close and bringing her nakedness against his.

"Tell me you love me too," Justin whispered. A finger traced the shape of her ear. Midnight eyes pleaded with passionate eloquence.

"I think I must," Leander confessed, unable to deny that demanding gaze, yet still not ready to examine all that her heart was absorbing. "You set me on fire." Her voice panicked at the telling admission. She tried to look away but couldn't. Her body shivered, naked evidence of the state of turmoil within. Never had she felt so vulnerable.

"That'll do for now, dear one." He had no doubt that what shone in those pansy depths was love — even if she might not be ready to admit it.

That time when Justin kissed her, he also put away thought of anything other than raw feeling. His tongue sent messages inside the velvety mouth, messages that her own answered in pleasing language. A keen edge of flame cut at him down low, sucking the air from his lungs, shooting waves of heat throughout. The shadowed room had seemed chilly while he was away from her fetching their food, but now it seemed close and warm. Within his arms he held all that he needed to enflame him, both inside and outside.

Their second coming together led Leander to more profound highs, peaks mercifully free of pain. The power encircling her . . . lifting her . . . sucking her up . . . emanated from him, and yet it had not existed until he made her his. She sensed that the force must have come from their joining . . . must have existed in a vacuum until he claimed her . . . must have wandered in aching desolation as it sought the catalyst to give it life. Like souls drifting toward a higher being, had Justin's and hers wept their anguish secretly in their search for the touch of the other? Could she ever again listen to a moan in the night winds and not wonder if the spirits of lovers destined to meet — or else die — might not be weeping over their loss?

Tenderness welled from some hidden source and threatened to float Justin away at the height of his passion. He felt marvelously light all over, felt he had just that night learned what life is all about. He longed to breathe his beloved into his every pore . . . hold her there forever . . . never let her rise to surface for others to see and share. Lea was his alone. He had dreamed her into existence.

Sleep worked its merciful magic on the lovers there on the bearskin rug. Still locked in close embrace and still murmuring husky-voiced endearments, they eased into peaceful blackness.

"What are you doing?" came Leander's morning voice.

Justin turned from where he was tucking his shirt into his breeches and smiled down at her before saying, "I'm getting ready to leave. Isn't that the way you wanted it—for me to ride away first? I'll leave your horse saddled for you."

Leander nodded, sitting up and clutching the robe he must have thrown over her to ward off the predawn chill. The fireplace held only coals now, and the lodge appeared gloomier than when she had first entered it the previous afternoon. She brushed at her tousled hair with nervous fingers, licked at lips gone dry.

"We'll meet here ten days from last night—agreed?" he asked, already busy at pulling on his boots. "If either of us can't make it, he'll leave a note tacked to the door telling when to return."

"I'll be here," she promised, shivering a bit. It must be from the damp air, she told herself. She shrugged into the robe and stood to tie the belt. The fur tickled her feet as she crossed the rug to slip her feet into the outsized slippers. "There'll be no need for me to write a note."

"Just in case," Justin said. He was fully dressed now and was appalled at the path his mind was taking. He wanted to renege on their agreement, wanted to demand she tell her full name and where she lived, wanted to see her in full sunlight, wanted to ask her to marry him—even set the date. The fear that he might never see her again rose more threateningly now that the pink tinge of dawn washed against the windows. Was it wise to give into her request? What if he pretended to leave but then hid and followed her?

"You're going to live up to your word and ride away without looking back, aren't you?" she asked, startling him with her perceptiveness.

"What makes you think I won't?"

"There's a look about your eyes and mouth which makes me suspicious."

"That, my beautiful Lea, is brought on by my wanting to crush you in my arms again before I leave."

"We agreed that we would walk away this morning without another touch."

"I must have been crazy to have made such an agreement."

"A prince always lives up to his word—remember? You told me yours is as good as gold."

"I love you, Lea. Remember that."

Justin stepped off half the distance to the door, each step sounding too loudly. He turned. She hadn't moved there in the semidarkness. He was sure that the memory of the way she looked in the man-sized robe with black curls tumbling every which way across her face and shoulders would haunt him over the next nine nights. As would the smoldering purple eyes. As would

255

the remembrance of the way she had felt in his arms —

"Go now, Justin," Leander pleaded, jamming her hands into the robe's big pockets to hide the way she was turning them into fists of protest. If he stood there gazing at her one more second with that naked, black-eyed hunger piercing the shadowy room, she would be lost. She mustn't weaken. By the time they met again, she would have all the answers worked out. "But don't forget to come back to me."

"Nothing short of my death will keep me from returning. Can you make the same pledge?"

Never more sure of anything in her life, Leander replied without hesitation. "Yes. Nothing short of my death will keep me away." She confessed silently that she would be only half alive until she was once more with him.

Justin turned then and left. Not until she heard the fading sounds of hoofbeats did Leander move and begin throwing on her clothing.

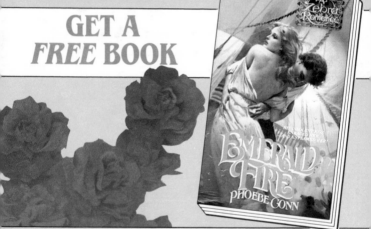

MAIL THE POSTAGE PAID COUPON TODAY!

START YOUR SUBSCRIPTION NOW AND
START ENJOYING THE ONLY ROMANCES THAT
"BURN WITH THE FIRE OF HISTORY."
YOUR GIFT OF A *FREE* BOOK IS WAITING FOR YOU.

Your FREE
Book Offer
Card

Zebra
HOME SUBSCRIPTION SERVICE, INC.

☐ YES! please rush me my Free Zebra Historical Romance novel along with my 4 new Zebra Historical Romances to preview. You will bill only $3.50 each; a total of $14.00 (a $15.80 value–I save $1.80) with *no* shipping or handling charge. I understand that I may look these over *Free* for 10 days and return them if I'm not satisfied and owe nothing. Otherwise send me 4 new novels to preview each month as soon as they are published at the same low price. I can always return a shipment and I can cancel this subscription at any time. There is no minimum number of books to purchase. In any event the Free book is mine to keep regardless.

Name _____
          (Please Print)

Address _____ Apt. No. _____

City _____ State _____ Zip _____

Signature _____
          (if under 18, parent or guardian must sign)

Terms, offer and price subject to change.

)1112186

PRINTED IN U.S.A.

A FREE ZEBRA
HISTORICAL
ROMANCE
WORTH

$3.95

Chapter Twelve

"Maybe you did do the right thing to spend the night at your papa's hunting lodge, missy," Jabbo said to Leander when they had time alone the morning after the storm. His normally placid face screwed up into worry lines, he scolded, "But you had no business leaving the house without getting word to me. No telling what-all could have happened to you."

Hiding the smile threatening to surface at his innocent yet apt phrasing, Leander retorted, "Criminee! You'd think that by now you'd know I can take care of myself, Jabbo. As I told Felix and you when you met me back near Frenchman's Bayou, I didn't plan for things to work out as they did. You've got to admit that was a monster of a storm, even if the sun is shining today as if nothing had happened." A secret corner of her heart basked in happiness at the thought of all that had taken place during the storm.

"Nobody realized you were gone till after dark," the big man pointed out, his voice still heavy with feeling. "Mr. Felix kept all of us down at the river filling sandbags till it was too dark to see. Sheeva thought you must be sleeping up in your room and didn't want to bother you till she had your supper ready. We spent a miserable night trying to figure out where you had gone." He shot accusing looks her way as they rode along in the black mud, their horses side by side in the lane leading to the stable up ahead.

"I'm sorry to have caused you to worry," she apologized. She hadn't seen such a troubled look on his face since Dom had died. Until Felix left them a ways back to get word to the other searchers, Jabbo hadn't made much fuss, and she was quite surprised to see the depth of his concern. "I'll try to use better judgment in the future."

Jabbo went back over his misery, as if he hadn't heard her. "Before dark set in, I saw those two clouds heading together, one from the south and one from the west, and I figured we were fixing to have a giant storm if they met. And did they meet! So much rain was falling that there was no way I could ride out to look for you till long after midnight. I had just thought about those horses in that pasture across Frenchman's when I heard Gabriel bark up ahead of Mr. Felix and me. If you hadn't come riding from the woods then, I don't know what I would have done. You ought to try searching for somebody in the dark when you don't know which way to start. Gabriel didn't have a chance to track, not with the water washing away every trail and scent." Dark eyes filled with both anger and relief searched her face. "Most of all the slaves were riding over other sections of the place looking for signs while Mr. Felix and I held to the middle. He had already told me he didn't expect we were going to find you when you showed up."

The black giant didn't add that the overseer hadn't seemed overly concerned when he had made the unsettling announcement. There was no reason to tell her, yet, that Felix Grinot was not her friend any more than he had been her father's. In time he would have to let her know. He needed more to go on than hunches, though, and he had little doubt that he would run across something before long.

"Everything is all right now. I'll apologize to everyone. Quit fretting about it, will you?" Leander's conscience bothered her more than a little. She hadn't realized how deeply Jabbo cared for her or maybe she would have started home as soon as the rain ceased. Some giddy part of her prodded her to confess silently that nothing could have dragged her away from Justin until dawn. "I'm just glad to be back home to get into some clean, dry clothing. Swimming across the bayou and leading that spooked Thunder soaked me good."

"You're probably going to catch a cold."

Leander made no further comment. When they reached the stable and she dismounted, she touched Jabbo's bulging forearm with an understanding pat. For the moment that they exchanged looks acknowledging some deep bond, she longed to tell him of Justin, of the marvelous discovery that she was in love, was loved in return. She sensed the time was wrong, though, and, after giving a bear hug to the frisky Gabriel, she went on into the house to face the upset Sheeva and her daughter Cara.

xxx

"I tole Mr. Petra and Mr. Lemange when you didn't come home the other night that you was goin' to come back with a devil of a head cold," Ona told her master downriver at Terre Platte. It was the third morning after the storm. She had been making the same announcement in the same "I-could-have-told-you-so" voice ever since he had returned home from his night in the hunting lodge.

Justin was resting on his bed, plagued by aches and fever — and the loss of his voice. With jaundiced looks, he watched the plump black woman bustling about, straightening the already-neat room. She seemed to hunt reasons to come to his room now that he had given up and gone to bed. Petra and the slaves seemed to have contained the floodwaters back on the far side of the plantation; now that three days of sunshine had reigned, danger appeared to have passed.

"Anybody got the sense you has and still ride off in a storm to check on dumb horses probably deserves what he gets," she scolded. Ona hadn't done more than nurse him yesterday when he had come in looking all washed out and feverish. But today, seeing that he was not coming down with something serious, she gave vent to her feelings. "You're goin' to be somethin' else at the Mardi Gras party, what with not bein' able to talk." She stopped before the garment hanging on a peg near the dressing alcove, sending appraising eyes over it. "And this costume, or whatever you call it, that Captain Galvez done sent from New Orleans, ain't goin' to help much. Don't seem like no friend would be shippin' up somethin' that looks more like two sheets all sewed together. Never seen a man wear a dress before."

260

Ona's full bottom lip protruded even more in disapproval, and a little snort drifted across to her irritated master. Glimpsing his hand lift in protest, she went on. "Never mind that you call it a 'toga,' it ain't nothin' but a dress, from where I stand. And to have one shoulder naked—Humph! Them Romans Mr. Lemange and you told me wore 'em must've been somethin' else! He may be a high-falutin' architect, but he's got ideas 'bout as strange as yours when it comes to dressin' up for a party. It's a good thing he learned how to wrap the sheet around you whilst he was off studyin' in Italy or you'd be showin' no tellin' what-all after the first dance at the party."

"I also told you I'm not going to the damned party," Justin rasped in an aggravated whisper.

He wasn't about to confess to the smug-faced slave that the idea of his wearing a toga hit him with as little enthusiasm as it did her. Deep down, he suspected Bernardo was playing a trick on him to have sent such a ridiculous costume. They had always liked pulling pranks on each other, but this time, Bernardo had gone too far. As for Ona—it was impossible to be nice to her. She had a way of taking over every time he let down his guard. When he regained his voice and was able to be up and about, he was going to set her straight. And Colonel Bernardo Galvez had best be on guard for what he was to receive from Justin in payment for the toga.

"Oh, yes, you's goin'!" Ona shot back, cutting angry eyes at him over her shoulder and propping a balled fist upon a cushioned hip. "You done promised the Ferrands you'd be there as a guest of honor—and that keeps it from bein' a 'damned' party. It's mostly for you and is the biggest party folks around here had in a long time and you's goin' to be there. You got three more days to get your voice workin' and get some color back in your face. How you goin' to ever be a part of these planter folks iffen you keep turnin' down all the invites? How you 'spect them to come to your parties in the new house iffen you don't go to theirs?" And inside, her practical mind asked how was her handsome master ever going to find a wife if he didn't go where available young women could be found. That new mansion Mr. Lemange and his crews were working on was perfect for a family — and far too big for a single man. He needed a wife and lots of children. Her eyes softened at the thought and she added on a more cheerful note, "Besides, you's always talkin' 'bout how you's a man of your word — and you done give your word to Mr. and Mrs. Ferrand."

Justin flinched. Ona knew him too well. Her words fell like the voice of doom. Yes, if he were to recuperate to some acceptable degree, he would have to go to Belle Terre for the Mardi Gras costume party. He had, indeed, given his word, had even accepted the invitation in writing. He closed his eyes and feigned sleep, hoping to hush the black woman and get her to leave him alone.

The fading sound of shuffling slippers told him his ploy had worked. Not until then could he allow his thoughts to dwell with uninterrupted pleasure upon Lea and the time he had spent with her. Only seven more nights and he would be with her again, could get everything out in the open and ask her to marry him.

Despite his stuffy nose and scratchy throat, he smiled. Maybe Ona was right in pointing out that bit about expecting the Creoles to attend his own parties — he would want every last one of them to come and meet his beautiful wife. What was one night at a boring affair when a lifetime of happiness would begin within the week afterward?

"Cara, you'll do as I asked you to," Leander announced there in her bedroom at Beaux Rives. Not often did the black woman question her mistress's decisions, and her comments about the costume Leander planned didn't please. "I'm not going to the party at Belle Terre to charm the bachelors. If you think my costume will horrify them and scare them away, so much the better." She leaned to look more closely in the mirror at the garb she had on. With her heart committed to the mysterious Justin, what did she care what others thought? The costume party had held little interest for her from the beginning. She hadn't looked forward to the scrutiny of those people she barely recalled any more than she had to that of those she would be meeting for the first time. Even the well-meaning Philip had confided to her at his last visit that interest in her whereabouts since the night the Ondine mansion burned was high among all who had communicated with his father and stepmother. The sardonic Antoine had intoned when he last called at Beaux Rives that someone had asked him if he were sure he had found Leander in Natchez or had he found her in "Natchez under the hill." Neither revelation did much to add to her already-shaky confidence about attending. If only the affair were a couple of weeks away instead of a couple of days, if only Felicity and Andre hadn't been so insistent, so gracious, persuasive . . .

"It won't be fitting for Miss Violette's daughter to be wearing such an outlandish outfit," Cara responded with more fire than usual. She was only nine years older than her mistress, but she felt she was old enough to be her mother. For Leander to be revealing her every curve in Creole society was plainly improper for one of her standing. She sighed. Her young mistress had always seemed cut from different cloth than her genteel mother.

"I'll be going as Miss Leander Violette Ondine, heiress of Beaux Rives—not as anybody's daughter." The reminder of her proper mother stung. To appease her need for approval, she thought of Josie and her ladies. They would go along with her notion to shock the Creole society, to show them that she didn't care what they might be saying about her mysterious absence of six years. "Since you've heard that everyone is buzzing about me, I thought I would give them something to whisper about."

"Your mother wouldn't have liked this."

"Stop saying that, Cara. I've made up my mind." Leander turned then to face the concerned slave. "You've done a good job in making the pants out of that piece of black satin I brought from Natchez. What you need to do to the shirt is make the long sleeves fuller and put a snug wristband. And don't bother to make buttonholes past here." She laid a measuring finger at the middle of her cleavage. "Don't frown. My fashionable gowns don't come a bit higher."

"Where on God's earth did you come up with this idea to go as a pirate?" Cara asked, shaking her head and knowing she had no choice but to go along with what seemed a foolhardy idea. She had confided to Jabbo what their hardheaded mistress was up to, and he hadn't been any more pleased than the personal maid. He had promised to try to intervene, but both knew he would have little more influence than Cara or Sheeva. Sheeva had already spewed out her disapproval yesterday when Leander first revealed her plans, but to no avail.

"I once acted the part of a pirate . . . back at the school in Mobile."

Leander's spirited mind didn't recoil from the lie. She had indeed acted the part of a pirate more than once . . . but it was on Dom's houseboat and in Josie's receiving room. And she hadn't had a costume nearly so appropriate for the role as the one she was directing Cara to sew. The old sailor's tales about pirates had always enchanted her. When she became older and yearned to give vent to her imagination and act out parts of his songs and yarns, Josie, Jabbo, and he had sat back and praised her efforts. She planned to give her best performance at the costume party, knowing full well that her actions would be scandalous. But how else could she show those who would be staid and suspicious that she was undaunted by their approval or the lack of it? And how else could she make sure that if any young lady having attended Miss Julia Shepherd's School for Young Ladies might be present, she wouldn't dare stoop to make conversation with the shocking Miss Ondine? She clung to Josie's oft-heard,

265

teasing remark that when people seem intent on talking about you, give them something to get their teeth into.

"Didn't Sheeva tell me there was an old trunk in the wine cellar that didn't burn?" Leander asked after shedding the red satin shirt and handing it to Cara to alter and complete.

The black head nodded. "Mr. Felix sent it up to the attic after poking through it." Cara had already accepted that the willful Leander would, indeed, do as she chose. And, she confessed, the young beauty was a sight to behold in the tight calf-length breeches and the bold shirt—one that she would be making bolder by putting no buttons higher than the bustline. "Why?"

"It might be the one with those things belonging to my grandparents back in France. I believe I once found a sword and scabbard in there and was almost spanked for charging about the grounds with it," Leander replied with a pleased little smile, brushing at her hair and squinting in memory.

"I guess you'd like for me to see." Her wide mouth spread in amusement at the thought that either parent would have laid a hand on their spoiled daughter—not when a winsome smile and a fervent hug could gain anyone's approval. Cara was all too aware that Leander was using the same tricks on her that very minute— and that she was responding exactly as everyone always had.

"Would you, Cara? You're ever so much help. I don't know what I would do without you." She sent a fond look at the black woman and realized a similar one was being returned.

266

By the Saturday of the party, Cara had everything her mistress had ordered in readiness — except a mask. Neither Leander nor she had ever seen one, and they had no idea how to make one. In a moment of what she deemed inspiration, Leander came up with the idea of using a triangle of the red satin to tie across her face and mouth, leaving only her eyes exposed.

Then came the question of what to do with her long hair. Cara suggested creating a more elaborate coiffure than usual, but Leander demurred, striving for something more dramatic.

"Didn't you say you saw some old hats in the trunk in the attic when you went to fetch the sword?" she asked. All the while, she was turning and peering into the mirror to get the full effect of her costume. The satin shimmered, both the red shirt and the black breeches. A wide sash of the red encircled her narrow waist and trailed down one side of the tight breeches. It seemed to her that the black riding boots came up too high, and she stooped to cuff the soft leather into large flaps falling at mid-calf.

"None of them were for ladies." What wild thing would the beautiful young woman dream up next? Cara had noted how tense and high-strung she had seemed ever since returning the day after the storm. And the caring slave had confided to Sheeva that their young mistress must not be sleeping well, that each morning the sheets were rumpled and pillows thrown on the floor.

"Good. Go get them for me, please."

When Cara returned with a large, wide-brimmed object of black beaver, Leander smiled and reached for the crumpled hat. She smoothed and plumped at the soft material, pleased to see how it responded to her touch and took a more recognizable shape. A forefinger tested a wide ostrich plume dangling from the hatband.

"This will do nicely," Leander said. "All you'll need to do is stitch the brim up on the crushed side, and I'll have a hat fitting for a dashing pirate." She lifted it to her head and showed her reluctant accomplice what she had in mind. "The feather is battered, but it'll serve fine for a pirate."

While the resigned slave set about to do as bade, Leander braided her hair into one thick rope and twined it about her head. Once she slipped the man-sized hat onto her head, little of her hair, except for the ever-present fringe of short curls about her forehead and neckline, could be seen. With the red satin scarf tied at the back beneath the hat, all that showed to mark her as Leander Ondine were the purple, black-fringed eyes.

"If you'll cut round holes and stitch them in black, I can pull up the scarf to cover my forehead. That way no one can see the color of my eyes," Leander told the frowning Cara.

With an outward show of resignation, Cara did as asked. Once more, her mistress experimented with the make-do mask.

"I love it!" the devilish part of her exclaimed in a voice muffled by the satin scarf. With an excited giggle, she strapped the altered scabbard about her slim hips and slid in the ornate sword some unknown ancestor must have worn to a distant battle. "No one will have the slightest idea as to who I am until the unmasking comes at midnight."

"No doubt about that," muttered the still disapproving Cara. "Who but you would want to cover up such pretty eyes? You don't even sound like yourself with your mouth all covered up like that. Sometimes you accuse me of sounding like I'm talking with my mouth full of mush—that's the way everything you're saying comes out. Nobody's going to understand a word you say." She didn't want to be downstairs when Jabbo got ready to drive her in the passenger cart over to Belle Terre. He was going to be madder than three wet hens because he had all but ordered Cara to talk some sense into Leander. And she knew that had the power been his, he would have ordered it. No telling what Mr. Felix was going to think if he happened to see her before she left. Her heart sank even lower at the thought of the cruel overseer—that was why she did her best never to think of him. Cara jerked her thoughts to the present. "What will your cousin think?"

"Felicity will understand," Leander replied carelessly. "She and I used to play dress-up all of the time, and she knows how much I like to pretend." Giving the image in the mirror a salute, she turned to leave. She was ready to get the miserable night behind her.

By the time Jabbo had let her know all the way on the drive to Belle Terre exactly how wrong he thought her rebellious actions and attitude were, Leander was having private doubts that Felicity would be as understanding as she had declared to Cara. After all, Leander was being presented as a guest of honor; the party was Felicity's first as mistress of Andre's mansion.

What if her unorthodox appearance shocked the Ferrands even more than their guests? She thought of Andre, then his sons, Philip and Antoine. Both of the young men had hovered over her with obvious admiration and respect each time they had called upon her at Beaux Rives. Would they now feel that she had been deceiving them all along in her role as proper young Creole heiress, and that the brazen young woman in the pirate's outfit might be the real Leander? She didn't want to examine the rising question as to which one was the real her and promptly shoved it aside.

Again she wished the party were taking place farther in the future, after she had once more met Justin at the hunting lodge—only five nights away, her fluttering heart reminded her—and had something definite worked out about their future together. Already she had decided that what she felt for him must be true love, that the incident back in Throw-away's bedroom would fade from memory. What fun it would be if she could be attending the party with Justin. She didn't even have to wonder if her mischievous lover would have approved her appearance. He would have loved it, would have encouraged her in her madness, would probably have tried to get someone to make him a frog costume. The ludicrous thought brought a grin to her face. A solemn-faced Jabbo brought her to the present then by stepping down to assist her to the ground, and she let the grin fade. She would have to face the evening alone.

"For God's sake, Pierre," Justin Salvador snapped. "Get it over with." As he had generously offered to do ever since having seen what Bernardo had sent, his architect and friend was helping him get into his costume there at Terre Platte. Justin had put off until the last minute getting dressed for the party and had found he was helpless when it came to draping the long length of fabric about him. Unlike Pierre, who had spent years studying in Italy, he knew nothing about the tricks of draping a toga. He stood naked except for an undergarment of white wool reaching to his knees. "This night will live as the most asinine of all my twenty-seven years."

Older and less fiery in temperament than the Spaniard, Pierre Lemange let his French heritage show in his amused smile and actions. "If you don't start speaking in French and paying attention to your pronunciation, you're going to have all of the Creoles bending double with laughter at your attempts to converse in their language. Sometimes the way you butcher my language makes me wonder if my two years of tutelage has been of any use." Meeting the angry eyes of his employer and friend in the mirror, he shrugged and added with a teasing chuckle, "All that's done to further the cause of romance can't be completely wasted. Ladies will swoon before this emperor."

Pierre laid one end of the purple-bordered, white wool against the broad chest, then carried it over the left shoulder, around the back, and brought it under the right arm to the front. Again he draped it over the left shoulder before dropping it to the back. In-sewn pellets weighted the straight-hanging folds and held them in place. The classical arrangement left Justin's right shoulder and arm bare. He grimaced at the

271

picture he made, looking down with distaste at the sandals consisting of little more than a leather sole and a few straps.

"What makes you think all of this has anything to do with romance, pray tell?" Justin intoned while Pierre rummaged in the package Bernardo had sent and came toward him with a small box in hand. "What in hell is that?"

"Gold-colored powder for your hair," his friend replied. "Bernardo thought of everything. The ancient Romans were high on this bit of decoration." Deftly he dusted the black hair, standing back to admire the effect. "It doesn't hide the streak in your hair, but it does make it less noticeable. The wreath of laurel leaves will cover it completely though."

"If I'm to be so disguised, why will I need to wear the damned mask? No one there is going to recognize me as I am now." Scowling, he turned away from the intimidating mirror. The thought struck him that had Lea been with him, had she been taking part in such an adventure, he would have become all caught up in the fantasy. He recalled the way she had seemed amused at his story of the frog and the prince, and felt cheered. After tonight — no, after five more nights . . .

Justin's department was delayed even further by Ona's insistence on seeing him on some trumped-up matter about what she had packed in the saddle roll for him to wear while staying overnight at Belle Terre after the party. And then, the telling blow to his ego, Principe fought against letting the robed figure mount him, snorting nervously and trying to bolt when his master put a sandaled foot in a stirrup and settled his

272

skirts across the saddle. He hung the face-sized mask upon the saddle horn and scolded his favorite mount for being a fool, finding that the hoarseness still claiming his voice was worsening as twilight approached. The thought that he was an even bigger fool than the spirited stallion loomed with certitude, bringing a frown to his handsome face.

In a fit of temper unbecoming to one who was being presented as a guest of honor at the Mardi Gras party, Don Carlos Justin Salvador charged off for Belle Terre on his reluctant steed. A few Spanish curses purpled the fading afternoon light. What would it matter if he arrived late? The entire evening could be nothing but a fiasco.

Chapter Thirteen

A wing of Belle Terre was set back at the stable side of the mansion, its porch jutting from the rear side of the large ballroom in the main portion. Seeing no one on the front veranda when Jabbo drove the small cart toward the stables, Leander hurried in the darkness to the side porch. Perhaps if she hid there and peeked at the arriving guests when they joined those already inside and saw what they were wearing, she could regain her conviction that she was doing the right thing to appear in her pirate's garb. Jabbo's mumbling disapproval had affected her far more than she cared to admit. Maybe he had been right; maybe she should have talked it over with him days ago instead of deliberately avoiding any private talk with him simply because she didn't want to hear his complaints.

Leander lounged against the low hand-railing in the shadow of a slim post, astounded to see the luxurious array the guests inside the ballroom were wearing. Appearing delighted in their roles as hosts, Felicity and Andre wore elaborate costumes in the purple hues of kings and queens. An enormous white wig hid Andre's graying hair. Felicity looked every bit a queen with her regal coiffure of blond curls topped by a diamond tiara. From her hidden spot outside, Leander stifled a moan. Felicity wasn't going to see one whit of humor in her cousin's outfit.

So engrossed was the crestfallen Leander in a kind of mental, self-flagellation that she didn't notice when a figure came from the direction of the stables and walked upon the porch behind her. She had already tied the red satin triangle across her face and tucked the ends beneath her hat, the one which had seemed so saucy back in her bedroom but now appeared as a bedraggled reminder of her earlier sense of humor. She was already regretting her last-minute idea to pull up the scarf to rest beneath the brim of her hat and cut eyeslits. The small holes limited her vision in the dark far more than she would have thought. There was little left for her to do but to go on around to the front veranda and go inside. Fingering the heavy sword slapping at her thigh and calf upon the slightest movement, she sighed.

"Why so pensive?" came a hoarse, masculine voice from the shadows of a post down a ways from the one she had been leaning against. The late-arriving Justin Salvador suspected the figure was that of a young woman, but as it appeared to be wearing some kind of breeches and high-heeled boots, he had his doubts. Had he realized someone was already on the side porch, he wouldn't have given in to some mad impulse to stop there before presenting himself to his hosts. "You must be about as eager to go inside as I am."

Leander whirled about, the sword thwacking against

the post with a loud report, and, in turn, sending a painful slap against her satin-clad behind. She sent a sympathetic hand to rub at the bruise, not realizing that the light from the ballroom fanned behind her and showed her movements clearly to the one facing her. His hair seemed to glow in a mysterious way, and for some reason, her pulse skipped in an erratic pattern. Was the figure an apparition?

"How long have you been skulking there?" she demanded with more bravado than she felt. It seemed obvious that the man was up to no good, or he wouldn't have sneaked up on her that way. One hand resting on the hilt of her sword, she peered in the darkness from behind the eyeslits, unable to see much more than a ghostly shape in the pale light reflecting from the windows of the ballroom. When no reply came, she asked again, letting her dissatisfaction with the entire evening and herself show in her voice, "What are you doing out here?"

"It's hard to hear what you're saying behind your mask," came the croaked answer as the figure moved to lean against the post next to the one she claimed. The voice was definitely feminine, Justin reflected, though it was heavily muffled by its covering — and far from friendly. And it wasn't hard to recognize that the buttock she had rubbed so tenderly was curved and shapely. If she were one of the flirting belles he expected to find present tonight, she must not think him worth the effort. He let out a breath of relief. Having found Lea, his dream goddess, he had no interest in any other kind of young woman. In spite of himself and his noble thoughts, he found the slight, costumed figure intriguing. What kind of outfit was she wearing? Without having given the matter conscious thought, he realized he had expected all the young women to appear decked out in the frills and furbelows of royalty.

"It's just as hard to hear what you're saying behind yours," Leander shot back. Upon hearing her words, she realized Cara had been right. She might as well be trying to speak with a mush-filled mouth. Even from behind the small holes in her mask, she could see more clearly now that he was closer. No wonder she hadn't heard him approach. Mere strips of leather formed a kind of shoe far from being masculine. Her eyes moved upward then, and she smothered a wave of laughter. The tall stranger was wearing a toga and a laurel wreath, the likes of which she had seen only in some of Josie's history books and in some paintings once hanging on the walls of Beaux Rives before the fire. He also wore a black mask which practically covered his entire face—the part jutting out to allow breathing reaching on down to conceal all but the tip of his chin. The eyeslits were elongated, sidewise cuts which lent an air of mystery about what lay behind them. Something in the air had seemed charged with an unsettling force ever since he first spoke, and she felt threatened. With breathless haughtiness, she accused from behind the satin covering, "We've not been properly introduced, sir."

"Nor or we likely to be until midnight—isn't that the way of masked balls?" Justin asked, straining to make himself heard. His throat hadn't taken on the soreness again as he rode in the fading light upriver to Belle Terre, but the hoarseness had moved steadily back as darkness fell. Maybe it was because he had ascertained that the guest was not interested in flirting with him that he felt he was where he belonged . . . for the moment. He had never seen a young woman wear a pirate's garb before and found the tight-fitting breeches and blouse fetching. "Whether we like it or not, we're both going to have to go inside soon."

She peered up at him from beneath her wide-brimmed hat. A mysterious blending of spirits seemed to be taking place, and from behind the scarf, she grinned. He must not be looking forward to the party any more than she.

"I suppose you're right," Leander replied. A spark of deviltry seized her, and she added, "We wouldn't want to insult the guest of honor."

Justin nodded sagely, wondering what the exquisitely formed pirate might say if she knew that she was speaking with him that minute. "He would likely never get over the disappointment."

"He?" Leander echoed, cocking up her head to study the strangely garbed young man more closely, setting the limp ostrich feather, angled forward from her hatband, to swaying. The crown of leaves encircling his head suggested he must be posing as a Roman emperor. Where in deuces had he come from? His French wasn't atrocious, but then who could tell when he spoke in a near whisper. It was then that she realized his right shoulder and arm were bare—and noticeably smooth and muscular against the creamy folds of the toga. Not that they could compare with her Justin's, she reassured herself. Still, anyone would have to admit that the tall stranger apparently had a manly build beneath the draped fabric. With hauteur she corrected, "I believe you're mistaken, sir. The guest of honor is the

Ondine heiress from Beaux Rives."

"That's not what my invitation said," he replied in a voice sinking from bass to whisper at aggravating intervals. He feared that before the night was over, he would be back to whispering every utterance. Damn! He shouldn't have listened when Ona and Pierre had kept reminding him of his duty to come. He could have gotten by with pleading illness. "The honored guest is the owner of Terre Platte."

"That's not true!" denied Leander vehemently, her eyes widening and sending out little flashes of white from behind the red satin eyeslits. "You're mistaken, sir. I'm sure the Ferrands wouldn't be giving a party in honor of a Spanish don. They're honoring Mrs. Ferrand's cousin, Miss Ondine."

"And I say what you tell is untrue. From what I've heard, she probably won't deign to attend."

Justin wasn't conscious that he stared when she drew up her slight body taller and brought gloved hands up to rest on the winsome hips and glared up at him. As she drew in an indignant breath, a glow from the ballroom reflected in the red satin of her shirt and bounced off obviously unbound breasts. The hint of nipples crowning the noble mounds and then the valley between those delightful hills drew his gaze. The pirate might be young, but she was no child. Thank God he was wearing the mask and she couldn't see that he was ogling like some gauche stripling. How was it that the sight of some strange young woman's voluptuous charms could rack him so when his heart belonged to Lea, when his beloved's perfect form had no equal? Ever since he had joined the pirate on the porch, he had felt drawn into some uncanny spell—it must be one of make-believe brought about by their masks and costumes . . . and darkness. With effort and a trace of guilt, he cleared his throat and forced his eyes back to her masked face.

"And just what have you heard to make you think that?" Her tone was sharp, even behind the fabric. Though she couldn't see his eyes, she suspected they were taking all kinds of liberty with her body—why else the unnerving, feathery feeling washing over her ever since he had joined her there in the dark corner? Obviously he had come alone. Was he searching for a young woman to escort inside? If so, he could look elsewhere. She noticed again that his right shoulder and arm were completely bare—and that both were unusually muscular. Not so handsomely formed as her beloved Justin's, she reassured herself, but with seemly grace. She still couldn't figure out what gave such a strange sheen to his hair. It seemed to be dark, yet . . .

"I've heard that she's a spoiled beauty who thinks she's too good for the new home her overseer built during her stay at some school for uppity girls in Mobile. It appears to me that if she were so snippety, she could have come back a time or two over the past six years and made some suggestions." Justin leaned around her to see into the ballroom, his eyes scanning the party-goers on the other side of the window. With a touch of amused scorn, he said, "If the infamous Miss Ondine is in there, you can bet that she'll be the one wearing the most elaborate costume of all—that of an empress, no doubt."

Leander smarted all over. Snippety? Infamous? She sucked in an angry breath. How dare this . . . this simpering, whispering excuse for a man dressed in a skirt utter such cutting lies about someone he obviously had never met? Bringing her hands to her hips, she glared up at him and hissed, "Well, at least she would know what might be fitting to wear to a Mardi Gras party. If—and note that I say 'if'—that despicable Don Salvador were to have been the guest of honor, he probably would have shown up wearing the mail of a plundering conquistador and set everyone's teeth on edge with his Spanish phrases and boorish manners. But I'm sure you've heard wrong. No Creole would invite him to a party."

With as haughty a lift to her chin as she could manage without dislodging the huge black hat with its drooping feather, Leander adjusted her sword and turned to walk away. The feather quivered in rhythm with her anger. The man was no one she cared to know or be civil to another minute. Since he had first spoken—no, croaked like a frog, she reminded herself—she had felt something inside tighten like a ball of thread. She had no intentions of letting him know that his arrogant attitude was threatening to unravel a loose strand of whatever was wound up inside. Going in to face Felicity and Andre and their growing number of guests would be far easier than staying to hear further insults. Seeing him in his toga had already convinced her that she wouldn't look any more ridiculous than he did. And it was likely there would be others dressed as much out of the ordinary as the two of them. The doubts which had driven her to seek refuge on the side porch had been foolish. Among the many guests, she could avoid having anything further to do with the insufferable young man—and would make that her goal of the evening.

"What makes you so sure no one would invite this man from Terre Platte to a party?" Justin was watching the way her slender hips swayed as she walked toward the steps of the porch. God! She was upset about something. The slender shoulders were stiff, the proud neck and head elevated to a haughty angle. He could almost feel the tension emanating from her, didn't stop to wonder why he allowed it to sweep him into its wake. Almost cursing at the unexpected hindrance from the folds of the toga, he took giant strides to reach her before she could leave the side porch and go around to the front of the house. A hand reached out to touch the arm covered in billowing red satin, but he drew it back. Not sure she had heard his hoarse question, he repeated it: "What makes you so sure no one would invite the man from Terre Platte?"

Leander strutted on down the four steps in her high-heeled boots, the sword swishing in time with her satin-covered hips, the streamers of the long sash fluttering behind her. In tones deliberately made loud enough to carry through the satin scarf, she turned to call over her shoulder, "Because he's a bloody Spaniard, that's why. Isn't that reason enough?"

Justin brought his finger and thumb up to rub at his earlobe, standing dumbfounded while watching the pirate move across the lawn toward the corner of the front veranda. She was certainly narrow-minded when it came to Spaniards, he mused with riled temper. And then he noticed in the light coming from the huge windows she passed that not only did she cut an arresting figure in her bold costume, but also she had the most fascinating, seductive walk he had ever seen. Conscience smote him a blow. The only reason he could be thinking such traitorous thoughts was that he had never seen his Lea walk in anything except over-sized robe and slippers. All of a sudden he felt less in the mood for a party than ever, despite the sounds of music from within the ballroom and of talk and laughter floating from the front veranda. How could he face the five nights looming ahead before he could see his beloved again? For some unexplained reason, the last view of the pirate rounding the corner left him feeling as beached as a whale after high tide . . . and terribly alone.

Once inside the front door, Leander walked straight to where Felicity and Andre stood to greet and visit with arriving guests there in the large hallway. She didn't notice that all heads in the vicinity turned to watch her progress.

"Felicity, Andre and you look absolutely regal. If you tell me I'm embarrassing you by wearing such a wild—"

Felicity's swift hug and delighted burst of laughter cut off Leander's attempt at apology. "Darling, you look perfectly divine! We already have one young woman dressed as a court jester. I love creative people, and I suspect that's why I've always loved being around you," she exclaimed, turning to Andre. "Doesn't she look marvelous dressed as pirate, Andre?"

The wigged head nodded and Andre's agreement showed in his smile and his comments. "Welcome, Leander. We're delighted to see you made it." He proved it by giving her a hug. "We had wondered why you hadn't joined us as we've already been told that Jabbo has put your portmanteau in an upstairs bedroom. My two sons and almost all of the guests have already asked if Miss Ondine had arrived."

"Of course we assured them we wouldn't tell," Felicity leaned to whisper, her pretty face flushed with pleasure, the diamonds in her tiara flashing from the overhead chandelier of burning tapers. "To keep everyone except the hosts masked until midnight is half the fun, and I'll love watching everyone try to figure out which masked figure is you." Excitement tingeing her voice and sparking her blue eyes, she added, "I promise you'll have a lovely evening, one you'll not forget for a long time."

"Pardon if I intrude," came a hoarse voice beside the trio there in the hallway. "I did wish to speak with my lovely hostess and handsome host before—"

Leander whirled about, her sword flying out and barely missing the newcomer. Yes, it was the young man in the toga. What was he up to? In a flash she saw why his hair had looked so strange on the darkened porch. It was covered with gold dust.

"Of course, my boy," murmured Andre, grasping the proffered hand and sending an amused looked at his toga-clad young friend. "We're happy you could join us. We need a Roman to lend the proper dignity around here tonight. After we heard that you had been down with a cold, we feared you'd not be able to make it. I hope the hoarseness I detect will soon be gone. Felicity, will you do the honors here?" His glance darted warily from the pirate to the Roman. His mien showed clearly that he hadn't put too much faith in his bride's little plan to bring together the owners of the two plantations downriver. Deceptions held no appeal for him, though he had gone along with Felicity's plan since it had seemed to mean so much to her.

"Darling," Felicity said, slipping an arm about her cousin's shoulders and sending an approving glance toward her other guest, "I've been eager for you two to meet, though I'm holding you to the bit of remaining masked until midnight. Since you're sharing the guest-of-honor spot tonight, I thought it appropriate that you at least be able to recognize the costume of the other." Assuming the air of the royalty she posed as, she looked at Leander and said with mock formality, "Miss Ondine, may I present the esteemed Don Carlos—"

Leander interrupted with undisguised fury, "Salvador, isn't it? The last name has to be Salvador." All inside she quivered. When had she ever felt so betrayed? Why had Felicity and Andre done this cruel thing to her? They knew full well how she felt about being around Spaniards. And they had deliberately not told her that she was sharing the honored guest spot with anyone, much less this nincompoop garbed in Roman splendor. "Am I right?" she asked in necessarily muffled tones. She longed to tear off his mask and hers and face him openly. "You're Don Salvador from Terre Platte, aren't you?"

"Yes," the Spaniard grated, the enormity of the awkward moment settling upon his brain. The pirate was Miss Ondine? For what reason had Felicity and Andre misled him into believing he was the sole guest of honor? Miss Ondine—my God! Small wonder that she had been so cutting out on the porch. He had made some snide comments, for sure. Not that she had been any more gracious with her obviously low, biased opinion of Spaniards, he reminded himself when she made no further comment. But Don Carlos Justin Salvador had not been brought up to be rude, and something pressed him to try to make amends. "Perhaps Miss Ondine and I should dance together and—"

"That won't be possible," Leander hissed. She was grateful then that the scarf covered her features except for a spot of chin. She wouldn't have wanted anyone to see the anger and disappointment taking over her face. From an eyeslit, she spotted a masked young Indian with curly brown hair standing in the doorway to the ballroom. Could it be Philip? "Please excuse me," she said to Felicity and Andre. She pointedly ignored Don Salvador. "I believe I've recognized a friend and prefer to join him."

With as much aplomb as she could muster with her limited vision, Leander turned away. She was unaware that her sword flew out in an arc or that the end of the heavy scabbard banged the toga-clad leg of the other guest of honor. All she could think of was getting away from the despised Spanish don.

The Indian warrior turned out to be Philip, and the two giggled over having recognized each other. Within a short time, Philip's deep-voiced banter had restored the outward layer of Leander's good humor, and they took their wine out onto the pillared veranda to a shadowy corner. Widely spaced sconces held chimneyed candles and lent a faint light. Other couples in lavish costumes and assorted masks stood about talking. As the evening was warm for February, some were strolling down the walkway toward the river. Torches dipped in whale oil lighted their way beneath the large oaks.

"You're the most beautiful young woman here, Leander," Philip said, lifting his wineglass in salute. He made no attempt to understand it, but there seemed about her that night something new and more exhilarating than upon previous meetings. "I wish you would take off the scarf so that I could see that face. Are you truly going to make me wait till midnight?" The way she had sought him out still had his pulses singing. Had she perhaps missed him? He had forced himself not to go down to Beaux Rives more than once a week since she had gone home. Mayhap she would be glad to see him call more often . . .

"No one is to unmask before then, silly," Leander replied, folding up her scarf to rest across the bridge of her nose so that she could sip from her wineglass. At the back of her mind rested the memory of drinking wine back in the lodge with Justin and she found herself smiling.

"Have you seen Antoine?" Philip tried not to let his jealousy of his older brother show in his voice. When she shook her head but retained the secretive, beguiling smile, he continued. "The last I saw of him, Maralys Soulier had him cornered near the orchestra, forcing him to dance with her almost every dance — not that he seemed completely unwilling for the daughter of one of the richest merchants in New Orleans to be hanging on his every word and batting her eyelashes at him." When she giggled, he paused to admire the pretty mouth and send her an appreciative smile. His was a demi-mask and covered only the area about his eyes. "He's posing as a judge — black robes and curled wig reaching down almost to his waist. And Maralys is dressed like Bo-Peep, or some such character from nursery rhymes."

"I'm impressed to see so many different kinds of costumes," Leander replied. "I wasn't sure that I would fit in with mine." She glanced down at her tight black breeches and cuffed boots, noticing as she lifted her eyes that ordering Cara to place the buttons of the shirt so low did expose more bosom that she had meant to. For some reason, seeing the lines of the red satin edging her breasts reminded her again of the night in the lodge when she had found the robe gaping there on the bearskin. That second, jagged memory brought to mind her beloved and she felt her throat fill, her heart do a somersault. If only he could be here with her . . .

"If you knew what seeing you in those breeches and boots does to me, you might run back inside and hide, or else draw your sword to fend me off," Philip whispered, leaning to let the words float into her ear but having to retreat because of the huge ostrich feather claiming the air above her face.

"Pardon me," a voice rasped nearby. "I hope I'm not intruding."

Leander jerked around, the feather whipping against the intruder's neck and bared right shoulder and causing him to backstep with speed. This time the plastered pillar of the veranda took the blow from the wayward sword with a resounding clang. When had the unwelcome Spaniard come upon them? With his wearing those sandals posing as shoes, who could have heard his approach? She stepped back as if she had come in contact with something dangerous. For some reason, she felt compelled to pull the satin back over her mouth.

"Don Salvador," she announced with venom, "we were having a private conversation. I believe that might have been obvious had you chosen to pay attention." Her gaze took in the straight folds of the toga, seeing its wide border of purple and not stopping until it perused the large black mask beneath the laurel wreath. "I always heard that Romans were refined and cultured. Is it your intention to wear their garments but ignore their customs?"

Justin's face flushed behind his mask and his eyes glittered behind the long eyeslits. Miss Ondine seemed determined to lash out at him with more than the unwieldy sword. His calf still smarted where it had thwacked him soundly upon her abrupt departure back there in the hallway. Only wounded ego and the determination to appear unruffled to his horrified hosts had kept him from pulling up his garments to check for blood. What in thunder had possessed him to force himself upon her and the plainly smitten Philip? Having spied young Ferrand trying to whisper into her ear there on the dimly lighted veranda, he had felt a strange compulsion to intrude, something not at all in character, he confessed. But the pirate had stirred a kind of rebellion in him all evening, and some part of him seemed bent on finding out why she had such strong feelings against Spaniards. He might deserve her anger, but she hadn't been exactly ladylike in her denunciation of him when she had known as little of him as he of her.

Acknowledging Philip's presence and having recognized the masked young man when the arrogant Miss Ondine had joined him earlier, he said to him, "It's probably good that you have your tomahawk with you, Philip. My suggestion would be for you to be on guard against a pirate with a tongue as cutting as her sword. Both might get the best of any man. Miss Ondine may be out to attack more than the Spanish tonight."

Philip, wondering what was creating the obvious tension between the two, tried to respond in a light vein. After walking into the hallway and seeing Leander and Justin talking with apparent civility to his parents, he had turned away, assuming that Leander had succumbed to Justin's ready charm. Had he been wrong? Was she still letting her old hatred of the Spanish control her? Now that he thought about it, she had seemed on edge ever since she joined him.

With an indulgent laugh, Philip said, "Miss Ondine is not yet accustomed to being around Spaniards. You might not know it, but she has been away at a school for young ladies in Mobile for the past six years. Perhaps if you showed her your skill on the dance floor, she would see how charming you can be and not be so eager to do battle."

"I don't feel like dancing," Leander spoke up. Though back at Josie's Inn when the ladies felt light-hearted and allowed the young Leander to join them in their afternoons of dancing she had never seemed to tire, she suddenly felt heavy-limbed at the thought of dancing with Don Salvador.

"That's just as well" came Justin's scathing whisper. "I hadn't planned on asking you to." And with a deferential nod at the open-mouthed Philip, he left and went back inside.

Shortly before midnight, Felicity noticed that the two she had felt certain might be destined for each had never danced together. After the fiasco of their intro-duction and Andre's whispered scolding of her for meddling, the pretty, blond hostess was determined that the two should have another chance to know each other. Several times she thought she had detected either

290

the black-masked face of Justin turned across the room toward the red satin of Leander's, or vice versa, but she couldn't be sure. Were they just being stubborn, or did they truly feel no attraction? Concern for her cousin and for the well-being of her other guests as well led Felicity to note when Leander had removed her scabbard and sword and allowed first Philip, and then Antoine, to lead her through the steps of the popular quadrilles. Countless other young bachelors had claimed her then for the lively galliards. All manner of costumed, masked revelers had danced the daringly dressed pirate about the candlelit room throughout the evening — except the one in the purple-bordered toga.

Felicity spoke with the musicians and crossed the large ballroom to find her cousin. Taking Leander's gloved hand in hers and leading her to a group where Justin stood listening to what he was apparently finding to be a boring conversation — poor man, she thought, to be hoarse on such a festive occasion seemed cruel — the determined hostess took matters into her own hands.

"Don Salvador," Felicity said, using her most beguiling manner, "Andre and I request that our honored guests lead off the pavan that I've asked the orchestra to play. We plan to have the unmasking soon." She could feel Leander's hand in her own tense, could feel the scathing looks shooting from behind the black-edged holes of red satin there in the candle-lighted ballroom.

Justin looked at the two cousins through the angled eyeslits of his mask and idly wondered if Miss Ondine might be half so pretty as Andre's bride. Probably not, he conceded, or she would have managed to show more of her face behind some less concealing mask. Still angered at her rebuff of him because of his heritage, he reminded himself that he did owe the courtesy to his host and hostess, even if he felt no wish to be polite to the arrogant pirate. What kind of spark was that stabbing at him from behind the red satin? He felt its intensity almost as surely as he had felt the blow from the heavy scabbard earlier.

"If Miss Ondine will allow me the pleasure," the Roman emperor replied with a formal nod in the direction of the pirate. He had given up trying to speak in anything but a whisper; his voice had completely disappeared. "I would be pleased to honor my hostess's request." He held out his hand for hers to rest palm-down upon its top before escorting the slender figure out onto the floor.

Leander could hear the orchestra tuning up to play for the stately, processional dance, one of many that the ladies had delighted in dancing with her, one she always favored because of its measured steps . . . until now. The miserable night was almost over. What else could go wrong? Grateful that at least she had only to rest one hand lightly upon the Spaniard's for the pavan and have no other bodily contact with him, she matched his formal nod with one of her own and placed her black-gloved hand just above his proffered one.

"I don't have an illness that can be caught from your touching my hand through your glove," Justin complained in a harsh whisper when they had taken the first two measured steps forward and prepared to take the double ones following. When it was time to move backward to repeat the pattern, he feared she might not follow him easily since she still held her hand above his. He assumed it was the pirate's several blows to his pride that was setting up a rising force inside. But for her to refuse to touch him whipped whatever warred within to a higher pitch.

"Dare I take the word of a Spaniard, Don Salvador?" Leander whispered back. She could see flashes of fire from behind that black mask. Good. He was as riled as she at Felicity's ridiculous attempt at matchmaking. And that had to be anger which roiled so persistently deep inside and set her stomach to churning, her heart to racing. Still strangely apprehensive about resting her palm on his hand, she was forced to when he began the backward steps or be left a quarter-step behind him. Others were beginning to take to the dance floor, but she could see only the masked face of the Roman turned her way in the fashion of the pavan. Even through the thin leather, her palm was achingly aware that it touched his hand.

" 'Tis as good as that of a pirate."

"I would warn you about pirates."

"You already have, Miss Ondine, in more ways than one. Besides, Romans were known to be men of perception." Justin paused with the music before beginning the forward steps again. The folds of his costume had hindered him in earlier, more livelier dances but they cooperated far better in the slower pavan, though they did have a tendency to swirl about his ankles when he stopped to begin a new pattern. Her small hand seemed ready to fly from his at the slightest excuse, and he lifted his to make the contact surer. Some force set into motion since seeing the pirate on the side porch refused to die down, puzzling him no small bit. It must be that her unreasonable bias against his people exuded from her every pore and attacked him.

"I would have thought a better word would be *deception*," she shot back, trembling a bit. The man was infuriating. "The skirts and gold dust could fool anyone into believing that the wearer might not be the gentleman he would seem."

Justin gasped but managed to continue the measured steps. God! But she had a sharp tongue . . . and a small hand warm and pulsating even through a glove.

"And what of an heiress who parades in tight pants? Isn't she apt to be less of a Creole lady than those who follow the conventions of fashion?" he parried, stung more than even his whispered words revealed. He would show her that she did not intimidate him with her aggressiveness.

Up close in the candlelight from the overhead chandelier, Justin could see more clearly the loveliness of her body. The long ends of the red sash floated from the small waist with each sensuous movement of her hips. The satin shirt molded the firm curves of her breasts in shimmering fashion. A part of him noted that she moved with more grace than any dancing partner he had ever squired; another part denied that she could have outshone his Lea were she to be beside him.

"I've had no complaints," Leander denied. She cocked her head in defiance, noticing the frayed ostrich feather had suffered from the evening's encounters and floated in broken splendor near one of her eyeslits. Her Justin had certainly found no fault with her as a desirable young woman . . . and it had been obvious that he hadn't been seeking out a society "lady." No doubt the Spaniard hoped to better his tenuous social position by marrying one of those "Creole ladies," the kind she couldn't help but notice that he had squired about the dance floor all evening. He was as maddening as she had suspected from the beginning. If it hadn't been for her meddling cousin, she wouldn't be caught up in this tailspin of wild feeling. Anger, no fury, that's what it was. The man seemed to have a way of bringing out the worst in her.

"Nor have I." A winged thought of Lea brought a smile behind the Roman's mask. Were she here with him, she would put the heiress to Beaux Rives to shame with her perfection. How she would laugh and smother him with kisses at the thought that anyone dared question his masculinity. A ripple of light-headedness threatened to make him miss a step.

"Your conquests would necessarily be Spanish." She knew from having seen the way the young women had fawned over him all evening that she was wrong, but she couldn't resist slicing at his obvious high opinion of himself.

"Why so?"

"With your French so bourgeois, I assumed that—"

Justin interrupted her slur with a Spanish remark in strained sotto voce. One word coming through clearly to her was *desagradable*.

"I must warn you that I speak your language," Leander said in flawless Spanish. She had to admit that he was a worthy opponent in their verbal duel, despite his hoarseness. "Surely you didn't refer to me as a disagreeable wench?"

Justin tried to make himself drop the convention of the pavan and turn his face from that of his partner. But something balked at allowing him to look away from the red satin scarf serving as mask. For a puzzling moment, he wished they weren't required to dance two arm's length apart as they glided forward and then backward in time to the music, her gloved palm resting lightly upon the top of his hand. A lift of chin and a sparkle winging his way from behind the black-edged eyeslits bordered on being familiar. It was plain that she was taunting him and enjoying the hell out of doing so.

"What a wayward mind you have, Miss Ondine."

"Only when it comes to Spaniards."

"I trust you know a great deal about them to have such bias toward my people." He had heard all about her father's having been shot as one of the Conspirators back in '69. She couldn't have been more than ten or eleven back then. Surely in her studies over the past six years at the school for young ladies she had learned that punishment for traitors was always harsh, no matter in which country or under which flag. That she could be bearing a grudge over something so out of the average Spaniard's control seemed ludicrous, even childish. And she was no child. Not that her presence or appearance had anything to do with the heady near-arousal he was feeling. It was the numerous glasses of champagne, coupled with the frequent thoughts of his night with Lea, he assured himself.

"Enough." Without warning, the memory of the night in Throw-away's room whirled through Leander's mind, threatening to drown her with molten fire. No wonder being so near the Spaniard had her all aquiver. All of a sudden, her hands felt branded to her partner's. Her heart skipped about crazily. Would the dance never end? Four more nights to go and she would never have to endure such torture again. Her Justin would see to that! She would confess all, and he would understand.

"Mayhap if you were around more of them, you would find that all of us aren't the boors you seem to think." Justin scolded himself. Why did he care what she thought about him or any other Spaniard? Strangely unsettling was the question of what was causing her hand to tense so noticeably—not that it had ever rested upon his in a relaxed way.

"Don Salvador," she hissed, "we truly have nothing to discuss."

They completed the final few measures without further words. Justin's skirt prevented him from making the stiff bow expected at the end. He suspected that his partner was laughing at his sudden flipping of the heavy folds from between his legs. Just as ridiculous to him was the pirate's lack of skirt to lift for a feminine curtsy. When she lifted an end of her long sash in each hand and executed a mocking but sensual curtsy in the form-fitting breeches, he couldn't keep from grinning behind his mask. God! She might be young, but she had poise. And a fascinating shape, all the way up from the well-shaped calves disappearing into the cuffed boots to the shadowed cleavage at the vee of the red shirt.

Antoine, the rakish judge, rushed to claim Leander for the final dance of the evening, laughing at the outsmarted Indian appearing too late. Leander felt little relief from her inner turmoil. She managed to endure Antoine's whispered invitations to meet him on the front walkway after everyone had gone to bed without letting him know how his innuendos repulsed her. She hardly noticed that when the dance was over, they stood beside the Roman and his last partner, the young woman Philip had told her was Maralys Soulier from New Orleans, the one seemingly smitten by Antoine.

Felicity and Andre made a grand show of tinkling a glass bell to gain the attention of the revelers. Midnight was upon them. It was time for unmasking.

Antoine had little choice but to bend toward the demanding Maralys because the Roman and the pirate turned to face each other. Excited laughter from the roomful of guests blended with ripples of chords from the musicians. In the next instant, the red satin triangle slid down. The black mask came off.

Leander stared at the Roman and took a step backward. Justin stared at the pirate and took two steps forward.

"How could you?" Leander whispered brokenly. A wild racing of her heart threatened to overpower her. She felt she had been sucked up into a whirlwind. Her knees were no more than week-old buttermilk.

"Lea," Justin managed to croak, reaching out a hand toward her. "Lea—?" What cruel joke had been played?

"Don't dare touch me!" Purple eyes raked over the handsome face. Indignation set the broken feather in her hat to quivering above an accusing eyebrow. She would have backed up further but all about her people were kissing, laughing, and shouting names, revealing earlier suspicions as to the identities of those about him. Besides, her legs had no bones. Her voice rose to hiss, "You're utterly despicable, you Spanish reprobate! How dare you do this to me!"

"Do what?" Damn not being able to do more than

whisper with all the din about them! How could the arrogant Miss Ondine with her hatred of the Spanish be his own sweet Lea? His mind reeled, unable to resolve all of its reviewing. And why was Lea angry and acting as if he had known all along who she was? Justin closed the brief distance between them, his senses attacking him unmercifully from all angles. His hand reached to touch her arm.

"My name is Leander Violette Ondine, though I never want to hear it upon your lips, you filthy Spaniard!"

Leander jerked away then, her eyes huge with unshed tears, her face pale beneath the big hat with the crippled feather. Blindly she wheeled, darting from the noisy ballroom and on up the stairs to the bedroom assigned to her. Her beautiful world had disintegrated at the stroke of midnight.

Chapter Fourteen

One of the Ferrands' overnight guests sleeping upon makeshift mattresses on the floor of the spacious downstairs study passed little of the night at rest. Even when his eyes closed heavily, Justin Salvador found no peace of mind, body, or spirit. The other bachelors sharing the quarters snored and shifted about normally, obviously having no difficulty in finding sleep after the night's festivities.

Justin could think of little other than his need to talk with his beloved, to find out why such anger and hurt had claimed her face as soon as she saw him. True, both had freely thrown barbs — but at disguised people, not at the real Leander and Justin who had fallen in love less than a week ago. If she would only listen to him, let him assure her that he had had no inkling as to her identity until the unmasking. He had pleaded urgently with Felicity, but without revealing anything about his having seen her cousin before that night. The suspicious Felicity had been adamant in her refusal to fetch Leander. Leander. Holy Mother! How could he have thought "Lea" the perfect name, once he heard "Leander"? One moment his heart soared; the next it swooped to dismal depths.

"Gone? She's gone?" Justin repeated the next morning when Philip answered the young Spaniard's question. He had wandered out into the main hallway soon after sunrise and accepted Philip's invitation to join him at breakfast. "Do you mean Leander has already returned to Beaux Rives?" The only good news of the morning was that his voice seemed to have returned to its normally deep bass.

Philip showed his puzzlement at the Spaniard's apparent agitation, even as he explained how Leander and Jabbo had driven away at the first rays of morning. "I did my best to get them to wait for coffee, but both assured me it was imperative that they leave early. Something about the need to tend to pressing matters." He ushered the guest out onto the whistle walk. Since no one else was up and about, they could find food more readily in the kitchen set behind the main house.

Though Justin seemed to be trying to accept Philip's explanation with casual interest, the younger man noticed a taut look about his mouth. Something stirred at Philip's jealousy as the two shared a sparse breakfast out in the kitchen. Was the black-haired Spaniard going to join Antoine's and his race for Leander's favors — and mayhap her hand in marriage? The memory of the seemingly testy exchange between the pirate and the Roman last night on the veranda rose. If that memory served him rightly, though, their manners had indicated more animosity than attraction.

301

Across the rim of his lifted coffee cup, Philip shot narrowed gray eyes toward his silent companion, the one he couldn't help but still like and admire, despite his unsettling thoughts. What was at the bottom of Justin's visible gloom upon finding Leander gone? A fierce look claimed the older man's handsome features, clouded the sparkle in the black eyes. Surely, Philip reassured himself, Justin meant no harm toward Leander, in spite of her heated spouting off about Spaniards at the least opportunity.

Justin wasted no time in bidding farewell to Philip, still the only Ferrand up and about at the early hour. Before heading for the stables, he tried to honor the younger man with a smile as he asked that his message of appreciation be relayed to Felicity and Andre, but his face felt frozen. He rewarded Principe with a lump of brown sugar when the ebony stallion didn't shy away from his master that morning, now that he no longer wore the strange, whirling skirts of the toga.

"We both had a rough time of it last night, didn't we, boy?" Justin replied in answer to the seemingly inquiring eyes. "Your problem is solved, but what about mine?" He tied the bundle containing the costume behind his saddle and mounted, turning downriver toward Beaux Rives and Terre Platte.

Upon the hurried ride of the previous evening, Justin hadn't done more than glance at Beaux Rives when he passed on the primitive road running across nature's low levee and connecting the plantations up and down the western bank of the Mississippi. Soon after taking possession of Terre Platte four years back, he had passed that way during the building of the two-story house, which Ona repeatedly referred to as the "red brick box," and had promised himself that he would call one of these days. From what he had learned of Felix Grinot, he had never been eager to find the time to stop by when making the infrequent journeys between the Ferrand holdings and his own. That February morning Beaux Rives held a special attraction. He could think of nothing more pressing than to call upon its mistress.

"No, sir, Mr. Salvador, Miss Ondine's not up to receivin' callers today," Sheeva told the obviously agitated man she had shown into the living room after the knocker clanged. "No, sir." Gabriel's protesting barks had alerted her that a stranger must be approaching, but she was still surprised upon opening the door to find the overpowering figure filling its space. Gabriel had done an about-face and was fawning all over the caller. Surprising her even further was the announcement of his name and reason for appearing. Didn't the man know how her mistress felt about Spaniards?

"Did you tell her who was calling?" Justin bit back all that wanted to pour forth. *Where is her room? I'll go to her and make her listen to me, talk out whatever is bothering her.* He then pleaded silently: *Leander! Don't let walls keep us apart now that we've found each other. Can't you hear me?*

"Yes, sir, I did that." Sheeva hadn't known what kind of dark spirits burned within her young mistress's eyes when she arrived home so early that morning, but she had already learned not to pry when the sparks seemed close to the surface in those purple depths. Whatever gnawed at Leander appeared ready to spill out at the least provocation. Both Cara and she had willingly followed her order to be left alone in her bedroom—until the caller arrived and demanded to be announced. He was not a man easily refused.

"And she said nothing else?" Leander yearned to hear each sound Leander had uttered. When the slave hid fidgeting hands beneath the snowy folds of her apron and looked down at the floor, he prodded, "What exactly did Miss Ondine say?"

Sheeva took a deep breath and raised her eyes. Up close, Mr. Salvador—or Don Salvador as some referred to him—truly did look like a demon, just as she had heard from talk among the slaves who kept up with all the tidbits of talk from the plantations. Wild, black eyes and unruly hair to match drew her eyes again to the narrow white streak reaching back from his left temple. As soon as she had opened the door and looked up to see the tall, imposing figure silhouetted against the wintry sunshine, she sensed that someone powerful stood before her. She had no wish to tell him what he asked to hear—but she feared he would know if she lied. Fingers crossed beneath the apron, the wide-eyed slave sucked in a deep breath.

"She said any bloody Spaniard darin' to call at Beaux Rives didn't . . . didn't deserve the time of day," Sheeva confessed in a hesitant, contrite voice. She eyed the iron sconces on either side of the mantel as if she had never seen them before, hadn't just that morning trimmed the candle wicks and cleaned the glass chimneys. At least she hadn't felt the need to add the string of curse words with which Leander had salted her statement, she consoled herself. And there was no way she was going to tell about the vase hurled toward the

304

door when Sheeva suggested that her mistress was being rude. Probably the man had heard the crash, but she would do nothing to satisfy his curiosity, not even if he plain-out threatened her. Lordy! If Missy were to find out she repeated even that much of what she had said . . .

"Thank you for your honesty," Justin replied after a little silence, the instant kindness of his voice inviting the slave's eyes to his own. Stabbing his already paining heart, Sheeva's recital temporarily robbed him of purpose. His eyes softened as he took in the worried look about the black woman's face and eyes. "I promise that no one will ever know what I insisted you tell me." He turned to leave the living room, hearing Sheeva's footsteps behind him. Not until he reached the front door did he face her again, saying, "Will you tell your mistress I'll return to see her—as often as it takes?"

Sheeva nodded and said, "I promise to let her know, Mr. Salvador." She heard him leave and sent troubled looks up the stairway. There was more going on between Missy and that Spaniard than met the eye, and she had the eerie feeling that things were going to get a lot worse before they got better. Nervous hands again sought refuge beneath the apron as reluctant feet climbed the stairs.

From where she lay upon her bed, Leander listened to Sheeva's message from Justin without comment or change of expression. For the rest of the day and night, she remained in her bedroom. Anguish steeped her heart, mind, and soul. The resulting brew was bitter, scalding. She replayed the scenes with Justin at Belle Terre over and over, taking a kind of perverse delight in torturing herself.

When had he first recognized her? On the porch when she first spoke? His hoarseness had kept her from realizing she had heard his voice before, but hers had surely been normal. She was certain that the loose mask of satin would not have disguised hers to such a degree as to prevent his recognizing it — not when he had heard it so recently under such intimate circumstances. Her face burned. She forged ahead with dogged determination to view the ordeal from all angles.

Philip and Antoine had seemed to have no trouble in placing her voice, and both had confessed that at first glance they hadn't known for sure she was the pirate. How Don Carlos Justin Salvador must have gloated to learn that at the hunting lodge he had beguiled the very Miss Ondine he seemed to loathe. What had he called her — "the infamous Miss Ondine"? Had he heard some of the ludicrous rumors floating about as to her whereabouts and activities over the past six years? Only the two of them knew to what degree he had lent authenticity to any heretofore false report of loose conduct on her part. She squeezed her eyes shut and groaned. If he so chose, he could give credence to the gossip. For some reason, she didn't care. What she seemed to care about were the memories of their time in the hunting lodge. They scorched her very soul.

Even at her lowest point, Leander could not permit herself to think that Justin had known who she was in the lodge. Each time that thought tried to surface, she scotched it. She knew too well that she had been the one to suggest holding back last names, to refuse to let the talk move into channels other than those of the moment. It had seemed so logical to believe him to have come from the smaller holdings behind her own. Logical? She flipped over onto her stomach, burying her face in the pillow. Nothing about the entire night had been based on anything as normal as logic, she scoffed in silent fury.

At some times, behind her closed door, Leander railed in whispers for having offered herself so boldly to the handsome Spaniard. At others, she attacked him with scurrilous language for having taken a young woman's innocence without once offering any kind of commitment. She had been a complete fool to have allowed the storm of passion overtaking her to lead her to believe what she had felt for Justin was love, to believe that when he told her he loved her, he had meant it. Unbridled passion, that's all it was — the very emotion that Josie had warned her against giving in to — the very one that another Spaniard had stirred to life that night in Throw-away's bed. Had it been more than a streak of desire between them, Justin would have asked her to marry him, would have never parted from her without more than a promise for a second visit.

By the second day after the Mardi Gras ball, Leander had come to terms with her festered wound. A touch of outrage made the hurt less raw. When the ache tempted her to hug her arms close about her chest in attempts to bring about surcease of the racking torture, she would call up that anger to gloss over the pain, to make it more bearable — anger at all Spaniards for having affronted her in every instance; anger at Justin for having deliberately taunted her at the ball, for not revealing who he was. A secret voice tried to add, with little success: *But anger mainly for his not being the Justin he had seemed at the hunting lodge.*

A need to escape her chamber of self-inflicted torment led Leander to plan a walk about the grounds late that second afternoon after returning from the Mardi Gras ball. She bade Cara help her bathe and dress, hoping that the diversion of such mundane activities might turn her mind to like thoughts. Her heart and soul felt wrung out, crumpled.

"The striped gown is a bit elegant for a stroll about the grounds, don't you think?" Leander asked the slave when she noticed what Cara had laid out for her to wear. The stripes of purple and black which had charmed her in Belle's shop that first day of shopping in Natchez appeared uninteresting.

"Sometimes dressing up can make a bad mood lift," Cara offered, continuing the styling of the long black hair as if nothing were out of the ordinary. Both her mother and she had whispered at length about what was going on in the mind of their mistress. They had never seen her in such condition since her return some six weeks earlier, so quiet after that single outburst yesterday when Don Salvador had stopped by, and so obviously removed from what was going on around her ever since. What the handsome Spanish don had to do with it brought far more questions than answers. They had attempted to query Jabbo, but the big man remarked that he knew nothing about who attended the ball or if anything there had upset Leander.

"Who says I'm in a bad mood?" Pansy-hued eyes

nailed the brown ones where they met in the mirror. The late afternoon sun angled patterns of shadow across the banistered porch outside the window, subtle designs reflecting in the mirror like an artist's grayed background on a canvas.

"You've not been out of your room since coming home yesterday morning, and you've hardly touched a bite on the trays Mama and I have brought up."

"Mayhap I am ill," Leander hedged, not wanting to admit Cara was right. Dom had always discouraged her from giving in to moods, urging her instead to aim for a steady course of behavior, no matter how she might feel inside. She saw the wisdom of his words but found the application vexing, nigh impossible, now that both heart and pride had been trampled on. Her heart bore scar tissue as a kind of protective covering, but her pride had never before been attacked in such wrenching manner.

Cara examined the pale face in the fading February light before asking, "Are you ill, missy?"

Leander shook her head and rose, shrugging at the slave's admonition that she wasn't quite through with her hair. When Cara saw that her mistress was determined to get dressed, she helped her into the lovely gown, commenting on how well the colors complemented Leander's eyes and hair.

"Tell Sheeva and Jabbo that I'm walking along the river with Gabriel until dark." When Leander noted the anxiety in her personal maid's eyes, she added with more warmth, "Cara, don't worry. I'm not ill and I won't go out of sight of the house. I need some time outside to myself . . . to think."

Flinging a black shawl about her shoulders, she left and went on down to the porch where Gabriel lay. The sight of the large yet still gawky dog brought a half-smile to her face, the first since she had left the ball. With excited barks and frisky movements, Gabriel followed her down the steps and the long walkway. Puffs of wind fenced with Leander's hair, winning little victories due to her stopping Cara before all the curls lay secured. An impatient hand brushed at escaping tendrils as she neared the end of the walkway close to the hollow tree. Smiling down at Gabriel's silent offering of a small stick to be thrown for retrieving, she knelt to give him a hug and toss the stick in the distance.

The game between mistress and pet took them into the edge of the woods near the faint road used by travelers. A rush of wind soughed through leafless branches, its sorrow echoing that in Leander's doleful heart. When she heard hoofbeats in the distance, she paid scant attention, figuring that her pet and she were hidden from any passerby's view. Gabriel noticed, though, and shot up the black-tipped ears, became rigid for a moment. A growl began low in his throat, but almost as quickly as it had come, the threatening sound faded into nothing.

"The rider had better be someone you know, boy, or I'll tell Jabbo you're no good at all as a watchdog," Leander teased the dog when he dropped the air of protector. He began to wag his tail and pant with that show of teeth which she often called a smile. "See if you can fetch this," she challenged, choosing a larger limb to throw. Since coming outside, she had found her spirits considerably lighter, though she doubted Cara's announcement that what she wore had anything to do with the change of mood. Enjoying her pet's noisy antics as he tried to retrieve the larger stick from a windfall of dead leaves not far away, she chose to be unaware of anything else.

"Good evening, Leander Ondine" came a deep voice from behind her.

Leander whirled about to see Justin Salvador standing with his hands behind him as he faced her, his horse tethered some distance back. Her breath hung back in her throat, but she told herself it was because he looked so different there at twilight in the shadowed, bare-branched woods. Did it have anything to do with the white streak striping his black hair, something she couldn't remember having noticed at the lodge or at the ball? A half-memory tried to remind her that she had seen such a mark in a man's hair before, but she couldn't make sense of it, couldn't make much sense of anything until she forced her stunned brain and heartbeat into motion and her throat to release the captive breath. Then she wondered if the disparity in his appearance lay in the noticeable solemnity about the face she recalled too well, the one haunting her over the past week? For a second, she considered flight but realized the panniers and swaying skirt would hinder escape, even if her suddenly hammering heartbeat would allow her to run. One hand pulled the black shawl closer. The other tried to control wayward curls surrendering to the whispering winds.

"How dare you come near me?" she quavered, hoping that the distance between them would keep him from hearing the unsteadiness of her words. Her misguided beliefs of the evils in the Spanish might have begun as tiny seeds, but they had grown, ripened into a passionate faith that lived near the surface of her heart. Always at the ready for her calling into force, they roiled upward into venom at the slightest demand. With determination she drew upon that anger to cloak the pain washing over her. Her voice came stronger then. "I sent word for you not to return to Beaux Rives, ever."

"And I sent word to you that I would keep coming back until I could see you," Justin responded. His voice was as uneven as hers, though neither noticed the quality in the other's. He cleared his throat. "I must talk to you, tell—"

"No Spaniard has anything to tell that I'm interested in hearing," she broke in to say, turning toward Gabriel then and wishing the scoundrel would come on back. Why was he ignoring the fact that a stranger had accosted his mistress? She could see the white dog still searching the pile of leaves with contented playfulness.

Justin's first sight of his beloved in a fashionable gown intrigued him in a way he wouldn't have deemed possible. His first thought upon seeing her from the road was that he was once more dreaming, that only in a dream would he have found her so beautifully gowned in wintry woods in the gloaming. Obviously unaware of his presence behind her, Leander had stood with an air of regality and beauty cloaking her slenderness, the same air, he realized, that had emanated from her when he first saw her sitting before the fireplace in the oversized robe. Not for the first time since discovering her in the hunting lodge, he puzzled over the intriguing question as to her existence. Had he not first dreamed her, would he have ever found her, recognized her as the only one he could love?

Before Justin had spoken and Leander had pulled the shawl closer around her shoulders, he had seen the provocative swell of her breasts above the scooped neckline of striped purple and black silk, the lovely line of her slender rib cage as it tapered down into the waist he had measured with his two hands. The memory brought tinglings to his yearning fingers, a new rush of blood through his veins. Billowing in the breeze before his bewitched eyes, her full skirt lay back in pretty, ribbon-caught drapes to reveal a ruffled white petticoat. He had not known what a divine creature a lovely young woman could be—first, a phantom; second, a warm and loving creature in his arms; third, a seductive, enchanting pirate with barbed wit; and now, superb young woman of style and dignity. His love for her in all of her encompassing guises sprinkled across his very being, like a private Milky Way in his heart's eye, ever twinkling, ever present, even when clouds might try to obscure or dissemble . . . ever wondrous.

"I came to say I love you, Leander, and that I want you to be my wife," Justin said, forcing himself to take only one step toward her. Keeping his distance demanded control. He longed to rush and pull her into his arms, smother the beautiful face with kisses. But he waited, his hands still behind him.

Leander felt her insides swoosh around as if everything had turned to liquid. She half-turned to look at him over her shoulder. In the tailored black breeches and coat, he could have been any young planter attending to business affairs. Only the soft ruffles of his white cravat relieved the somberness of his attire and his visage. What had he proposed to her in such stiff fashion? The style did not fit. Was he feeling guilty for having taken her virginity? What he felt for her couldn't be love or he would have never dallied with her affections at the ball by keeping his identity secret.

"Am I supposed to say 'thank you' for trying to salvage my reputation?" she demanded. At his indrawn breath and leveling of black brows, she turned to face him, thankful for the anger which allowed her to camouflage the terrible hurt inside. "I don't need anything from you, Justin Salvador, and especially not your name. Go away and don't come back."

"But I need you," he replied. "I told you that night—"

"That night never happened," she interrupted to say with lifted chin. Seeing again the manly beauty of his face and form upset her. How she would have loved it to find him not nearly so handsome as she had remembered. The sight of him matched the memory too well. Sharp blades might as well have been slicing her into thin, bleeding fragments. "Forget it. I have." The lie ripped at her somewhere down deep. "You go your way; I'll go mine. Everything has changed since then."

"Why has it changed? I'm still the same man who fell in love with you—"

She broke in with frost-laden words, "That wasn't love."

"Believe me," Justin pleaded, his pride stinging from her cold denouncement, "that was love, *is* love. You can't deny that you felt something, too."

"I can deny it, and I do. I could never be in love with a Spaniard, even if he hadn't tried to dupe me at a ball." When the black eyes widened in apparent shock and disbelief, and the wide mouth seemed ready to issue a reproof, she went on. "You had to have known who I was from the minute you heard me speak on the side porch. I had no way of recognizing anything about you, not with your hoarseness and that outlandish toga." The words spilled out in a heated rush, as if they wanted to be freed before she changed her mind.

"I give you my word that I had no idea who the pirate was until midnight." So that, along with her old hatred for the Spanish, was what had riled her so at the unmasking. She had suspected him of playing a game, one in which she hadn't known the rules. His heart enlarged with sorrow at what must have been excruciating pain for the young, trusting Leander he had left behind at the lodge. How could he convince her that he would never have done such a cruel thing? "Will you take my word? Will you believe me when I say that our differences are of little consequence?" He drew a tad of hope from her hesitancy, from the way her forefinger lifted to get lost in a tantalizing, tousled curl. He took another step toward her. A dead leaf crackled beneath his feet.

"No." A thicker veil shadowed the purple eyes. What was he up to? Couldn't he tell she despised him? "I'll scream and slap you if you come any closer."

Justin sighed then and brought his hands from behind him. "I brought these for you." He took what delight he could from the surprised look upon her face

315

when she saw the limp bouquet of daffodils. When he had seen the few blooms dancing in a breeze beneath a tree near his door, Leander had come to mind and he had known he must see her before the day ended. Deliberately taking advantage of her distraction, he moved close enough to present the yellow flowers, unaware that his sweating clutch had wilted the crisp stems into large, forlorn green strings. "I wanted to give you something when we became engaged, for I don't have a proper present for you yet." He held out the gift of love.

"I won't take them," Leander said in a labored voice, "because I have no intention of becoming engaged to you." For some reason, the intensity of the rich yellow inside the small tubes drew her eyes in the same way the sparkle of Felicity's tiara had at the Mardi Gras ball. It must be because they're the first of the season, she thought. The fading light seemed to bring a glow to the weak-necked daffodils, one which reflected upon her face and rent the veil from her eyes for a brief moment. "Please leave Beaux Rives. We have nothing more to say to each other."

Justin smiled for the first time then. His heart expanded. He had seen the naked wonder in her eyes as she stared at the flowers, had glimpsed again that starry spark of purple shining only for him that night before the fireplace. When her guard was down, as it had been upon seeing the daffodils, Leander had not kept hidden the fact that a strong feeling for him lived within. Hope spurring him on, Justin had no doubt that she loved him. What bothered him was that if she knew the seeds of love were implanted, she refused to admit it. The smile increased, danced in the black eyes. He could wait. Justin Salvador was a patient man when it came to planting crops and tending them to fruition — and to wooing and winning Leander Ondine.

"I'll go now," he said, "but only if you'll accept my gift." When she lifted eyes once more veiled, he added with the old forcefulness back in his deep voice, "Take the flowers as a token of my apology for whatever it is that you think I did to hurt you. Surely you wouldn't want me to have to throw away something so beautiful."

Making sure that she kept her gaze upon the daffodils and trying to avoid contact with the hand proffering them, Leander accepted his gift. The exchange called for some touching, though, and both flinched at the sharp tingles racing up fingers and arms. Leander had no way of knowing that for her to take his gift signaled to Justin that she was accepting far more than a bedraggled bouquet of early spring blossoms. The knowledge that they were warm from his having held them was scrambling her befuddled brain and setting off ridiculous flurries of heat throughout her body.

"I'll return soon," Justin promised, his smile lighting the darkening space between them.

"Don't bother," she retorted, anger once more in control. "I don't welcome Spaniards here."

"No bother," he said, spying a big black man ambling down the walkway from the house. "I suspect someone is coming to look for you and escort you inside, now that it's almost dark." He walked a few steps toward his horse in that sure-footed way she had noticed that night in the lodge. Flurries of dead leaves marked his path.

"I mean it. Don't come back," Leander said, glancing over her shoulder to see Gabriel bounding toward Jabbo up on the walkway. A lot of good he had been as a watchdog, she thought with dismay. He should have charged any stranger approaching her. And he never had found the big stick she had thrown. "I won't open my door to Spaniards."

"But, Leander," Justin called from over near his horse now, "I'm not just any Spaniard." The cockiness of a young man in love lent a lilting bravado to his final words. "I'm the one you're going to marry."

Leander watched with opened mouth as the jaunty-walking Justin leaped from the ground onto his saddle and waved a cheery farewell there in the deepening dusk. When Jabbo called to her, she was still staring in the direction of the disappearing horseman, the limp bouquet in her hand.

Chapter Fifteen

"Isn't there something you need to tell me about?" Jabbo asked his mistress the next morning. They were riding over the back part of Beaux Rives to check flood damage. Both had already expressed relief that the swollen streams were receding into their beds.

Leander's guarded eyes met the intelligent dark ones studying her with concern. She had deliberately avoided private time with him ever since the party. On the way home the morning after, he had given in to her pleas that she had a headache and didn't feel up to talking.

"Not that I can think of," she lied. Her gaze wandered off to assess the distant fields and the shrunken streams. "We're lucky not to have had more damage than we've seen, aren't we? I hadn't known whether to believe Felix's assurances that the water had run off. If no more giant rains hit, we ought to be able to plant on time, don't you think?"

Diligently, Leander had studied the sparse records

the overseer had kept over the past six years, calling upon memory of what she had heard Felix and her father discuss on those times when she was allowed to sketch while they talked in the study. She had questioned Felix and Jabbo about those aspects of planting and breeding horses that made little sense to her untutored mind, ignoring their initial reluctance to speak of such matters with one of the opposite sex and demanding answers anyway. After the first session or two, sometimes private and sometimes with both men present, they had seemed to accept that the strong-willed Leander would not allow herself to be relegated to the living room and reign as the normal, flighty young heiress. She made it clear that she intended to help manage Beaux Rives and do a creditable job of it. During such discussions about the workings of the plantation was when she first realized that the slave had been more of a confidant to her father than the white man, almost as aware of the workings of Beaux Rives as if he had been the overseer.

Jabbo nodded. "What about that Justin Salvador? I need to know what's going on there."

"Nothing is going on there," she shot back with venom. "He is a dirty Spanish dog. What else matters?" She urged Bagatelle into a double gait to gain some time before Jabbo could catch up and ask more.

"You need not try to hide things from me, missy. You know it won't work. He visited with Gabriel and me that morning after we came home from the party." Easily he had caught up with her, though Victory was not a true double-gaited horse and was jostling the big man about with its unrhythmic half-trot.

Leander slowed Bagatelle, her surprise showing as she once again met those demanding eyes. "And pray tell, what did the two of you have to talk about?" The squeak of saddle leather and the muffled attack of hooves upon the black soil seemed especially loud as she awaited his answer.

"He was mighty curious about where Gabriel came from, for one thing. I could hardly believe the way that dog took right to him. Right off, they acted like lifelong friends."

Leander made no comment. She was too busy reflecting upon Gabriel's reluctance the previous evening to dash over to protect her upon Justin's arrival. So the charming Spaniard had won over her dog. Fury set her teeth into a clamp. Had he captivated her slave-protector as well?

"What else?" she asked when she could trust her voice.

"He seemed like a true gentleman," Jabbo replied. "Asked all about the horses grazing out behind the stables. He said he has a fine herd himself, the brood animals having come from his father's stables in Spain. Jerez breed, I believe."

"How nice that the two of you had such a pleasant visit," Leander grated. How dare Justin worm his way into conversation with Jabbo — or any of her slaves! She recalled how highly Sheeva had spoken of his looks and manner that morning she had sent word for him to leave and never return to Beaux Rives. The man had nerve, as well as an exalted opinion of himself. Thank the Blessed Virgin that she had found out all about him before dashing over for the planned meeting at the lodge. She shooed away the mocking reminder that their reunion was to have been the next afternoon.

"What I think you should tell me is why he came at all," the giant black said. "And then why he returned late yesterday afternoon."

Leander jerked her head toward her companion. When riding about the plantation, she chose to wear the severely tailored black habit Belle Monroe had created for such occasions. The simple cravat of the white blouse bore no lace, its only decoration a small monogram of white silk thread. Completing her riding outfit for business ventures were the black boots worn to the masquerade, leather gloves, and a small, close-fitting hat of black felt. Trimming the hat, now perched atop the ebony curls at a rakish angle, was a band of purple ribbon stitched in mannish fashion at the base of the low crown, the short streamers falling and fluttering from a flat bow in the back. "How did you know he came back?"

"I saw him from the porch before I came to fetch you in for dinner."

"You were spying on me?"

"That's my main duty, isn't it?"

Jabbo had a way of putting everything in neat slots, Leander mused with a touch of exasperation. She sighed and stared at a distant cluster of moss-draped oaks left standing in the middle of a pasture to protect grazing animals from the elements. Most were towering swamp oaks, fat-based from their frequent stints in standing water, bare-limbed, a darker gray than their mossy drapings wafting mournfully in the breezes. One or two live oaks stood out proudly from the others on a little rise, their narrow, green leaves intact until the new ones would push them to the ground before summer. Against the pale blue of the February sky, the sight stirred the artist in her.

"I'm tired of this conversation, Jabbo. Let's head back to the house and check the southern pastures." She reined in the direction she wanted to go, sure that he would follow.

"If you go ahead with plans to increase the herds, we need to see about some cross-fencing in that large pasture," Jabbo told her after they had ridden in silence for a spell. At her questioning look, he went on. "Your papa always talked to me about his dream to build a big herd of horses here and how he would have seasonal pastures for them. Thought his ideas made a lot of sense."

"You're right," she conceded. She still found it hard to believe she had ended his interrogation so easily. Besides, what could she have told about Justin Salvador and her? That she had brazenly offered herself to him the night of the storm? That he had thrown her gift back in her face by toying with her at the Ferrands' masquerade ball? Her face burned each time she allowed the shameful memory to surface, as it did now. And his ridiculous declaration of love and his proposal of the previous evening were too laughable to repeat to anyone. No man worth his salt would ask one to marry him who so openly professed that she despised him. He was up to something; she was sure of it. She hadn't been able to figure out any plausible answer during her restless night, but she would.

Jabbo and Leander located patches of grass beginning to turn green and discussed possible locations for future fences to form the seasonal grazing areas. Jabbo had learned a great deal from her father, Leander reflected. She hadn't realized that they rode beside the property line between Terre Platte and Beaux Rives until she heard a forceful whinny and thundering hooves from the other side of the rail fence.

"Look, Jabbo," Leander exclaimed. She reined in the suddenly nervous Bagatelle. "Isn't that the most beautiful specimen you've ever seen?" She watched his eyes widen with appreciation as he, too, looked at the black stallion prancing up and down on the other side of the fence, its silken tail lifted and trailing in splendor.

"That must be Don Salvador's stud," Jabbo said. "You're right, missy. He's some fine piece of horseflesh. Guess since the flood, they've begun using this pasture next to us because I've not seen any horses over there since we've been back."

"Thor is not nearly so handsome nor as young. We'll be years building a better herd with Thor as our only stud." Her eyes narrowed in deep thought. A frown knitted her eyebrows a shade closer. With a rare petulance, she asked, "Why does the Spaniard have such a fine animal and we don't? We Creoles were here first."

"We'll get our herd," Jabbo assured her. Victory, the huge gray gelding he rode, seemed unimpressed with the stallion's prowess and stood in place without the coaxing Leander's mare was demanding. "Don't be so impatient." The bitterness riding her voice and face disquieted him. That she had not given answers to his questions about Don Salvador didn't bother him. Her very silence had told him far more than she realized. Something was going on between the handsome Spaniard and his mistress. In time, Jabbo felt confident that he could gain answers. "Thor's yearling is coming on nicely, and he seems to have better lines."

"But it'll take years and years for him to make a difference," Leander complained with a vexed sigh. A finger found a curl resting across the shoulder of her tailored jacket and worried at it. With openly jealous admiration, she eyed the shiny black coat and elegant form of what must be the Terre Platte stallion. Regal power seemed to exude from the high-stepping horse as he sought to impress the appreciative Bagatelle with his beauty and virility. When the animal galloped up to the fence with a noisy snort and lifted its black head proudly in a daring stance, a narrow slash of white across the slightly dished nose brought to Leander's mind a picture of its owner with his streaked hair. Her hand tightened on the reins. What an inane thought, she scolded herself as she urged the reluctant Bagatelle back toward the Beaux Rives stables. The Creoles didn't need the damned Spaniards . . . or their horse-flesh.

"Who is the gentleman who wishes to join me for tea?" Leander asked Cara that afternoon after the slave delivered a message. She looked up from the book in her lap, making no effort to rise from her chair beside the fireplace. February had breathed back a spell of cold to remind everyone that spring was still just a promise. Since returning from her morning ride with Jabbo, she had given in to her wish to laze before a cozy fire.

"He asked that I say it is someone you'll be glad to see—and that he wishes to surprise you." The black woman serving as personal maid came nearer then, sending a critical eye over her mistress's hair and gown. Yes, the deep blue wool was elegant in its simplicity and would do nicely for afternoon tea in the living room. Swirls of darker braid formed looping patterns at the border of the scooped neckline and again on the bias circlets forming ruffles above her wrists. Similar patterns edged the overskirt where it was caught back from the paler blue petticoat of minute tucks. "I 'spect I'd better neat up your hair in the back."

"Not until you tell me who is calling," Leander replied. The hint of arrogance learned from her father, which Felix had noted the first day of her return but few others had recognized, rode in her voice, lent a fierceness to the set of her mouth. She didn't like the idea that it might be Justin—though why he would come calling after her clear dismissal last evening baffled her. That he must be even more devious than she had suspected brought the sinking feeling inside, she told herself. "If it's that Spaniard, tell him—"

"It's not Don Salvador," Cara interrupted from over near the dressing table. She readied the comb and brush. "Will you come over here, or shall I bring the brush over there?"

Rising and putting her book aside, Leander let out a breath of relief and gave herself over to the talented hands of Cara. It must be Philip, she reassured herself. Mayhap the little skipping of heart ever since Cara delivered the message was a sign that she wanted someone to call—someone other than Justin, of course.

"What a surprise to see you," Leander blurted when she stepped into the living room. "I hadn't expected my caller to be you." She watched Antoine's lean, hawklike face ease into the smile which gave him such a handsome, sophisticated air. For a second, she wondered if she would have rushed down had she known it was the older brother rather than Philip. Antoine's persistent overtures toward her were becoming more and more distasteful.

"But you are glad to see me, aren't you, beautiful one?" Antoine responded in his usual cocksure, bantering way. He lifted her hand and brushed a kiss against its top before going on, "How lovely you are in blue." Glinting dark eyes cut a path around the modestly curved neckline, then dropped back to the hint of cleavage. "I've had you on my mind ever since the night of the masquerade ball. I was distressed to learn of your early departure the next morning and feared you might be ill."

Disliking the way Antoine's touch always triggered a feeling of repulsion mixed with uneasiness, Leander retrieved her hand and went to sit on one of the two sofas facing each other in front of the fireplace. At each step, as always when alone with Antoine and sometimes when in a crowd, she could feel his eyes raking across her backside. Even through petticoats and panniers, his gazes could burn in a way she found both hot and cold. More than once she had turned to catch him in the act and had almost flinched from the demonic gleam in the assessing eyes. Why would he have her on his mind? She had not been very nice to him the night of the party, had spent far more time with Philip than with anyone.

"How kind of you," Leander murmured, wishing he wouldn't sit so near and that Sheeva would come soon with the tea tray. "As you can plainly see, I'm not ill." Did he catch that she was referring to his intent scrutiny of her face and form? If so, it didn't seem to deter him. "It was imperative that Jabbo and I return home early that day."

"So Philip informed us." Accepting her explanation, Antoine relaxed then and became aware of more than the young beauty beside him. Glancing about the spacious room, he eyed the simple windows and furnishings with a sardonic lift of eyebrow. Upon earlier visits since her return, he had noticed how the new Beaux Rives could not compare to the older, more luxurious mansion—or even to his father's. Such an heiress as Leander needed a far grander setting, one more in keeping with the great wealth she would own outright before the year was out. What she needed, he told himself, was a strong husband with a good sense of Parisian style and social graces. "Felix could have used the touch of someone wiser in making selections, don't you think? Too bad you were locked away in that girls' school and couldn't feel safe enough to come home." When she made no reply and merely gazed at him with no visible emotion in those incredible violet eyes, he went on. "I had this urge to see you and decided to join you for tea."

Sheeva came through the double doors then with the silver tray and, after quiet greetings, set it upon the table in front of the sofa. She sent a critical eye at the fireplace, obviously satisfied that there were logs and crackling flames aplenty. Turning to leave her mistress and her guest alone, she explained that the hallway was too drafty to leave the doors open.

Gesturing toward the tapestry bell pull hanging beside the fireplace, Sheeva said, "Just give a tug on the pull if you need me before I return to check on things, Miss Leander. I hope you and Mr. Antoine enjoy your tea." She left then, the tall wooden doors coming together with a little clack.

Leander went through the ritual of making and pouring tea, glad to have a reason to escape acknowledging his perusal. The tiny sandwiches disappeared as they talked and sipped at their tea. For some reason, Antoine had ceased his leering and become more sociable than she could remember since their time together in Natchez. She felt a pang of guilt that she often had the feeling that he was several people all wrapped up in that tall, wise-eyed form. Too handsome for his own good . . . and too knowing for hers.

What was behind Antoine's mention of her absence at school in Mobile? Was it a chance remark, or had he heard some gossip at the ball? She doubted Antoine ever made any comments by chance. Had the young woman from New Orleans who seemed smitten by him — Maralys Soulier, that was her name — attended Miss Julia Shepherd's School for Young Ladies and told him that she had never seen or heard of Leander Ondine? Philip had confided to her at the party that Maralys was about his age. Even so, she could have been at school sometimes over the past six years. If she knew Antoine as she suspected she did, he would have most certainly questioned his frequent, obviously adoring dance partner.

"Leander," Antoine said, rising and slipping the fingers of one hand inside his partially buttoned vest, "I think you and I should talk about us." He reached the fireplace and paused before turning to face her with slightly elevated chin. Only that morning he had practiced the pose before his mirror, liking the way it gave him the appearance of a young man sure of himself. And a handsome one at that.

"What is there to talk about?" She wondered if Antoine had an itch. It seemed strange to see a young man stick his fingers inside his vest that way. And why was he cocking his head and peering down at her through his lashes? A glance at the fireplace showed no escaping wisp of smoke to make his eyes smart.

"You must surely know how I feel about you," Antoine intoned. She seemed properly impressed with his dramatic pose, he mused. Desire for the beautiful young woman lifting her puzzled face to his washed over him with more force than the blazing fire behind him warmed his backside.

Leander didn't want to hear more. "I think you and I have a lovely friendship, Antoine." That was as much of a falsehood as she intended to offer.

"It's more than that, my dear, and I think you know it," he said in a voice suddenly thick with wanting. Gone was the exaggerated pose of a French dandy. He rushed to sit beside her again and caught her forearms in both hands to prevent her surprising attempt to draw back. She wasn't fooling him with that show of innocence. No one who could strut about so seductively in the form-fitting pirate costume could be what

330

she would have had him believe since their meeting in Natchez. Where in hell had she been over the past six years? From his sly questioning of Maralys, he had learned that the young woman from New Orleans had indeed attended the school for young women in Mobile back in her teen years. Wouldn't she have at least *heard* of the younger Ondine heiress from Louisiana? When he had mulled over the situation, he recalled that Leander never once had volunteered information about the happenings back at the school as Maralys had done repeatedly on the night of their first meeting at the Mardi Gras party. Was Leander that different from other young women?

"Let me go. You're hurting me," Leander said, struggling to be free of the pinioning hands.

"We belong together, Leander. Say you'll marry me." The quick little indrawn breath and the flare of purple deep in her eyes set Antoine on fire. His touch did affect her, he exulted. He fell against her, crushing those voluptuous breasts against his pounding chest and pinning her against the high back of the sofa. His devouring lips claimed the lovely mouth that had been tempting him since he had first seen her back in The Cockatoo Tavern. God! How had he managed to wait this long to taste such nectar? Not that he hadn't tried more than once. His tongue invaded the protesting mouth, testing and probing in the telling way of a conqueror.

Leander squirmed and struggled, maddened that his arms pinned her own to her sides, that the infuriating attack on her lips had been unexpected and unpreventable. The instant one of his hands relaxed its hold and

331

moved to touch her breast, she brought the freed hand to push against him with the force of one bursting with fury. When Antoine continued to moan deep in his throat and plunder her mouth, she drew back her hand and slapped his face. The sound echoed like a pistol shot in the close space between them.

"Why did you do that?" Antoine snarled, releasing her and watching with disbelief when she jumped from the sofa and went to stand beside the fireplace, her hand upon the bell pull. Instinctively his hand had shot up to nurse the painful smarting of his cheek. "You know you wanted me to kiss you."

"Whatever made you think that?" she hissed, taking a firmer grip on the wide pull. "Shall I pull this and get Sheeva to show you out — or to send for Jabbo to do it?"

"No," Antoine said, sending the free hand out in silent pleading. The other still covered the paining cheek. "No, don't do something that foolish. We can talk this out, just the two of us."

Leander narrowed eyes and mouth. Could she trust him? She had no desire to embarrass the Ferrands by having Jabbo toss out the older son, but she wanted no repetition of what had happened either. "Swear it."

"Swear it?" he echoed, trying to ignore the sting on his face. During her stay at Belle Terre over the holidays, he had seen her revert to such childish behavior when he tried to catch her in shadowed corners. Once she had even kicked him smartly in the shins and run off giggling like a schoolgirl, calling over her shoulder that she was going to tell his father if he didn't keep his hands to himself. At such times, as now, he couldn't help but wonder if he were wrong about the latent, full-grown passion he suspected lived within. "What good would swearing to it do?"

"It might keep me from yanking on this pull," she countered. Her heart still raced, but she recognized its pattern was not one of pleased excitement. Was she afraid of Antoine? Until she knew she had the upper hand, she wasn't going to let go of the pull. She expected Sheeva to appear at any moment to check on her needs concerning the tea tray and silently called for her to hurry. "Do you swear to keep your distance if I don't summon help?"

"All right, I swear if that will please you. Surely you've had more men than me to get carried away with your charms." He saw her hand relax on the bell pull at his first statement but tighten again at the second.

"What makes you say that?" Had that Spanish rogue done a bit of bragging among the men after the party?

Antoine noted the heightened color in her face, the flash of suspicion in her eyes. Was he right about her being wiser than she would have anyone know?

"You weren't at Miss Julia Shepherd's School for Young Ladies those six years, were you?" The question was a wild shot, but he felt it might be on target. At her gasp and release of the bell pull, he went on, "Just where were you and what were you doing all that time, Leander? Living at the infamous Frenchie Dumain's tavern posing as a young lady—"

Leander stalked to stand before her accuser, eyes killing him with purple daggers, hands itching to slap him again.

With undisguised fury, she cut him short, saying, "How dare you say such things to me, Antoine Ferrand? Frenchie is my friend and more of a gentleman than you've turned out to be. Are you the one who started the rumor that I might have been found Under the Hill at Natchez instead of on top of it in a decent tavern? You know as well as I that The Cockatoo is a respectable place to stay. Come to think of it, where were you staying—in one of the gambling places Under the Hill? I can tell from the look on your face that you know more about those lies than you're telling, you scoundrel." She drew hands up to her hips and glared down at him, not at all sorry that the print of her palm hadn't quite faded from the lean cheek. "That is the most dastardly thing I've ever heard of anyone doing to a supposed friend. Wouldn't your father love hearing all about this?"

Antoine straightened his cravat and flicked at a spotless ruffle peeking beneath a well-tailored sleeve. He had no wish to discuss his activities in Natchez—or even think upon them. His luck at the tables had been abysmal. He was yet trying to wheedle from his father money enough to cover his losses. And having as little luck there as he was at the moment, he mused.

"You're reacting like a child, my dear. I was merely teasing; couldn't you tell? Why would I circulate such tales about the one I intend to marry?"

Antoine hadn't actually started the rumor, but when one of the young men idling about the store down at Point Thoms, the Spanish village downriver, had mouthed the possibility a few weeks ago, Antoine had not set him straight. In his mind, such degradation against Leander could do little but hold off the suits of other Creoles until he could win her. Already he had found that she wasn't going to be an easy prize. He would need all the help he could get.

"I thought that one so bold as to dress as a pirate could take a bit of adult banter," he countered, taking a deep breath, not at all sure any more that he had learned one thing of use to him—except that she had a temper he didn't care to rile again. If she had been a cub before, she was full-grown tigress now. "Actually, I came here today for the sole purpose of asking you to be my wife. Would I have done so had I told such lies about you, or believed them if I heard them?"

Leander threw back her head and laughed, the scornful sound whipping across Antoine's pride more painfully than the hand had upon his face. Shining curls returned to caress her face when she lowered her head and queried mockingly, "Marry you? Why on earth would I want to marry you?"

"Just a minute," he intervened, stung to the core by her harsh refusal. Spitfires always had attracted the wild side of him. She had no way of knowing that her display of temper made her more desirable, more of a challenge. God! How he would love to tame her, crush her into submission. "I confess I owe you an apology for my ungentlemanly forcing of my kiss upon you. Forgive me that and let's start over."

Antoine summoned the charm he knew he could muster when the need arose. He tilted his handsome head and sent Leander a smile to disarm her, deliberately softening the desire in his eyes to a warm approval she couldn't object to. Since his return from Paris last year, he had learned to his dismay that the coffers at Belle Terre were low. Even if he inherited anytime soon, which was unlikely, the plantation and the town house in New Orleans would be all that was left for Andre's heirs. Now that his father's new wife — one without dowry — would receive half before Philip and he came in for their shares, he knew that marriage to one of wealth was his only hope for continuing the way of life he had come to expect. And what if Felicity bore children? Belle Terre needed large sums of money right away to continue its mammoth operation.

For that prospective bride of means to be the desirable vision before Antoine at the moment made the prospect even more pleasing. Such devious thoughts had fed his mind since he had first found her in Natchez. "I truly love you, Leander, and I did come to propose to you. I must have gotten carried away. I swear never again to touch you . . . unless you with it also. Please forgive me."

A shudder at the unlikely thought of ever wishing his touch again made Leander clutch her arms across her breasts. She need not have worried that she was wanton, some part of her noted. She had despised his wet, searching mouth on hers. Not believing a fraction of what he was saying, she turned her back on him and went to stand before the fire. One hand clutched at the cool marble mantel and served as a resting place for her forehead. Damn Antoine! He had set her back with his accusations — and his asinine proposal. How much did he know about where Jabbo and she had been? She surmised that to pretend to forgive him might be the smoothest way out of the predicament. The two of them would have to fake some kind of acceptable give and take, what with the double relationships of being neighbors and half-related by Felicity's marriage to Andre.

Sheeva opened the doors just then, her face wreathed in a smile. "Another gentleman to see you, Miss Leander." Before she could receive more than a questioning look from her mistress clutching at the mantel and staring over her shoulder, the caller appeared beside the doorway.

Justin Salvador took in the little scene before him with narrowed eyes, but made no other show that he sensed something was amiss. He greeted both Leander and Antoine with casual good manners and looked pointedly at the empty tea cups.

"Sheeva assured me she'll bring more hot water and tea. Sorry I missed the first pot. I'm running a bit late today," the newcomer said while the two showered him with barrages of ill-tempered looks. With an air of one expecting the answer to be negative, he said, "I hope I've not come at a bad time."

"Not at all," Antoine said with a bite of sarcasm. "We were just discussing . . . the masquerade ball and all the varied costumes." Assuming a world-weary air, he went on in deliberately sarcastic tones. "Yours was among the most . . . amusing."

"Thank you," Justin replied, sending the man a bright smile. He well knew that Antoine's caustic comment was anything but a compliment, but he refused to allow his face or voice to show it. "A friend, Bernardo de Galvez, sent it up from New Orleans. I gather togas must be quite the thing to wear this year at costume balls in the capital. We can be proud that though we live a goodly distance upriver, we manage to keep up with the fashions there."

Hogwash! Justin's sensible self jeered. He couldn't have cared less for what went on in the social circles of New Orleans, but he wanted Antoine to see that he could pull on the air of a dandy when the need arose. The big issue at the moment was what had been going on in the room. If he weren't mistaken, that was the fading imprint of a hand on Antoine's carefully averted face. Justin tried not to look too pleased

Antoine almost conceded "Point" aloud to the Spaniard. He dismissed the initial attempt to whittle him down to size. What grabbed his interest far more was the change coming over Leander from the moment Justin appeared. An unsettling atmosphere in the room, already charged by the earlier scene, seemed to increase almost perceptibly. She seemed to tense up all over and stand taller, her hands clasped tightly before her. Her color bloomed. Was the flush left over from her furious outburst at him? Was she deliberately sliding her eyes from Justin's or was he imagining it?

Then the big question gnawing at Antoine since Sheeva had opened the doors popped forth. What was a Spaniard doing in Beaux Rives? Why didn't she order him to leave? Too easily he could recall Leander's diatribe at Christmas against all Spaniards and her vow never to be around them. And yet Sheeva had brought Justin to the living room without prior announcement, as though he had been at Beaux Rives before and was familiar to the housekeeper. Watching the devilishly handsome Justin approach Leander at the fireplace, Antoine wondered if the owner of Terre Platte was joining Philip's and his suit for Leander's hand. An amused smile slanted across his face. He could well imagine what the high-spirited beauty would tell any Spaniard were he to be allowed time enough to get out the question. He tried not to look too smug.

Leander managed to respond to Justin's polite, casual talk as they stood before the fireplace. Her heart did all kinds of crazy flipflops. Antoine glued his eyes upon them in such a way as to make her feel the disturbing newcomer and she were on stage before a critical audience of one. She dared not make a scene and order Justin to leave, else the wily Antoine would have fodder for a gossipy tale. Now that he had shown what she viewed as his true colors, she distrusted him even more than she had from being around him at Belle Terre over the holidays. Somehow she must convince him that her account of her whereabouts over the past six years was true. No matter how independent of spirit Leander might be about her own reputation, she sensed that for anyone to learn the details of her connection with a whorehouse—no matter how innocent—would create a scandal tainting her beloved Beaux Rives, one that might never be laid to rest completely. She had no intention of allowing such to happen.

And so Leander played the part of a Creole belle with two suitors having arrived at the same time, calling upon the conversations back in Natchez with the shopkeeper Belle about her niece Roseanne. If the opportunity arose later, she promised herself as she threw herself into her role with cunning, she would give Justin a piece of her mind about his barging in on her after she had forbidden him entry to her home. And she would make sure never to be alone with Antoine again.

"Antoine has just been asking me about my schooling in Mobile," Leander lied to Justin while Sheeva replenished the tea tray. She arranged her full skirts prettily about her there on the sofa opposite Antoine, motioning for the housekeeper to slide the small table across in front of her. When Justin would have sat beside her, she tossed her curls coquettishly and said, "Please sit over there by Antoine so that I can talk with both of you more easily. Now that I think about it, there were a few amusing incidents happening at Miss Julia Shepherd's School which you gentlemen might enjoy hearing about."

Leander saw Justin eye her askance before he sank onto the sofa indicated. Off and on she felt like the logs being licked by the flames in the fireplace. Mayhap it hadn't been wise to have the men facing her. Both seemed agog. Was she guilty of what Dom had often accused her of doing when she put on shows for Jabbo and him — overdramatizing the part?

"Do you want me to leave the doors open?" Sheeva asked before she left the room. She sensed that to have closed them earlier hadn't been the thing to do. Something sure had Miss Leander all flustered and carrying on in a way she had never seen before, she mused. Was it because two handsome suitors had arrived at the same time? Somehow, she couldn't believe anything that ordinary was causing her mistress to give off that glittery smile and speak in that new, breathless way.

"Please do," Leander said in dulcet tones the staring

Sheeva hardly recognized. "These two gentlemen are on their best behavior today." A demanding, cutting look at both hardly matched her voice. For different reasons, both averted their eyes from those accusing, violet attacks. "The three of us will appreciate the extra warmth."

After Sheeva did as bade and left, both men shifted about on the sofa, crossed and recrossed their legs, and watched their hostess pour their tea. They made no pretense of being interested in anything other than the beautiful young woman posed before them in feminine majesty behind the tea tray. The graceful hands, busy at their little tasks, drew their gaze as often as did the flushed but composed face.

"Since you're late, Justin, I'll serve you first. Will you have cream and sugar?" From behind half-lowered lashes, she saw him startle from an intense study of her features.

"Sugar only." Justin couldn't figure out why she hadn't torn into him and ordered him to leave. It had to have something to do with the presence of the suave Antoine, the son of his friend he found he couldn't care for, the one so unlike Philip as to seem born of different parents. If Leander were interested in the Creole — and the thought stabbed at his heart — wouldn't she have preferred an unexpected caller to leave? She hadn't exactly welcomed him, but neither had she protested when he entered. And her feigning the role of feminine charmer he found utterly fascinating. But why was she putting on such an act? Which was she trying to fake off — Antoine or him? He took the cup when she handed it to him and stirred with the small spoon while

341

he puzzled.

Antoine accepted his unwanted cup of tea with a casualness he didn't feel. Not a sign of the earlier upheaval showed upon the lovely oval face. What had simmered her down so quickly? A sidewise glance at the handsome man beside him gave him the answer— and yet it made no sense. If she were interested in the Spaniard, wouldn't he have noticed some kind of exchange between them at the party, the first time they could have possibly met? The only time he could recall seeing the pirate and the Roman together after Felicity and Andre had introduced them upon their arrival was when they had danced the pavan near the end of the evening. And judging by his observation from a vantage point on the side of the ballroom, they were as busy exchanging what seemed heated remarks as they were following the stately patterns of the dance.

While Leander and Justin carried on stilted conversation, Antoine sipped and pondered. Their brittle talk and manner plainly revealed that they played a game of cat and mouse. The two had no love for each other. The Paris-educated lawyer had always prided himself on his ability to read the actions of others.

"Oh, yes," Leander replied when Justin asked about the comforts of the school in Mobile, "we were fed and housed well. Shepherd Hall had two stories and an enormous clock tower with a clock forever five minutes behind its hourly strikes. All of the buildings sat behind a tall brick fence." Thank the Holy Mother for Belle's sharing of Roseanne's letters, she reflected. "The teachers lived in the same dormitory as the girls, but on the lower floor."

"And were they women?" This from Antoine. She seemed to be speaking from certain knowledge. Could Maralys have been mistaken about Leander's not having been at the school?

"All except one." The reply came immediately. "Professor Beauvoir taught mathematics." She sipped from her cup and went on, as if lost in happy reverie, "Miss Greenough is the teacher I won't likely forget. She taught us languages and logic."

"She must have been a fine teacher," Justin remarked. He had relaxed against the back of the sofa. To find out more about his beloved filled him with contentment.

"She was that," Leander agreed. "But what will make her live in my mind is the tale about an incident taking place in her class of older girls. I always thought of it when I saw her and had to work to keep a straight face."

"Tell us," Justin urged, loving the way her face and eyes shone from the glow of the fireplace. Did she recall that tomorrow afternoon was their trysting time at the lodge? Dared he hope she might appear? He fought against letting the image of her naked on the bearskin back in the lodge take over and suffocate him. Her obvious love of the dramatic, which had so enthralled him upon his mention of the frog and the prince, added extra sparkling beauty to the black-fringed eyes. She was femininity in finest form.

"Well," she said, setting down her tea cup with little sound and offering sandwiches from the small plate, "it seems that she marched into the room one day to begin class and found a dead mouse in her desk drawer. She shrieked and carried on in a frightful fit of temper.

When not a one of the twelve upperclasswomen would confess to having placed the mouse there, she punished the entire dozen by sending them to bed that night with nothing to eat but bread and water." A little sigh served as pause for comment from her enraptured audience.

Both Antoine and Justin made appropriate sounds of concern tinged with amusement, their attention riveted on their animated hostess.

Purple eyes dancing and enhancing the act, Leander continued. "Late that night the girls talked and found that none had put the mouse there and that Miss Greenough had punished them unjustly. The story goes that no group plans of retaliation were made and that they straggled back to bed with growling stomachs and swelling tempers. The next morning while they sat in her classroom, the prim lady came in and opened her desk drawer to take out her roll book." Leander let a smothered giggle escape before going on. "Twelve dead mice lay inside. She screamed and fainted dead away, unable to hold class for the rest of the day. After that, her students referred to Miss Greenough by the name of the color she turned upon seeing the little gray corpses in her desk—Miss Green."

The professed product of Miss Julia Shepherd's School for Young Ladies tossed her raven tresses and joined in the polite laughter coming from the men following her story so closely. On the inside she crowed. Miss Maralys Soulier from New Orleans couldn't deny that such a tale circulated about the school in Mobile, might very well have been one of the twelve. It was difficult not to lift her eyes to Antoine's to claim victory.

But she didn't.

Justin's constant appraisal of her face and hands while she related Roseanne's story had Leander all flustered by then. Surely he wasn't attaching significance to the fact that she had allowed him to remain? The man would be insane to think he had bested her by invading her home. She had needed a third person to balance the scene between Antoine and her while she sought to lay to rest his doubts as to where she had been since leaving Beaux Rives the night of the fire.

Leander would have been hard pressed to recall the remaining events of the afternoon. Assuaging her mental torment, both callers left at the same time soon after the shadows stretched inside the living room through tall windows. She hurried up to her bedroom, throwing herself facedown upon her bed. Had she been running a race with Gabriel out upon the levee road, as she sometimes did, she couldn't have been more exhausted.

Chapter Sixteen

The gray, cold skies outside the study at Beaux Rives the next morning matched the atmosphere inside its walls. Leander sat hunched behind the desk, frowning at the contents of a letter that a ship on its way upriver had dropped off at the pier. For protection against the pervasive chill racking her, she drew about her shoulders the lovely shawl of natural-colored wool, the one which had seemed such a fashionable trifle in Belle's shop. The once-intriguing workmanship and long falls of fringe made no impression. What did it matter what she wore or how she looked when the only salvaged piece of her world was threatening to tumble down down about her?

There had been no need to confer with her overseer since the morning of the torrential rains and threatening flood waters ten days ago, but the desire to do so now raged within. Already she had sent Jabbo to fetch Felix. Upon awakening that morning, Leander had recalled that this afternoon was when she had originally planned to return to the hunting lodge to meet

Justin. Perhaps it was that wounding thought which had led her to plan to spend the entire day going over business matters. None such tragedies of the heart brought the pained shadows to her eyes at the moment, though. What was keeping Felix?

Without preliminaries, Leander jumped in with her accusations the minute Felix came through the door and closed it behind him. "You have some explaining to do. What is the meaning of this notice of taxes and fees in arrears?"

Felix took his time reaching the desk and taking the proffered letter. What had she learned? He was in no hurry to find out. He sank upon the chair pulled close and read it through before looking up, no easy task for one of such little schooling. "Seems plain enough to me. We owe money to the Cabildo."

"You don't seem surprised," she remarked. Her tone matched the gleam of suspicion in her eyes. "How long have you known that Beaux Rives was behind in assessments? This is obviously not the first notice, yet you've made no mention of it to me, and I've found no old correspondence."

"Well, I figured we would wait and see if our crops don't bring enough this fall to pay something to keep them quiet down there in New Orleans." With a flourish he let the letter float back upon the desk. If that was all that had her upset, he had nothing to worry about. He permitted himself to drink in the Violette-like beauty across from him. The fringe of black curls about her face fascinated him. "They never have complained before when I came up with some kind of payment." Felix felt confident she could never find out that he had made regular payments to a cohort in the

Cabildo, the monies being set aside for the two to share once the waiting period passed and Beaux Rives became his outright. Friends in high places had not come cheaply.

"That's not the proper way to carry on business, Felix, and you know it. I gather that the plantation has been behind ever since Papa . . . died." She hated it when his piglike eyes roamed her face as they were doing.

"Even before that, missy," Felix said, slipping in the name everyone about the place had called her until she returned all grown up. It seemed to him that he was the only one she had refused permission to continue the privilege. Her lack of invitations to dine with her more than a few times right at first rankled, made him want to lash out. That he had been allowed to see her only at a distance over the past ten days seemed a deliberate act to put him in his place. Why couldn't she appreciate all he had done for Beaux Rives? "He didn't pay much attention to business after your mama passed away, though you were probably too young—"

"What my father did has no bearing on this conversation or this problem," she hastened to say before he could berate Etienne further. "I resent receiving this threat from Lieutenant Charles Garcia, the Commissioner of Land Assessments, to take control of Beaux Rives unless full payment of overdue monies is made before the end of the year. How could you neglect to tell me such might be forthcoming? I thought you were working with me to make Beaux Rives grow, not against me." Leander heard herself sounding harsh and accusing, but she didn't care. The gray-faced little man reminded her of a sneaky animal trying to find a hole to crawl into while a storm blew over.

"If you want," Felix offered, wishing he dared call for Sheeva to bring coffee but figuring the time was wrong, "I could write a letter explaining that we need more time. I've got a few friends in high places in the Cabildo." Let her chew on that a while, he mused.

"I have no desire for you to write a letter to anyone," she retorted. His brag didn't slip by unnoticed. How would he know some Spanish official in "high places"? "I want you to explain to me why you've not paid the money as it came due over the past six years from harvest sales. From my checking over the books, it seems that there have been good harvests. Yet the bank account is barely large enough to cover the purchase of seed and goods for planting this year's crops. What has happened to the money?"

Felix straightened and threw her an angry look. "For one thing, I spent a lot building this house."

"And why did you need to build it if you thought I had died in the fire?" That question had been building inside for some weeks now, ever since she had first gone over the books and accounts. "Besides, this place couldn't have cost all the profits for six years." With a contemptuous, Etienne-learned gesture for the boxy room with its lack of luxury, she fixed a demanding gaze upon the shifty-eyed Felix. "Something is going on that I don't know about. I want answers, Felix, and I have a right to hear them."

Resenting the assertive tone which reminded him too sharply of her father's accusations during that final year of his life, the overseer snapped, "I've done the best I could do, considering everything. If you don't like it . . ." He caught himself before completing the

349

threat. "As your legal guardian and caretaker here until December sixteenth when you'll become eighteen, I made the decisions I thought best. There's not much you can do about it, unless you decide to up and marry before then and let your husband serve as guardian." He observed the pale face and blazing eyes, taking perverse pleasure in having riled her further. If she intended to try to ride herd over him, she might as well learn to take as well as give, he reasoned. A quirk at the corner of thin lips hinted at the warped amusement the situation offered. "From what I hear, you already got two or three getting in line to propose."

Leander declined to comment. She stood and turned to gaze out the window. Why had she bothered to send for him? He was no help at all. It seemed obvious that he had either squandered the profits or squirreled them away for his own use, neither an action she could prove. A forefinger wandered in and out of a long black curl falling across her shoulder. In the distance through dead-looking tree branches she could see the mast of a ship drifting downriver. Swags of gray moss on drooping tree limbs formed the only softening features in the dreary scene. Without any sunshine, the grounds didn't have that hint of green showing yesterday.

"If you're planning to marry for the money you need to get Beaux Rives out of debt, your best bet is the Spaniard," Felix said, a sneer lending ugliness to what he knew was a repugnant suggestion to Leander. When he learned from his private sources of the forceful Don Salvador's visits, he had found it hard to believe. Had Leander cast aside her frequently voiced prejudice against all of Spanish blood? Having been witness earlier to one of her railing tantrums against the

Spaniards and having heard of others through his grapevine, he doubted it.

Leander stiffened her back but made no reply. The coldness outside permeated her being and did nothing to relieve the knot growing at the pit of her stomach. Somehow she had to find a way to accumulate the required sum to pay off the assessments against Beaux Rives. If only she could close her eyes and it would be two years in the future when she might have an increased herd of finer blooded horses to sell. If only she could be sure that the year's crops would be bountiful and bring in larger than normal profits. If only —

Felix's dry voice cut in on her thoughts. "You'd be wasting your time to marry either of the Ferrands. I hear Andre hasn't much left in the bank after his costly courtship and honeymoon. If either of those Ferrands proposes, you can bet he's hoping for money from you to keep Belle Terre from going under. And when they find out you're worse off than they are, then I suspect their courtships will be over."

In a controlled fury, Leander spun away from the window to say, "Felix, you may be my guardian by some quirk of Spanish law, but you don't have the right to talk to me about such things. Thank you for coming in today. I'll give this latest development some thought and see what I can come up with. If you're sincere about wanting to save Beaux Rives, your main job is to put in the largest crops ever — cotton, indigo, corn, whatever the markets in New Orleans want — and see that the harvest is good. We may need to cut some timber, but we'll come up with that payment before the deadline at the end of the year. Are you with me on this?" She held him transfixed with the proud stance of her father and the beautiful features of her mother. What Felix would never comprehend was that on the inside, she was uniquely her own person.

"Sure, I'm with you." He rose then, thinking that if he were to help her by carrying out her plans, she might then show some of the gratitude toward him he so justly deserved. She didn't know it, he enthused, but before the year was out, she was going to need him on her side in the worst way. Some half-formed plan by which she could repay him dazzled his thoughts, brought his tongue to lick at slack lips. "Things do seem in a mess right now, Leander, but I vow they'll look a heap better come September. I know the officials won't push for payment till after the first of the year. Don't you worry your pretty head about a thing. I'll do my part."

Felix longed to stick out his hand and force Leander to shake it, but he sensed she would recoil from the gesture. First he would need to make her appreciate him. Instead of reaching out to touch her, he pushed fingers grimed with dirt through thinning gray hair and smiled at his lovely young mistress. A gleam deep in the small eyes was the only hint at what went on in his mind.

Long after the maddening Felix had left her alone with her misery, Leander sat at the desk. Where had he kept such papers about overdue assessments that she hadn't found them? She sent questing eyes about the cheerless room. Several large, leather-bound volumes stood upon the shelves to one side of the fireplace. A pair of tall vases with hideous Chinese dragons sat upon the lower ones. Remembering her father's penchant for using such ordinary articles to hide precious documents, she walked to investigate. The vases were empty, as was the marble umbrella stand beside the door. In the third book she pulled down, a thick tome named *Columbus' Discoveries of the New World*, she found what she searched for. Several folded documents lay pressed tightly between the pages.

Going first to turn the lock on the door, Leander took the sheets to the desk. The first she read tightened the already painful knot in her belly. To make sure she was reading the Spanish correctly, she read it a second time aloud in a disbelieving voice.

Signed by Felix and the infamous Lieutenant General Don Allejandro O'Reilly, who was listed as the official representative of the Bourbon King Charles III and Acting Governor of Louisiana, it revealed an agreement between the undersigned Felix Grinot and the Spanish official. Touted for having taken the oath of allegiance to the Spanish flag and delivered "certain acts of good faith," Felix Grinot was designated as successor to "Beaux Rives and all property of the Traitor Etienne Ondine if no legal heirs have come before the Superior Council to present the original deed by the last day of December, 1775." The document, official if she could judge by the impressive seal of the Spanish Crown set in a splash of pinkish wax, was dated the last day of December 1769—three months after the death of her father.

Leander flung the offending news as far as she could, the crackling sound of its skittering across the wooden flood fueling her anger. Damn that scheming bastard Felix! He had wasted no time in making his claim. During a moment of insane rage, she snatched up the declaration and considered throwing it into the blazing fire. But common sense prevailed. When she had threatened to do the same with the one declaring Felix her guardian, Antoine had advised her that she would be wasting her time, mayhap setting herself up for further trouble. He assured her that he, as a lawyer, was certain there were identical copies of official documents on file in the offices of the Spanish government in New Orleans — the Cabildo, as everyone called that august body.

Muttering a spate of obscenities learned from Dom as she pondered the overseer's covert actions, the distraught young woman prowled about the room. Her thoughts roamed over the ways in which the devious Felix had sought to gain what was hers. He well knew that the original deed had burned in the fire, along with everything else outside a few of the contents of the wine cellar. To present a deed obviously no longer in existence was impossible. How cleverly he had set up his case! Upon the date of the document, he must have believed with certainty that Leander was buried between her parents.

Felix had been downright toadying when he had produced the document naming him as her guardian, the frowning Leander recalled as she paced up and down. She remembered that on the second morning after her return, he had been in the study with the paper in hand when she came downstairs for breakfast. No telling how long he had worked there making sure that those others he had reason to hide were stashed away. Had she not informed Jabbo in front of him that morning that the overseer was not to be shown into the office in the future unless she were present, he more than likely would have scuttled the papers off to his own quarters in the smaller house built for him. No doubt he had counted on her not taking time to examine the books on the shelf, knowing that it would take all of her working hours for some time to go over the routine ledgers and business papers he couldn't refuse to allow her to examine.

Small wonder that Felix had built a house scaled down to suit his more bourgeois tastes and needs. What would he have known about rebuilding one on the scale of the former, even had he found the money to attempt it? And then fell the question as to what he had done with the profits from the crops. Leander ceased the furious pacing, quaking all over at the injustice of having to accept him as her guardian. Both rage and a new fit of trembling filled her with anguish at the realization that the sneaky little man had stood to gain the entire Ondine holdings without question had she not come back. The memory of the way he had stared upon first seeing her the night of her return speared her attention. Had all of the visible emotion showing upon his face been from shock? Or had some, perhaps, come from disappointment? No telling what drastic steps Felix would be willing to take to remove her from the scene again — if it weren't for Jabbo's watchfulness, that is. The eerie thought led to another, and she sank upon weakened knees before the fireplace, her troubled eyes searching the wavering flames, as though for answers.

What were those "certain acts of good faith" Felix had rendered unto that short-termed governor she had heard called "Bloody O'Reilly?" The term had always seemed to her to be apt. Wasn't he the hired soldier who had ordered his men to arrest and then shoot the Conspirators after the so-called trial? She intended to find out what such a ruffian might term "acts of good faith" that could be worth such a reward as Beaux Rives. Until she did, no one would learn what she had discovered.

"Damn you, Spaniards! I hate you, every one of you!" Leander hissed in a low, venomous voice while she knelt on the hearth, staring into the untended, smoldering fire. Her breath seemed to work as a bellows, turning some of the live coals into hissing, flame-topped chunks, others from dead-looking gray to blazing red. Her hands had clenched into loose fists some time ago, but they tightened further as she again spoke aloud, "You've killed my father, but you'll not conquer his daughter. I'll show you Spaniards! I swear that you will never wrest Beaux Rives from me." Fascinated at the way the force of air from her impassioned outburst coaxed new flames to jump into life and lick at the charred logs, Leander rose with a grim smile. The speaking of the vow there in the quiet of the room had fired up something else as well—her long-nursed hatred of the Spanish.

Before Sheeva came to summon her for the midday meal, Leander had read every page the wily Felix had secreted away. With care she returned them to the volume and replaced it on the shelf. She wouldn't need to see them again to know each word by heart. Old tax assessments seemed to have been ignored. Why? The question begged for answers. She marked that each notice bore the same signature as that on the one received today. Already she had in mind a plan which would take her to New Orleans before the year was out, one which would no doubt confound her overseer and mayhap others as well. One of the first places she would visit would be the Cabildo. The first man she would ask to see was one Spanish Lieutenant Charles Garcia.

Leander marched to her desk. She found paper, dipped the quill, and composed a letter. Old memories of practicing penmanship under the supervision of her tutor guided her. Her father's distant, older cousin had purchased the Ondine trading houses to free the adventurous Etienne and his bride to seek a new life in New France. More than once, Etienne had passed along to the tutor a nicely penned letter from the cousin to serve as models for the young Leander.

Easily the name Jean Paul Ondine surfaced, as did the remainder of the oft-copied address: Ondine Warehouse, Garonne Four, at Bordeaux, France. King Louis XVI had worn the crown for less than a year. Would the young monarch care that a gift from his grandfather was being despoiled? Would Jean Paul make the effort she was asking, send a delegate to approach the Crown and request a reissue of the deed bestowed upon Etienne Ondine? Not until the third try did Leander feel satisfied that the letter stated her desperate plight. She would have to pray that Jean Paul was yet alive and was the gentleman her parents had believed.

That afternoon, a horseman dashed up the walkway toward Beaux Rives. Something about the hurrying hoofbeats and Gabriel's excited barks brought Sheeva on the run, stirred Leander from her work in the study. Within a short time, all had digested the horrible news that the slave from Belle Terre had brought. Andre

Ferrand was dead, apparently from some kind of seizure in the chest. His heart seemed to have stopped while he sat dozing beside the fire that morning after a late breakfast with Felicity. Antoine and Philip had found him in the final stages of what appeared to be a peaceful death.

Jabbo had Bagatelle and Victory saddled and waiting at the hitching posts to the side of the porch by the time Cara summoned him to fetch down Leander's portmanteau. Her face drawn, Leander silently accepted Jabbo's assistance to mount. Next to her heart, she carried the letter to Jean Paul Ondine. The Ferrand slave had told that a ship had already picked up the message to summon a priest from downriver, that services would be held upon his arrival. The idea to ask the Father to send the letter to Bordeaux struck her, even as she listened to the announcement. That way she could be certain that its dispatch would not attract attention from Felix or the Spanish.

Leander would have chosen to wear the austere black riding outfit, but Cara was in the process of cleaning and pressing it and couldn't get it ready in time. She settled the full skirts of the purple velvet riding costume about her and led the way up the faint river road toward Belle Terre. The rakish hat of matching velvet did little to lend her an air of fashion. Sadness seemed to claim even the lovely ostrich plume tucked in the side brim. Leander's thoughts centered on her cousin. Widowed at nineteen and after only three months of marriage, Felicity would be bereft.

Along with all who gathered at Belle Terre to mourn, Leander found the next three days tiring and taxing. Once Father Raphael from New Orleans arrived on a midday ship that third morning, the grieving family and friends gave Andre up to last rites and burial in the plantation's cemetery beside his first wife, mother of his sons. A cold, steady rain from a properly gray sky made the tedious task even drearier.

Leander was surprised to see the depth of emotion on the handsome, yet unalike, faces of Antoine and Philip. For a brief time, the sons seemed to have reverted to the status of lost children. She seemed the one who could bring the most comfort to the sons as well as to the widow. Spending private time with each and doing her best to offer cheer and hope, she hardly had time to notice or care who else gathered to pay last respects to the revered Andre Ferrand.

Even so, she sensed each time the only Spaniard in the group of friends came and went. Private grief and respect for Andre's family prevented her from lashing out at Justin. Inside the kernel of hate throbbed. She avoided contact with him, refusing to acknowledge those piercing black eyes she could feel singling her out. A secret satisfaction at having found the opportunity to speak at length with Father Raphael and gain his assistance in getting her letter to the cousin in Bordeaux gave Leander a spark of new hope. The Spanish had not conquered her yet.

"Leander, please don't talk of leaving tomorrow," Felicity begged on the fifth day after the burial, tears threatening to rain down the sad face. "I don't think I can stand sleeping alone yet. Having you in the bed is so reassuring when I awaken in the night."

Leander teased, "You're pulling your old tricks on me to get your way. What was it Docie used to say about your cunning — you catch more flies with honey than with vinegar? You know very well that I often kick the daylights out of you before I'm aware of it."

"You could move into the guest room, then," the wan-faced blonde said. "I'm not ready to be alone here with just Philip and Antoine."

"Then pack up and come to Beaux Rives with me," Leander insisted, taken with the idea the moment she uttered it. The black-draped mirrors in the halls and receiving rooms were probably having a morbid effect on everyone. "I've much to see about, now that it's time to break soil and prepare for planting. You could ride with me as I watch the work going on. March is almost here, you know." They were resting on plush chairs in the sitting alcove of the master bedroom. With a sudden, flashing smile, Leander held out her hand toward her cousin. "Touch my hand and I'll make your dreams come true."

A crooked smile tugged at the pretty mouth still puffy from days of weeping. "You can't pretend to be my fairy godmother anymore, Leander." From her throat came a half-strangled sob which tried to pass for a laugh.

"Only if you believe." Leander kept out her hand. "Remember? That's the only requirement. Don't you believe anymore?"

"I want to, honestly I do." The fervent words seemed to come from some faraway Felicity.

"Then do it," Leander urged. "Touch my hand, close your eyes, and believe that things will get better. Think of how many times you helped me over scraped knees and disappointments by acting as my godmother." Even after the sobering past eight days, Leander could recall the heady magic of those times of childish belief in such powers. When Felicity hesitantly laid light fingers upon that outstretched hand, Leander laughed. "I knew I could count on you."

"Oh, Leander," Felicity moaned for the hundredth time since Andre had died, "you've no idea what sadness is. Stop trying to cheer me up. My life is over and we both know it. You're so lucky to have control of your world and have so much to look forward to. Some young man will come along and love you as Andre did me and ask you to be his wife . . ." Self-pity filled the blue eyes with tears, sent the lovely lips to quivering before she could complete the pretty picture she envisioned for everyone on earth except herself.

Leander had accepted Felicity's numerous invitations for compassion and sympathy and taken on the role of mature comforter, despite the fact that she was two years younger. Never did she attempt to correct her cousin's naive assumption that Leander had no personal problems to tear at her own heart, nor did she have any intentions of doing so. Once Justin had tried to follow her from the living room, evidently planning to talk with her privately. Heart hammering with what she was sure must be repugnance for all Spaniards, she had retreated into a side room until she could hear his footsteps wandering away. And when she lay awake beside the sobbing widow night after night, her thoughts had a way of dwelling upon the tangled web of deception and debt awaiting her attention back at Beaux Rives. If, as Felicity chose to believe, she did control her world, Leander reflected, she was doing a poor job of it.

"I'll say this only once, Felicity," she announced, sitting up straight and fixing the tear-ravaged face with stern looks. The black of their gowns seemed out of place in the sunny alcove facing the Mississippi. "I'm getting fed up with repeating the same condolences every hour on the hour. If you don't know by now that everyone, and I do mean everyone, sympathizes with you and grieves privately for Andre, then you're acting plain stupid." She went on before the shocked Felicity could protest. "I think the smartest thing you can do is go home with me for a few weeks. I want you and I would enjoy being with you. But if you're going to sit and cry and moan over your state of widowhood from now on, you might as well start tomorrow right here in your house. I see no need merely to seek a change of scenery for the same old act. You may be required to wear black on the outside for the coming year, but that doesn't mean you're to let it color your brain. The time for mourning is over—if you intend to go on living."

Felicity stared with opened mouth at the previously soft-voiced Leander. She watched her rise and move toward the wardrobe. Narrowing her eyes and sitting up straighter, she asked in a more nearly normal voice than she had used since Andre's death, "What are you doing?"

"I'm moving my clothing to the guest room. If you plan to go home with me, be ready by noon tomorrow." She folded the few gowns over her arm and went to the doorway. "And don't ask for food to be served up here tonight—unless you plan to eat alone. I'm going to dine downstairs with Antoine and Philip. In case you've forgotten, they've lost someone dear to them, too. They've lost their father, and they've loved him for a longer time than you've even lived."

And with that hard-to-deliver announcement, Leander left. When a slave tiptoed in to get the remainder of her belongings, she found the young widow sleeping almost peacefully across the big canopied bed. Leander breathed a sigh of relief upon hearing the good news.

Jabbo followed the cousins the next morning at a discreet distance. He knew they had much to discuss on the two-hour ride. Talk in the kitchen while he was eating breakfast centered on the reading of Master Ferrand's will that morning.

"Can you believe that Andre had almost no cash?" Felicity asked Leander for the third or fourth time. Hearing her husband's will read by the lawyer up from New Orleans had done as much to sober her as Leander's ultimatum of the previous afternoon. "He never let on to me that he couldn't afford all the things he bought me. I feel terrible that Maurine didn't insist on giving the dowry I know Papa meant me to have. She was getting back at me for not marrying her precious son."

"As for Andre's scarcity of cash, running a big plantation and keeping up a drove of slaves takes a lot of money," Leander explained. She was learning much about business and figured Felicity might as well begin to take notice. "Even if Andre had had reserves, he would be using them now to get ready for planting. Didn't you say that Philip appeared satisfied that he could manage to put in the year's crops on what was left?"

The blonde nodded, still in partial shock at learning that she was half-owner of a river plantation and a town house in New Orleans, plus a number of slaves, cattle, and horses—but that she had practically no money to spend. If the year's crops and harvest weren't extraordinary, she would still have none to speak of in the fall.

"Philip didn't seem surprised, but Antoine turned pale and put on a mean mouth when all was read," Felicity said. A frown wrinkled her brow for a second. "I remember hearing his father and him having words behind closed doors just last week, and I suspected it was about Antoine's gambling habits. But of course, Andre never bothered me with such matters."

"I can't believe he was doing you a favor" was her cousin's caustic comment.

"Wonder what the debonair Antoine will do now that he hasn't Andre to furnish him with money to live on?" Felicity mused aloud. All kinds of plaguing thoughts were arising as she rode down the river road toward Beaux Rives. Though the cloud of grief still hovered in her heart, her mind seemed to be clearing at each mile.

"That's simple," Leander replied. "He can go live at the town house in New Orleans and find a job as a lawyer. It seems plain that he has little desire to join Philip in seeing to the plantation." She couldn't help but hope her solution seemed as logical to Antoine and that he would be gone shortly. To see him leave the area would keep him from trying to repeat the miserable scene of two weeks ago. It seemed obvious that Felix's snide remark had been right. Antoine was seeking a rich wife. And how absurd that he should have thought she might fit into that category. Absurd that day, she mused, but even more so now that she had learned of the indebtedness against Beaux Rives.

"I'm glad you acted mean to me and made me come home with you," Felicity confessed with childlike candor when they could see the two-story brick house rising up ahead through trees wearing a fuzz of green on upper branches. "It makes me feel good to realize that we're family and that you love me."

From beneath the purple velvet hat, Leander grinned at the pretty blonde. "How can you be sure that I invited you because I care for you? I might have had a devious purpose in mind and need some cheering up myself. You never can tell, can you?"

In that way both recalled from frequent childhood times together, Felicity stuck her nose in the air and pretended great insult for a moment. She then sent blue eyes to meet the loving violet ones awaiting. Admiration embroidering her words, she declared, "You've always been so strong, Leander. I can't imagine that anyone would ever need to cheer you up about anything."

Chapter Seventeen

The cousins found the change of locale helpful in lifting spirits. By noon the next day, Felicity had chatted at length with Sheeva and Cara and renewed old acquaintances. While Leander attended to business in the study, the young widow strolled about the grounds and visited her horse Fortune in the stables. Gabriel bounced along beside her at each step, obviously eager to add one more conquest to his string of admirers. Tower, the slave serving as head stableman, convinced her that Fortune was contented in new surroundings.

In the study, Leander pored over plans for the planting of fields. Earlier, at her request, Felix had come up with some based on his actions over the past year. After spending a goodly portion of the morning going over them with Jabbo, and adding his ideas to Felix's, she felt far more confident that the year held promise of being fruitful.

"Do you think we can really get better prices in New Orleans if we plant earlier than the others around here?" Leander asked Jabbo before she left him to join Felicity for the midday meal.

"Your papa always worked on that theory, missy, when winter didn't hang on past the end of February." Sitting on the chair before her desk, his hands resting on charts lying before him, Jabbo continued in the rich, sonorous voice she had been listening to ever since she could remember. "He gambled on the weather, of course, by planting a week or so early, but generally, if I remember right, he would tell me he gained more than he lost. Spring does seem to be coming early this year." He glanced beyond her at the grass greening down the gentle slope leading to the riverbank where drooping willows echoed the weak color. He noted a swelling of buds at the tip ends of some tree branches lifting toward the blue sky. Those would be the cottonwoods, he thought with new pleasure at being back home. They always beat the oaks.

"I'll talk with Felix and tell him I've decided to plant as soon as the fields can be readied." Leander studied the wise, dark eyes when they looked up from another appraisal of the planting charts. Though tempted to confide in the giant black man, she held back. Not for him were the worries and doubts she nursed in secret anguish. To keep the plantation productive and solvent was the owner's problem. "Despite the odds, I like the stakes too much to pass on this." She cocked her head in an attempt to appear jaunty, sure of herself.

"Are you holding your cards close in the game with Don Salvador?" Jabbo leaned back against the chair and crossed his legs, not surprised that she was slow in answering. Sounds of scolding blue jays came through the closed window. A quiet caring interlaced what might have sounded like an impertinent question between an ordinary slave and his mistress.

Leander averted her eyes and pursed her lips before replying, "If there ever was a game there, it's over now. I've told him not to return to Beaux Rives."

"He talked with me each time he called at Belle Terre to pay his respects to the Ferrands. He seemed to have thought a lot of Mr. Andre." His words hung in the suddenly tense space between them. "I feel I came to know him quite well."

"Talked — about what?" A lump tried to fill her throat. She hated having to think of Justin. The memories of their making love in the lodge never ceased to war within her during the long nights. The only good coming from such unsettling thoughts was that it caused the earlier ones from the night in Throwaway's room to pale by comparison. What was it about the two Spaniards that had overpowered her? Justin was as much a scoundrel as that stranger, as undeserving of a single thought — much less the tons he received without her willing them to haunt her. She cleared her throat and rubbed at the back of her neck, weary of talk about Justin, even before it began.

"Horses and planting."

His elbows resting on the wooden arms of the chair, Jabbo formed a tent with thick, pinkish fingers and pitched it across the wide nose. Meaty thumbs anchored beneath the broad chin. The questing gaze above the concealing hands examined the demeanor of his mistress. She sat across from him, her back to the sunlit window facing the veranda, grounds, and, on down the slope, the Mississippi. Mentally Jabbo was marking the way the black-haired beauty ducked, letting their eyes meet, the way she worked too hard at appearing only slightly interested. What was eating her?

Ever since having first seen Justin at Beaux Rives the morning after the Mardi Gras ball, Jabbo had suspected that the handsome young man had a yearning for Leander. And when, upon his questioning the day they first saw the awesome stallion across the fence, she had refused to tell him much about Justin's visit with her in the woods late on the previous afternoon, he had become suspicious that there might be something brewing between the two young people. For some reason, she appeared more nervous about discussing Justin this morning than earlier. What had happened?

From what Justin had told Jabbo as they chatted on the grounds of Belle Terre during the days of mourning for Andre, Leander had refused to grant a single moment of privacy for the two of them. Had they spoken with each other since the afternoon the Spaniard had barged in on Antoine's tête-à-tête with her at Beaux Rives? Keeping his face impassive, the black man pondered the question. He could come up with no possible way the two could have exchanged more than a few words since then. But something had apparently changed her attitude toward him since she had allowed him to join Antoine and her for tea. Afterward she had seemed a bit wan and weary, he recalled, but when he had asked the next day about her visitors and heard her comments, she had worn a look of satisfaction bordering on the smug. He remembered thinking that Justin must be competing with Antoine for her hand. No expression or tone of voice had suggested that Leander had found the Spaniard's surprise visit completely unacceptable. Would he ever be able to guess what went on in that clever mind?

"So you talked of horses and planting," Leander commented, the testing voice breaking into Jabbo's musings. "I suppose he would sound knowledgeable about such things." No answer from the mouth still tented behind huge hands. What were Jabbo's eyes demanding she tell? He seemed deep in thought. "And what else did the arrogant Spanish don and you find to discuss?" Her pulse floundered around, then sped up.

"We both found that we were interested in your welfare." So she was curious, just as he had figured she might be. A smile hovered about the concealed mouth.

"You dared talk about me to someone?" She tried for an imperious tone, tossing her head enough for the black curls to shift positions where they fell across one shoulder.

"Missy, you know I wouldn't say anything but good about you," Jabbo reprimanded. He took down the tent and sent her a reassuring smile, the white of his teeth almost startling in the black face. Straightening on the chair, he lifted his head menacingly. "Don Salvador knows not to get pushy with me."

"I don't want him back here, and I've told him so." The confession came on a ragged, exhaled breath. Every aspect of the Spaniard seemed determined to gnaw at her in one way or another. Was he some reverse side of that faceless stranger? If only she could blot out both instances . . .

"Do you want I should throw him in the river if he shows up again?" Jabbo leaned a fraction closer there across the desk from her, a slight frown trenching his forehead. They both knew he could, and would, if she gave the word.

"No," she replied after a pause in which she straightened papers already straight and reset the quill in its holder at a different angle — not better, just different. How could she justify setting Jabbo on Justin without doing a lot more explaining about the situation than she wished? "I can handle Don Salvador on my own. He's just another Spaniard who needs to be put in his place, and I'm the one to do it."

"Whatever you say," spoke Jabbo without much conviction.

"Leave him to me," she insisted. Leander rose then, watching the giant of a man nod his acceptance of her order. She lifted eyes he could tell were troubled and said, "Carry on as usual if he does return here. Actually, I doubt he will."

Without a backward glance, she swept from the study with a silken rustle of skirts, leaving Jabbo to stare after her with a perplexed look wrinkling his face and revealing his forty-odd years. He was more certain than ever that some kind of mysterious link existed, however tenuously, between Leander and Justin Salvador. And he felt with like certitude that it had little to do with the fact that the man was a Spaniard. What he didn't know was whether or not his mistress realized that as well. If he had been looking for something to puzzle over, he chided himself, he had found it. His steps as he left the study were the same long ones a seven-footer normally makes, but they sounded slower and heavier in his ears.

Leander and Felicity were on their way back from the stables that afternoon when Gabriel let out a deep bark and dashed around the corner of the veranda.

Within a few seconds, the dog bounded back with bursts of happy sounds, the black-tipped ears flopping their own kind of pleasure. Behind him on the grassy path came Justin Salvador, the streak of white in his hair gleaming in the late afternoon sunlight.

"What a pleasure, ladies," Justin called, honoring them with a half-bow and a huge smile before strolling on to where they had paused. "How are you this fine March afternoon?" So Ona's report at breakfast that morning about the cousins' return to Beaux Rives had been right. His devastating love for Leander chased away the doubts he had entertained as to the wisdom of appearing so soon after the death of Andre. The need to see her, hear her voice pressed upon him more than his wish to observe any social codes. God! She was breathtaking in the form-fitting black riding costume, the high-heeled boots he recalled from the Mardi Gras ball gracing her slender feet. Sunlight danced in and out of the ebony curls, as if it could not refrain from reveling in such beauty. Not until then did he realize that her hair was as sooty black as his own, that he had never before seen her in full sunlight. The sight of her dazzled and stunned his senses.

Forcing himself to include Leander's companion in his field of vision, Justin wondered if they knew what lovely contrasts they presented on the path beside the house, one so brunette, the other so blond. Only their slender yet curving forms suggested kinship. Something about the set of Leander's mouth and chin, even across the little distance, warned him that his reception was not to be the same as on the afternoon he had found her with Antoine. Though she had purposely avoided him at Belle Terre later, he had credited her actions to being overwrought at Andre's death. In truth, he had gleaned hope from that last visit to Beaux Rives that she was warming to his courtship. At least she hadn't ordered him to leave or set Jabbo against him, though he was beginning to suspect he might not be so lucky this time. Even in his besotted state, he recognized purple fire blazing from those incredible eyes. What could have altered her mood so drastically in less than two weeks?

The obviously happy dog dashed up and licked at his hand, reminding him that he needed to do more than drink in the sight before him. Letting a hand touch a soft, furry ear, then give a pat to the broad head, but never dropping his eyes, he remarked, "Gabriel is quite effective as one to greet callers, wouldn't you say?"

"What are you doing here?" Leander demanded. Under his scrutiny, she had stiffened, realizing for the first time that she hadn't left the riding crop behind in the tack room. Her fingers closed over it painfully. She longed to slash at Justin with it, to scream at him, drive him away for good. Damn this having to control her feelings and bottle up all that begged to be hurled at the Spaniard! He had no right to intrude into her life, especially since she had told him not to. She couldn't help but notice that a white cravat spilled across his brown riding coat and showed how darkly olive the handsome face was, how sparkling the teeth behind smiling lips. It dawned that it was her first close-up view of him in full light. Something within tightened like a string pulled too tightly, and she labeled it as hatred for all that he was, all that he represented. Had there ever been a man who could walk with such

373

arrogance and yet give the outward appearance of graceful, manly ease of movement? Lips clamped in disapproval of all that threatened, she glared at the caller.

"Leander, don't be mean," Felicity said, blue eyes darting with disapproval toward her stormy-faced cousin. During the silences between the brief exchanges, she had looked in puzzlement from Leander to Justin. They seemed locked in a staring contest, and she couldn't for the life of her figure out what was bringing it on. A believer in social graces, as well as a bit of a peacemaker, she chided, "Is that any way to treat a gentleman caller — and your neighbor as well?" Hoping to camouflage what she viewed as unforgivable rudeness from Leander, she spoke to the young man who had halted on the path. "Please forgive her, Justin. She's been so fractious all day that I can hardly get along with her myself. I'm happy to see you and I hope you've come to join us for tea." She smiled at the still hesitant young man.

"I don't care for tea today," Leander snapped, wishing Felicity would mind her own business, tempted to hiss that thought into the ear close to her own.

"Good," Felicity shot back, not deigning to look at her fully again. The way Leander clutched at the riding crop made Felicity suspect she might be even angrier than her mien and manner hinted. "Justin can join me then, for our ride this afternoon has made me frightfully thirsty and tuckered out. Would you accept my invitation?" By then the blonde had walked on to stand before the young man, the trailing back section of her black riding habit draped over one arm in careless fashion. "I want to hear those stories you once told Andre about the horse races back in Spain when you were a boy. He tried to recall them for me not long ago, but he got them so mixed up, we both ended up laughing at the hodge-podge he was coming up with."

For some reason, Justin's presence, his deep voice offered the young widow a needed comfort. Here was someone with whom she could share pleasant memories of her husband, someone who hadn't seen him as a father or a master, someone properly grieved but not steeped in sorrow. Later she would make Leander explain her inexcusable manners. She doubted anyone lived who was harderheaded than her cousin. That Justin was a Spaniard must be what had her all riled up, she reasoned. Leander's narrow views on the subject needed to be brought to a head soon and settled. For now, Felicity put aside such tedious thoughts and walked to take Justin's arm, forcing him to turn from Leander and escort her to the veranda, and then to go on inside the house.

"You did what?" Leander asked on rising notes the following afternoon, her furious stare bringing red to Felicity's fair cheeks. She had come by the guest bedroom to see if the young widow was ready to go downstairs for tea or coffee, unprepared for her cousin's calm announcement that she had asked Justin to join them. "As you pointed out in 'grand manner' last night during our quarrel, your asking him to come inside with you yesterday might have come from your sense of embarrassment over my behavior toward him—a somewhat misguided sense, if I may say. But why did you ask him to return today? Don't tell me you're going to be one of those widows already measuring the sizes of a man's shoulders and purse before the dirt on the grave settles."

Anger leaping within blue eyes, Felicity rose from where she sat reading to face Leander standing near the doorway. "You don't even have to work to be mean, do you? You've always had the foul habit of saying whatever jumps into mind without once stopping to think how it might sound, how it might stab. If this is the way you plan to treat me, I won't stay here another night. Surely even one as immature as you must have been able to see that I loved Andre. You can't possibly mean what you just said or hinted at . . . about Justin and me."

A measuring look from accusing eyes took in the faintly apologetic glimmer in the purple ones, the perceptible quiver of the lower lip. But Felicity waited. Tension mounted at a dizzying pace. She hadn't lived two more years than her cousin, almost three months of them as wife to an older man, and not learned a bit more about people in general. Hers hadn't been a world cut off, deliberately made small, as had Leander's. And hers hadn't been a world revolving only around her, Felicity reminded that inner, musing self. In truth, hers had been almost the opposite after her father died, leaving her to endure life with an unloving stepmother and her leering son. The time had come for Leander to own up that she could not control everyone and everything.

Leander stared back, the hateful words aimed at Felicity echoing in her heart with something akin to pain for the cousin she loved, the label "immature" rankling deep within. When they had exchanged heated words the night before, although nothing as hurtful as what she had uttered had surfaced then, the blonde had done little but offer barb for barb and flounce off to her own bedroom. Both had seemed to welcome the excuse to revert to childish behavior and vent some of the tautness building since the funeral. This afternoon, though, Leander observed that an imposing quality seemed to lend a new dignity to the too-thin figure, add a commanding light deep within the sorrowed, blue eyes, spread a look on the wan face that seemed to shout that its owner was ready, able, and willing to defend whatever needed defending. Even against the only remaining member of family.

When she managed to speak, Leander heard her voice quake. "I'm sorry, Felicity. You're right. I didn't mean what I said about your . . . being interested in another man only two weeks after the loss of Andre. And I know you loved him." She took a step forward when the expression on the stony face didn't change, a hand out, imploring. "Will you forgive me?"

Even in her turmoil, Leander noted the change that the seldom-used question wrought upon her cousin's face and eyes. Had she already made the first step toward altering the label from "immature" to the desired "mature"? Over the past few moments, she had realized how much she longed for Felicity's approval, as well as her forgiveness. Mayhap if she confided some of her worries, Felicity would have more compassion for her plight—tell some, but not all.

"Yes, I'll forgive you because I love you," Felicity responded with warmth, glad that Leander had recognized the need for altering her obstinacy. Secretly, the older cousin judged the younger far wiser and more knowledgeable in numerous areas than she herself was.

"Shall we go downstairs now?"

"No, let's talk until your . . . our guest arrives." Leander went to claim a place on the chair opposite where Felicity had been sitting. "I guess you have reason to think I'm fractious and mean just for the devil of it, but I do have problems."

"What kind of problems could you possibly have?" Felicity's shock and disbelief showed clearly in tone and look. "With your looks and position and your entire life before you, what could upset you? I was angry when I accused you of being immature, and I beg your forgiveness. Frankly, I find you the most grown-up thinking young woman I've ever been around. Now that I think of it, you always were advanced for your years." At Leander's grateful, tremulous smile, she added, "What troubles you? Surely it can be no more than an affair of the heart. Has Antoine made a pass at you?"

"Why would you ask that?" Veiled eyes hid her thoughts.

"I've watched how he looks at you when he thinks no one is noticing. He reminds me of some giant animal sizing up a smaller one that he plans to eat the first minute it turns its head."

Leander threw back her head and laughed long and hard, something neither had heard much of for too long a period. She couldn't have described Antoine's mannerisms any better had she tried, she thought as she wiped at a tear spilling beside her nose. Even so, she had no intention of telling about his kiss and proposal. Watching with puzzled amusement, Felicity did little more than return a lopsided grin.

"Actually," Leander said when both sobered, 'I'm

378

concerned over raising the money to pay some back assessments due on Beaux Rives at the end of the year. That reprobate Felix has let them stack up over the past six years, though I can't imagine why he wouldn't want to pay those first. He might know how to oversee the work, but the man has no head for business." Her mind added that when it came to looking out for his own though, he seemed to have no problems.

Felicity showed proper horror and amazement as Leander filled her in on the disappointing actions of Felix and the sorry state of monetary affairs at Beaux Rives. Leander carefully kept back the suspicions about Felix's collusion with the Spanish, the picture of the official document she had found in the study rising to set her teeth on edge while they talked. As soon as she became eighteen, she intended to name the cousin as next of kin and oust the overseer from possible future claims. Sometimes, as now, she wondered if December would ever come.

Trying to offer encouragement, Felicity assured, "I'm so sorry to learn of these worries, Leander. I had no idea. If Andre had left me any money, I would gladly lend it to you. As I've already told you—"

"No, no," Leander cut in to say. "I'm not telling you all of this to get money or sympathy. I guess I needed to tell it aloud to someone I can trust—and that limits the number."

"What does Jabbo think? Of course you can trust me, but you know you can trust that big, kind man as well. I think he would kill for you if the need arose."

"Such matters shouldn't be shoved on a slave, Felicity." Leander sent a forefinger to curl and recurl a strand of hair across her breast. "As mistress of the plantation, I must shoulder all such problems myself. If you didn't have Philip to run Belle Terre, you would be in the same fix. I learned from Papa that the owners have a responsibility to protect and care for the slaves in more ways than the physical. Getting them to work for you is only part of the business of owning slaves. It would be unfair to let Jabbo know of a problem that he can't help me solve. How could he know anything about money matters? I learned while living with Papa after Mama died, and then with Dom and Jabbo, that men aren't always as strong as everyone likes to believe. There were lots of things I kept back from them because when I would tell them everything on my mind, they would go around all sad-faced and blue for days. They couldn't stand not being able to do anything about my problems. I learned to share only the things they could solve, or at least try to."

"I never had thought about it, but what you're saying makes sense. I remember how Andre didn't seem to like it when I would tell him of my loneliness at Belle Terre. I wasn't trying to get him to do something about it, just understand why I was so eager to have a baby. I stopped talking about it altogether." Felicity sighed and shifted her gaze from Leander's face to the sunshine patterning across the second-floor veranda and on through the window to pick up color in the woven rug. "To see my monthlies come the day he died hurt almost as much as losing him. How I would have loved having his child."

"I'm sorry." Leander felt her throat go dry at the memory of her own recent fear. She had felt the opposite when her monthlies had appeared yesterday morning. The thought that the wild lovemaking in the

380

hunting lodge nearly a month ago might result in a child had tagged along with all of the other worries haunting her. To have even one problem solved had been enough to send her on her knees last night to tell her beads with rare fervor. "We never know what we'll have to face next, do we?"

"I'm glad you said that," Felicity said, leaning forward. "You yourself have to face up to something that you keep hiding from." At Leander's haughty lift of chin, she went on. "Now don't get riled. You know that I'm going to lecture you about your ridiculous attitude toward the Spanish. Yes, I am, so don't toss your head and push out that bottom lip at me that way. Nobody continues to bear the grudge against them that you seem to. Time has eased the pain for everyone but you. All of us have prospered more under the Spanish than under the French. Andre pointed that out to me more than once. When will you admit that Justin and others like him have as much right to be in Louisiana as you and I?"

"Never!"

"You're back to the immaturity, you know."

"I don't care what you say. They didn't shoot your father as they did mine."

"But mine didn't join with the Conspirators and openly give money to the effort to oust the Spaniards, either."

"That was my father's stand as a French patriot. How can you question his beliefs? How can I go against what he would have wanted me to do had he lived?"

"I don't question his right to take any stand he chose, but I doubt that he meant for you to carry on like a

381

banshee trying to fight the whole government. It didn't pay off for him; why do you think it will for you? What you need to know is that Uncle Etienne defied the authorities at the trial, mocked them, even dared them to shoot him as a traitor."

"Good for him," Leander shot back. "He told me that he would never beg for their pity, and I won't either."

"Nobody is asking you to do anything but forgive and forget the past."

"How can I?" Leander asked, a little broken note threading through the wistful question.

"Give Justin Salvador a chance to be nice and neighborly. Quit hiding as if you're afraid—"

"I'm not afraid of him—or any bloody Spaniard!" A fleeting memory of that night in Throw-away's room when she had brought the candlestick down on that devil's head reassured her that she wasn't lying. But if Felicity suspected fear lay behind her avoidance of Justin, what must he think? Never did she want him to think she was afraid to be around him.

"Then quit avoiding him so obviously. What else can he or I think when you act so rude and refuse to be in his company?"

Felicity pondered her words after they floated over to Leander. What else but rudeness and the preposterous hatred of the Spanish could cause a normally gregarious young woman to treat a handsome young man the way she had seen her treat Justin? The only other answer she could come up with startled her. Was Leander attracted to Justin? She peeked from beneath lowered lashes at the half-frowning face across from her. No, there was no chance of that being the case. Or was there? She would pay closer attention from now on. She hadn't forgotten Justin's apparently heartfelt appeal to her the night after the Mardi Gras ball to fetch Leander down to speak with him. What had that been all about? And Leander's hasty departure the next morning had seemed strange, even then—but stranger now that she had reacted so negatively to his appearance yesterday afternoon. A hand going to smooth at a stray curl tickling her ear, Felicity found something to think upon other than the bleakness of her own future. What if—?

Leander stopped the blonde's mental observations by saying, "Think what you like. I have nothing to fear from Justin Salvador."

"Then I dare you to go down with me and greet him like a proper hostess when he arrives. If you've nothing to be afraid of, show him that, and show me too. What must he think of someone who is rude without reason? Aunt Violette would have shamed you and you know it."

Leander digested that final bit of truth and swallowed at the lump in her throat. True, her mother had prided herself on her good manners and hospitality, had tried to instill an appreciation for them in her only child. Damn that Felicity! She had always known how to work her to get her to do what she didn't want to do. Dare her, would she? Flipping long curls to fall down her back and lifting her skirts to free her feet, she rose, saying, "You win . . . this time. But I can be pushed just so far, and you had best not forget it."

With a secretive smile at her unexpected success, Felicity rose and followed Leander across the room to the doorway. "I knew you would listen to reason."

Leander ignored the little stab. There was a hell of a

difference in a dare and reason, she fumed. She did not trust Felicity to be saying what she truly thought. Not for very long at a time had she forgotten how the sweet-talking cousin had planned the Mardi Gras party in such a way as to force the introduction of her Spanish neighbor when Leander had vowed never to meet him socially. How could one so pretty and innocent-appearing as Felicity be so devious on the inside?

Cara met the cousins at the bottom of the stairs, saying, "I was just comin' up to get you. Don Salvador is waiting in the living room." She sent inquisitive eyes toward her mistress, hoping that her actions weren't going to result in a dressing down. The frequent outbursts against Spaniards weren't easy to forget.

"Thank you" was all that Leander said. A closer look at the familiar black face made her call Cara back before she went on down the hallway. "What happened to your cheek, Cara? I don't recall seeing that bruise there when you dressed my hair this morning."

All day the slave had worked to avoid close inspection from Leander. She sighed and said, "I stumbled comin' down the stairs with a tray while you were in the study."

Self-consciously she brought a hand up to hide the deep bruise on her cheekbone. "It's not bad, missy." Again she turned to retreat.

"You would tell me if someone struck you, wouldn't you?" Leander asked, catching Cara's arm. When the young woman refused to lift her eyes, she went on. "If Tower and you are quarreling, that's one thing. But if he's hitting—"

"Why would you think Tower might slap me?" Cara asked, puzzled. The image of the adoring slave in

384

charge of the stables came to mind, lending her strength and courage. She glanced up and down the hallway, going on when she saw no one, "What have you heard about Tower and me?" What did Leander know about what went on between certain people on the plantation? Jabbo might be learning more than was good for him and sharing it too readily with their mistress. She swallowed at the brassy taste in her mouth.

"I know that he wants to ask for you. And now I'm wondering if perhaps he's slapping you around and that you don't care to take him as husband." Leander did her best to read the obviously deep emotion showing in the brown eyes now meeting her concerned gaze. Was it resentment at being forced to submit to such questioning? Or was it fear?

Cara affected a nonchalant smile and replied in reassuring tones, "I can promise you that Tower never slaps me, missy, and that he never will. I got this fat cheek from a fall. We don't have everything worked out yet for talking to you about marriage. He'll be coming to you when I give him the right answer. Mama told me you ordered coffee today. Shouldn't I go get her to fetch the tray now?"

Leander nodded and watched the slave go toward the kitchen. She turned back to a wide-eyed Felicity and asked, "Do you believe she was telling the truth?"

"I think so. Surely she would have wanted you to know if someone were beating her so that you could have the culprit punished."

"That does seem logical, doesn't it?" Leander remarked. She was probably imagining things, she assured herself.

For the time being, she brushed aside what must be no more serious than Cara had told and walked with Felicity toward the living room. Dipping into the hidden reserve of hate with a generous swab, Leander smeared it over the chambers of her heart. She was armed for battle. A Spaniard waited just beyond those closed doors.

Chapter Eighteen

Justin Salvador prowled from window to window in the living room at Beaux Rives that March afternoon while awaiting the arrival of Leander . . . and Felicity, of course. Would his beloved show up? Or would she disappear as she had yesterday and leave him to the mercies of the young widow?

Turning at the sound of feminine voices and the scrape of a doorknob, Justin smiled to see that his prayers had not been in vain. Quiet greetings and exchanges among the three might have been those found in any of the great houses up and down the river. Except for a veiling of eyes, Leander appeared the polite hostess. By the time Sheeva brought in a tray with coffee and tiny slivers of a golden cake arranged in spokelike fashion upon a crystal plate, the trio had found a topic of conversation pleasing to all.

"Horses can bring income as regularly as field crops, if the stables produce fine animals," Justin said, leaning back against the sofa and sipping at coffee black and hot. He had been quick to praise Leander for her choice of beverage. Not that he despised tea, not when he could be drinking it with her, but he preferred the stronger, more fragrant brew.

"I take it yours do," Leander responded. She glanced down at the skirts of blue taffeta spread around her on the sofa opposite where Justin and Felicity sat. A flare of ruching at the edge of her bell-like sleeve seemed crushed and she plucked at it to stall meeting the penetrating black eyes.

"Philip and Andre said more than once that the Salvador stables would, in time, improve the quality of all the horses in Louisiana," Felicity added. "I heard them say that last year's foals were sired by the stallion you sold them, Justin, and that they were the finest they had produced."

Felicity had spent the first portion of the afternoon studying the facial expressions and comments of her companions. Sometimes a half-guarded look upon the face of one or the other led her to suspect there was a definite attraction between them. At others, their strained words seemed those of antagonists with ancient grudges. When she caught Justin sneaking longer looks at Leander as she played the role of caring hostess and served more coffee, passed the plate of cake, Felicity suspected that far more than admiration for a beautiful young woman put that steady gleam in the black eyes.

Justin expounded with equal modesty and pride on the quality of the horses on his plantation, even recounting some of the experiences from his days as a youth on his father's horse ranch back in Spain. That Leander seemed interested in what he was telling gave him all kinds of hope that his persistent courtship was winning her over.

Leander listened to the deep voice with its unique resonance, noting that the French rolled with finer accent than upon their earlier meetings. Had her ridicule of his French led him to seek a tutor? She dismissed the idea as quickly as it formed. It was unlikely that he found himself lacking in any area.

Upon entering the living room, Leander had taken in Justin's stylish attire with grudging approval, telling herself it was all right to admit that Justin was the most handsome man she had ever seen. Handsome could also apply to animals, she assured herself while covertly taking in his appearance, so why not to a Spaniard? The usual white cravat was edged with blue hemstitching, the exact shade of his waistcoat. Did he always wear white because it accentuated the olive skin? Black pants, tight as was the fashion, disappeared into tall leather boots, a departure from the more common knee-breeches above white silk hose and low-quartered shoes. An unusual vest of a darker blue and embroidered with black and silver crosses seemed to define his garments as one whole. She wondered if the designs on the silver buttons of the vest might be reproductions of a family crest. And then she realized she was staring at the manly chest as it rose and fell in quiet rhythm, was eyeing the broadness of the shoulders rather than the cut of the waistcoat, was admiring the olive-skinned hands rather than the way the hemstitched ruffle fell from beneath the coat sleeves. With a noisy clatter that surprised her, she replaced her cup and saucer on the tray before her. She drew in a breath of control, kept her eyes fixed upon a crumb of cake near the edge of the plate. Her hands still trembled when she clasped them and laid them on her lap, but her brain was once more in charge.

"We saw one of your studs while riding this afternoon," Felicity was saying, not missing the way Leander had become more and more interested in Justin's talk of horses. "Leander and I both agreed he is breathtakingly handsome."

Justin nodded and said, "That must have been Rio Sepe, my alternate. He's pasturing next to Beaux Rives for the time being, as Petra, my stablemaster and overseer, convinced me to bring in a younger stallion to serve second spot this year."

"Yes, he is magnificent," Leander said, enthusiasm undisguised. Since that first time Jabbo and she had admired the animal across the fence, she had wished more than once that she could afford such an addition to her stables. With sudden inspiration, she added, "If you're not running Rio Sepe with the mares, would you be interested in selling him?"

"Are you saying you might like to buy him?" Justin countered. He took in the cool gaze of a young businesswoman, a new guise for his beloved. Did anything faze her? At her nod, he said, "Jabbo and I talked about your horses when we visited at Belle Terre. I haven't seen the mares but he seems to think you have the beginnings of a fine herd here. Actually, I don't wish to sell Rio Sepe, but we might be able to work out some kind of arrangement."

"I doubt that," Leander shot back, her back stiffening in a way that lifted her full breasts to a more arresting tilt. She wanted no favors from the arrogant man. She probably should have never let on that she even admired the stallion. "I would be interested in a business arrangement only — such as an out-and-out sale."

A part of Leander's mind told her that she had no money to be spending on studs, that she was lucky he had refused to discuss a sale. The gold she had stolen from the Spaniard back in Throw-away's room may have tripled at the dice game, but she had used over half of that sum to buy lodging, food, and clothing for Jabbo and her in Natchez. The remainder lay hidden at the bottom of her trunk upstairs in her bedroom. She would need it to make her trek to New Orleans in the fall.

Felicity saw with increasing puzzlement that the two were fencing with looks defying description. She sought to change the subject.

"Justin," Felicity said, "I haven't asked how the construction of your house is coming along. I was so impressed with it when Andre and I returned from our honeymoon in New Orleans. From the river, it looks like a jewel atop that little rise. Andre told me how you built up the land before you began building. When do you expect to have it finished?"

Leander shifted interest from Felicity back to the black-haired Justin. The news that he was building a new home at Terre Platte shocked her. Her curiosity rose and, despite her resolve to ignore him for the remainder of the afternoon, she found herself following his reply with interest.

Justin smiled at the blonde sitting beside him on the sofa and said, "I wish I knew when the house will be ready for me to move in, but work has slowed considerably now that Pierre is trying to complete the interior." When he viewed a little frown of perplexity on Felicity's face, he went on. "Pierre Lemange is the architect who designed the house. To my great relief, he also signed on as builder and has stayed with me over the past two years of construction. He works on site with the slaves and varied craftsmen brought up from New Orleans. I joke with him that I think he has fallen in love with my horses and woods so much that he isn't trying to get through with the work." By the time he finished talking, he was including his obviously interested hostess across the low table.

"We would love to ride down and see it," Felicity replied, darting a look toward Leander that begged her to continue to be a polite hostess. "Wouldn't we, Leander?"

"I can't think of anything I would like better," Justin said with barely a sidewise glance at the young widow at his side. The black-haired beauty across from him fascinated him more with each passing moment. In his mind's eye, he was already seeing her inside his new home, presiding over trays of afternoon refreshments, filling his eyes and heart with her loveliness. "My only apology will be for the interior."

Avoiding giving an answer to Felicity's question and without thinking to hold back her thoughts, Leander asked, "Why would you apologize for the interior?"

Justin almost showed his hand by letting a gloating smile surface. She wasn't as disinterested as she would have him believe. An idea struggled for recognition.

By the hardest, he kept a passive face while answering. "Neither Pierre nor I have the ability to carry out the proper artistry for the inside that we both feel the outward lines call for. There is a man available in New Orleans, but he's booked until the end of the year. The place calls for the elegance of detail found in other planters' houses along the Mississippi." The generous mouth pursed in apparent deep thought.

"What you need is a wife to guide you," Felicity teased, reaching for a wedge of cake and nibbling at it. From behind lowered lashes, she watched Justin watch Leander—and Leander shift her eyes from his.

"You're right," Justin said after a noticeable silence. "I suppose I should wait until I find the right one, but over the past few weeks, I find I'm eager to get the house completed." The half-formed idea clicked. With a new timbre in the dark voice, he continued. "Leander, I suspect you would know how to create the grandeur I have in mind. From what I've heard, the original Beaux Rives was the finest of the mansions in the area." He deferred to Felicity's fine home at Belle Terre by saying, "Not that your own is not grand; it's just that I've heard the other was far larger and more ornately detailed."

"Indeed it was," Felicity responded, a remembering smile easing away some of the sadness in the blue eyes. "Aunt Violette had the most exquisite taste. I've always thought Leander inherited her artistic talents from her mother. Unfortunately, her brother—my father—didn't pass on such a blessing to me. I'm assuming that Andre's first wife was less attuned to such aspects of making a home."

Glad to see that he hadn't offended, and even happier to learn that Leander must possess artistic tendencies, Justin went back to addressing her. "Growing up in Beaux Rives and then having attended such a fine school in Mobile, you must be familiar with the details of the finishing arts and the decorating to follow.

Mayhap Felicity and you can join me tomorrow and tour the house. You might come up with some ideas about how you would have the place look."

"I doubt we will be able to come down tomorrow," she demurred, blood rushing to her cheeks as she read the unspoken messages in those black eyes. The conceited ass! He was blatantly reminding her that he had asked her to be his wife, mistress of the new house — the one who might like to see to its finishing touches. What must Felicity be thinking? She avoided looking at her cousin. No telling what she might be reading into Leander's startled face. "I'm going to be very busy overseeing the preparation of fields. Felicity might get Jabbo to escort her down, though."

"No," Felicity was quick to say. "I don't want to be out calling alone so soon after Andre's death. He talked of the difference in our ages soon after our marriage, pointing out that I would undoubtedly outlive him. You both knew of his thoughtfulness about family. He insisted that when I was left alone, he wouldn't want me to hide from the world." Genuine sorrow knitted the pale eyebrows, shadowed the blue eyes for a moment before she went on in a lighter vein. "But I'm already defying convention by coming to visit Leander so soon. I am dying to see the house, though. It would be such a nice diversion." She pulled a dramatic, sad face and sipped at the last of her coffee. "Of course if you prefer to ride herd on your overseer rather than lend me comfort . . ." Letting her words fade upon a whisper, she pretended great interest in the empty cup.

"Surely after all these years, Felix Grinot is capable of seeing that the field hands clean out the fence rows and get the soil turned over." Justin made no bones about his belief that Leander had lied. "And the invitation is for mid-afternoon, not for the entire day. Won't you reconsider and reward Felicity . . . and me by saying you'll come?"

Leander fidgeted on the sofa under the questioning gazes of blue eyes and black. She heard the little clinks of pewter against porcelain as Felicity refilled the three cups sitting on the tray between the two sofas, heard Justin's quiet "Thank you," heard the tiny scrape as one of them lifted cup from saucer and carried it to mouth. A questing forefinger found a curl to fondle on her shoulder for a moment or two. The tucks and rosettes on her petticoat drew her attention. Again she fluffed at the blue taffeta sleeves. From behind lowered lashes, she could see them pretending interest in coffee. If she refused to accompany her cousin to Terre Platte, Felicity was going to enjoy hurling accusations again that she feared being around the Spaniard. Deep down, she confessed that she was curious as to what kind of house Justin had built. No doubt it was a horrible example of Spanish architecture and would offer her a chance to belittle his culture, carve him down to size, so to speak. She might even get a chance to get him in private and tell him again that she had no intentions of allowing him to continue calling at Beaux Rives. She didn't want him to be getting ideas that her courtesy to him today had anything to do with a changed attitude about his preposterous proposal of marriage.

"All right," Leander said, reaching for her own cup. "I'll make tentative plans to ride down tomorrow with you, Felicity." Purple eyes signaled to blue: "You won . . . this time." Then fixing Justin with a shrewd look, she asked, "What if I were to see ways you might make the inside attractive? Could you be sure your future wife would approve? How would you explain that a neighbor planter made such suggestions? Or would you perhaps tell her that you hired someone to perform such a personal service?" The look of surprise on the handsome face pleased her, almost brought a smile of glee. Now she had him on the defensive.

Glancing at Felicity before answering and wishing for the hundredth time that, as pleasant as she was, she weren't present, Justin said, "I am sure my future wife will love anything you might suggest." Black eyes twinkled a stronger message. She was taking advantage of Felicity's presence, and he had to admire her for it. Seeing the smug look on the beautiful face, he threw out a challenge of his own. "In fact, if you were to consider taking on the task of planning interior details, we might work out some exchange of services."

"How could that be possible?" What was he up to?

"I have something you want."

"I can't imagine what it would be." She felt a rush of blood to her cheeks. His gaze was devouring her.

Justin paused before he answered. "Rio Sepe."

"Your stallion? Yes, I suppose you do have something I want, after all." How foolish of her to have suspected that he was making reference to their love-making, to her unabandoned responses to his body. She felt warm all over.

"I was sure that I did." He suspected that her mind had rushed back to that night in the lodge, just as his was doing. The wide mouth tilted upward even further.

"Sometimes it doesn't pay to be too sure of anything."

"I'm learning that . . . the hard way."

"I'll bet you don't learn much any other way." Sliding a glance toward Felicity, Leander wondered if she were as blind to the double meanings of the conversation as she pretended. An open look of curiosity wreathed the pretty face, but the blonde made no effort to join the lively repartee.

"Point well made, but then you always seem able to get right to the heart of a matter."

Leander ignored the jibe and countered, "I thought you said Rio Sepe wasn't for sale."

"He isn't."

"Then what do you have in mind?" The second the words slipped out, Leander regretted them and lowered her lashes. She shouldn't have baited him in front of anyone, much less Felicity.

A huge smile lighted Justin's face. The sooty fringes of her thick eyelashes formed fascinating semicircles above pretty, rounded cheeks. His fingers itched to touch her. With daring and a slight thickness in the resonant voice, he responded, "Come tomorrow and we'll talk about it."

In the ensuing silence, Felicity jumped in with banal remarks, surer than ever that some kind of bond stretched between Leander and Justin. Strangers would have no call to converse in such highly charged manner, she mused. She could not figure out how they had managed to effect such a relationship, but she knew the sparks flying between them came from some deep-seated passion. Was it hate, as Leander had claimed?

After Justin left Beaux Rives, Leander feigned interest in working in the study and left her cousin to find her own entertainment until dark. She had no wish to give Felicity a chance to interrogate her privately about the afternoon's happenings. At mealtimes, both always observed etiquette and spoke only of pleasant trivialities. She would be safe at the evening meal and would declare fatigue afterward so as to escape to her bedroom. The ride over to Terre Platte the next afternoon would take the better part of two hours. Before that time, she could get a better hold on her feelings and be ready to fend off the nosy Felicity. Too many times during Justin's and her seemingly casual banter, Leander had caught the gleam of suspicion in the blonde's eyes.

"It seems odd that no one has ever mentioned the building of a new house at Terre Platte," Leander remarked the next afternoon when Felicity, Jabbo, and she neared the site of the original home of the former owners, Jacques and Marie Turrentine.

Leander observed the way Gabriel raced from road to underbrush and back, apparently loving a chance to explore new territory. The dim road never veered out of view of the muddy Mississippi racing southward a small distance beneath them, its sand bars deluged from spring rains and drainings farther upriver. Watching a tree uprooted from somewhere spin around out in the wide river and disappear in one of the countless suckpools in midstream, Leander recalled the numerous times she had observed the river's treacherous main current from the safety of Dom's houseboat in the backwaters. A sigh for those peaceful years aboard *The Lady* escaped. How well she remembered that the Mississippi flexed its awesome muscles with greater force in the springtime. Each year when she saw the debris-filled water rise and stretch against its lower, western banks bordering Louisiana, an even dimmer memory from earlier childhood reminded her of a flood from both the Mississippi and the bayous running across Beaux Rives. More than once, she had overheard her father and other planters talk of the need to build up their lower side of the river permanently for future protection against such floods. Across the way she eyed the strangely soaring banks on the opposite side, their bluffs reminding her of English Landing and Natchez.

"How could anyone mention your neighbor's new house when you forbade anyone to speak of him?" Felicity asked, reining her horse around a patch of briars claiming space along the road. The planters in the area seldom used it as a main route of travel, except in times of treacherous currents in the river, as now. Small boats could not maneuver safely under such conditions. Only large ships dared traverse the Mississippi when the river rose to such heights. "I think you'll be quite surprised when you see it."

Jabbo followed at a discreet distance, half-listening to the cousins talk at intervals, half-musing about his mistress. Her announcement in the morning that the trio would be riding down to Terre Platte after the noonday meal had surprised him. How had Justin managed to lure Leander to his place? The giant black had made plans right away to do a lot of looking and listening once they arrived.

"Nothing that man can do will surprise me," Leander shot back, deliberately urging Bagatelle up ahead so as to escape further talk. Sleep had eluded her far into the morning hours, yet she felt strangely exhilarated. No doubt it was her love of riding and drinking in the scenery, she told herself. And she did enjoy seeing Gabriel having such a grand time.

With a gloved hand, Leander brushed at the fringe of wispy curls ever-present about her face and turned her attention from troubling memories, her companions, and the threatening river below on her left. Large trees were sparse in the woods on the right side of the road where the frisky dog kept wandering. A few soaring, moss-draped swamp oaks and blackgums, plus numerous smaller locusts, cottonwoods, and black willows beneath the high-branching big trees gave the impression of more density than existed. What gave the illusion of a big forest were the multiple vines and bushes already bursting from the rich, black soil and filling in the spaces beneath the budding trees with more shapes and shades of green than Leander could sort. She glimpsed some white blooms peeking above the greening ground growth and wondered if they might not be from parsley hawthorne trees. Already she had spotted and sniffed at the fragrance from pale fragrant blossoms on swamp honeysuckle, their parent vines twining rampantly up small and large trees alike. A slow, drinking-in breath rewarded her with the lovely smells she always associated with those earliest years spent in the wooded areas around Beaux Rives. Surely that couldn't be a hint of sweet bay so early in March, she reflected when a hint of a heavy sweetness rewarded her nose.

All three riders paused to stare, once the first view of the new house rose ahead. Stuccoed walls of pale pink lifted majestically atop a noticeable rise beyond a stand of live oaks. Uneven beards of gray moss accentuated outstretched branches bearing their ever-present green leaves, but they failed to capture more than fleeting attention from the trio. At a loss for words, they recovered from that first shock and rode on toward Justin's new home, Gabriel bounding on ahead with bursts of barks.

The splendor of the pink, two-story house with its four chimneys of pinkish-red brick outdid its surroundings. The gentle slope running down to the road, where it leveled off enough for the crude road, then on down to the river seemed to be of perfect proportions to lend majesty to the handsome structure. With an air of dignity, it ruled all that it looked upon from the crown of the small rise. Numerous slender, unadorned columns of white edged the verandas on both floors, verandas, the visitors could see as they neared, that wrapped three sides of the enormous house. White shutters opened back from tall windows, those facing the riders winking blindly in the afternoon sunlight. Before they had done more than pause beneath a shading oak near the front steps, they saw the mammoth white door open.

"Welcome to Terre Platte," Justin said, leaving the door opened behind him and rushing down the several brick steps to greet the visitors. Gabriel had already claimed first attention and now trotted beside the Spaniard. Justin felt no need to use one of the white wrought-iron railings for safety or support. His feet seemed not in contact with anything. The vision of his beloved in the purple velvet riding costume jolted his every sense. The matching hat and saucy feather atop black curls gave Leander such a regal air that Justin felt he might be in the presence of royalty.

Neither Leander nor Justin knew how it was that the visitors came to be greeted further and ushered down from their horses, guided up to the veranda, then on inside the house. But all of those things did take place, and obviously in fairly normal manner, for neither Felicity nor Jabbo found anything extraordinary about the activities. From somewhere slaves had appeared to usher Jabbo, the horses, and Gabriel out back to the stables while their master applied himself to a rarity at Belle Terre—lady visitors.

Leander hadn't expected that seeing Justin in his own surroundings would jolt her as it did. Was it the grandeur of his home? Or was it the obvious happiness jumping in those black eyes that attacked secret parts of her in a disarming way? Adjusting her hat with a shaky hand, she decided it must be the former. After all, the mansion was even grander than the original Beaux Rives, grander than any home she had ever seen. On the outside, that is. When he guided the callers through the interior, it became clear that what he had bemoaned on the previous afternoon was true. The inside had yet to be turned into a work of beauty to equal the imposing pink-stuccoed facade with its white shutters and white wrought-iron railings on the upper veranda.

"What do you think?" Justin asked while Felicity wandered off into a far room.

"About your house?" Leander replied, wondering why he needed more praise than Felicity and she had heaped on him upon arrival. It annoyed her that she had found she could not find one aspect of the house to complain about. Realizing that she held a losing hand, she had concealed and voiced sincere appreciation for his home.

"No," he answered with a touch of exasperation. "What do you think about taking on the job of working with Pierre on the interior?"

"I doubt I can help much," she said, letting her eyes take in the staircase that landed in the great hall running down the length of the house. Never before had she seen one that flared out at the base. Or one with ornate wrought-iron railings. The use of so much wrought iron must be a Spanish touch, she thought. And very effective. Was that a scrolled "S" in the design? "I've had no experience."

"Neither have I, but I know what I like when I see it. I know I'll like what you choose to do." He sent black eyes to survey the bare rooms they could see from where they stood near the front door. "The room to our right will be the ballroom." He loved the way the black curls danced when she turned her head to look where he indicated. "See how the staircase leads one to walk straight into it?" Leander's gaze followed his gesturing hand, and she nodded. In an intimate tone, he said, "Down that very staircase is where you'll come to me as my bride."

"Have you gone mad?" Leander hissed, darting a look over her shoulder to make sure Felicity was not around. They stood now in the shadows of the staircase soaring to a banistered landing running across the top. "You're a fool to make such preposterous remarks to me. I've told you that I have no interest in marrying you, Justin Salvador." Purple eyes blazed with indignation.

"You won't need any," he replied with a pose of sureness and a look of open appreciation for her velvet-clad body. "I have enough interest for both of us." He touched her arm and felt a shock tear up the length of his own.

"Our paths should have never crossed. We have nothing in common, and even if we did, I would never consider marrying a Spaniard. If you don't already know that, you do now." She recoiled at the feel of the hand on her arm, a bit surprised that he didn't loosen his fiery grip.

"Our paths were destined to cross and then stay together, Leander. You knew it that night at the lodge, just as I did."

"I knew nothing of the kind," she denied, not wanting to recall that first meeting. Tumult reigned inside. "I say that our paths should forever have been parallel—and shall be from now on."

"Think about how parallel lines seen in a distance, like fences or paths, always come together on the horizon." He could see the dawning of what he was saying in the half-veiled eyes and smiled. "That's the way our lives were meant to be. Merging into one upon meeting at the right time."

"You have a strange sense of what is meant by the 'right time,' " she huffed, trying again to move away but with the same lack of success as earlier. "Take your hands off me," she muttered with a note of threat.

"Or you'll scream?" he teased there in the half-light beside the staircase, daring to move the free hand to capture the other purple velvet arm. Before she could believe he would dare such bold action, Justin pulled her hard against him and kissed the protesting mouth.

Leander felt that she had been tossed into a blazing fire. Patches of heat stabbed at her all over. Only his pinioning of her arms kept her from shoving him away. How dare him to force himself on her? With surprisingly little heart for ending the searing kiss but determined that he not know how it shocked and affected her, she struggled to free her mouth from his. She panicked that he held such control over her, though it was only physically, she told herself in a rush. Damn him! What if Felicity came back out into the hall? With the same quickness he had shown when he had grabbed and kissed her, Leander set sharp teeth into Justin's bottom lip.

"Why did you do that?" Justin released her as readily as he had seized her. Though the kiss had thrilled him, he was angry now. Black eyes shot sparks as he brought a testing finger to his swelling lower lip. No young woman had ever before repulsed him with such vehemence, and his pride rankled. Some inner voice reminded him that some such rejection from the violet-eyed beauty of his dreams seemed to have taken place. Without thinking, he brought a finger up to the slight scar barely visible above the right eyebrow. But the wound had been real, the reasonable part of his mind told him. Why would he be connecting it with the ethereal vision in his dreams? She had not existed until he met Leander in the hunting lodge. An eerie feeling of having experienced violent rejection from Leander at a previous time washed over him, shadowed the fuzzy images coming from those early dreams. His brain whirled. Only Felicity's call and sudden appearance at the end of the hall kept him from studying with more intense scrutiny the eyes blazing up at him with purple fury.

"Justin," Felicity was saying while approaching the

couple near the staircase, "I love everything I've seen. I believe that Leander's touch would give the house the elegance needed inside." Wondering at the whiteness of her cousin's face, she remarked, "I hope you've told him you'll help him out, Leander."

"As a matter of fact," Justin replied, an innocent-looking smile on his face, "she agreed just a few minutes ago." The look he sent Leander dared her to disagree. "Though I suspect her wish to have Rio Sepe running with her mares had far more to do with the decision than any desire to be helpful to me." When she seemed about to spout the denial her eyes signaled, he added, "Don't be concerned, Leander. I won't divulge to Felicity or anyone the terms of our agreement. After all, this is a business deal between two neighbors. I have the same love of privacy that you seem to have." The threat in his voice waved as boldly as a red flag.

Leander stared in disbelief, paying little attention to what Felicity was telling about a room she had seen upstairs. Was Justin daring her to refute what he was making up so that he could reveal their secret? She gathered from the narrowing of the black eyes and the firm look about his mouth that he would do almost anything to force her to agree with the ridiculous lie. The anger and puzzlement claiming his face after she had bitten him had shown her a side of him she hadn't suspected existed. All of a sudden, she saw him as someone formidable if motivated—and why not? After all, he was a Spaniard, and didn't they have the reputation for fiery tempers? If she were to anger him further by calling him a liar right then, he might delight in telling Felicity all about their having met at the hunting lodge. She cringed at the degrading thought.

Leander was sure that she could see deviousness lurking in those black depths, even as Justin pretended interest in what Felicity was saying. While a forefinger lost itself in a curl, a reasonable side of her appealed to the side longing to tell him off at any cost. Didn't she want Rio Sepe at Beaux Rives more than she wanted to call Justin's hand? After his offer of the previous afternoon, she had mulled over the way the blooded stallion's services could improve her own herd and lead to greater profits. In spite of herself, the artistic part of her had begun making mental notes of ways to create a place of grandeur and beauty from the moment she had stepped inside the unfinished house. Such an arrangement as he had suggested could lead to more security for her beloved Beaux Rives in a much shorter time. Nothing was more important than Beaux Rives. And for a despicable Spaniard to be the means of helping her achieve her goal to restore it to its former state seemed a blow for justice.

"Justin, I couldn't have stated our arrangement better myself," Leander said, when Felicity ended her recital. She preened to see the surprised look upon his face. He had thought he held all the cards, she exulted. "So long as each of us respects the privacy of the other, we should have no problems working out this business deal. That is, if we both understand what we mean by privacy."

"I'm sure we do," he remarked. He hadn't known what she might say but he hadn't expected her to seem so cocksure of herself when she was forced to give in. That she obviously believed he would tell about that night in the lodge bothered him, and yet that was what he had wanted her to believe so as to bend her to his will. What had been going on behind that beautiful face? He had a strange feeling that he was no longer the one who was winning.

"Do I have your word that ours will be a business relationship only?"

"You do," he answered, admitting that he might be lying but gambling that the ends would justify the means.

"How soon can you turn Rio Sepe over to Tower at my stables?" She didn't really trust him, but she figured she could handle him if the need to do so arose. He wouldn't forget any time soon the way she had bitten him.

"How soon can you begin making plans for the interiors?" The hint of arrogance intrigued him.

"I asked first." Let him see she was not intimidated.

"So you did." Justin took in the coolly poised young woman before him, admiring the way she had refused to be baited but puzzled at what gave that triumphant look to her face. The main thing was that she would be coming to Terre Platte frequently. Anticipation had erased the earlier anger over her biting him the moment he had come up with the plan to tell Felicity the lie. "Is tomorrow too soon?"

"The minute Rio Sepe is turned over to Tower, I'll ride for Terre Platte with sketch pad in hand."

Neither heard Felicity's little sigh of relief or noticed that she wandered toward the front veranda where Ona was setting up a tray of refreshments on a table formed by a plank that Jabbo was angling across sawhorses. The two slaves carried on a low conversation in tones suggesting they might be finding they had a lot in common.

In the lengthening March shadows inside the empty house, Leander and Justin were too busy measuring each other by new standards to notice what went on in any other part of the world. Without the need for words, both knew that the game to be played over the next few months required different rules.

Chapter Nineteen

"Philip Ferrand, I don't need your permission to work on Justin's house," Leander was saying pointedly to her childhood friend a month after Justin and she had made the business agreement that afternoon at Terre Platte. "Ever since you came that week to escort Felicity home and learned what I was doing, you've tried to play the role of boss." She sliced disapproving looks toward the curly-haired young man to add dimension to her haughty tone. He might be devilishly good-looking and fun to be with, but she had heard enough of his scolding about how it must look for her to be over at Terre Platte almost every day for the past several weeks. "As for what people might say, I could care less. Some days I work on sketches and plans at home. Right now we're waiting to hear about orders from suppliers in New Orleans. When I have to ride over, Jabbo escorts me. And if he's needed about the place and returns early, Justin rides home with me. Whether you believe it or not, ours is no more than a business arrangement. I can never forget he's a Spaniard."

The two were sitting at a table beneath the curving arms of a water oak near the kitchen behind Beaux Rives. Philip's gray eyes deepened with emotion as he watched Leander pick and choose from among a huge pile of wildflowers. They had just returned from an afternoon's ride in the forests behind the pastures. Until he had brought up Justin's name, they had been having a pleasant time.

"You should care that people might talk," Philip remarked, feeling far older than Leander, though he could claim only five years on her. Aware of her increased loathing for anything Spanish, he entertained no jealousy of the handsome Justin. "You'll be expecting to marry some day, and gossip can—"

"Fiddle-faddle!" she spouted with disgust. "I'm a long ways from marrying."

In fact, Leander had become so adamantly against listening to Justin's references to her becoming his wife when the house was completed that he had made less mention of the preposterous idea over the past week. There were times that she thought him insane to keep repeating himself when she never gave him the slightest encouragement. At least, she mused there in the shade, he hadn't tried to kiss her again after that time she had bitten him. Touch her arm or hands, maybe, when the action was so sly as to escape the notice of Pierre or the workmen, but no attempt to kiss. In fact, Justin had become almost personable—and it bothered her to be finding him such an interesting person to be around.

"You don't have to be a long ways from marrying." Philip's teeth flashed white there in the shade as his

411

attractive, heart-shaped mouth spread into a wide, teasing smile. His eyes raced over the face of his companion as she pursed lips and cocked her head while trying to decide which flowers to stick first in the tall urn on the table. Ever since she had brought comfort upon the death of his father, he had felt drawn more and more to call upon Leander and seek out her cheerful companionship.

Eyes narrowing to size up the effect of tall stems topped by purple blooms, Leander put them into the urn and stepped back to observe. Wildflowers always brought a special happiness. Her mother had taught her the names of most of those growing near the house on the numerous treks they had made through the woods. The very first time Violette had showed the eager little girl how to draw, she had used wildflowers as models. Leander could look upon very few that didn't bring up wonderful memories. She put out a finger to trace the feathery purple petals of the tall lead plants.

"Why would you say that? I'm not dying to have a husband," she finally replied to Philip's rather vague comment.

"That's what Antoine told me before he took off for New Orleans." He leaned back against the chair to enjoy the pretty picture Leander made with the wildflowers.

"Oh," Leander said in what she hoped was a casual tone, "you know how that older brother of yours likes to run his mouth and pretend he knows everything." That Antoine had come to Beaux Rives twice to tell her he was going to the capital to seek a position as a lawyer and to beg her to marry him and go along had angered her more than it flattered. Upon the second proposal, she had told him she had no money and that he was wasting his time trying to pretend to court her for any other reason. The way he had continued to try to kiss and fondle her aggravated her, led finally to her ordering him not to return without an invitation. Intent upon building the bouquet to please the artist in her, she continued to insert different flowers and then exchange them for others. "By the by, how is Antoine doing in New Orleans?"

"He wrote that he has a position in the Cabildo as assistant to a judge. And from his comments, I gather he is already on the party circuit, courtesy of Miss Maralys Soulier." Philip had lost his jealousy of the older brother when Antoine let it slip during a drinking binge that Leander had snubbed his suit. "She's the youngest daughter of one of New Orleans' wealthiest merchants. I expect she leads him in a lively dance."

Leander let out a tinkling laugh, remembering the way Maralys had clung to the lean, darkly handsome Antoine at the Mardi Gras ball. "Maybe she'll be the one to settle him down," she said when her eyes met the laughing gray ones across from her in mutual amusement. It was highly unlikely that anyone would ever settle Antoine Ferrand down, their exchanged looks seemed to say.

"Who is the one to settle you down, dear one?" Philip asked with a deeper, darker timbre to his voice.

The thought of being near Leander for the rest of his life suited Philip in all the ways he deemed commendable — she was beautiful to look upon, delightful as a companion, talented in many ways, and far smarter than any woman, young or old, he had ever been around for any length of time. A stirring in his loins reminded him of another way she appealed to him, a way which taunted the young, restless part of him at night when he lay awake thinking of her. He had known women in New Orleans, yet he realized that the way he felt about Leander was more than lust. With a satisfied smile, he recalled how she hadn't protested over the past few weeks when he began taking liberties to hold her hand, curve an arm around her waist as they walked in the woods, or buss her cheek upon arriving or leaving. The thought of holding that delectable body in his arms, of pressing his mouth fully upon hers, brought a veritable storm all throughout his body. Unlike Antoine, he placed no value on dowry. Strong and able, Philip had confidence he could manage Belle Terre without a purse from a bride.

Leander went ahead with her separation of the wildflowers, very aware of the appraising looks Philip was sending her way. Sensing something of his thoughts without knowing how she did so, Leander sent the handsome — no, "pretty" was a better word, she thought with affection — young man a look from beneath silky lashes not much thicker or curlier than his. How would it feel to be in his arms, those muscular arms that always seemed so eager to lift her to saddle, then to catch her when she dismounted? Just that afternoon when they returned from their jaunt in the woods, Philip had held her against his lithe frame far longer than was necessary. She hadn't protested, had actually felt a rush of feeling from his nearness. Was she beginning to care for him in the same way he seemed to be caring for her? The thought of his kissing her brought a flush to her cheeks. From beneath that attractive mop of curly brown hair, the gray eyes flirted there in the shade. The violet ones did not return the same messages, but neither did they shy away.

"Why would I want to be settled down by anyone?" Leander teased, a note of laughter in her voice. She had no real wish for him to continue. "I probably would hate it."

"I would like the job of trying," Philip replied, soberness adding a look of maturity to his boyish good looks. When Leander pretended not to have interpreted his meaning, he went on, his voice tender and husky, "I'm asking you to marry me, Leander. I think I must have always loved you, even when we were children. Coming to see you several times a week keeps me sane—or mayhap I should say insane." He tried to end in a joking manner but knew he failed. "Serious" might as well have been written all over him.

All of a sudden, Leander found it necessary to become concerned with the way the stalks and blooms in the urn looked and return her attention to them. Inside her heart quavered. The young man watching her was no pretty-faced companion from childhood days as she would have liked to tell herself; he was a virile, handsome French Creole asking for her hand. And from the way he had held her against him that afternoon, she knew that he desired her in the way a young woman longs to be desired. Was she ready to hear such a question from Philip—or anyone? That she had heard it so often during those first weeks while at Terre Platte didn't keep it from sounding new when it came from someone other than the arrogant Spaniard.

"Philip," Leander began, not sure how she could tell him that she wasn't ready to consider his proposal. She squared her shoulders, then glanced toward the back door. Was that the deep voice she heard almost daily coming from inside the house behind them, the voice which too often haunted her dreams but to which she denied a place in her conscious mind? Her finely shaped head lifted on the slender neck like that of a wizened doe scenting danger.

"Missy, here's someone to see you," came Sheeva's soft voice from the back door. "I told him Mr. Philip and you was out back."

"Thank you, Sheeva" came the familiar voice Leander suspected she had heard. Following the sturdy form, Justin came out onto the whistle walk then. His feet making taps upon the bricked surface and his heart rushing upon seeing the sight before him, he smiled. Beneath spreading oak limbs, Leander stood beside a table covered with a mound of colorful flowers, her face glowing as she went about separating stems and colors and arranging them in a large porcelain urn. That Philip Ferrand sat across from her with indolent ease and the air of one belonging there made little impression on the besotted Justin. He had long known that the two had grown up together and enjoyed each other's company.

"Leander, Philip," Justin called when the pair acknowledged his approach by lifting eyes and putting on smiles. Quiet greetings out of the way, he settled his gaze on the object of his affections. Was that a spark of some new nervousness in those purple orbs? He wouldn't let himself believe his appearance caused it. Not yet would her face pinken for him as it was doing. But soon . . . "Sheeva tells me you two have been on a lark."

"We have," remarked Leander, accepting his unexpected appearance in a way she would have sworn only a month ago that she never could. Even when she was being her most unreasonable, she had to admit that she had come to look upon him as more than the ordinary Spaniard. Not much more, she assured that inner rascal of hate rearing up to jeer at such a confession. She was glad to see him only because his coming kept her from having to reply to Philip's proposal. "We had the loveliest ride. Philip thought he could take me to a bank of a bayou where we would find violets, and he did. Aren't they lovely?" She reached for a small cluster of light purple flowers and held them out with one hand, her gaze drinking in their beauty, then her nose burying in their fragrance about the time Justin eased upon one of the chairs around the table. "And look," she enthused, "we found the lead plant in full bloom, already taller than I am." Aware that the handsome Justin watched her with open admiration, she picked up long stems with slender branches topped by small purple flowers running down the ends to a point. She added them to some already in the tall container.

"I don't know the names of all the flowers coming up around here, but I guess I'll have to learn," Justin remarked after a cursory glance at the younger man. More and more Philip seemed to be making himself a regular part of the scene at Beaux Rives. The coral-red blooms those graceful hands added to the bouquet gave out a sweet fragrance. He noted the cut of the summer riding costume, liking the way the lavender broadcloth followed the fine lines of her breasts and tiny waist. Over the past weeks of seeing her frequently, he had observed with appreciation that whoever had designed her wardrobe had done a superb job of setting off her beauty. Even when a smudge marred her cheeks and wisps of her coiffure curled out in defiance, as now, Leander was perfection. Silently he pleaded for her to fix those pansy-colored eyes on him. "All of them are pretty. What is that one called?"

"That's trumpet honeysuckle," Philip answered. He caught Justin's sidewise glance and sent him an amused smile. He knew that the question hadn't been directed at him. What he did know was that Leander had let him hold her hand that afternoon as they strolled about the woods, that she hadn't pushed him away when he held her overly long upon dismounting, and that she had not given him a quick "no" to his proposal. Feeling a bit smug from being a Creole and knowing such things without having to give them thought, he went on. "It grows on a vine in the trees and blooms from early spring until the first frost. Surely you must have noticed it over the past four years."

"I suppose I wasn't paying much attention to such things," Justin replied. Not until he had met Leander had he cared about much other than making a success of his horse ranch, he realized.

"And we call this swamp fetterbush," Leander said when she placed stiff stems with tiny pinkish flowers bursting from beneath each waxy leaf into the opening of the urn. She couldn't explain why Justin's interest in wildflowers pleased her so, but she knew that it did. "I asked Sheeva to serve tea this afternoon instead of coffee because Philip prefers it. Is that all right with you, Justin?" She allowed herself to look at him fully then. As she had noted when he first came from inside, he wore the usual, sparkling white shirt and cravat that set off his olive complexion, even in the deep shade of the water oak. An unbuttoned black vest over matching breeches seemed the exact hue of his hair—except for the white streak, of course. In spite of her wish that the opposite be true, she confessed that the good looks of the Spaniard outshone those considerable ones of the French Creole.

Sheeva appeared with the tray of refreshments before Justin had to reply. Leander completed the bouquet and set it in the curve of an exposed root of the oak in order to admire it while they drank tea and ate the small buttered biscuits Sheeva had brought. The three found much to discuss, what with planting season going on.

As neither caller seemed eager to be the first to leave, it was nearly dark when both rose to go at the same time. Leander's face wore a harried look as she waved them off. To see the two young men together had forced her to make comparisons—and contrasts. No matter that Justin had shown himself to be charming and gentlemanly over the past few weeks, he should not have come out so far ahead of Philip in the afternoon's unplanned ratings.

"What was the important business you wished to discuss with me, Felix?" Leander asked in the study after dinner that night. Her attempts to put off a meeting with the overseer until the morrow had failed. She leaned back against the chair behind the desk, noticing as usual that the gray-haired little man had few redeeming features.

"I see how Ferrand and Salvador keep snooping

around here, and I want you to know that as your guardian, I have a right to be told what's going on." After several stiff drinks from his jug of brew, Felix had screwed up enough courage to demand a meeting with Leander. More and more she was sending messages to him by that giant Jabbo, finding less time than at first to speak with him personally. Taking orders, even indirect ones, from a slave didn't set well. His interest in Leander's callers were keen. He had no wish for surprises. "Are you planning to marry one of them?"

"I assured you earlier that I would tell you if I made any plans about marriage," Leander informed him with open disdain for his thinking he had the right to question her about such personal matters. She tossed her curls in annoyance and gave him a haughty stare. "I have no plans to marry soon."

"Don't guess you would say if you've had proposals," Felix said, hoping she would feel friendly and tell him about her admirers. His source of information about Leander's personal life was revealing less and less. She seemed to resemble Violette more each time he saw her, and lately he had caught himself seeking convenient hiding places to keep from being seen while he gazed upon her beauty from a safe distance. Each time he was with her, though, he saw again that only the outside was like his beloved Violette; inside she was tough, single-minded. Was the clever daughter of Etienne Ondine keeping things to herself so as to prevent his learning about them? His fists knotted at the thought. Before the night was old, they would make demands in the right places. He figured all young women talked more about their suitors than he was being told Leander did, and somebody close was bound to be listening.

Leander did not deign to reply. Had she had an inkling that such meddling was behind his demand to see her tonight, she would have told him herself to go butt a brick wall. Her mind bent on the increased pace of planting, she assumed he wished to consult with her about the progress being made so as not to be held up by a talk with her on the morrow. She kept a steady gaze on the face across her desk, not liking the way a mysterious darkness seemed to weave in and out of Felix's piglike eyes as they studied her. If there were enough color to justify the term, she reflected, she could say they almost glittered. The man had the wild look of a hunted animal about his drawn face. Why this interest in her possible marriage? Surely he was aware that both Philip and Justin had been calling upon her frequently over the past weeks. Had some slave told that both had shown up at the same time that afternoon? If so, why would the news upset him?

Felix bolted from his chair and paced up and down in front of the desk, his jaws working as if he chewed upon something distasteful. Her apparent calm drove him into a frenzy. How was it she always ended up being in control whenever the two had a confrontation? Stopping just as quickly as he had begun the wild movements, he put both hands on the desk and leaned toward her, saying in an oily voice, "You see, Leander, you don't have to settle for no pup like Philip or no Spanish scoundrel like Salvador." The indifference of her stare goaded him to say more than he had intended to that night. "The only way you'll ever get even a part of Beaux Rives legally is to marry me."

Leander gasped and leaned against the back of her

chair. "You must be out of your mind!" The beady eyes held her transfixed for a frightening moment. "What makes you think I would ever consider marrying you?" She forced herself not to let the obscenities pushing at the back of her throat come out. Wild thoughts about how she had little choice but to remain his ward until she was eighteen circled in her brain. And then another joined them, one just as revolting. Or she could marry before she was eighteen and force him to show his hand, one he might could win this early in the year. "I would choose the 'pup' or even the 'scoundrel,' as you term Philip and Justin, before I would consider you." A wash of rage and humiliation erased earlier shock. She rose to stand, looking down at him regally, the Etienne-like pose making her seem taller, more imposing. "I suggest you get out of here before I yell for Jabbo to throw you out."

"You can do that," Felix admitted, his voice revealing his crumbling confidence, "but it won't help you in the end. Without my help with the officials, sooner or later, or without proof of ownership, you're going to lose out on Beaux Rives. Mind you, I know what I'm talking about, missy." What gall for that slip of a girl to defy him, the one who had overseen the running of Beaux Rives since it was founded!

Not about to reveal her knowledge of his agreement with the officials and the necessity for producing a deed that had obviously burned in a fire over six years ago, Leander replied, "I am the only child of Violette and Etienne Ondine—no other proof of ownership will be necessary, no matter who sits in power in New Orleans, no matter whom you think you know in high places." Would time run out on her before she was ready to face

Felix for an accounting? Inwardly, she prayed that she would hear soon from the cousin she had written in Bordeaux and that his news about having a second deed drawn up by the old king's grandson would be positive. Outwardly, she appeared every inch what she claimed to be, the Ondine heiress.

"Good night, Felix," Leander said with the same coldness that had pervaded her being since his "suggestion" that she marry him. She had no intention of elevating it to the status of "proposal." The man was a lunatic. "Don't ask to see me again unless your talk concerns your duties as overseer." When he made no move to leave, she put a hand on the desk and leaned forward to ask, "Did you hear me say 'good night'?"

Felix wheeled and stomped from the room, not bothering to waste another breath on the maddening young beauty. Damn her! How he would like to seize her and . . . He knew exactly where he was going and with whom to vent his fury and frustrations.

The next morning at Terre Platte, a dark-skinned young man was with Justin when Leander and Jabbo arrived. A previous agreement with Justin that he would accompany her home that day freed Jabbo to return immediately to Beaux Rives to oversee the planting of the gardens behind the slave quarters. As the two young men came toward her from the front porch, she noted that the stranger was thicker of build and not so tall as Justin. Both walked in that straight-backed way of military men, though only Justin's manner of moving seemed easy and natural. She got the impression that his companion might have gained his manly rhythm through study . . . or much practice.

"Oh," said Leander when Justin introduced his friend, "then you're the Bernardo de Galvez who so kindly sent Justin the costume for the Mardi Gras ball." Her eyes danced sidewise to enjoy Justin's discomfiture at the reminder of that evening of misery. "He has told me much about you over the past weeks and the ways you two play practical jokes on each other."

"I hope you believed only half of what he told," Bernardo replied, a finger smoothing at his heavy black mustache. "He has already told what you thought of him in that costume."

"I doubt that," she shot back with a good-natured smile. She liked the way Bernardo sized her up with appreciation, yet gave no hint of a flirtation. Mayhap he was married already or at least in love, she mused. "I haven't even told him *all* that I thought."

"Come, you two," Justin insisted, glad to see the way his beloved and his best friend took to each other so readily. "There must be better things to speak of than that asinine toga." The memory of how that evening almost lost him any further contact with Leander kept him from liking to dwell upon it. It had also led him to ask Bernardo to dress out of uniform during his brief stay. There was no need for Leander to learn all at once that his best friend was colonel of the Louisiana Regiment, second in command of all Spanish forces in the colony. Perhaps if she could first accept him as a Spaniard, and she seemed to be having no trouble succumbing to Bernardo's considerable charm, she could later accept him as Governor Unzaga's right-hand man.

Leander listened to the easy exchanges between the two young men while she went about checking the accuracy of earlier measurements and sketches. The two had obviously been friends over a long period of time, and their constant joking and telling of tall tales brought giggles and smiles to her face.

Later, when Leander was ready to return home, only Justin accompanied her.

"I figured your friend Bernardo would come along for the ride," she said once they were mounted and moving along the road.

"He came for a rest as well as a holiday," Justin replied. "I was glad he opted to take a siesta while I'm seeing you home. He was kind enough to oversee some shipments of goods I had ordered from New Orleans. We'll have them unpacked for your inspection when you return."

"How exciting," Leander responded. Sorry to have shown personal interest in his affairs, she added, "For you, I mean." They rode side by side, the woods and undergrowth on their left providing fragrant shade.

"Why not for you as well?"

"Don't be silly. I'm merely the one putting together the interior. You're the one who will be living with it."

"You always become angry when I say this," Justin said, "but you're going to live in it with me as my wife, darling."

"Don't call me that," she retorted. "And quit repeating that ridiculous lie. I am not going to marry you and you well know it."

Justin sighed, hoping that she could hear it above the sounds of saddle leather and horses' hooves. "And here I had thought we might go an entire week without a quarrel."

"If we have, it's because you've slowed down on your

425

harping about a marriage between us."

"So you've noticed, huh?" he asked on a note of surprise. "I'll bet you've missed it, haven't you?" He shot her a devilish smile, one jumping into quiet laughter when she huffed and looked away toward the river on their right.

Leander's unsettling experiences with Philip's proposal and Felix's repugnant suggestion that she marry him led her to retort, "Maybe others have made sure that I not feel I'm being left on a limb."

"What does that mean?" When she continued to give him a haughty profile and refused to answer, he asked, "Who else has proposed to you?" A grim set to the full mouth, he demanded, "Did Antoine Ferrand propose before he left for New Orleans?" No change on her countenance. Justin thought over all that Ona had reported and put it with what he had observed. "Or is it Philip who has asked you to marry him? He's more like a brother to you than a suitor. Even I can see that."

"Who says your eyes are that discerning? And anyway, this is none of your business, Justin Salvador."

Justin made no pretense of hiding the unreasonable jealousy racing through his veins and said, "I can see that I have little choice but to go ahead and present a betrothal gift. It's time everyone knows that you're to be mine."

"You are the most conceited man that I've ever known," Leander replied with unconcealed anger. Her eyes raked him without mercy. "I have never told you I will marry you and you know it. How anyone can continue to ignore what's as plain as the nose on his face is beyond me. Don't you realize that I can never marry a Spaniard—and least of all you!" She reined

Bagatelle to travel as far from his Principe as possible on the narrow road.

Justin digested her words, her tone, and her loveliness. The last was the only one making a dent. God! She was ravishingly beautiful when she was fired up that way. He wanted nothing more than to stop their horses and gather her close.

"I've heard you repeat that little speech over a dozen times, if that's what you mean," he countered after a spell of silence. "But I know what lies ahead for us, Leander, and I'm not letting some blind side of your heart keep me from seeing that we're meant for each other. You'll see it in time."

"I can promise you I won't."

And all the way back to Beaux Rives, they exchanged no more than measuring looks. For a while there, she had feared he might try to grab Bagatelle's reins, then steal a kiss, but she was wrong. The furrowed, olive brow cleared in a short while, and she relaxed. Mayhap he, too, had enjoyed their times together when he seemed content to let the matter of marriage drop and wished to have repeats of those easy talks, she mused. Already she was sorry she had let out the hint of Philip's proposal. She felt guilty, especially when she hadn't given him an answer, one way or the other. Her mind was too jumbled to make decisions about marriage to anyone—not that she had ever considered one to the Spaniard, she assured herself.

When they saw her red brick house up ahead, Leander slowed Bagatelle to say, "You don't have to come any further. Thank you for escorting me home."

"You're not to get rid of me that easily," Justin replied. "I have something I want to give you but I wanted to wait until we're inside your home."

Leander squinted a suspicious look up at him. "What is it?"

Justin ignored her and continued on ahead toward her house, knowing that she would have little choice but to follow. Not until they had dismounted and gone inside did he say more.

"I wrote Bernardo and asked him to bring me a selection of gifts," he told her after she permitted him to go with her into the living room. He tried not to care that she had been almost adamant in her refusal to invite him inside. Sometimes it was harder than at others to remember she was young and required gentling with a light touch. Ignoring her obvious gesture for him to sit across from her, he dropped down beside her on the sofa. From the packet he had brought from his saddlebag, he pulled a velvet-covered box. How could he have eyes for its contents? All he cared to see was her face when she saw what he offered. "I chose this for your betrothal gift."

Her mouth already set to dress him down for his audacity, Leander stared at the opened box held toward her. No words came for what seemed an eternity. In the distance, she could hear Gabriel hot on the trail of a swamp rabbit in the woods off to the side of the house. Earlier that week she had watched a pair of mockingbirds building a nest in the thorny locust near the veranda; they now called and twittered in domestic bliss. Down the hallway, a door banged shut with the finality of a gunshot. Had Sheeva seen them return? Was she on her way with a tray? Just outside a raised window, a dirtdauber hummed noisily as it deposited river mud from its mouth and hair-sized limbs onto a slender, tunneled nest glued to the wooden shutter.

At last the stunned mind and voice worked in harmony, and Leander said in low, awed tones, "The pearls are beautiful, but I have no intention of accepting them. Save them for your future wife."

Blood claimed Leander's cheeks, and she wondered if it came from Justin's intense scrutiny. Without conscious thought, she put her hands behind her there on the sofa, as if they might betray her and reach out for the lovely necklace. The luster of the pearls, from the largest in the center to those tapering ever smaller to the clasp of small diamonds, fascinated her, brought a faint memory of having seen her mother and her friends wear such lovely jewelry. A wild wish to remember forever the exact shade of the lustrous, pinkish glow of the necklace surfaced, helping her to put aside the compelling desire to reward aching fingers with a caressing touch of each pearl. Still held in back, her hands and fingers intertwined more tightly.

Justin let go of a deep, indrawn breath, its sound loud in the small space between them on the sofa. Lowered sooty lashes denied him a peek into the windows of her soul. He had seen the tremor upon her lips before and after she spoke but couldn't determine its cause. He had wondered if the pink washing her face and neck indicated pleasure denied. Or was it anger at his assumption that she might accept his betrothal gift? In his eagerness to glimpse a rent in the armor of misguided pride Leander wore as protection, Justin missed completely the sign he longed to see. Not once did he notice that she had sent her hands to hide behind her as soon as she saw the pearls, that she kept them there until he closed the box and returned it to his pocket.

"They'll keep," Justin muttered hoarsely, angry at himself that he had chosen the wrong time to push her to recognize his proposal as legitimate. "My timing was wrong, Leander. Are you upset with me?"

Leander lifted her eyes then, freed her hands, and tried to compose an answer. What truths lay hidden in those starred, black depths so near? Surely Justin must have faced long before now that she meant it when she kept refusing to consider marriage to him. What kept him on such a determined path? She had worked out a logical explanation of their puzzling relationship. He did not love her . . . any more than she loved him. Their coming together at the lodge had been happenstance, pure and simple. Under any other conditions, they would have had no use for each other, no time to do more than pass polite remarks and go their separate ways. The two of them could have no future together.

All that worldly-wise Josie had told Leander of physical attractions fell into slots of truth when she thought of the way Justin affected her, faced up to the fact that such must be the case with him. Even now, recognizing that her body cried out for his, she mistrusted such passionate needs as a basis for marriage. Had she not had two Spaniards rack her body with fiery caresses? Once had been enough—twice was too much. The kind of marriage she wanted would be based on love, not base desire. And no Spaniard would ever claim the daughter of Etienne Ondine as wife!

"Go home," Leander ordered in icy tones, rising and marching toward the door. "You need to recall the agreement about ours being a business relationship," she called with a glance over her shoulder. "I'm living up to my part of the bargain. Why don't you do the same?" Bending gracefully to lift the train of her riding costume, she swept out of sight.

Justin had risen when she did, but he had not taken a step. Whatever had raced through her mind just before she had escaped from the sofa seemed to have troubled her. A pang of regret for rushing his suit saddened his eyes. Her cold words of dismissal cut at his heart. The earlier hope that he had made headway with Leander sank out of sight. There was nothing left to do but return to Terre Platte.

Philip found a pensive Leander when he called a night or two later. After accepting her invitation to dine with her, he walked with her toward the river beneath a full moon. Although she had been easy to talk with, she had lacked her usual vivaciousness. He tucked her arm in his and they laughed at Gabriel's pursuit of his own shadow there on the walkway.

"Have you an answer to my proposal?" Philip asked when they reached the pier and stood looking out at the rushing river. He brought his other hand to cover hers where it fit into the crook of his elbow. Touching her soft, warm skin sent thrills all over. "Leander, I love you and want you to marry me."

Aware that he was bending his head toward hers, Leander lifted her eyes there in the moonlight to look at Philip. The tempo of night sounds seemed especially frenetic that night, and she wondered if they contributed to her rare mood of unrest. Mating season, she mused with the realism of a horse breeder. Smells of sweet bay laid a telling hand on the general fragrance of the night air, and she sniffed with appreciation. A smile for all that was gentle and promising that perfect night lighted her face and eyes while she admired the handsome face moving closer each second.

Philip's lips moved lightly against Leander's. She felt so right in his arms, he thought with exultation. When her arms came up around his neck, he pulled her closer and gave in to his desire to kiss her with abandon. Sweet. Everything about her was sweet. The taste of her lips, the smell of her hair, the feel of her softness against him. When he leaned away enough to look into the uplifted face, her beauty almost suffocated him. Eyes dark and mysterious in the moonlight reflected a moonbeam with a delicacy he had never seen. Half-parted lips glistened from his kiss, their fullness tempting him to taste again of their honey. When she made no sound, no attempt to pull away from the close embrace, Philip gave in to temptation.

Having wondered more than once what it might be like for Philip to kiss her, Leander had no reservations about his taking her into his arms. The touch of his well-shaped mouth upon hers was pleasant, warming, not at all objectionable. She tried to imagine those hands now caressing her back moving in like manner on her breasts and hips but couldn't. When he kissed her the second time, Leander felt her heart break a little for all that was absent from Philip's embrace. The reverence she would like was present in abundance. The words of endearment came out as husky bits of adoration, and she found no fault with them—but no special pleasure, either. Her body fitted well against the hardness of his own, but no fire raced from the touch of his mouth on hers, the feel of his thigh against hers through her clothing. With a sigh bordering on a sob, she broke away.

"Dear Philip," Leander said, placing her hands on either side of the handsome face, "I wish I could say that I love you in a way a wife should love her husband, but I don't. I'll forever love you as my dear friend." When he jerked his eyes away and took his arms from around her, she dropped her hands and went on. "I know this isn't what you wanted to hear, but I could never be less than honest with you."

Philip hurt clear down to the soles of his feet. Almost every hour over the past few weeks had held thoughts of Leander, hopes that she might feel about him as he did her, dreams that she would belong to him someday. Never having been smitten by any of the numerous young women who seemed to invite his attentions, he was shocked to learn that he was being rejected by the only one he longed for. Not pretending to be a man of vast experience with the opposite sex, he saw no course but to withdraw from active courtship of Leander. Having her for a friend was better than not having any kind of relationship with her at all.

"If honesty pains that deeply, I believe I can do without any more of it for a long while," Philip replied when he could once more be sure of his voice. A night wind cooled his hot face. He watched the river flow on southward as if nothing unusual had happened.

"Mayhap it's time for us to go back inside," she said after a silence of her own. "You'll need to be getting back to Belle Terre."

Leander heard bullfrogs complaining to each other from the swamp south of where they stood. Locusts and cicadas in the trees behind them notched up their calls to a raucous, treble chorus. A mosquito sang nearby, its whine annoying her. A gentle breeze rose from the water to ruffle her hair, but she made no move to smooth it. She joined Philip's intent study of the Mississippi moving majestically in the moonlight. What had earlier seemed like promise in the scented air had settled into just another spring night in Louisiana.

Chapter Twenty

During the weeks leading into May, then June, Leander and Justin continued to see each other several times a week. If there was no need for her to journey to Terre Platte as often as before, now that the groundwork had been laid for the completion of the interior and was proceeding under the capable direction of Pierre Lemange, Justin rode up the river road to call on her at Beaux Rives. Since the day he had blundered and offered the betrothal gift, he had reverted to the earlier tactic of gentling the headstrong beauty into submitting to serious courtship. His love for her never faltered; neither did his determination to marry her.

Leander doubted Justin's frequent visits were based on what he sometimes declared to be their "strong friendship." The black eyes still took liberties with her body, liberties setting her blood to racing in that way she felt showed a shameful weakness in herself. There were times when they strolled or rode horses that his hands seemed to appear from nowhere to touch her, brush against her clothing. She yet fought frequent night battles over the debilitating physical attraction the Spaniard held for her—even found memories of the stranger in Throw-away's room still chewing at her self-esteem.

Even so, the French Creole found herself talking more and more freely with the Spanish don. If Justin had not been one before, he developed into an attentive, sympathetic listener. Without going into details of her secret worries over losing the plantation, Leander discussed her trials in assuming the role of mistress of Beaux Rives. To her surprise and delight, he never seemed to talk down to her, often gave sound advice.

By the end of summer, Justin had become such a regular visitor that, as often as not, Leander no longer asked Jabbo to leave when the Spaniard would appear where the mistress and her slave might be discussing the brood mares and the successes of the borrowed stallion Rio Sepe, or the need to send men to hoe the weeds from a back field of cotton they might have stumbled upon during a ride across the property. As long as the talk veered from talk of marriage, Leander seemed to accept Justin's presence with a casualness akin to that she showed Philip. She became adept at masking the surge of desire that the mere sight of him could bring. Had she thought of it, she might have compared the change in their relationship to that of the crops in the fields. Time and nourishment were promoting solid growth in all areas.

Harvest began in September, and Leander's eyes

counted money instead of piles of cotton, stacks of indigo, shocks of corn. Eagerly she made lists of all that she could offer the warehouses in New Orleans. Pleased at the faith his mistress showed in him and mindful of tips from Justin, Tower worked in the training circle with the unbroken colts, turning the more promising into marketable saddle horses. No word had come yet from the cousin in France, but she had hopes that the next ship would bring news of a reissued deed. The household moved with its own rhythm of summer and harvest, what with all available hands helping to nurture, gather, then preserve the bounty from the large garden Jabbo had helped plant. To Leander's surprise and gratification, Felix had lived up to his promise to see that Beaux Rives delivered its finest harvest to date. Within a week, Felicity would be coming down from Belle Terre to accompany her to New Orleans.

Brimming over with anticipation and untapped energy, Leander wandered down toward the river. Whistling for Gabriel through two fingers jammed in her mouth, she admired all within view. The old hollow tree reared up to her left, one less limb left at its towering top after a recent hailstorm. Gabriel came bounding, headed upriver, and she followed him. Beneath a cottonwood, she sank to sit cross-legged and gaze out across the river. Soon she would be able to sell the harvest and settle the assessments against her beloved Beaux Rives. Her father's dream to restore the plantation to its former solvent state was about to come true. The thought of the colts to come out of Justin's Rio Sepe added to her good mood. Leaning back against the papery bark of the cottonwood, she recalled

one of Dom's favorite bawdy songs and let her voice
ring out:

> Land Ho! Come home again!
> Sail Ho! Where have I been?
> Sailed to the East,
> Sailed to the West,
> Found there be one
> That I love the best.

> Fair Bridget's me gal
> Who's a kind of a pal,
> Till the light is off
> And our duds we doff.
> Then she's all lass
> With a hot little . . . mouth.

> Land Ho! Come home again!
> Sail Ho! Where have I been?
> Sailed to the East,
> Sailed to the West,
> Bridget's the one
> That I love the best.

The sound of applause and deep laughter followed
Leander's spirited singing there beside the river. She
jerked her head around to see Justin smiling down at
her with what was undeniably admiration and amusement.

"I don't appreciate your sneaking up on me," Leander faltered, almost at a loss for words at having been
caught in such an undignified predicament. She had
worked hard to keep hidden that hoydenish part of her

revealed that night in the lodge. How much of the boisterous song had he heard? What would she say if he asked where she had learned it? Anger at a Spaniard's putting her on the defensive took hold, glossed over any feeling of benevolence for the one she had come to know so well over the spring and summer. "Go away!"

"Why send me away?" Justin countered, surprised to see her cheeks flush and her eyes flash. The sight and sound of her dramatic outburst reminded him of that lighthearted beauty discovered in the hunting lodge. He had longed to find that side of her again, had sighed to think it might have disappeared forever. "Gabriel and I both would like to hear another song." He looked down at the big dog resting his front paws against his thighs and giving himself over to Justin's fondling hand upon head and ears. "Wouldn't we, big fellow?" When she made no reply, he added, his eyes on the black-tipped ears, "I still am surprised that every time I see Gabriel, I think I've seen him somewhere else."

Leander rose with a huff, saying, "No amount of kindness to me or to my dog pleases me this afternoon. I'm going inside and work on the harvest count." She brushed at her mussed skirts and stalked back down the road toward Beaux Rives, not caring that Gabriel and he tagged along behind her. The Spaniard's intrusion on her privacy had burst her bubble of much needed happiness.

Justin made no attempt to follow Leander inside, going instead on around to the stables to find Jabbo and Tower and visit with them. She had not even turned back at the front door to acknowledge his apology for upsetting her. For the past few weeks, she had seemed almost friendly to him, and he had let his hopes soar. Well, he told his heavy heart, sometimes losing is the only way to get another game set up.

"Felicity, you've been through that trunk a hundred times already since you arrived yesterday," Leander scolded her cousin a week later. They were preparing to go down to the pier to await the ship that would stop for them on its way downriver to New Orleans. One of the slave boys had ridden a horse upstream to flag it and had already rushed down with news that the ship would soon be pulling over to pick up Jabbo and the young women. "If you don't have what you need now, you never will."

"It's just that I'm so excited," Felicity exclaimed, outdone all morning over Leander's lack of proper interest in the wardrobe she herself was taking. "Andre and I had such a wonderful time in New Orleans that I can't help but look forward to returning."

But Leander was already down the stairs, calling for Cara and finding only Sheeva hurrying toward her. Sheeva had served as her maid that morning, and had she wished to be picky, she would have informed her that her talents with hair had much to be desired. However, the matter seemed trite on such an important occasion.

"But I thought you said Cara would be here before I left," Leander complained when Sheeva offered a lame explanation about Cara's not feeling well. "I merely wanted to tell her 'good-bye' and ask her to do something for me while I'm gone. It seems she could have managed to get out of bed for that." Now that she thought on it, Cara had seemed more than usually quiet and absentminded of late. "I'll charge you with what I wanted her to do for me. Watch for any letters arriving here by upriver ships. I'm not sure how many weeks we might be gone, and I don't want Felix looking over any letters sent me. Take any that might come straight to my room and put them beneath my mattress, do you hear?" When Sheeva nodded but kept an abnormally sober face, Leander asked, "What did you say is wrong with Cara? When she was in bed last week, you told me she had run into some fence-row briars, but when I saw those places on her neck and face, I could hardly believe she couldn't have backed out before she received so many cuts."

"She just feels porely, missy," Sheeva replied, a veiled look about the usually clear eyes. "She says to tell you to have a good time down in New Orleans. And don't you pay no never mind to that Neenie who stays in the Ferrands' town house. You know, she was the slave what nursed both Philip and Antoine before she got sent down there, but she always did Mrs. Ferrand's hair. She might be old and a grouch, but she can do up hair like crazy."

Down at the pier, Leander stiffly bade Felix take care of everything while she was gone. As he waited for the ship to tie up and throw out a gangplank, the overseer showed plainly by look and manner that he still resented her decision to go to the capital to sell the harvest herself. By rights, he should be going. Her demand that he sign the paper giving his ward the right to conduct the business of Beaux Rives had led to more unpleasantness. Grudgingly Felix had signed, angered that he could never seem to be in command when the two clashed. His questions as to why Leander was intent upon handling the sale of the harvest had resulted in her once more having to order him from the study. At the last moment that night less than a week ago, she had half-threatened to bring back a replacement for him when she returned. With renewed determination, Felix had sought through his grapevine to find out what lay behind her decision to journey to New Orleans. His lack of success maddened him into a seething rage.

Leander's impulsive idea to replace Felix had grown into a mental promise since it had slipped out that first time, but she never again spoke it aloud.

Farewells to Gabriel didn't work too well, so Jabbo asked Tower to take him to the stables and pen him up until the ship was well out of sight. Leander noticed how straight Jabbo walked in his best black suit. And back in Natchez he had tried to talk her out of buying anything nice for him, she mused with a grin. That he was proud now to be cutting such a fine figure was easy to see. She saw him pat his inside coat pocket after they boarded the cargo vessel and found kegs to sit on near the bow. Good. He had brought along his copy of the harvest count also. The thought shot through her mind that Jabbo was fully capable of serving as overseer, that she might should discuss it with him after they reached New Orleans and took care of business matters. A glance at her stuffed reticule reassured her that she had all necessary papers with her.

"Why are we slowing?" Leander asked, tearing her gaze from the soaring banks on the east side of the Mississippi, the one belonging to the British. She knew that when they reached English Landing downstream, memories would tear at her. Up ahead she could see a man standing alongside a trunk on a jutting pier. Her face flushing, she turned to Jabbo where he stood at the railing not far away. "Well, I can see the pink stucco walls now. It looks as if we'll be stopping at Terre Platte. Do you know anything about this?"

"No, Miss Ondine," Jabbo answered in the formal manner he had adopted in Natchez and yet used in the company of strangers. Only the three were in the prow, though.

Leander glared up at the giant black, not believing him for one minute. How else would Justin have learned the exact time of their departure for New Orleans? She had been cool to him since that day he slipped up on her during her abandoned singing.

Not until the ship was once more underway did Leander acknowledge Justin's presence with a curt nod. He had scrambled around visiting good-naturedly with the Spanish captain and crew before ambling over to find himself a seat near the ladies.

Felicity tried to make up for what she deemed Leander's reversion to childish rudeness. Tossing black curls and giving the two involved in polite conversation a good view of her back, Leander continued to drink in the sights across on the English banks. When the few buildings atop the bluff at English Landing came into view, she marshaled self-control and stared with what she hoped was no more than the normal curiosity of a river traveler.

There on the banks of the cove beneath the soaring bluff sat Josie's Inn. And the spot once claimed by *The Lady* was easy for one who had lived there six years to recognize. Leander half-expected another dilapidated houseboat to be tied up beneath the willows, but the muddy water was deserted and still. *Fight down the vision of the flames,* she told herself. *Remember Dom as he was when he was alive and cheerful.* She swallowed at the knot of sorrow clogging her throat. From her first sight of the two-story building, the sad-faced young woman thought it looked exactly as she had last seen it the past November. But when the ship passed directly in front of it, Leander almost cried out. The sign now read The Nightingale Inn. What had happened to Josie?

Not for the first time, Leander wished she had not given in to Josie's demand that she never write to her. Her troubled eyes met those of Jabbo where he stood beside the railing nearby. The question hung between them long after the ship raced with the current, on past the British fort at the spot called Baton Rouge, so-called, Dom had once told her, because the early Indians in the area had planted a red stick there to mark the boundaries of hunting grounds. Where was Josie? The following question stirred up memories Leander had no stomach for: Where was Throw-away? She could never think of the retarded young black without conjuring up memories of the passionate Spaniard found in her room, the one first stirring up all those disturbing currents of desire deep within. Though the afternoon breeze was warm on that September afternoon, Leander shivered.

Justin was too caught up in his own thoughts about Josie's Inn to notice the intense scrutiny that Leander and Jabbo gave the place. To see the changed sign ended his half-formed wish to return to visit with Josie now that he had found Leander and tell the charming, sympathetic woman how his dream had materialized.

His brain whirled with jagged memories of the strange, whiskey-blurred night he had spent in that back room. Not since had he imbibed so unwisely. The events of that evening refused to fall straight in his mind. His thumb and forefinger tugged at an earlobe.

Felicity let her blue eyes drink in the familiar shapes of the buildings atop the bluff, remembering the good times of her childhood at English Landing rather than the miserable years after her father's death, those prior to her marriage to Andre. She smiled to recall the joys of their wedding day and of their brief months together. Having accepted over the past six months that Andre's love had enriched her but that her life with him belonged now in fond memories, she sighed. As if by some mysterious command, all four turned faces toward New Orleans as soon as the settlement faded from view behind them.

Before dark that night, the travelers were feeling at home in the Ferrand town house. Her black face split with a huge smile, Neenie had welcomed them and introduced her gangling, teen-aged grandson Quint who cared for the horses and carriage.

Justin had insisted on accompanying the trio to the Ferrand town house, using the excuse that Jabbo might need his help. Actually, he wanted to find out if Leander might have thawed a bit toward him. When he saw she had not, he left them after escorting the young women inside and telling Jabbo the location of Bernardo de Galvez's home where he would be staying. Vowing that by tomorrow evening, he would have Leander laughing and talking to him again, Justin directed the hired lackey carrying his trunk to follow him the three blocks to St. Anne Street.

When Antoine returned from his office at the Cabildo, he greeted the two young women with hearty kisses. Both overlooked his boldness, figuring that to make an issue of his unwelcome caresses would probably make him even more rash in the future.

Upon his arrival back in the spring, Antoine had evidently claimed the master suite on the second floor looking out upon Royal Street. He made no gesture of even offering it to his father's widow and her cousin. Felicity had not looked forward to staying in the exact place where she had honeymooned with Andre and felt only relief. A large bedroom at the end of the hall on the second floor suited the needs of the two young women. Jabbo found a room off the spacious stable at the back of the lot running the depth of an entire block.

Jabbo walked the proper distance behind Leander the next morning as she headed for the warehouses on the riverfront. When Antoine had answered her queries that morning at breakfast about the location of the markets for plantation crops, he had offered to accompany her. Determined not to be around the wise-eyed Antoine more than necessary, she had refused.

After the fourth buyer had studied the lists she presented and made an offer little better than the earlier ones, Leander sighed and turned to Jabbo. "I'll check with Antoine tonight to see if there might not be other places to sell."

"What's the problem, missy?" Jabbo asked once they were back out on the banquette and headed back toward Royal Street. He couldn't remember having seen the lovely face so strained in a long while. The black forehead wrinkled.

Leander noted the concerned features and put on a

smile before replying, "Nothing. I just want to make sure I'm getting the best possible offer."

A number of horses and riders on the narrow streets clattered by as the two walked along. Leander assumed that Jabbo's great size caused the numerous stares sent their way. Everywhere she saw men and women moving along the walkways, some pausing before single store windows, others entering the varied shops and eating places marked as often with carved wooden signs portraying their line of businesses as with mere printed ones.

Stopping at a corner, Leander turned to say to Jabbo, "Antoine pointed out the bell steeple of St. Louis Church this morning, so I guess we must be nearing the Cabildo where he works. He said there were two identical buildings housing the Spanish government, one on either side of the church." Tomorrow, she planned mentally, she would ask Felicity to come with her to call at the office of the Commissioner of Land Assessments. When she first met Lieutenant Charles Garcia, she wanted to appear defenseless. The last thing she wanted was to put him on guard. She would have no trouble convincing Jabbo that she had nothing more in mind than shopping with her cousin.

With undisguised interest, Leander and Jabbo eyed the large area in front of the imposing structures, cleared all the way down to the curving Mississippi that appeared to be higher than the capital city, or at least on level with it. There seemed little doubt that what Felicity had told on the trip downriver was true. The space was indeed large enough to serve as parade ground for the Spanish soldiers housed in two long barracks built facing each other across the cleared ground.

The sight of several soldiers in uniform distressed Leander, but she forced herself not to give in to the urge to flee. After all, they had no cause to come after her . . . yet. A part of her mind noted that silver chains arched over the insteps of each soldier's polished black boots. With surprise she realized that the Spaniard in Throw-away's room might not have been the owner of the legs she had glimpsed that frightful afternoon from within the hollow tree.

"Jabbo, why are there so many slaves on the street? They seem to be shopping and carrying on business like everyone else," Leander said, turning to look up into his face for an answer.

"They're called Free Men of Color, missy," he replied.

"Oh, now I recall that you got around those mountain men by claiming to be one, didn't you?" she exclaimed, the memory of the dice game bringing an extra sparkle to her eyes. "How did they become Free Men of Color instead of slaves?"

"From what your papa told me and from what I've overheard through the years, most of them came here with money from selling their sugar plantations in Santo Domingo to make new lives for themselves. Others followed, especially carpenters, tailors, and those with special skills like that." Jabbo sometimes forgot what an unnaturally sheltered life his mistress had led. As afterthought, he added, "And some are slaves who were freed by their owners."

Leander digested all that Jabbo told, but especially the last bit of information.

"Good afternoon" came a familiar voice.

Leander whirled about to see Justin smiling at Jabbo and her. To see one with such a jaunty air after the disturbing thought that even her early crop might not produce the needed monies pleased her, lifted her own spirits in a way she did not bother to examine. "I thought you told me that New Orleans has some three thousand people living in it."

"I believe that's about right. Don't tell me you're going to make me account for all of them." Justin searched the violet eyes. Was that a spark of happiness at seeing him?

"No, but I want to know how you happened to find us in such a large place."

Justin tossed back his head and laughed. "There aren't too many wandering about fitting your descriptions, you know. Besides, you happen to be standing at one of the busiest corners in all of New Orleans, Leander. I suspect that if one were to stand here an hour or so, he might see at least half of those in the capital pass by. I wouldn't have had to follow you to find you. Will you allow me to buy you a coffee in the shop down the street?"

"You followed me yesterday," she shot back accusingly.

"You told me you wouldn't be needing to come back to Terre Platte until some more supplies arrived. What better time for us to select furniture than while you're in New Orleans to sell your harvest?"

Justin turned to tell Jabbo that he would escort his mistress the few blocks to the Ferrands' town house. When Leander made no out-and-out protests, the big black man smiled and told her he would see her back at the house.

"We don't have an agreement that I'll help choose furnishings," Leander reminded. Watching Jabbo walk away and move across the Place d'Armes, the thought occurred to her that Justin had accomplished what she had vowed no one other than she had the right to do. He had given orders to Jabbo. And Jabbo had taken them. Oh well, being in her first large town might be giving her a light head, she mused. And it did seem foolish to make the black man wait while the two chatted. Somehow, the more she looked at the debonair Spaniard with the silvery streak in his hair, the farther her troubles seemed to skip away. For the life of her, she couldn't recall what had brought about the most recent disturbance between them. It seemed that their relationship constantly teetered from high to low — all levels caused by him and his erratic behavior, she reassured herself. Maybe to stop for coffee with him would be a nice diversion. She had learned to conquer that unnerving physical attraction. Besides, it was her first visit to the capital.

"Of course we do," Justin assured her as he took her arm and guided her back down to a coffeehouse. "How else can anybody complete an interior if he doesn't include furnishings?" he asked with what seemed perfect logic. He spotted a table near the opened doorway and led her to it, pulling out her chair and getting her settled before he sat down. "Besides, since you're going to live there, you might as well choose what you'll like."

"You can't drop that asinine subject, can you?" For a minute she forgot they weren't back in the vast spaces in which they usually held their confrontations and let her voice lift with too much force.

"You know that I love you and that I won't rest until

you're my bride, don't you?" Justin seemed to have no compunction about giving full volume to his response either.

"I asked my question first," she hissed, aware that people nearby were beginning to look over at them. Were their voices that loud? Was it obvious they were quarreling?

"No," he corrected, ignoring her attempts to shush him with little frowns and hand gestures. "I asked mine first back in March—or don't you recall?"

"This is the most absurd conversation." She shot sidewise glances about, glad to see that a waiter was coming to take their orders.

"I can remember several more absurd," he said after asking for two coffees. Enjoying the way she was beginning to look flustered and rosy about the face, he grinned. Did she have any idea how beautiful she looked? His eyes took in the fashionable, scooped neckline of her mauve silk dress, then dipped to worship the perfection of exposed neck and swelling tops of breasts. His heartbeat skipped.

"Stop looking at me that way."

"How am I looking at you?" The whisper came with such feigned little-boy innocence that Leander couldn't help but roll her eyes with exasperation.

Their coffee cups came but were soon pushed aside. They merely gazed across at each other with mutual admiration for the other's persistence and plain obstinancy.

"I have a confession to make," Justin said, a smile hinting that it wasn't of great consequence.

"The church is just around the corner. A priest will be happy to oblige."

His eyes told her how delightful he thought she was while he continued. "I *was* following you a while back."

"I knew it!" Her eyes shot purple daggers for his deception. "You tell lies quicker than the truth. It's no wonder I never believe you."

"I wanted to ask Felicity and you to let me come for you this evening to have dinner with Bernardo and me at his home. Now don't draw yourself up like that," he said when she leaned back against the chair and upped her chin. "Bernardo is a respectable bachelor with a nice home and staff only three blocks from the Ferrands' town house. You've met him and know he's a gentlemen."

"He isn't choosy about his company, is he?"

"When you consider he wants to entertain your cousin and you, you might think so."

Despite little misgivings, Leander finally gave in. To escape the company of the pompous Antoine would be good for both Felicity and her. Besides, she had really liked Bernardo and felt sure that her cousin would enjoy having an excuse to be out in New Orleans at night.

That evening, Bernardo de Galvez greeted his guests in the uniform of the Colonel of the Louisiana Regiment. Leander flinched at the sight but managed to recover her poise. She suspected that Justin had deliberately kept back such information, and she had no wish for him to feel he had put one over on her. To see how sparks seemed to fly from the moment Felicity's blue eyes met the brown ones of the Spanish officer took Leander by surprise. Justin was as attentive to her as Bernardo was to Felicity, and the evening was an obvious success. Leander loved hearing laughter bubble from Felicity's pretty mouth in that old, remembered way.

"Leander," Felicity whispered the next morning when they approached the huge building housing the Cabildo, the seat of the Spanish government, "are you sure this is what you should be doing? From what you've told me, this Lieutenant Charles Garcia is likely a cohort of Felix's. Aren't you afraid to ask about taxes on Beaux Rives?"

"Shush," Leander said in a low voice. "We've been over this on our walk down here. I merely want to meet him and show where my guardian signed that I can handle all business affairs for the plantation. Felix had no idea that I wanted more than permission to bargain for the harvest, and he didn't pay much attention to the wording I put in the letter. I'll bet he tried like the devil to find out from every slave about the place why I was so determined to come to New Orleans—except Jabbo, of course." A grim smile lifted one corner of her mouth. Felix and Jabbo had never had any love for each other, and since her return, they had seemed even more like antagonists than she recalled from the past. "You're the only one who knows of my concern over money."

"What if we run into Bernardo?" Felicity glanced around the entry hall of the building.

Leander smiled for real that time, saying, "We'll tell him we're just seeing the sights." The glow on the blonde's face reminded her of the previous evening and the way Bernardo had charmed the young widow. And vice versa.

Easily they found the office of the Commissioner of Land Assessments and went inside. When Leander asked that her cousin and she be granted time with Lieutenant Charles Garcia, she was surprised that the soldier showed them in right away.

Lieutenant Charles Garcia bowed low over the hands of the two lovely young callers, his mind racing over what Felix Grinot had written back in the spring. A sharp pain in his chest reminded him of much he preferred to forget. Lieutenant Garcia had little use for one so obviously rotten as Felix, yet he had more or less inherited the rascal when Governor Unzaga replaced Governor O'Reilly. Any man who would go to such lengths to turn in his long-time employer as a traitor against the Spanish Crown was not to be trusted in anything. While polite conversation went on between the young women and him, the lieutenant kept regretting his part in the overseer's devious plan to wrest ownership of Beaux Rives.

Wishing to remain in Louisiana when it was time to be pensioned off in less than ten years, Lieutenant Garcia had saved little toward a nest egg. Felix's plan had seemed foolproof at his revelation that the Ondine heiress had perished in the fire and that the original deed had also burned. The wily overseer would pay the plantation's annual assessments — doubled as were all against properties of the known Conspirators — directly to the lieutenant in exchange for his letting the records show default until Felix became owner. Felix's plan was designed to hinder any claim from a legitimate heir. Lieutenant Garcia recalled the overseer's brag that he was gambling no one from France would come since he knew of no close relatives. If anyone were to appear though and have in hand a duplicate deed, the past-due taxes would be so high that to claim the legacy would be extremely costly and might lead one to relinquish it. At any rate, the monies set aside would provide a goodly sum for both the Spanish officer and Felix.

"This letter," Leander was saying, breaking into the officer's thoughts, holding out the last notice of assessments in arrears, "disturbs me, Lieutenant Garcia. I can't imagine why my overseer neglected to make the payments as they came due each year." She lifted the pansy-colored eyes in apparent innocence and pleading. "Surely such large taxes can no longer apply, now that my father is dead and I have returned from school in Mobile. Perhaps the doubled assessments against those accused of treason might not be so unfair if the planters hadn't paid with their lives for taking part in the Conspiracy. Since my father did pay the ultimate price, shouldn't a reduction of taxes be in order now?"

The lieutenant reread the letter, letting his thoughts dwell upon the beauty and dignity of the Ondine heiress sitting before his desk. What she said made sense. Mayhap he could rectify some of the wrongdoings against her. Dare he approach Governor Unzaga on the subject to see if he might present her case to the Council? After all, feeling against the French had all but disappeared over the past few years. All of the Spanish officers, himself included, enjoyed the hospitality of the finest homes in New Orleans. Had not Governor Unzaga himself set a precedent when he married a relative of one of the traitors? And no one had seemed to be appalled. Since then, several of his friends had also married Creole beauties. He still had hopes of finding a wife to comfort him during his upcoming retirement from service.

"Your petition touches me, Miss Ondine," Lieutenant Garcia replied, his hand moving to stroke his suddenly paining left arm. "I shall speak with Governor Unzaga upon the matter and get in touch with you." At her encouraging smile from beneath half-lowered lashes, he found himself adding, "That is, if you grant permission for me to call and deliver any messages."

With an air of one flattered but flustered, Leander gave the gray-haired lieutenant the address of the Ferrand town house and ushered her silent companion outside. When they left the Cabildo behind and Felicity tried to question Leander about what could be expected to happen next, she received no answer. Leander didn't know herself what the next move might be.

Without anyone's having planned it, the meeting of the four young people over dinner at Bernardo's home became something of a ritual that first week in New Orleans. Felicity confessed in private that the Spanish colonel appealed to her as no young man ever had. Leander convinced herself that she owed it to her cousin to accompany her. Neither wanted gossip to start about a young widow's being in the company of one Antoine had referred to in casual conversation as "the most eligible bachelor in New Orleans."

During the days, Leander and Jabbo made the rounds of all the buyers. Finally making a decision to accept the best offer and get the matter settled, she tallied the numbers on her sheets and accepted the usual half-payment, agreeing that the second half would come when the buyer received the goods. That afternoon, after she figured the staggering difference between what she would receive and what she owed in back assessments, Leander set out to put the money in the bank her father had always used. A loan would be necessary as the funds would not clear Beaux Rives' debt. No word had come from Lieutenant Garcia. She knew not to put much faith in what the Spanish officer had said abut conferring with the governor to help a Creole. Were her petition for reduced assessments to be granted, there was the question of paying those from the past seven years.

Even though Leander approached Louis Bordreaux, president of the bank handling the accounts of Beaux Rives, and found the Creole gentleman friendly and full of good memories of her father and some visits to the lodge, she received no loan to pay assessments. The kindly gentleman explained that policies of the capital's banks were to lend money only for seed, slaves, or improvements to land and that she would have to find the sum for assessments from some other source. He seemed highly disapproving that taxes had been allowed to fall in arrears. A second and a third bank gave her the same excuses. She hid her disappointment deep inside.

"You ladies deprive me of your company too often," Antoine said that evening when he came from his office and found Leander and Felicity having a late tea in the living room. "I can't tell you how surprised I've been, Leander, to see Justin Salvador calling for you two and escorting you about. My, my, what a change for the one who last Christmas refused to let his name be mentioned in her presence." He sent Leander a probing look, his handsome face wearing the air of one pleased with himself.

Felicity laughed and remarked, "Antoine, you never lose your charm, do you?" She shot Leander a warning look not to rise to Antoine's bait.

Seeming to have lost interest in taunting Leander when she made no quick reply, Antoine announced with a touch of arrogance, "I've been escorting Maralys Soulier to a round of parties since I've been here. Her parents both came from France. The father owns one of the largest stores near the river. They insist on throwing a small party for my houseguests and introducing you to their friends. Would this coming Saturday evening be convenient?" He looked from one to the other, noting their puzzled nods before going on. "Very well. I'll tell Mrs. Soulier and she can send around invitations." Before leaving them and going up to his room, he added, with a smug look directed toward Leander, "You might like to know that Governor Unzaga and his wife Sophia will be among those invited. The Souliers aren't snobs though and will make sure that a nice mixture of types will be there. The old barriers against the mixing of French and Spanish at social affairs have long disappeared."

Felicity and Leander both dreaded and looked forward to attending such a grand party. What would they wear? How would they dress their hair? What would they do if only Spanish were spoken and Felicity would be unable to converse without Leander's serving as interpreter? Leander shared her fears about having to face Maralys and be questioned about Miss Julia Shepherd's School for Young Ladies. Glad to be able to reassure her cousin, the excited blonde told that she had learned from Antoine that Maralys was all of twenty-two and had not been at the school since in her teens. If she had been in Mobile at the same time as Leander claimed to have been, it would have been only during that first year. Leander breathed easier. From Belle's tales of Roseanne's experiences, upper-level students ignored the younger ones.

After learning from Justin and Bernardo that they too had received invitations, the young widow declared to her cousin in the privacy of their bedroom that she would have a grand time, no matter what. In the same way that Leander ignored Felicity's hints to learn more of her relationship with Justin, Felicity gave out little information on the depth of her feeling for Bernardo de Galvez. Leander couldn't fail to see how the two talked with eyes and body motions as much as with mouths. Would they be able to hide their attraction to each other at the party?

Chapter Twenty-one

Arriving at the imposing Soulier home on Antoine's arms, Leander and Felicity blinked at the splendor about them. A large ballroom to the left of a sumptuous foyer already held several fashionably dressed guests. Maralys, along with her parents, greeted the arrivals. The way Maralys's wide brown eyes worshipped Antoine's face told Leander that the buxom young woman considered him her property. Though Antoine's expression did not echo the identical message, it did nothing to daunt the apparent hopes of the dimple-cheeked heiress to one of New Orleans' finest stores.

As if planned, Justin and Bernardo stood talking with a group near the arched entry into the ballroom. The second that Leander and Felicity appeared, they moved toward them and escorted them about, introducing them first to one and then another. The sheen of Felicity's blond hair and the glow upon her face above her "widow's weeds" seemed even lovelier from the stark contrast.

Leander had wondered if the pale blue brocade from Belle Monroe's shop, trimmed with pearls embroidered in flowering swirls, would look grand enough for such an occasion. The low-necked gown draped across the peaks of her breasts and curved upward to hang perilously close to the tips of her shoulders. Below the tiny waist, the blue brocade skirt was caught up in side swags, revealing a petticoat of creamy satin with identical, pearl-embroidered patterns spaced about. Felicity had insisted that a strand of tiny pearls Andre had given her be interlaced in the upsweep of ebony curls at the crown of her head. After Justin's compliments and a few covert, admiring looks from young women no more elegantly gowned, she felt reassured.

When Justin introduced Leander to Governor and Mrs. Unzaga, she found it difficult to call up the hidden hatred of all Spaniards. Despite her intentions not to, she found the governor charming. His wife Sophia seemed eager to let Leander know that she, too, was a French Creole. She spoke freely of Creole families Leander might have known or heard about.

"You may have heard your father mention my uncle Jerrel Fontaine. I believe they were quite good friends at one time," Mrs. Unzaga told Leander in a low voice when the two men became busy talking about the horse races to take place on the following afternoon out near Lake Ponchartrain. At Leander's obvious look of recognition at the name Fontaine, the attractive young woman added, "Yes, Uncle Jerrel was also one of the Conspirators who were executed. Had someone told me six years ago that I would have even considered a suit from a Spaniard, I think I would have struck him. But when I met Luis three years back and he courted me so eagerly, I came to know and love him. Now it's hard for me to think of him as anything more than a citizen of Louisiana." She lifted a jeweled fan and waved it prettily before her face.

Astonished, Leander swallowed hard and replied, "You must admit that he is a bit more than an ordinary citizen. Mayhap being governor gives him an edge over most Spaniards." What else could she do but play the social game and hide her revulsion? Her eyes darted to the impeccably dressed young man who had brought her over to meet the colony's foremost couple. Justin wore the usual white cravat, though one trimmed lavishly with lace this time. A red satin vest embroidered with gold brightened the black coat and knee breeches, turned them into festive attire. She admired the gleam of an ornate, gold watch chain against the red. The well-turned legs looked splendid in white silken hose. Was she putting more emphasis on his nationality than she should? Her mind whirled from unwelcome thoughts as the young women chatted and waited for the men's talk of racing to die.

Returning his attention to Leander, Governor Unzaga asked, "Have you run into Lieutenant Garcia tonight?" He looked about the now-crowded ballroom. "He told me before we left the Cabildo yesterday that he would be here and that he was looking forward to seeing you again, my dear. Like me, Charles is an older fellow, though, and he may have elected to have a quiet Saturday night."

Justin puzzled. Where and why would Leander have met the Commissioner of Land Assessments? No taxes would be due on property until after the first of the year, so she wouldn't have been calling on him to pay money—unless Beaux Rives was in arrears. He well knew that Felix Grinot had produced average or better crops over the four years he had been his neighbor. As he watched Leander talk with the governor, a trace of a frown shadowed the lovely brow. Justin sensed something distressed her.

"Lieutenant Garcia was most gracious," Leander remarked in a remote manner.

"And highly in favor of your petition, I might add," the governor replied with enthusiasm. "I will be presenting it to the Council and suggesting that they vote to begin setting the annual assessments against your property by the standards used for all others. As for the other matter Charles mentioned, I'm afraid there is little to be done about that. Water under the bridge, so to speak. Even if wrongs were committed, records must be kept straight." He leaned closer to say in little more than a whisper, "But don't let it worry you. We'll not be quick to enforce the law. You can have until the last day of the year to pay up. That way you can use money from the sale of this year's harvest when it comes in."

Justin couldn't hear the last statements the governor made to Leander, but even the first ones stunned him. That she had taken it on her own to call upon Spanish officials and discuss business awed him. Would he ever know all about the beauty he loved? And there she stood in that fashionable blue brocade dress talking freely with the governor, looking like the most helpless piece of femininity in the room. The first clue to some inner agitation was the deepening of the purple in her eyes. The way her forefinger worried at a curl resting on her shoulder told him that something did perturb her. Whatever Governor Unzaga had confided seemed to have erased the glimmer of hope showing on her face when he first began discussing some kind of petition. The need to get her off for questioning consumed him.

With a finesse learned over the years, Justin deftly sidestepped the Unzagas and the other guests, guiding the dazed Leander outside to the large courtyard. Other couples wandered about admiring the lush bougainvillea vines hugging the brick walls. The uncertain light from torches set about smudged the brilliant colors of the flowers to mysterious, dancing pastels.

"What is wrong?" Justin asked after he gestured for them to sit on a bench in a shadowed corner. When she batted eyelashes and sent fingers to check the pearls weaving in and out of crown curls, he snapped, "Don't play the vain, empty-headed female with me. Something is wrong and I want to know what it is."

Leander flashed him an angry look, saying, "I don't make it a habit to tell my problems with the Spanish to another of like blood."

"You told Lieutenant Garcia, obviously."

"That was different."

"Why?"

"Because he was the one who could help me. You heard Governor Unzaga say that my petition will be presented." Leander looked away from those demanding black eyes. "You already know more than you should. Leave it alone. I can handle it." The defeated tone of her voice lent no conviction to the brave words.

"Leander," Justin said, tipping the averted face toward him, "I thought even you admitted by now that we're more than just neighbors." His finger traced the oval shape of her face. "More than just friends." She seemed entranced. "Every day I've come to love you more. Every night I pray that you'll consent to be my wife. Won't you tell me what the governor said to upset you so?" He allowed his fingers to brush at the wispy curls across her temples. He could feel her pulse dancing wildly. The desire to kiss that half-opened mouth warred with the one to gain her confidence — and conceded defeat. He dared not chance angering her by kissing her at this point.

"All right, Justin," Leander said with ragged breath. His nearness and his hands upon her face were overpowering her in that way she had known they would if she ever allowed the two of them to get into such an intimate situation. Self-restraint was becoming increasingly difficult. Had she not been so desperate to escape the governor and get her thoughts together, she would never have allowed him to lead her outside. Most of the other guests were wandering back inside. She could hear strains of music floating out through the opened doors and windows. "But first take your hands away."

Justin obeyed, albeit reluctantly. Leander's recital of her woes with Felix and overdue assessments came in a quiet rush of words deliberately devoid of emotion. She didn't seem to expect any comments from him during the telling. When she dropped her eyes from his and let out a deep sigh, he put an arm around her and pulled her head to rest against his shoulder.

"Why have you kept this from me, Leander?" His heart had wrenched at each revelation of the agonies she had suffered. Alone. That she had endured them alone seemed to make them all the more terrible. At her explanation as to why she had not confided in

Jabbo, Justin couldn't find words to express his admiration of her sense of commitment to the slave. As mistress, the troubles belonged to her alone.

"It doesn't concern you, and I shouldn't have told you," she confessed. She despised her weakness for his touch and the sound of the deep voice so near.

"Doesn't concern me?" Justin asked. "Doesn't concern the one who loves you and wants to make you his wife forever? How can you hurt me with such foolish words?" His arm tightened to keep her from leaving his embrace. "No, don't get your dander up and try to rush off. Hear me out, will you?" He loosened his grip enough to cuddle her against his arm and yet gaze upon her face.

Leander was in shock from having confided all to the handsome man peering down at her. Whatever had possessed her? Finding more comfort in his embrace than she cared to admit, she nodded her consent to listen.

"I have more money than one man could need in a lifetime. Everything I am or have is as much my wife's as mine. You know how I've begged you to marry me, Leander. Won't you consent to be my wife and let me clear Beaux Rives of debt for you? I'll personally run off that Felix Grinot the minute we return upriver. Please accept. Let me help the one I love."

"But I don't love you, Justin," she said when she could get her mind working. What was setting her on fire was his touch and that was not love, she agonized. Inside, she felt some part of her was melting, spreading throughout all her limbs. "How could you want to marry someone who doesn't love you, who despises Spaniards?"

Justin lifted his head and let out a deep laugh before telling her, "I'm willing to take the chance that you love me already — and that if you don't, you will come to in time. I suspect all you would have to do is remember our night in the lodge when you had not the least idea that I was a Spaniard and your heart will remind you that what we found that night was love between two people — not some vague attraction between a Creole and a Spaniard." He bent his head toward hers, not stopping until their lips touched. A great rush of feeling tore at him and he pulled her closer against him, letting his tongue find again those velvety recesses he had claimed that night during the storm, had longed for ever since.

"Will you marry me, Leander?" he asked when the long kiss ended. They stared at each other in the shadowy corner of the courtyard. He kept her pulled close as they sat side by side there on the bench. Black eyes begged darkly purple ones.

"If I told you it would be only to use your money to save Beaux Rives, would you still want me to marry you?" she countered, surprised that she had no wish to deceive him outright, even if he was a Spaniard.

"Yes." His voice was firm, sure. His heart reassured him that what moved her to accept his kiss with such fervent response could be nothing other than love. All he had to do was lead her to examine her own heart and admit that she had loved him since that first meeting. In time, she would recognize it. He knew it with certainty.

Leander dropped her eyes then. His were probing too deeply into her very soul. Her breathing became more erratic.

"All right," she said with trepidation, "I will accept your proposal — but only to save my dream of setting Beaux Rives back to its position as a prosperous plantation."

"Your dream, Leander?" This came out in doubtful tones.

"Yes. My dream." What was he hinting at?

"Are you sure it isn't your father's dream, the one he told you about after he had given too heavily to the cause of the Conspirators?"

"Where did you hear such a lie?" She stiffened in his arms, would have pulled away had he not tightened his hold.

"Here and there, but mainly from you in snatches of talk about your father those last years after your mother died." Had he gone too far? The fiery eyes were scorching his face. The softness in his arms was becoming rigid. "Not that it matters to me, love. You can have any kind of dream you want. But mean it if you tell me you'll be mine."

Leander sent the handsome Spaniard an assessing look, reaffirming, "I gave my answer and named the conditions. I won't back down . . . if you don't."

"Never." He smiled then and asked, "May I bring the pearls over tomorrow?"

"You brought them to New Orleans with you?" The memory of the lustrous necklace had never left her.

"Sure. I hoped I might find somebody interested in accepting them." His teasing smile coaxed one of similar vein to her own lips.

Justin would have devoured the honey of her mouth again had not Bernardo called to them just then from the doorway of the ballroom. It was time to go inside to

468

dine.

"I can't believe that you're going to marry Justin Salvador," Felicity was still saying to Leander the next day at odd intervals. "I thought you would never see that he's the man for you."

"He wouldn't be if he didn't have the money I need," Leander pointed out, not for the first time. "And I told him so."

"Pooh! I can see the sparks fly when you two get together. You're not fooling me, though you're trying to fool yourself."

"What about you?" Leander retorted, aggravated at her cousin's knowing tone each time she brought up the subject of the relationship between Justin and her. "Aren't you finding Bernardo to be more than a handsome companion to entertain you in New Orleans?"

"I don't deny that I do," Felicity confessed, her pretty mouth drooping at the corners. "And here I am, a widow with six more months of full mourning to endure. He must think I'm the most fickle person in the world." Tears formed in the blue eyes. "What will I ever do about him, Leander? We'll be going back upriver soon, and I just know I'll never see him again."

Leander hadn't realized Felicity was so serious about the Spanish officer. She watched the blonde twitch at the black lace on her sleeve with nervous fingers.

"I think Bernardo is as smitten with you as you are with him," Leander said after giving the situation some thought. "And if he is, he will be willing to wait until enough time has passed for him to court you openly. Look how careful he has been to make sure you've not been seen in public as a twosome. No one knows how often we go over for dinner—and Justin and I are always about. If he weren't in love, I doubt he would be so mindful of propriety. From what I hear, Bernardo is likely to succeed Governor Unzaga in a year or so, and he is probably just as concerned with his own reputation as he is with yours. For a governor to have a wife with a tainted reputation would never do, and you well know it."

Felicity cheered up as Leander pointed out other ways she could tell that the politically important Bernardo de Galvez was in love with the young widow. Leander was relieved that the subject of Justin seemed to have gotten pushed aside. She hadn't liked lying awake most of last night pondering the decision to marry him. What about all the lies she had strewn about to smooth the way for her return? Would he want her if he knew all about her past? Then that old hatred would sneak out and hiss that he was only a Spaniard, after all, and that she had told him from the beginning that she was marrying him only for his money. He was getting no more than he deserved. The Spanish had caused the death of her father and the fall of Beaux Rives. It was only right that a Spaniard provide the pathway to evening the score.

On the following days as Leander and Justin dashed about New Orleans to tend to business and shop for furnishings at Terre Platte, she seldom heeded the nasty voice of that old, buried hatred. Instead she surrendered to the heady wine of being young and openly adored by a handsome fiancé, one who seemed to have boundless wealth to spend. With his beloved on his arm, Justin walked into the office of the Commissioner of Land Assessments that first week of their engagement and asked to see Lieutenant Garcia. Both exchanged shocked looks when the soldier temporarily in charge announced that Lieutenant Garcia had died of some kind of seizure over the weekend. Within a brief time, the replacement had found the records and accepted Justin's gold. The debt against Beaux Rives was no longer.

Maralys and Antoine spread the news of the engagement of the Ondine heiress and her Spanish neighbor. Invitations to parties piled up on the silver tray in the foyer of the Ferrand town house. Within a couple of weeks, Leander had renewed acquaintances with the Creole families her parents had known and met new ones, as well. Her fears of close examination about her claimed years at Miss Julia Shepherd's School for Young Ladies never materialized. Obviously her "act" had satisfied Antoine, who, in turn, must have convinced Maralys. Talk at parties seemed centered on the present and the future, not on the past.

Spanish friends of Justin's opened their homes to the handsome couple also. Leander was hard put to find fault with their friendliness, manners . . . or use of the French language.

"Why do the Spanish converse mostly in French?" Leander asked Justin one night as they left one of the many parties given in their honor.

Justin smiled a bit crookedly before saying, "Because the French refuse to learn Spanish, won't even teach it in the schools. In the first years, officials tried to enforce the use of their own language, but everyone here ignored the edict. To carry on the business of governing and to become accepted by the people of New Orleans, the Spaniards had little choice but to take up French." He sent his free hand to cover the small one nestling in the angle of his bent elbow. In the dim light from the streetlamps, he admired the oval face lifted to his while they strolled on the banquette leading to Royal Street. When she looked so woebegone, he figured her thoughts dwelt upon her father's being shot as a traitor, and his heart ached for what must be an everlasting agony for his beloved. He longed to help her accept that what had taken place was one of the cruel necessities life dealt individuals when the business of government took precedence over the desires of citizens. "When you think on it, you can see that we Spanish haven't trampled down the French. It required a lot of give and take on both sides to turn Louisiana into the thriving colony it is today. Population is growing each year, as is trade."

Leander dropped her gaze. Was her fiancé trying to convince her that her views toward his people were completely wrong? When they kissed good night at the front door of the Ferrand town house, she fought harder than ever against letting his caresses set her blood on fire.

The next day the couple strolled to the warehouses of dealers handling furniture imported from both Spain and France. The only pieces on the premises for immediate possession were those for the master bedroom. Leander fought blushes when the clerk began questioning her about the kind of bed she preferred. Leaning casually against a post in the large warehouse, Justin grinned and offered little comment. When she stole a glance toward him, he winked lewdly and fell in love with her all over again when the blushes materialized and she had to ask the clerk to repeat whatever he was saying. He couldn't recall ever before having seen her so flustered.

From sketches and descriptions, the engaged couple chose what they would like ordered and shipped up-river. That Leander tended to prefer the lines of French goods bothered Justin not at all. To see her eyes smiling into his, to have her arm linked with his, to be able to kiss her and call her sweet names, to know that she had set the day after her eighteenth birthday as the date she would become his bride—only those things held importance. December seventeenth might be a mere two months away to most, but to Justin Salvador it loomed like a year. When he agonized, though, he had to admit that having a definite date set was better than not having even a commitment. He felt like a man who had gambled his entire stake on one turn of a card and won.

"It isn't proper for you to buy my trousseau," Leander told Justin one night when they were sitting in the courtyard at Bernardo's home. She had welcomed the chance for the foursome to dine quietly after the spate of parties over the past weeks. Though it was late October, the night was warm and pleasant. Lamenting after dinner that he must attend a meeting, Bernardo had escorted Felicity the three blocks to the Ferrand town house. The engaged couple were truly alone for the first time since the night she had accepted his proposal. "I have enough money to buy my own."

Leander thought of the gold coins won in the dice game. The pile was still larger than what she had taken from the soldier's boot back in Throw-away's room. Despite her concerted efforts, the memory of that disturbing night refused to disappear completely. She

473

had brought the money with her to New Orleans, hoping that it might add enough to the sale of harvest to pay the assessments. When it had not and she had accepted Justin's offer of marriage and promise to pay the debt, she had forgotten about it. Justin now filled almost every waking hour and thought, whether or not she willed it. "The groom shouldn't buy the bride's wedding dress and trousseau."

"What is proper for others doesn't necessarily apply to us," Justin assured her, stealing another kiss and letting his fingers caress the delicate neck. He loved the way she leaned into his hands, warm and pliable. "I want to shop with you and choose what you'll be wearing for me to admire."

Leander gave in to the increased flames racing through her and clung to Justin as he kissed her with more ardor. When his hand dipped to fondle her breasts, she moaned low in her throat, overcome by fresh desire. Memories of the way it had felt for Justin to make love to her back in the lodge swept her into a kind of frenzy. Surely to have such feelings for the man she was to marry did not mean she was wanton — though it certainly did not indicate she loved the Spaniard or ever could. Her earlier labeling of what she felt for him still rang true in her mind — mere physical attraction. She refused any conflicting messages from her heart to interfere with that decision.

"I want to give you the world," Justin declared when he ended the scalding kiss and touched the gleaming pearls at her throat.

"The pearls are enough for a betrothal gift. I've told you how much I love them. What else could I need?" She didn't tell him how their warm solidity touching her skin reminded her of the way she felt when he pulled her into his arms. Secure. Treasured. Beautiful.

"Surely there must be something you'd like to have. Name it, and it's yours." Did she know that starlight played in her eyes and dazzled him?

Leander studied the handsome face, let her fingers trace the heavy brows and linger at the place where she knew the tiny scar sliced. "Could you help me free Jabbo?"

Justin laughed, the joyful sound echoing in the small courtyard. "You always surprise me. A lifetime with you will never be dull. Here I thought you had seen a bauble in a jeweler's window, and you're thinking of that giant black protector of yours." Seeing a defensive tightening of those tantalizing lips, he added, "Of course I realize that Jabbo is more like family to you than slave, darling. I didn't mean to make light of the devotion you two have for each other." To prove his sincerity, he brought her exploring fingers down to his lips and kissed each one separately.

Leander almost lost her breath at each lingering kiss upon her fingers. Lying back in his arms there on the bench, his betrothal pearls warm against her skin, she felt she might be in some fantasy world, one all cordoned off from the real one. What was it about his nearness which made everything seem more wonderful? Even the stars above twinkled with unusual brilliance.

"My answer is 'yes,' " Justin told her after another thrilling capture of her mouth. "We'll call on Governor Unzaga tomorrow and see what steps you need to take." With concern, he asked, "Are you sure you want to free him? You might never see him again. Is that what you want?"

"I want to offer him the job of overseer at Beaux Rives and pay him what I pay Felix," she replied. Her lips set in a pensive pattern, she went on. "I'll let him decide what he wants to do. If he were to choose to return to Jamaica, I would grieve, but I would buy his passage. I doubt he'll want to go back. You see, Beaux Rives is home to him now."

"If he chooses to stay, it would work out fine for both of us," he remarked, pleased that she was aware of the uncertainties involved in offering Jabbo his freedom. "We could live at Terre Platte and let him take over Beaux Rives."

"That's what I was thinking."

"At last," Justin called to the stars overhead, "we've agreed upon something."

Had they cared to be literal, they could have said that they agreed upon more kissing, more fondling, more murmuring of endearments. But they were too busy carrying out those delicious acts to waste time on rationalizations.

Justin rose and lifted Leander in his arms, murmuring his intention of carrying her inside. Already drunk from his kisses and caresses, she made no protest when he opened a far door leading from the courtyard. A bedroom lighted by a single taper seemed to be awaiting lovers. Snowy sheets lay turned back to the foot of the wide bed. A musky fragrance reminding Leander of the way Justin smelled in the mornings when he would call for her to go shopping permeated the room, telling her that the room must be the one he used.

"Allow me to undress you," Justin murmured when he stood her beside the bed, his eyes paying court to her beauty. With gentle hands, he loosened the back of the blue taffeta gown, smiling into her face while it rustled to the floor with a sensual whisper. The petticoat and panniers delighted him, but she had to show him how the basketlike contraptions tied around her waist. He flung them on a nearby chair and kissed her thoroughly before lifting the chemise over her head and exposing her breasts. With half-teasing grumbles at all the garb she wore, he eased off silk stockings, satin slippers, and be-ribboned underdrawers. Midnight eyes feasted on her naked perfection. "You're even more beautiful than I remembered," he said, his voice thick with yearning.

Before Leander could wonder if she might like stripping Justin's body, he had done it for her. He turned to walk toward where she sat upon the bed, noticing the way her eyes widened at the sight of him.

"So are you," Leander replied with awe gilding her words. The olive skin of the well-proportioned body glowed in the dimly lighted rooms, seemed to invite her touch.

"Men aren't beautiful," he teased as he guided her to lie beside him on the bed. On the inside, though, he loved having her say that he was.

"You are, Justin." And she knew in that instant that he truly was beautiful. Her fingers traced the lean cheeks, the muscular shoulders, the swelling biceps. To touch lovingly and be touched in return seemed the most precious part of making love, she mused. Warm waves of contentment undergirded by earthy desire were already lapping against the hungry sands of her soul.

A searing kiss, a duel of tongues, then a need to

express some of what was washing them into a sea of feeling led them to pause and adore with looks and words.

"No man has ever loved as I love you, because there has never before been a Leander," Justin told her, planting small kisses on her forehead while a hand cupped an uptilted breast and teased the taut nipple.

"How can you be so sure you love me? What does that word mean to you?" Leander was serious. A puzzled look deep in the purple eyes lent credence to the questions.

"Love means not being truly alive except when you're with the one you love," he announced, as if what he spoke were a known truth.

"Is that good? To be so dependent on another human?" In her brief time upon earth, she had learned that being independent was a necessity for survival. She thought of the parents who had loved her, hugged her, made her feel special . . . but gone so long now. Justin was speaking of another kind of love, as was she.

"All good. As good and natural as the relationship of the sea to the shore—without the one, you'd not have the other."

"I've heard that the sea tries to destroy the beach, that the beach tries to hold back the waves." How many times had Dom related tales of storms he had seen at sea and on land?

"Sometimes they may seem cruel to each other, but they exist as a team. 'Tis all a part of nature's law—the same one applying to lovers." He bent to kiss her eyelids closed, loving the tickle of curly lashes against his lips.

"You're trying to woo me with words," she protested.

"And my object is to win your love." His hand moved to caress her other breast.

"I might not be what I seem." She flirted from behind half-opened eyelids, liking the way the fire leapt in answer deep in the black eyes. Her fingers tiptoed through dark chest curls, found his hardened nipples.

"I know."

"Why the smug smile, Justin Salvador?"

"Because I suspect you're far more than what you seem, and I look forward to spending the rest of my life discovering each delightful facet. Like a rare gem, you're perfect, Leander Ondine."

"I'm far from it." Why would he make such a ridiculous statement? She moved restlessly. "I sometimes lie."

"So do I."

"How do I know you're not lying now?"

"You don't." At the startled look upon her face, he laughed and kissed her again. Gently at first, like the first wave of high tide. Then with increasing force.

A reservoir of passion crashed and rolled over both then. They cast aside words and clung to each other as though shipwrecked in a vast, shoreless ocean. Like a sea god intent upon worshiping his goddess, Justin paid tribute to Leander's loveliness with kisses on the silken swells and dips of her body. Her senses scudded before the consuming wave of rapture rushing over her too-long neglected need for love and tenderness. She might have been the shore Justin had told her existed because of the ocean; if so, he was surely the sea bringing splendid life to a desolate beach.

Leander's body was no longer virginal, unpathed, but such seemed a triumph. She knew now how to float with the passions Justin's nearness and touch created, how to reach out to his own wondrous shape and channel his desire to run in harmony with hers. With the same wonder as before, she sent fingers to find the shape of the fine head, to get lost in the black mane, to cup the form of an ear with reverence. Remembering how Justin had thrilled her with such a trick, she traced the inner edge of his ear with the tip of her tongue.

"You're driving me insane," Justin whispered, "but I love it. And I love you." Tenderly he unpinned her hair and spread the black sea of curls upon the pillow, burying his face in its fragrance and breathing in the sweet smell of her. How could she not know that what they shared was more than raw passion? Already his pulses threatened to render him deaf from the roar. He felt his entire body was enlarged with delicious wanting, crying out for what only hers could give. As if his hands could not get enough of sliding across the satiny skin, they repeated paths already taken, pausing longer at those spots that brought her into obvious throes of happiness. And each time she trembled with apparent longing and anticipation, he found that his body echoed what she seemed to be experiencing.

Justin's latest capture of her breasts pushed Leander farther toward the brink of ecstasy, brought a plea that got lost far back in her throat and turned into a whimper. Her heart came alive with new bursts of beats that seemed ready to pound her into quivering mounds of flesh, mounds screaming for more of his touch. Restlessly, she moved against the warm length of him, catching her breath at the new tide of desire washing over her from the promise of his hardness against her. Kissing him back with the same wild abandonment he was showing, she awaited what she knew would be the perfect release from tormenting attacks upon every cell.

Both existing now in a world of tossing, uncharted passion, Justin rolled to complete their journey through the turbid sea of sensation. Leander welcomed him, her legs hugging him closer. Those fragile barriers that had held back the force of their love gave way now to rising undulations of frenzied delirium. As though a tidal wave had sucked them up into its vortex, their souls aimed for the highest point . . . roared with that erupting tide . . . skimmed its apex . . . hung suspended for a convulsive moment . . . erupted with glorious poignancy . . . reached in vain for an unseen star to guide them . . . receded with a pang of heart-rending regret . . . then lay still in the calming backwaters of spent love.

Justin fondled the precious shape of her before he rolled to lie beside her, to cuddle her next to him, to whisper in a ragged way, "I love you, Leander. Do you think you might be able to say that back to me someday?"

Leander lifted puzzled eyes to those pleading black ones and answered with complete candor, "I hope so, Justin. I hope so." A dainty forefinger traveled the length of his handsome nose, went to outline the sensuous mouth. "Will you give me time to find out what I truly feel about you?"

Her breath came sweet as a night breeze across his face. Justin buried his head between the lovely breasts, answering from that delectable hollow, "Don't take too long. I would hate for our first child to be born before his mother realizes she is in love with his father."

Leander joined in his muffled laughter at his absurd rationalizing. But down deep in her heart, something painful stabbed at her, cutting off the laughter. Their child . . . children . . . would be half Spanish!

Chapter Twenty-two

By the middle of November, Leander, Felicity, Justin, and Jabbo were traveling up the Mississippi to their homes. Leander felt her world had become a crazy patchwork of clashing ideas and goals. Excusing herself from where Felicity and Justin sat on makeshift seats in the prow of the ship, she went to stand beside the railing and sort out her thoughts. So much had happened during the two months they had spent in New Orleans that the events seemed to run together.

First and foremost, Beaux Rives was free of debt, thanks to the generosity of the Spaniard who could make her blood run hot with desire and who would claim her as bride in a month. If her cousin in France had not already procured a second deed from King Louis XVI and sent it across the ocean, she would still have problems in claiming her legacy upon reaching her eighteenth birthday on December sixteenth. Justin had assured her that before they left for their honeymoon in Spain, they would stop over in New Orleans long enough to get the matter settled. Not to have a deed in hand when she appeared before the Council, despite the support of a Spanish husband, seemed mighty risky, and she fretted. She couldn't bring herself to trust Spaniards.

The thought of standing up to Felix Grinot upon arriving home did not daunt Leander. Her blind gaze upon the roiling, muddy waters, she planned to produce the papers showing Felix's collusion with the Spanish Governor O'Reilly and demand he confess what he had done to deserve such an award as Beaux Rives. Antoine had already told her the talk among officials, that Felix had turned in Etienne as the most rabid Conspirator. Then she would tell him of the death of Lieutenant Charles Garcia, the last of those older officers conspiring with Felix who had stayed behind after Governor Unzaga replaced O'Reilly six years ago. She would save the best for last: not only was she ousting him as overseer but also she was replacing him with Jabbo.

Now that Jabbo was legally a Free Man of Color, he could assume the position of overseer without fear of reprisals or rejections from other planters or their overseers. When she recalled Jabbo's declarations that for her to free him had not been necessary to make him feel he was special, she smiled to herself. His adamant refusal to consider settling anywhere but at Beaux Rives had brought a peculiar swelling to her heart. From the moment she had handed him the official document signed by Governor Unzaga, the giant black man had carried his broad shoulders even more proudly and stepped a bit jauntier. Neither had revealed why he had selected Wilding as his last name. Without discussing it, both had sensed how pleased

Dom would have been. Once she became mistress at neighboring Terre Platte, she could yet keep a hand in the running of Beaux Rives whenever she wished.

Justin watched Leander as she stood by the railing apparently deep in thought. His heart swelled with pride at the sight of her. Her beauty was unique, flawless. She was not like any of the other young women he had met in Louisiana. Even though she had attended the finest of schools and could practice elegant manners without effort, his beloved had an innate charm, an exuberant sense of the joy of life that no other possessed. Her independent spirit called out to his own, seemed to meld with it, even enforce it. The memory of her natural, spontaneous responses to his lovemaking, without false modesty or coyness, brought a surge of warmth to his groin. She was perfect in every way.

"Felicity," Justin leaned to say to the dreamy-eyed blonde sitting beside him, "Leander and I made out our list of guests to invite to the wedding, but I kept forgetting to remind her to add the names of your cousins in Mobile. How many do you suppose might be coming? Since many guests from New Orleans will be staying at both Beaux Rives and your place, you might prefer that the relatives stay with you."

Lost in the reverie having to do with the romantic Bernardo de Galvez, Felicity startled and replied, "Leander and I don't have any relatives outside France. I don't know what you're—" Felicity came to herself then, heard what she was saying, and let out a strangled ending, "—talking about."

"You know, the cousins of her mother's and your father's that she stayed with when she wasn't in that private school," Justin said impatiently. What was bringing that look of consternation to the pretty widow's face? He recalled her vague reply. "What was it you said about not having any relatives outside France?"

Felicity frowned prettily, claimed a splitting headache, and promptly laid her arms upon a nearby keg and settled her head across them. Leander was going to kill her! If she hadn't been woolgathering about Bernardo and his declaration to court her in the spring, she wouldn't have been caught off guard. By the time Leander returned to sit with Justin and her, Felicity didn't have to feign a headache. She ached all over.

If Jabbo hadn't come then to announce that the ship was nearing Terre Platte, Justin might would have pursued the strange answers and actions from Felicity. The more he thought upon it, the more he decided to wait and talk with Leander privately. The sometimes flighty Felicity might truly be half out of her mind with a headache — or a heartache, he told himself when he recalled how attached Bernardo and she had become over the past two months. The matter of invitations could wait another few days, for ships passed almost daily between New Orleans and Mobile.

Justin forgot the matter of invitations when he called at Beaux Rives the afternoon after their return from New Orleans. He was too delighted to see Leander, talk with her, steal a few impassioned kisses and embraces.

Feeling sure of herself the following morning and rested up from her journey, Leander sent for Felix. He listened, unbelieving. When she laid out the evidence to back up her accusations, the little man blanched.

Beady eyes jumping from the documents to the cold, accusing face of Leander, he offered a full thirty minutes of jerky, unbelievable explanations.

"Felix," Leander said, tired of his lies and ready to get him out of her sight, "you might as well face it. You will leave here tomorrow — and without a recommendation. If I could prove you are the one who testified against my father, I would and have you locked up. But I have no real proof, other than this document signed by both Bloody O'Reilly and you. I also have witnesses as to what you have said and done against my family and me." She was thinking of what Antoine had told her was common talk at the Cabildo. He had assured her that such testimony was unlikely to stand up in court, but she wanted to shut Felix up and get him gone. If threats worked, she would use them. "Now that your cohort Lieutenant Garcia is dead, you have no one on your side. Those you have trusted have turned against you."

"What has that damned slut told on me?" the grim-faced overseer demanded, his head raised so high that his Adam's apple jiggled.

"To whom are you referring by such foul language?" Leander shot back with disgust.

"You know who. That stupid Cara. What has she told about me?" The weak face screwed up into one of anger and hate.

Leander sank back against her chair behind the desk in horror at the thoughts racing through her mind. Memories of the so-called accidents that Cara had been having over the final months of summer spewed forth. She recalled how she had once threatened to speak to Tower about his possible mistreatment and how the young woman had assured her that the stableman would never strike her. Though the slave had seemed fit when Leander returned home, she remembered how Cara had been unable to come see her on the day of her departure.

"Have you been beating up on my personal maid in attempts to learn about my business?" Contempt and anger lent a chilling harshness to the question. "Have you, Felix?"

"Whatever gave you such an idea?" he countered, standing and ramming grimy hands in his pockets. "I know Cara doesn't like me because of that old business with her sister, and I just figured she had been blabbing lies. I'll go now if that's the way you want to repay me for all I've done here the past seven years since the house burned." His voice took on a self-pitying whine; his thin shoulders drooped even lower.

"You'll get no pity or thanks from me, Felix Grinot."

"You're going to be sorry if you try to put that bully Jabbo as overseer. Nobody's going to want to work for another black." He gave her a sneering look. "Of course since you're going to become Mrs. Justin Salvador, I don't guess you care much what happens to Beaux Rives anymore."

"I care as much as I ever have, not that it's any of your business. As for Jabbo, he will make a better overseer than you ever did." When he raked her with a cutting look and seemed ready to make a quick reply, Leander stood and said, "Good-bye, Felix. I expect you to be gone before dark tomorrow." Even when he slunk on out the doorway, she felt soiled from his having been in the study.

Leander sent for Jabbo and told him all that had

gone on between Felix and her.

"I'll keep a watch on him," Jabbo promised, disturbed that such hateful words had passed between Leander and the sneaky overseer. It bothered him, too, that he hadn't suspected Felix was forcing his attentions on Cara. Why hadn't she told him? Why had Tower, who he knew loved Cara and wanted to marry her, not stepped in to help? Was Felix so clever that he held something over every slave? Jabbo's frown was fierce.

"Better still, keep a watch on Cara," she replied after a moment's thought. "He left here with blood in his eye. Though he is furious with both of us, she is probably the only one he would dare seek revenge on."

Late that afternoon, Felix commanded Cara to meet him at their trysting place before dark. Devastated at having lost his chance to own Beaux Rives and perhaps marry Violette's look-alike daughter, the half-demented little man rushed to a slough left from a change in the course of Frenchman's Bayou. Cut off from the main body of the bayou, the muddy, sluggish arm of water served as a lair for a family of alligators. Back when he was having the affair with Cara's sister Leone and other young nubile slaves, Felix had found the secluded banks perfect for indulging in his bestial sexual appetites. The threat to throw uncooperative partners down the steep bank to the alligators below always made the most unwilling young woman submissive. His sharp knife served as secondary assurance of getting his way. Cara wasn't the only slave at Beaux Rives to bear beneath her clothing a thin scar in the shape of an F.

"What you want with me in the daylight?" Cara asked when she appeared from the trees and stood facing Felix. She had run almost the entire way, afraid Leander or Tower would miss her. "I've not told nobody about your making me meet you since you whipped Tower with that bullwhip the second time last year. We both know you can do what you want with either of us." She lifted her head bravely.

"You've been blabbing to your mistress. You told her I asked you about her reasons for going to New Orleans, didn't you?" He motioned for her to come close where he stood near the edge of the bank. When she hesitated, he drew his knife from its holster. "And about my trying to find out if she was talking about getting married, too."

"No, sir, Mr. Felix," Cara denied, her eyes round and frightened at the red fire in his eyes. From remembered beatings and mistreatment, she urged her feet to shuffle forward. "I've never told Missy anything about you . . . and me."

Felix grabbed her arm then and yanked her to stand with her back to him. With the knife resting close to her throat, he said, "I'm going to beat you like I never have before for tattling on me, you whore. And then I'm going to throw you to the alligators. Nobody will ever get a chance to see the bruises this time, so I won't have to hold back." Carried away with his devilish plan and encouraged from having slugged whiskey all afternoon, he threw back his head and cackled.

Taking advantage of his temporary loosening of the blade against her throat, Cara slipped the kitchen knife secreted in her apron pocket and slashed backward, sticking the blade in his thigh where it stayed. The sharp pain and shock cut short Felix's laughter, sent him back a step, causing him to lose his hold on her.

With a lightning twist, Cara turned and whacked the hand holding the knife, laughing hysterically to see it fall to the ground near her.

"I hate you, Felix Grinot!" she yelled, stooping to retrieve his knife and rushing toward him. "Hate you for all you've done to my sister and to me and to Tower. Go ahead and kill me. You've made my life a hell anyway. I wish I'd stuck that knife over more toward the middle." A new spate of hysterical laugher replaced the jeers.

Having hobbled his horse after trailing Cara secretly, Jabbo followed the loud voices and appeared to see Felix stumbling backward toward the edge of the bank, cursing the delirious Cara, threatening to kill her. She advanced until she could reach him. He swung his fist, forgetting his own pain for a second when he heard the cruel blow, saw her head snap back. Recovering, Cara slashed at his arm and lost the knife to him just as Jabbo called out and ran toward them. Pig-eyes bulging in the contorted face, a thigh bleeding heavily from the protruding knife, Felix lost his footing and fell backward over the bank.

The earlier screams and raised voices drifted across the boundary to a back pasture on Belle Terre. Pierre Lemange, architect and builder of Justin's new home, was out riding his favorite horse on the warm November afternoon. When the commotion continued, even became louder and more frantic, Pierre removed the pistol from his saddlebag, left his horse, and hurried across the small wooded area. The sight awaiting shocked him, sent waves of revulsion throughout.

Pierre saw Jabbo leap into the slough, obviously trying to rescue whoever screamed so piteously from below the steep bank. A young black woman lay writhing upon the ground, moaning and holding what might be a broken jaw. When Pierre rushed to look over into the shallow, muddy water, he saw an alligator as long as his body grasping the leg of a screaming white man. Jabbo, his powerful black muscles bulging, was trying to pry loose the deadly, pointed teeth. His biggest problem seemed to be trying to stay clear of the great, whipping tail of the angered beast. At last he managed to free the leg and yelled to the man to scramble up the bank. But the man seemed to have gone berserk and instead of heading for the bank, he tried to escape downstream in the hip-high water. Before he managed to limp more than a short distance, he stumbled and fell facedown. An alligator, even larger than the one Jabbo still wrestled with, opened jaws with lightning speed and clamped onto his head, backing off into deeper water and dragging its struggling victim beneath its surface. Feeling useless, Pierre noticed that the flailing legs had lain still even before the reptile disappeared downstream with its catch.

"My God, Jabbo," Pierre called from the bank, his pistol at the ready. "Tell me where to shoot to kill the brute."

"Between the eyes," Jabbo answered, not sure who had offered help from up there but not caring either. Holding open the jaws of the threshing alligator was becoming more than even his strong arms and hands could manage much longer, and yet he couldn't let go. He was unable to back away far enough or fast enough to reach safety if he loosened his hold. The spiked, punishing tail had continually mauled one of the big man's legs, bringing fresh blood to the water. Aware that help was available, he boomed, "Make a slipknot in a rope and drop it on top of its head when I hold it still. I'll grab it." Jabbo gave his unknown benefactor time to check Felix's tethered horse for rope. When he heard the expected call, he made his move. The big hands released the opened jaws and then pressed to clamp them shut. After a violent struggle between man and beast there in the muddy, bloody slough, Jabbo won. With both arms he held the thrashing, bucking animal's jaws together.

Pierre took a step down the incline to a ledge and dropped the looped rope accurately. With awe he watched Jabbo snatch the rope with one lightning quick hand and slip it over the pointed end of the giant jaws forced together for that brief moment by one tensed arm. His injured leg took another stunning blow from the writhing animal before he could scramble through the shallow water toward the bank. Jabbo managed to leap and cling to an exposed tree root on the steep bank while Pierre shot at close range. A second shot followed quickly. Letting out an ear-splitting roar, the wounded alligator splashed wildly with his tail before it revealed the success of the closely aimed shots, one through an eye and the other through the middle of the flat forehead. By the time Pierre rushed to aid Jabbo's awkward ascent up the near-vertical incline, the monstrous reptile was bucking in death throes, the cruel tail still writhing and seeking a target there in the bloody, shallow water.

The shots brought Cara to her senses. She struggled to her feet to help Pierre drag the exhausted Jabbo upon the bank. Aware of the roars and splashes from the dying alligator in the slough behind them, the three lay still upon the ground, drained for what seemed a long time there in the fading November light. From what she heard the men say, Cara learned that Felix was dead, was already a meal for an alligator. Her quiet flood of tears were for the maimed Jabbo, though. Pierre tore his shirt into strips, using them as bindings to staunch the flow of blood from the mauled leg. Leaning on both, Jabbo managed to use his good leg and mount his horse. There seemed to be no need for talk as the three headed for Beaux Rives.

By midnight, Leander and Sheeva had tended to Jabbo's mutilated leg muscles. Tower came to help and determined that no bones were broken. Only then did Pierre leave for Terre Platte. Sheeva used the needle and catgut from the stable medicine box to stitch together the gaping wound. Applying a soothing salve and using clean cloths as bandages, Leander bound up the injured leg. Even after Jabbo breathed the regular pattern of deep sleep, she sat on beside his bed. The wavering flames in the fireplace drew her shocked gaze. Though she had come to despise Felix, she felt no joy that his death had come as it had. When she thought of Jabbo's dislike of the cruel overseer and the indignities he had suffered due to the little man's disregard for him as a person, Leander felt a kind of awe that the giant black had risked his life for one of so little apparent worth. None of the events at the slough made any sense.

Justin arrived before the sun was up all the way. Pierre had not returned to Belle Terre until late and had assured Justin that Jabbo was going to be all right. When Justin entered the downstairs bedroom, he found Jabbo dozing. Flinching to see the circles beneath Leander's haunted eyes, he carried her upstairs to her bedroom and called for Cara to get her into bed. Her jaw swollen but not broken, a solemn-eyed Cara moved to carry out the orders neither Sheeva nor she had been able to make their mistress obey.

That afternoon, when Leander awoke and came downstairs, she learned that Justin had stayed beside Jabbo most of the day while she slept. To her delight, the giant black man grinned at her in that way which convinced her all would be well with him.

Justin returned before dark, telling Leander that he had come to eat dinner with her and keep Jabbo and her company. When Cara and Tower came to visit the wounded man, the engaged couple retreated for a private visit in the living room.

"These past twenty-four hours have been hell for you, haven't they?" Justin asked. They sat side by side on one of the sofas, his arm gentling her head to rest against him. "I know how much Jabbo means to you." The caring words spread across her pain like a balm.

"He has been the father I lost so long ago." Neither judged her remark incongruous, for neither thought of Jabbo's color as being more than a characteristic of his body — like his great size. Leander exhaled a scraggy breath at the thought that Jabbo could have so easily died while trying to rescue the evil Felix.

Justin smoothed the troubled brow with butterfly kisses. "Tell me all about yourself. There are more gaps than filled-in places in what I know about you."

"There's not much to tell." What was bringing that serious set to his mouth, the one she always thought of as tilting upward into a permanent look of pleasure? A curious wish to take her fingers and mold the corners into a smile overcame her. Once she touched those lips and achieved the effect she longed for, she teased, "My life hasn't been that unique."

"Tell me anyway."

"Well," she began, surprised that the solemn look had already claimed the handsome face again. "I was born on the second floor of—"

"No," he interrupted to say, "I know about your childhood here at Beaux Rives. What about those years after the house burned, after your father died?"

Leander lifted her head from his shoulder to let her eyes meet the questing ones so close. "You know that Jabbo and I traveled to Mobile to my cousins there. I entered Miss Julia Shepherd's School—"

He broke in again. "Felicity said there are no cousins outside of France."

Justin felt her body tense there in his light embrace. The glow from the overhead candlelabra bathed her face with golden light, picked up the bewitching blue-black tints in her hair. He watched the pansy-colored eyes darken, draw a curtain against him as if he were an outsider, even before they hid behind sooty lashes. Why didn't she spout a denial of her cousin's story?

"What made her say that?" Leander queried, her heartbeat speeding up. Her fingers interlaced there on her lap. She could feel her body becoming rigid. The encircling arm became an imprisoning vise when his hand tightened cruelly on her shoulder.

"I asked her how many might be coming to the wedding, where to send invitations," Justin responded in not much more than a whisper. Why was she trying to escape? The normally fair-skinned oval face was turning into a white mask.

"Why is this so important to you?" she fenced, her mind scurrying in desperation. Why had Felicity told him? Why had she not warned her that she had? She recalled then that she had blamed Felicity's remoteness during the return trip on her grief at having to bid farewell to Bernardo. Had it been due to something else as well? Not for a moment did she suspect Felicity had revealed her secret to Justin on purpose. Her brain was too busy scrambling for plausible answers to figure out what the blonde must have told and why.

"I told you. I want to know all about the one I love." Her attempt to draw away made Justin all the more determined to keep her beside him. The hand on her shoulder gripped harder.

"What difference do such things as cousins in Mobile or no cousins in Mobile make?" Leander parried. If she were to admit to him that all she had told about the six years before she reappeared at Beaux Rives were lies, would he try to back out of marrying her — ask for reimbursement of the sum paid on back taxes? She couldn't afford to gamble such a high stake, not when it came to the security of Beaux Rives and all who depended on it for life's necessities. Trying to distract him, she darted him a flirtatious invitation from behind half-lowered lashes. "Can't we talk of more pleasant matters? As you said, these past twenty-four hours —"

"Don't try using feminine wiles to worm your way out of this." The words and the coldness of the black eyes peppered her like well-aimed darts. "Are there cousins in Mobile? Where did you go when the house burned?"

Leander jerked herself free from the controlling

497

hand on her shoulder and slid down to the far end of the sofa. How much had Justin learned?

"Criminee!" Leander exclaimed in little less than a shout. Anger at his persistence kindled purple fire in her eyes. "Is this what is meant by the Spanish Inquisition?"

His head cocking in disbelief, Justin stared at the purple eyes glaring across the small distance, the daringly lifted chin. That word "criminee" crashed into a fragmented memory, fell into an empty space there. He had heard it said in feminine tones only once in his lifetime. Like a wheel ever laboring uphill toward making a complete revolution, the turnings of his mind reached a telling point.

"My God!" he muttered, the taste of truth bitter on his tongue. The dizzying mental puzzle came full circle. "You! It was you in the bed with me back at Josie's Inn last November. You! My God! Why have I been so blind, allowed myself to be so duped?" His hands whipped through his hair and mussed the black perfection. An avalanche of blood flushed the olive face. The black eyes seemed glued to her face.

Leander's puzzlement gave way to hated knowledge. All at once she recalled having noted something strange about that faceless Spaniard's hair even in the nearly dark bedroom—it was the thin white streak. The memory of that night rose up in lurid detail, seeming more vivid than the nightmarish drama taking place in her living room at that moment. A painful, indrawn breath turned into a gasp, and her hand flew up to stop its coming out. Her horrified gaze flew to the tiny scar in his left eyebrow, the one she had fondled and kissed. Holy Mother! Her hefty blow with the pewter candlestick must have put it there. She even remembered how she had wished she had killed him. The hand on her mouth no longer held in all sounds.

"This can't be true," Leander managed to blurt. She had never before seen Justin lose his temper. The sight of him on the verge of losing control frightened her, drove her to lean farther into the corner of the sofa.

"You were there, weren't you?" his voice whipped across the space, its force almost tangible. "All the other whores lied when I went to ask about you. The faking Miss Josie told the biggest lie of all, leading me to believe I had dreamed you, that none of her 'ladies' had violet eyes." At each new revelation, Justin's voice took on more fury. "Dreamed you, did I? What a stupid fool I've been! I should have wondered how such a 'fine Creole young lady' could have learned the bawdy song you sang that day beside the river."

"Wait, Justin," Leander began, not sure why he was as upset as he appeared to be. Once he knew the entire story, he would calm down. If he knew about the soldiers hunting her, about Dom . . . A pleading hand begged for his understanding. "There are so many things you don't know—"

"So very true, my dear," he grated, slashing her with cold stares, inching down the sofa toward her, but ignoring the supplicating, outstretched hand. "Suppose you enlighten me, now that the truth is out. You didn't go to any school for young ladies, in spite of that ridiculous act you put on right here in this very room that afternoon for Antoine and me. How it must have tickled you to have us both eating out of your cheating little hands. Somehow, you ended up downriver at that whorehouse. When I found you in that bed, you were exactly what I thought you were when I woke up." Fast and furiously, he spat out the hateful, accusing words. "Not only are you a whore, you're a thief as well. Have Jabbo and you had secret laughs at my wondering where Gabriel came from? And did my gold spend well? Did it buy the fancy wardrobe you two wear?" He grabbed both her hands then and pulled her face to within inches of his. "Tell me about you, by God, or I'll make you wish you had. Give me some answers, Leander Ondine—or is that even your real name?"

Stung at the cruel, unjust accusations and frightened by his vehemence, Leander replied with that hint of her father's arrogance, "You well know that's my name or you would have never tried to make me your wife. Don't you think I know that you proposed just so you would have an entry into Creole society? You've never fooled me a minute with your claims of being in love with me. Does being a bloody Spaniard give you the right to expect your wife to be perfect? I never once made such a pretense. Get out of my house!" She would have slapped him had her hands been free.

"*Your* house, is it? *Your* dream, is it? Do you think the whole world revolves around you and what you want?" Justin snarled. He still grasped her wrists tightly, still spoke right in her face. The knot inside him writhed and twisted from pain to anger, then reversed with maddening persistence. "I may be what you term a 'bloody' Spaniard, but I don't need to marry the likes of you to be accepted by your precious Creole society. Not that it ever made a damn to me, but I made it on my own, long before you left your chosen professions of whore and thief and returned here."

"You know that I'm no whore," Leander denied, her

voice strangling and jerking out in the tones of a stranger. Her blazing eyes challenged him to deny that he had found her a virgin that night in the lodge. That vile lie seemed the cruelest stab of all. That no denial, apology, retraction — no decipherable message at all came from the livid face or cutting eyes seemed more hurtful than if he had begun a new tirade. "As for the puppy and the gold . . . I can explain if you care to hear. None of this is as it seems."

"No, by damn, it's not. It's worse than it seems, one hell of a lot worse. You took me in and played me for a fool, and I'll not forget it in a lifetime. If there's one thing I can't stand, it's a lying cheat."

Leander struggled to free her hands. When he suddenly let them go as if they were objects of filth, she fell back against the end of the sofa and announced with disdain, "I'm calling off the engagement. I wouldn't marry you if you were the last man on earth." She would find another way to salvage Beaux Rives. Rage roared within. If he was so determined to believe his own warped interpretation of what took place that night in Throw-away's room, then let him go to hell. Her breathing becoming more and more ragged, she reached to the back of the necklace to release the catch, preparing to fling them in his face. All of a sudden the betrothal gift seemed to be choking her.

As if he had read her mind, Justin reached and snatched the pearls downward, saying, "You don't deserve the string holding them together."

A jerk that sent a stripe of pain to the back of her neck and then a snap, loud there in the tense space between them, and the lovely pearls rolled down Leander's neck and onto the tops of her heaving breasts.

Justin's hand froze in midair, once it did its dastardly deed. Both seemed mesmerized at the sight of the luminous balls dropping down like permanent tears to get lost in her cleavage and clothing.

"Get out!" Leander yelled, recovering first. With all the dignity she could command, she stood and motioned toward the doorway, pearls scampering down her cleavage and in every direction across the floor. "I'll return your pearls if I ever find all of them. I hope I never see you again."

"But you will, dear Leander," Justin threatened in heavy, double bass. Steely black eyes narrowed in emphasis. "You have stolen my dog and my gold, made an ass out of me for nearly a year—plus you are in my debt even more now. You'll live up to our bargain, just as I did when I paid your past-due assessments. You'll become my wife and bear my children, whether or not you want to. We've promised half of New Orleans and all the planters up and down the river a wedding, and there's going to be one—one they'll never forget."

"Why would you saddle yourself with such a burden as a whore and a thief?" She tried to hone her voice sharp enough to bring blood. Her hands knotted in fists and rested on her hips. Had her looks been knives, they would have slain him on the spot.

"Because I have already bought and paid for her," Justin sneered in answer. "I may be a 'lousy' Spaniard, but I'm the one with the gold, remember? Get Cara to restring those pearls. I want to see them around your neck when you become my bride." Without a visible softening of features, he spun around and marched to the doorway. He might as well have been handling a sale of horseflesh, so impersonal did he seem. Once there, he turned to say over his shoulder, "In case I don't see you before, I'll meet you at the bottom of Terre Platte's staircase at noon on December seventeenth as planned. Be on time." He slammed the door and escaped.

If he heard a yell and the crash of a vase against the closed door of the living room, Justin Salvador made no show of it. He stalked across the front porch and leaped upon the startled Principe lipping on a patch of grass near the steps. With a forward lunge, he grabbed the trailing reins and pressed for home. Each racing step Principe made away from Beaux Rives restored a piddling grain of Justin's trampled pride. He doubted anything could ever ease his broken heart.

"You might as well tell me what has you all down in the mouth," Jabbo told Leander a few days later. At first he had thought she was saddened and concerned over his injuries, but now that he could sit up and hobble about on a crutch Tower had made, he realized that something far more serious gnawed at her.

From where she sat beside his bed, Leander lay down the book she had been reading aloud. Propped up against two large pillows, Jabbo looked more like himself than he had since his ordeal with the alligator. The blue-black of his skin no longer had a faded, washed-out look. The few sprinklings of gray in the finely matted black hair seemed more noticeable against the white pillowcases. But then so did his teeth when he smiled at her in that patient, waiting way she recalled from as far back as she could remember.

"Maybe I can't forget how foolish it was for you to

risk your life for someone who hated you, whom you must have hated in return," Leander countered, letting her gaze skip outside the window beside the head of the bed. What leaves were left on the trees were brown and papery, dead without realizing they were doomed to fall. Up near the house, a scraggly branch of a cottonwood rose and fell in the wind rising from the river.

"I never hated Felix, nor did you," Jabbo said in that slow way of his. "God-fearing folks don't go around hating people, even if they seem not to be friendly."

"Who said we're God-fearing?" Leander quipped, thinking to bring a gleam to the solemn brown eyes.

"We both know we are, even if we don't talk about it. Your mama and papa brought you up loving and knowing about God, and they helped me learn too. Don't you remember how the visiting priests used to come here and hold services for all of us in the big ballroom?"

Leander nodded, not sure she liked the way the talk was going. She felt guilty enough and angry enough to want no reminders that there was good in the world somewhere. Inside, a tormenting ball of misery wound up tighter.

"By the way," Jabbo said, seeking a subject to bring a peaceful look to her face and eyes, "I heard Miss Felicity telling how Father Raphael gave her permission to wear a dark blue gown when she stands up with you at the wedding. That was mighty decent and understanding, wasn't it?"

Along with Cara and Tower that last night Justin was in the house, he had heard the raised but muffled voices coming from behind the closed doors to the living room. Since her face had stayed long ever since, he suspected that whatever plagued her had something to do with Justin Salvador. Maybe if he could get her to talking about the upcoming ceremony . . .

"I guess," she admitted, not warming up to talk about the wedding. She felt no anger toward Felicity for not warning her about Justin's probable interrogation. Her cousin had no knowledge of what had gone on between the two of them at Josie's Inn. The issue had to come out into the open sooner or later.

"Don Salvador will make a good husband for you, missy."

"How can you say that?" Leander huffed. "You know what I think of all Spaniards; yet here you are, praising that conceited planter. He doesn't think much of you, judging by the way he hasn't even come over to see about you in three whole days." Violet eyes fixed him with a so-there look.

"When you're always talking about hating the Spaniards, you don't really mean that, missy. You might still hold a bit of a hurt inside about what they did to—"

"I do hate them Jabbo. I can promise you I do," Leander cut in to say with vehemence. "And especially Justin."

Jabbo studied the trembling lips, the faraway look in the haunted eyes before saying, "If you fill your heart with hate, you won't ever have room for love to grow there. Hate harms the one doing it, not its object. I learned that a long time ago, missy. When I arrived in New Orleans and your papa bought me and took me to a doctor, I would have killed him simply because he was a white man, had I gotten the chance. I was so full

505

of hate, I wasn't hardly human." Her eyes seemed fixed on something outside the window, but he recognized the darkening back in the depths that had always signified comprehension of something new.

"And what happened?" Leander bent her gaze on the broad black face then. She thought she had heard every speech he held in reserve to teach her about life, but she had never before heard this one.

"First you papa and your mama, then all the other slaves, ignored my open hatred and treated me with kindness. Nobody would let me die, when sometimes I thought that was all I wanted in this world. When I finally got well from the unmanning my master in Jamaica gave me with the same tools used to geld a stallion, your parents handed you to me to watch over. You weren't quite a year old. They trusted me to care for their most valued possession. I remember how their gentling had already led me to expect more good than bad from life here on Beaux Rives. Pretty soon, I didn't have any room left in my heart for that old devil hate because it was brimming over with love." He didn't add, "For you."

But Leander heard the words anyway. She leaned over from the chair and laid her head down on the foot of the bed, her face turned away from Jabbo. She hadn't shed tears in front of him since that day she learned of Dom's death. The enormity of what the giant black had told her filled her with sorrow. He had tried to save Felix because his heart harbored hate for no one. Her shoulders heaved as cognizance cut a keen path. She was doomed never to know love or happiness, for she had a heart full of hate. She knew no way to get rid of it. No wonder Justin had turned on her, had refused to listen to her explanations.

For the first time in his seventeen years of being responsible for the young woman weeping into the sheets on his bed, Jabbo reached out a hand to touch her just for the sake of touching. The shape of her skull beneath the pile of black curls felt exactly as it had when he had had call to cradle it when she was a child. He remembered catching her to cushion her falls when she was learning to walk, picking her up when she would fall asleep in the shade near where he hoed in a flower bed and taking her inside to her bed, rescuing her when she would try to climb too high in a tree . . .

"I'll tell you what," Jabbo said in low, crooning tones he hadn't used in years. "There's not a single reason you can't wipe out that hate. You're the only one who can." When the sobbing became more audible then and nigh brought tears to his own eyes, he added, "In fact, I wouldn't be at all surprised if you looked real hard in that fine heart of yours, you'd see it's already gone."

He heard the wind whip a few leaves against the windowpanes, heard the book fall from her lap to the floor, watched the shadows lengthening in the room. When the shoulders became still and the little grieving sounds died, he withdrew his hand as gently as he had eased it to lay upon that familiar head.

"You know," Leander said, taking time to wipe at the tears with her hands before turning to face him, "I think a brisk walk with Gabriel before dark might be just what I need. Now that you're feeling so much better, you won't mind being alone for a little spell, will you?" By then she had risen and picked up the fallen book, placing it on the table beside the bed. Her eyes met his with a brilliant self-knowledge which warmed him all over.

"You always did have the best ideas, missy. Go on now and get yourself outside. Breathing in some of that fresh river wind is probably just what you need." When the door closed quietly, Jabbo sighed and relaxed his gray-streaked head against the pillows.

Chapter Twenty-three

Delving into her heart more deeply than at any time in her life, Leander spent the following sunny morning riding across her land. Without planning to, she ended up on the bank of Frenchman's Bayou. Little rain having fallen that autumn, the water at one spot was no higher than Bagatelle's knees. Talking to the horse as she so often did when riding alone, she watched the noisy antics of fox-tailed squirrels playing chase overhead in the canopy of interlacing branches and trailing moss. Rustling dry leaves danced up in echoing swirls as Leander loosened her hold on the reins and gave Bagatelle freedom to find the way through the forest. Beneath the oaks, prancing hooves crunched fallen twigs and dried acorns.

"Jabbo would say the squirrels are storing acorns for winter," she confided to the easy-gaited horse, catching a glimpse of a fuzzy, orangey tail flipping out of sight on a nearby oak. Bagatelle lifted ears already pert and seemed to move her neck more energetically.

Now that most of the leaves had fallen from the towering swamp beeches and oaks, Leander could spot the circular mounds of dried leaves and twigs that squirrels had lodged high in cradling limbs to house them during approaching winter. Extreme temperature drops seldom occurred in Louisiana until after Christmas, she reflected, so they still had a few weeks to prepare.

"Well, what do you know, Bagatelle?" Leander asked in that musing tone she used when speaking "horse." "You've brought me right to the hunting lodge." Her heart had chided her ever since she crossed the bayou. Its thumps seemed to threaten her when she noted a foreign object on the grayed wooden door.

The memory of Justin's and her promise to meet there within ten days of that stormy night back in January hit the raw edges of her heart with the pain of smeared salt. And by the time that tenth day came, she made herself remember, she had found he was both a Spaniard and a scoundrel. That Lea and Justin who had loved so sublimely during the cloudburst had been no more real than their pretended princess and frog from the fairy tale.

Honesty reared up to snatch Leander back from ignoring a truth, making her admit that her impressions formed at the Mardi Gras ball had since proved false. Still, she could not forget her anguish at the time. And on that trysting date, news had come of Andre's death. She recalled how she had rushed to Belle Terre to be with Felicity, determined to forget Justin and their night together.

"What have we here?" Leander asked, not ready to

rein Bagatelle back toward the bayou. A giant leaf or whatever was stuck to the door begged for inspection. She dismounted and went closer, footsteps on the leaf-covered porch loud in the deserted forest. Held by a rusted blade was a folded piece of brown paper with curling, water-spotted edges. Yes, she reminded her hopscotching heart, they had agreed that a note would be left if one had to miss the date, but after the debacle of their clash at the Mardi Gras ball . . . Could it be—? Her fingers trembling, she freed the paper, unfolded it and read:

Darling—I will love you always and wait forever to make you my wife. Beautiful princess, don't forsake me.

A Sad Frog

Not understanding why tears pushed at her eyelids, Leander digested the faded, weathered words a second time before mounting and heading back toward Beaux Rives. Justin had come that day back in February, even though she had told him never to come around her again. Why? Had he truly loved her before he had learned she was the one in Throw-away's bed? She agonized all the way home. What were the answers? Even the questions brought wracking, new pain.

Gabriel at his side, Jabbo was hobbling slowly across the whistle walk when Leander came from leaving Bagatelle in Tower's capable hands. He wondered at the stormy specks back in her eyes as she bragged on his prowess in getting around.

"Don Salvador came over while you were gone

riding," Jabbo said. He watched her take a little shuddering breath.

"Is he coming back later to call on me?" Leander stooped to ruffle the fur on Gabriel's neck.

"He said he wasn't. Guess he's pretty busy, what with the bedroom furniture and some other goods arriving from New Orleans yesterday. Also a ship stopped here and left some packets while you were out riding."

With what Jabbo thought was too little interest in packets for a bride-to-be, she turned and went inside. Whatever chewed at her still was at work, he mused. Would she get it resolved in time? His heart wrenched. The wedding was but two weeks away.

To Leander's disappointment, the packet contained no letter from the distant cousin Jean Paul in Bordeaux, though it did hold one from Josie. Eagerly she ripped through the sealing wax to read that the man in English Landing whom Josie had always loved had become widowed the past summer. She had sold her inn and gone with him to their former home city of Charleston where they married. Josie told that she had learned from a friend in New Orleans of Leander's upcoming marriage to Justin and that she was sending both Throw-away's and her best wishes. Briefly she told how it was that Throw-away had unknowingly put Justin into the bed with a female that night.

Had she not been so close to tears, Leander would have laughed at the incongruousness of Throw-away's innocent, simple-minded mistake wreaking such havoc in two lives. Justin would never believe Josie's explanation was more than additional lies. With a sigh for Josie's happiness, and a longer one for her own misery, Leander turned to the major portions of the packet.

The carefully wrapped bundles held the elaborate trousseau Justin had bought her in New Orleans. While Cara lifted out each item and raved over its beauty, Leander stared at the wedding gown hanging in the dressing alcove with trepidation. A cold spot knotted up inside her belly. How could she walk down that staircase at Terre Platte in that pristine gown and meet a groom with frigid, accusing eyes?

Late that afternoon while wandering about the grounds, Leander still puzzled over that question. She paused, surprised to see that she stood beside the old hollow tree. More weathered now, with fewer branches lifting toward the wintry sky than on that day when she had hidden from the soldiers, it seemed to beckon. Thoughts dwelling upon that fateful afternoon over seven years ago, then rushing on to include the years with the loving, caring Dom and Jabbo, she stooped to see if she could still fit inside the hollow.

Bemused at her childishness, Leander found not only could she enter, but also she could stand. There in the little cobwebbed niche was the rolled-up piece of vellum, damp but intact. The piece of charcoal she had been using was crumbly, yet still in place. Her foot struck something metallic. With the vellum in hand, she peered down in the shadowed space and gasped. Even in the half-light, something glowed, almost gleamed.

A sweep of her foot and the gleam multiplied. Gold coins stared up at her. There must be hundreds in a box beneath the rotting debris on the ground inside the hollow tree, she exulted, letting the vellum fall. She slid down in the narrow space, squatting close enough to the ground to touch them, to push her hands down into

513

a seemingly bottomless pit, to make sure they were real. Yes! Very real. Then she recalled that her father had told her their last night together that he had asked Jabbo to hide the gold from his recent sales of a bumper harvest and nearly all of the horses. Why had she never remembered it before now? Why had Jabbo never told her?

But even as joyful tears formed, Leander realized that it had never been her policy to discuss money matters with the big man or in his presence. He would have had no way of knowing she desperately needed money. His world had been one of enforced simplicity; he depended on her as he had always depended upon masters to care for his needs. Until she had freed him recently and he had elected to return to Beaux Rives as overseer, business matters had not been his concern.

Covering over the treasure with loose leaves until Jabbo was well enough to come for it, Leander picked up the vellum and squirmed backward from the hollow. As she walked toward the house with bouncy steps, she sniffed the comforting smell of woodsmoke drifting from the chimneys. An early December sunset formed a colorful backdrop for the blackening shapes of the trees, house, and outbuildings. Leander wondered if the myriad shades of pinks and purples on that western horizon would ever again seem as lovely.

When the dazed young mistress of Beaux Rives reached the porch, Gabriel came from around back to nuzzle her. She sat upon the top step and hugged him close before unrolling the vellum to see again that childish sketch of the snow goose. Holding it up high to keep the inquisitive dog from licking it, she realized it had writing on the back side and investigated. Her little yip of disbelief startled Gabriel, ended up as a huge smile on her glowing face.

"Gabriel," Leander explained to the attentive animal, "you're looking at the original deed to two thousand arpents along the Mississippi assigned to Etienne Ondine and his heirs forever." Accustomed to her conversing with him, the dog seemed to try to understand, tilting his head first one way and then the other while the black-tipped ears lifted like flags. Letting out an indulgent laugh at his obvious confusion, she went on. "See. This is the scrawl of King Louis XIV, and down below is the Royal Seal."

A forefinger traced the embossed seal with reverence. It sounded so much more believable to say it aloud, she mused—even if the only ears to hear belonged to a dog. Inside, her heart and mind celebrated: There was no longer any need for her to wed a Spaniard to save Beaux Rives. She had money enough to repay Justin for his expenditures, with plenty left over to operate the plantation on a grander scale. She was free.

During her last talk with her father—the one she had blindly refused to dwell upon before now—he had told her he meant to pass on some information to her besides that about the hidden gold but had been unable to recall it. Leander gulped back the memory of his drunken state, let the memory unfold in its entirety. Had what he meant to tell was that the roll of vellum in the umbrella stand was the deed to Beaux Rives and not a cast-off for her to sketch on? Somehow, she sensed it was. If she had forced herself to relive the final night with him before that very afternoon, would she have recalled about the gold, or at least sought the vellum as a keepsake? Not that such made any difference now, she realized.

A surprised look upon his face when Leander burst into his room, Jabbo listened to her garbled account of her findings. Never had he seen her so excited.

"I don't guess it ever crossed my mind about that gold since we came back here," he confessed when she slowed down for a breath. His healing leg propped upon a footstool, he sat in front of the fireplace in the downstairs bedroom. His heart lifted at each little squeal of happiness she made. "Those were such troubled times that I seldom thought back on them. I buried it that last night Master Etienne was here. He never said what he had in mind to do with it, but I reckon something like this must have been behind his blurred reasoning. You know, he never was himself after your mother died."

The brown eyes looked inward for a moment, then closed the door on that painful view. With renewed faith in the present replacing the sadness in his eyes, Jabbo went on. "Now that I'm to be overseer, I'll have to start paying attention to how debts and taxes get paid, won't I?" He leaned toward where she sat across from him. "Why haven't you already let me know you had money worries? I'm sure I would have recalled burying it had you told me about them." At her brief but clear explanation, Jabbo nodded in understanding, a relieved smile upon the broad face. "We're lucky some windstorm didn't blow over the old tree and show what was hidden to Felix."

As she rode Bagatelle down the river road toward Terre Platte the next afternoon, Leander felt the bulge of loose pearls in her coat pocket. What would the arrogant Spaniard think when she poured them on the floor before him? Let him be the one to get them restrung. Taking Jabbo's place as her protector, Tower rode at a discreet distance behind until she motioned for him to come alongside.

"Cara tells me you may have something you wish to talk over with me," Leander said, amused to see the embarrassed set to the slave's mouth.

"Guess you know what it is, missy," Tower mumbled, shooting her a sidewise look. "We want to be married."

"When the traveling priest comes next to hold services at Beaux Rives, I'll ask him to perform the ceremony. Everyone will be happy for Cara and you."

"Can we 'jump the broom' till Father's next visit?" Tower asked, ducking his head at his audacity.

"Of course," his mistress agreed, smiling at the memory of the simple ceremonies she had attended in the slave quarters when a child. In the absence of priests and churches up and down the river, weddings sometimes consisted of the engaged couple's gathering their families and friends together to witness their stepping over a broomhandle laid upon the floor. Often the master, or sometimes the overseer, would make the solemn announcement afterward that the two were married in the sight of God and man. Then when the traveling priest next came, he would officiate at a religious rite. Though Leander recalled her father's saying that the church had in the beginning protested against such "pagan" actions, it had already become an accepted practice by the time her parents came from France as newlyweds.

A few more exchanged remarks and Tower slowed his horse, obviously content to entertain himself with private thoughts as he followed his mistress.

Leander had plenty to think about herself. To ward off the chilly December winds, she had thrown a shawl over the purple riding costume. Dipping her chin into its soft folds, she rehashed all that had kept her tossing until the cocks crowed that morning. Since she no longer needed Justin's money, there was no reason to continue with the farcical marriage scheduled to take place in less than two weeks. Justin had never loved *her*, Leander Ondine; he had confused her with some perfect, illusory person from a fantasy world. Once she repaid the money, he could no longer claim to have bought a bride. With a grim smile, she acknowledged that she could now develop her own herd of fine horses, even purchase Rio Sepe or one of equal caliber as permanent stud, could turn her home into one of luxury. Beaux Rives would be as her father dreamed—and as she, too, dreamed, she added almost as afterthought. No longer would she have to be indebted to any Spaniard.

A short ways farther up the hard-packed road, she asked herself why she wasn't feeling happy that she would soon oust Justin from her life. Never had she denied that the physical attraction was real, but her mind had warned her repeatedly that such could not be binding, should not flavor decisions about the future. The river on her left kept rolling southward, no answers upon its muddy, swirling surfaces, no ships in sight to give her something new to think about. The stark banks rising dramatically on the opposite side held no fascination for her on that sunny afternoon.

On the travelers' right the denuded forests loomed bleak and forbidding, bare branches soughing against

518

each other in agitation from gusts of wind. Only a few straggling vines and undergrowth low upon the ground were still verdant and showing life. A flock of scavengering blackbirds swooped into a stand of tall trees up ahead, their flapping wings and raucous cries needling her, aggravating Leander's ears. The saddle squeaked with each third hoofbeat, the monotony of the sound setting her teeth on edge. She felt wound up tightly inside, like a ball of rolled-up yarn with a loose end threatening to unravel at the slighest tug.

What did she feel for Justin Salvador, Leander wondered for at least the hundredth time since he had stormed out of her living room last week with the imperious order for her to be on time for their wedding. Was there more than that earthy desire to melt in his arms?

She recalled that as a child, she had loved to swing on a board fixed to rough ropes hanging from an outreaching limb of a huge tree behind the mansion. She never could figure out if she preferred the swinging forward or the swinging backward to complete the arc in the air. Both had brought keen exhilaration, one she could still summon to mind and relive in poignant detail.

The downswing filled the young Leander with a sense of expectancy, bathed her face with a rush of fresh wind, sometimes came close to stealing away her breath in a delightful way. The backswing made her feel she was sailing off the earth, entering into some imaginary land, being snatched backward into an even more beautiful world than the one she faced. But just before she could accomplish her escape, the air would hold her suspended for a second, then come dancing to kiss her face, fan out her hair as she raced downward and forward in mid-air toward the overhead sky.

Guiding Bagatelle to the smoother side of the crusted road, Leander wondered if her feelings for Justin might not vacillate in a similar way. Always heady, sometimes promising, at times threatening, at others, thrilling—but ever challenging. When she ended their relationship, whatever category it fit, would she not miss its effect? Had she not always protested at having to leave the swing after only one full motion? Always she had wanted more.

Before Leander had her thoughts sorted out, the pink walls and white columns of Belle Terre stuck their beauty above the bare limbs. Her breath lodged in her throat. Memories of the past months of shared planning and laughter within the mansion's empty rooms roared through her mind like a cyclone. Before the summer ended, she had admitted that she was finding conversation with Justin to be heady and stimulating, no matter what the subject. For hours on end, she had forgotten that his heritage was Spanish, had accepted him for what he seemed—an intelligent, charming, witty young man. And certainly the most devastatingly handsome one she had ever seen. Ah, she chided herself, there's that old demon Physical Desire again. The reins in her left hand seemed damp, even through her gloves. The hateful knot inside pulled itself into a tighter ball.

"Where is Justin?" Leander asked when she knocked at the front door and Ona ushered her in with a huge smile. She could hear the clip-clops of the horses as Tower led them around back to the stables. She was glad she had insisted that Gabriel stay behind with

Jabbo to keep him company. To see the way the big dog always bounded to greet Justin would have been more than she could have borne. Closing the door behind her, she again addressed the black woman; "Ona, is Justin around? I need to speak with him." The pearls felt warm, almost alive through her pocket.

"Yes'um, Miss Leander," Ona replied, sending a hand to smooth at the kerchief tied about her head. "He's here. I jes' left him upstairs lookin' at the bedroom. I got all that new furniture shinin'. That man's been plain silly over gettin' married to you ever since comin' back from N'Orleans. Till jes' last week. Some kinda fierce spell done moved in on him. I'se sho' glad to see you come over 'cause I was feered y'all done had a tiff." The round face split into a pleased smile; the merry eyes twinkled. "Run on up an' brag on how the bedroom's gonna' look. I was jes fixin' to go on back to the ole house and see 'bout my other chores."

When Leander made no reply, Ona shuffled in the flapping slippers on toward the back door at the end of the hall, turning to say, "Mr. Pierre an' the master tole us Jabbo doin' fine now. We proud to hear it. I wants you to know all us at Terre Platte thanks the lucky stars an' the good Lawd for bringin' you back to river country. I doan mine tellin' you, I would'na thought so at first but now I knows you is exac'ly what the master needs. See iffen you can put that smile back on his face." With a knowing look and a jaunty wave of her hand, Ona left.

Thinking that her message would indeed put a smile on Justin's face, Leander called his name as she climbed the staircase. She removed her gloves to allow her hand to glide caressingly across the top of the satin-

521

smooth railing of mahogany. Halfway up to the landing, she turned to look behind her at the view across the wide hallway into the large ballroom. Her heart warmed to see the results of her contributions. Justin's Rio Sepe had provided future colts for Beaux Rives; she had added style and beauty to Terre Platte.

A glance at the closed front door beneath the fan of transom across its top showed Leander the striking Cross of Christ panel design she had favored, the wrought-iron rams' horn hinges made in the blacksmith's shop out back. Another of her ideas had been to repeat the pink and white of the exterior in the receiving area, paling the pink a shade. Her eyes drank in the restful beauty of the tall walls. The detail on the ceiling cornices was outstanding, was repeated on the mantel there in the ballroom as well as on the mansion's other five. Under Pierre's direction, the slaves had punched, gouged, and fluted the woodwork on blue poplar according to her sketches, then painted it white.

With appreciation, Leander noticed that since her last visit before going to New Orleans, the workers had accomplished much. Someone had apparently scrubbed the smooth floors of yellow poplar planking, then hand-rubbed them with oil and waxed them to a softly gleaming luster. The smells of wax and paint smacked of exciting newness. Tall windows in the ballroom with their twelve-over-twelve panes of English crown glass twinkled in the late afternoon sunshine. The chandeliers Justin and she had chosen had arrived and been installed. Over the fireplace, with its framing and hearth of white marble, a huge, gilt-edged mirror reflected the hanging fixtures in sparkling splendor, just as she had visualized. Tapers with uplifted wicks already filled the numerous holders. She sensed that a mysterious mood of expectancy permeated the house.

"Justin?" Leander called again, once she forced herself on up the stairs, on across the landing to the doorway into what she knew was the master bedroom. In her mind's eye, she saw the fireplace, a smaller replica of the one in the ballroom, saw the windows facing upon the upper veranda toward the Mississippi, saw the plastered walls of sunny yellow bordered with carved white cornices — all as she had first created on her sketch pad.

"What are you doing here?" was all Justin could get out when he turned from gazing out the window toward the river and acknowledged that what he had been hearing actually was Leander calling his name. His first thought was that something was wrong. The tall bed stood between them, but his eyes ran over her face and form quickly to check for possible injury. No, she was as lovely as ever. The purple velvet riding costume set off her beauty in a way which tripped his heartbeat into a veritable race with itself. Though the saucy hat angled back enough for him to view her face and eyes, he had the crazy notion to jerk it off so that he might see all of the black curls. Clearing his throat of the fullness that the sight of her brought and concealing all that was wreaking havoc inside, he asked, "What brings the unwilling bride before the assigned date? Surely not the wish for the company of a Spaniard."

Leander's gaze stumbled on the bed before she looked at Justin beside the window. The sight of him across what was to have been their marriage bed twisted the inner knot tighter, compressed it into searing pain. That old physical attraction she despised tried to take charge, sent a taunting, almost lewd mental image of her in his arms there on that lofty mattress before she could squelch the preposterous idea. Criminee! She had come to tell him off, she reminded herself while taking a deep breath, not to fall into his arms like the wanton his touch had always created. Even so, when she met the unfathomable look from the mesmerizing black eyes, she felt a sharp sense of loss.

"Justin, I came to tell you that I've found hundreds of gold coins my father must have hidden for me. I can now repay you for all that you've spent on my behalf."

Had his face always been so perfectly formed, Leander wondered. Had the streak in his hair always gleamed that way? Her mind seemed to be imprinting his likeness onto some permanent surface. To look at those full lips and know that they would never again set her on fire, murmur endearments, or smile in that way meant only for her nigh tore her heart into shreds. Of course, she reflected, all of those actions had been lost to her ever since that last night at Beaux Rives when he had lashed out at her. It was just that she had not been with him since then, hadn't truly faced up to what lay ahead, even had the marriage taken place as planned.

She heard her rehearsed speech unfold in the uneasy silence. "As soon as Jabbo is well enough to retrieve the gold from its hiding place, he'll bring over what I owe. You no longer have to take damaged goods for your money. I've come to call off the wedding."

Leander suspected that a kind of subdued pandemonium controlled the space between them. What would it take to set off the threatened explosion, let it destroy itself and cleanse the atmosphere? She felt suspended in a partial reverie. She was both taking part in the eerie scene and yet remaining an observer. As Justin stared across the bed at her, the ball of inner tension gathering ever since that night in Throw-away's room coiled tighter, imprisoning a core never examined.

The seeds of hatred of all things Spanish had grown too rank in her heart, had consumed too much space for too long a time. Only a scythe as sharp and cutting as Jabbo's gentle words that day in his bedroom could have ever led her to consider examining what lay hidden in her heart other than that old hate. His telling remarks came back: "If you fill your heart with hate, you won't ever have room for love to grow. Hate harms the one doing it, not its object." All at once she wanted nothing more than to unravel that self-spun cocoon, spin out those concealing filaments holding in her essence, expose what lay secreted. Taking in a shaky breath, she willed the topmost strand to unravel.

"I'm lying again," Leander told the tight-faced Justin when he made no effort to break the uneasy silence. Another thread loosened. Did those strong jaws lose a touch of rigidity, or was it a play of afternoon light? The air between them was yet fraught with silent tumult. He watched her with such alertness that she wondered if he could see her pulses pounding at her temples.

"About what?" Justin asked after a long pause. Seeing the violence in the purple eyes twanged at his heart. The laugh indentures normally cornering his mouth had turned into faint vertical lines in the olive face ever since her brief recital had commenced. Like a lantern with fuel running low, the light in his eyes dimmed, flickered, then repeated erratically.

What else could Leander Ondine do to flay his heart and soul into more disoriented segments, Justin agonized. The black-haired beauty leaning against the closed bedroom door was no phantom, never had been. She was blood, tissue, and sinew . . . and flawed, as he was, as all mortals. How could he have been so misled by hazy, romantic notions as to believe she was perfect, was destined to belong to him simply because he fantasized about that possibility, desired it be true? He had courted her as if he might be playing a game, one not unlike those they had enjoyed that night in the lodge, one with the outcome of no more significance. He had been a fool.

Cognizance of the fact that Leander had seen the difference in games and reality before he had himself brought Justin up short. The war within still seething, he scrutinized the lovely oval face, the pleading eyes. No longer able to keep his distance, he took steps to reach the foot of the bed.

Before him in regal purple velvet stood one ten years younger, but one who had shown far more wisdom than he in analyzing what was to be between them. Never had Leander pretended to be the perfect vision he had thought to have dreamed. That she be beyond normal guidelines of measurement had been his wish, his alone. Blinding insight told him that no perimeters should attempt to bind up love. All at once Justin's illusory world unfurled like a wind-inflated flag, jolted him into viewing the real culprit playing havoc with their relationship. It was he.

Leander walked to stand before him there at the end

of the bed they had selected in New Orleans. She heard the trailing skirt of her riding habit whisper against the polished wood. Now that she was so close, she could smell the masculine, woodsy smell she had come to associate with him, one she realized had become as familiar over the past months as her own. Another imprisoning thread rolled free inside when his eyes didn't compel her to retreat. Only a bridge of mutual compassion across the chasm of their misunderstanding offered salvation. Was it firmly in place? If so, could they cross it? Any positive sign from him she would welcome as a benediction. He might as well have been a statue.

"I was lying when I said I wished to call off the wedding," she whispered, surprised that a scalding lump hampered the passage of words from her throat. The black eyes seemed to be harboring a fierce storm. She wanted to shrink from the sparks attacking her. With amazing speed, the filaments of the hidden cocoon in her heart were uncoiling, spinning loose. A remarkable truth was bursting to be recognized. Justin's hand shot out, and she wondered fleetingly if he might not be going to strike her.

An impetuous movement and Leander was on her knees, seizing that outflung hand, kissing it, covering it with tears, saying with just-born knowledge, "Justin, Justin, can you ever forgive me for being such a fool?" Her voice tried to break, but she willed it to continue. "Here I've come to tell off the arrogant Spaniard, and I find I'm hypnotized, cast into some spell—and all because I can see no one in this room except the man I love, must have loved since I first laid eyes on him in the darkness in Throw-away's room last November.

527

Have pity on me, Justin, and forgive me." Only then did the pansy-colored eyes lift in tear-kissed splendor to invite entry into those tantalizing depths.

Having jerked his hand out to hug her close and tell her what an idiot he had been, Justin had knelt to face her the moment she grabbed that hand and dropped before him. Not until she had finished her timeous plea and lifted her eyes did she realize he had pulled her within the circle of his arms, that they were on their knees facing one another there at the foot of the bed, that the currents dizzying her came from their touching.

"I can forgive you to the extent that I love you, Leander," Justin told her in those tender bass tones she had thought never to hear again.

Merciful Heavens! How he longed to take those messages read in her eyes as absolute truth. Simply because he had not dared to hope for such a coup, a frisson of doubt persisted. Had he heard correctly? Leander loved him—a "bloody, lousy Spaniard"? He looked into her soul and saw forever. He fought the impulse to let out a victory yell, to shout to the world what he read there. Instead, he willed a forefinger brush tenderly at a tear lingering on the lovely curve of her cheek.

Humility and a new reverence for the Leander who could admit love with the same passion as she had once declared hatred swelled Justin's voice as he confessed, "And to tell the truth, I love you so much that I can't imagine how terrible your crime would have to be for me not to grant you total forgiveness."

Not a moment longer did he keep his lips even that bare inch from hers. Groans of relief and joy vibrated in both throats as worshipful arms and mouths celebrated their reunion.

Hungry lips eager to erase old hurts and doubts parted with reluctance. Starred eyes exchanged soul-felt promises. Embracing arms relaxing at last, Justin's strong, muscular ones reached to help a weak-kneed Leander to stand along with him.

"Who came with you?" he queried, not asking if he could remove the pert hat, just slipping out the long hat pin and doing so as if he might have been following a well-discussed plan. It landed on the bed, along with the discarded shawl. When she told him it was Tower, he said, "I'm going to go tell Tower I'll escort you home later. With our wedding so close at hand, we have much to talk about, don't we?"

Leander nodded, her gaze eating him up as he walked to leave the room. The fine, proud manner in which he carried the tall body brought a memory of the way he had moved from the doorway toward her that afternoon in the lodge, as though he had known she would welcome him. Nothing had been the same since. Funny how the threads were no longer binding deep inside. She felt all soft and blurred around the edges.

"Stand still," he ordered when she would have come to him there at the doorway for another hug. "I want to brand in my mind forever the way you look this moment." A long, drinking gaze savored the curved shape of her in the purple costume, the wide matching eyes framed in sooty silk, the kiss-puffed lips below the finely shaped nose, the shining jet wisps curling about the smooth oval face. With an audible sigh, he left after promising, "I won't be gone long."

And he wasn't, though both felt the brief time

dragged on for an eternity. Once Justin returned, he joined Leander where she sat radiant-faced on the green velvet sofa near the window. As though from long practice, she fitted her form to his when he sat and hugged her close for a kiss. Her heart nigh choked from swelling pleasure, as if it were feasting on a delicious draught of nectar. For a time, whispered "I love you's" were the only words tumbling forth. In between murmurings, Justin released the piled up curls one at a time until they fell in a fragrant black cloud about her shoulders. At each freed curl, the coiled strands inside her stretched out farther, as a crumpled ribbon does before a heated flatiron.

Neither could have explained how it was that they ended up on the bed, clinging shamelessly to the other there in the waning December light. When the forgotten pearls began to roll from her pocket and lodge beneath them, Justin puzzled for a moment. Reaching to capture one between a thumb and forefinger, he cut his eyes at her and howled with laughter.

"You minx, you paid no attention to my order," he mock-scolded in between smothering, teasing kisses. Could he ever get enough of her precious femininity spiced with deviltry? "I would have been disappointed if you had."

More in love than a second earlier, Justin reverted to the original plan, neither expecting nor receiving resistance. Somewhere on the floor of the bedroom lay Leander's jacket, blouse and skirt, stockings and shoes — and a small fortune's worth of pearls scattered about. Flung here and there were the articles she had peeled with loving, wandering hands from those muscled arms and shoulders, those lithe hips and manly legs. Whether the flirting undresser or the one being so willingly undressed felt the greater thrill seemed unworthy of discussion. Enjoyment of the senses ruled with loving abandonment.

Leander felt that Justin's hands must be linked directly to those unwinding strands of silk falling so quickly into a mass of lustrous passion deep inside. Not only was he stripping the outside of her, she exulted when he removed the last stitch, but also he was clearing out all obstacles in that secret chamber of her heart with each sensual movement. Naked at last, they gloried in giant head-to-toe hugs, delicious forays of exploring fingertips into begging zones, sweet joinings of feverish lips and tongues. Throughout, awe-struck eyes probed those only a kiss away, sending and receiving starry messages of love, adoration, and vows for eternity.

Justin's heart rejoiced at each wondrous touch upon her body, at each matching one she gave to his. In secret he had endured the suffering of having lost hope of winning her love. His mouth working a breathtaking, inward magic upon her breasts drunk in by both, he felt humbled at having won what he had sought for over a year. Leander loved him, Spaniard or not. Her throaty moans of ecstasy from the worshipful motions his mouth and hands made upon her loveliness now wrapped at the sharp edges of that old pain, soothing them, softening them into bearable scars. He promised himself that forever they would remain as firm reminders of love's fragility.

Could Justin have but known it, the agonizing ball of pain which had threatened to suffocate him ever since their clash several nights ago resembled the one that had grown ever deeper within Leander since the night in the lodge. As he unknowingly tugged and loosened those encumbering strands which had enveloped the recognition of her love for him, the cordage of his own coiled-up despair gave way—a line here, a line there. His every sense tingled, hungered, rejoiced.

The final unwinding for both began when Justin claimed Leander in that way she longed for. Each sensed that their union was all the finer because it had so recently seemed unobtainable. Rather like separate pools of syrup when touching, they fused into one mass of warm sweetness. Their coming together fit their own rules, rules they made up as they moved in that expectant, delirious rhythm of man and woman. Leander's love, so long cocooned, was attentive to his, spinning out like a gossamer web . . . inviting his to come closer . . . cajoling . . . capturing it with feminine sureness . . . entwining it with her own . . . embellishing it with a silken brand . . . marking it forever as hers alone. And Justin's love, vulnerable for so long, responded with eager, open surrender, seeking to be taken in . . . pulsating with unspoken tenderness . . . rushing to receive and claim all the satin secrets his beloved offered.

Somewhere in that elusive lovers' infinity, their yearning spirits met with splendor . . . collided with searing, satin explosions . . . merged with awesome rapture . . . and recognized that only in such ecstatic fusion could they exist as one perfect entity. The feverish clinging as they parted soulfully from that invisible apex only reconfirmed what they would ever know from that moment on. Each would exist in a kind of partial existence until they once more came together in that singular way of lovers.

A blanket covering their nakedness against the chill, Leander and Justin nestled together in the fine afterglow of making love. Outside, the night winds from the Mississippi sprang to life, sighing against the windows as the sun began to disappear.

Justin sat up in protest when Leander insisted on telling what Josie's letter had revealed about how it was that Throw-away had assigned him to her bed. Ignoring his declarations that whatever had taken place in her past made no difference to him, she went through the whole bit, including the way his caresses had set her aflame, even the stealing of the puppy and the gold coins from his boot. His loud guffaws at the lively unfolding set off giggles she couldn't control, and they ended up falling back against the pillows, arms and legs entwined in pleasing intimacy. There was so much yet to tell, their dancing eyes reported, that it might take a lifetime to get them all into words. The plastered walls of the bedroom seemed well designed for years of such confessing, forgiving, teasing, laughing, and uninhibited lovemaking. Up to that point, they had held their ground with dignity.

"Then it was fate that brought us together," Justin announced when they could finally look at each other without breaking up. When had he ever felt so carefree, so fulfilled? *"Querida,"* he added, devilment sparking the black eyes.

After poking his ribs as punishment for the endearment that had angered her so that night at Josie's Inn, Leander said, "I don't agree." Soulful eyes looking inward then and a forefinger twirling a curl, she reflected aloud. "Mayhap if people bend their minds strongly toward what they seek, knowingly or unknowingly, they direct their own fate."

"Could be, could not be," Justin replied, fascinated as always, at the startling beauty of his beloved, at the intricacies of her mind. He scooted up to lean against the headboard, bringing her with him. "So wise. So beautiful. You're my angel."

Leander's laughter pealed out before she cautioned, "Don't get carried away again with false pictures of me. I'm not an angel, as we both well know." She couldn't resist touching the scar in his eyebrow, then leaning to kiss it.

"To me, an angel," he insisted in that intimate, growling way she loved. Deep within the black eyes, a demonic spark flared. " . . . Only slightly damaged."

"Actually," she retorted, tossing her hair and slicing him a sassy look from beneath thick lashes, "that's about all a lousy Spaniard deserves."

There in the last vestiges of the December sunset, their laughter merged and rang out again. Before the final note reached the by-now startled walls of the formal master bedroom in the elegant mansion known as Terre Platte, Justin's hands and mouth had become questing, serious, were again setting both aquiver. Murmuring her eternal love for him, Leander met each frenzied caress with one of equal ardor. And when neither could no longer control those consuming, inward fires, they found another blazing path to blissful, satiating lovemaking.

Leander and Justin were unaware of the enormity of what took place that afternoon. The here, the now seemed the only matter of importance. But love knows its own time and had guided them with eternal patience and wisdom. When they became man and wife in less than two weeks, they would find that the lively pattern for their glorious life together as man and wife had already been set.

Epilogue

Wedding guests came in droves to attend the wedding of Mademoiselle Leander Violette Ondine and Don Carlos Justin Salvador that December 17, 1775. Almost all traveled on ships plying their way upriver from New Orleans. Some stayed at Beaux Rives, some at Belle Terre with the Ferrands, others stopped off at Terre Platte, finding space either in the old house or in the new mansion where the ceremony would take place. Their finest clothing, rarest jewels, personal slaves, and highest spirits arrived along with them. More than a few brought a curiosity bordering on the love of the lurid.

Who would have ever thought that the Ondine heiress would have consented to marry a Spaniard, older French Creoles whispered among themselves, especially those who had known Violette and Etienne in the days of French rule. Old, wise eyes left as much unspoken as lips said. Those who had done little but meet the engaged couple, but who had made the invitation list through "proper" connections, hankered for a look at the much-talked-about pink mansion, as well as a close-up view of what was rumored to be the most handsome couple to have wed in Louisiana in years. Excitement and anticipation led to much laughter, flirting, and revelry.

Hardly anyone present put away the memory of that wedding as of little consequence. Truly, it was a time to remember.

Felicity Ferrand, the bride's cousin and attendant, recalled it as the first time Bernardo de Galvez, Colonel of the Louisiana Regiment, spirited her off in secrecy to kiss her and ask her hand in marriage. Bernardo would never forget the moment the lovely blond widow consented to become his fiancée when the mourning period for Andre passed. When he apprised her of the possibility that he would be leading battles against the British encamped across the Mississippi from Spanish Louisiana before their lives could be peaceful, tears filled her blue eyes. The ensuing kisses and embraces sent lasting thrills through the hearts of the lovers. Two years later in 1777, Bernardo de Galvez succeeded Luis Unzaga as governor and proudly introduced the beautiful Felicity as Spanish Louisiana's — and his — First Lady.

With the old proud lift to his handsome head, Antoine Ferrand announced to all gathered at Terre Platte on the night before the Ondine-Salvador wedding that the smiling, buxom Maralys Soulier hanging onto his arm would become his wife before summer. If any besides Felicity and Leander wondered how much of Maralys's charm lay in the large dowry her father had settled on her, no one spoke of it. The couple seemed to find all kinds of reasons to get lost in smiles and private talk, despite the large crown present.

Over in a corner of the large ballroom that same night, Philip Ferrand was unaware that he was losing his heart to the brown-eyed, blond niece of an old friend of his father's. Long after his marriage to pretty Annabelle Duhon two years later, Philip and she would remember how they had first met at Terre Platte on the eve of the prenuptial celebration of the Ondine-Salvador wedding. In fact, their first son carried the name Justin.

The slaves from Beaux Rives and Terre Platte talked for years of their private parties out behind the mansion. And why not? It was the only time they had partaken of champagne and every single, tasty dish served inside to the boisterous well-dressed guests.

As time for the nuptials came the next day at noon, whispers among the guests seated and standing in the hallway and the ballroom rose and fell at intervals. Father Raphael waited before a mammoth, improvised altar of fragrant winter roses shipped from New Orleans; swamp ferns brought, for some unknown reason, by the groom from near a hunting lodge on the far side of Frenchman's Bayou; and trailing ivy vines. Tucked in a corner beside the soaring staircase, a quartet of musicians from New Orleans plied their strings with quiet skill.

First came the dashingly handsome bridegroom from down the long hallway, accompanied by his friend Bernardo in his dress uniform of Colonel of the Louisiana Regiment. Their military bearing as they stepped toward the altar quite awed the women guests. Felicity, striking in dark blue velvet, moved to wait alongside the men.

Eagerly Justin turned in his well-tailored black coat and breeches to watch for Leander's descent down the staircase. A white satin vest embroidered with gold thread and a snowy cravat with multiple rows of heavy lace showed how smooth and olive was his skin. When his full mouth spread into a joyous smile and his black eyes glistened with new sparkle, all knew that he was seeing his bride approach. The gleam of sunshine dancing through the tall windows paled beside the glow on the Spaniard's face.

The guests talked for years of all the myriad happenings at Terre Platte that December day. If there had ever been a more beautiful bride than Leander Ondine, none could name her. The pristine gown of silk fanned in perfect bell shape from the tiny waist, swaying in provocative rhythm to the music as she was escorted to the tall man with the telling slice of white in his shining black hair. Some remarked how unusual it was that the bride seemed blind to self, seemed unaware that she presented a breathtaking sight with her raven curls brushing naked shoulders and barely covered breasts beneath a diaphanous veil of floating illusion. Beneath that filmy covering, a particularly lustrous string of pearls glowed around her neck. The wide, pansy-colored eyes shut out all except the beaming Spaniard awaiting her at the altar.

Many women sighed and shed a few tears for the sheer romance of the union of what they confided must surely be star-crossed lovers. Most of the men sneaked looks at the dreamy-eyed bridegroom and secretly envied him such obvious perfection in a wife.

But what the Louisianians whispered about for years to come was the fact that the poor, orphaned Leander had had no family member to give her away. Those not present at the wedding sometimes doubted the follow-up tale, told with solemn declaration as absolute truth: An enormous black man, attired in elegant black coat, breeches, and a black-and-white-striped vest of satin, escorted the radiant bride down the staircase, across the hallway, into the pink ballroom, and placed her gloved hand in that of the eager bridegroom.

ROMANCE FOR ALL SEASONS
from Zebra Books

ARIZONA TEMPTRESS (1785, $3.95)
by Bobbi Smith

Rick Peralta found the freedom he craved only in his disguise as El Cazador. Then he saw the exquisitely alluring Jennie among his compadres and the hotblooded male swore she'd belong just to him.

RAPTURE'S TEMPEST (1624, $3.95)
by Bobbi Smith

Terrified of her stepfather, innocent Delight de Vries disguised herself as a lad and hired on as a riverboat cabin boy. But when her gaze locked with Captain James Westlake's, all she knew was that she would forfeit her new-found freedom to be bound in his arms for a night.

WANTON SPLENDOR (1461, $3.50)
by Bobbi Smith

Kathleen had every intention of keeping her distance from the dangerously handsome Christopher Fletcher. But when a hurricane devastated the Island, she crept into Chris's arms for comfort, wondering what it would be like to kiss those cynical lips.

CRYSTAL PASSION (1645, $3.95)
by Jo Goodman

When Ashley awoke from her drugged sleep, she found herself in the bedchamber of a handsome stranger. Before she could explain that her guardian had tricked them, the rapture of the stranger's searing, searching caress drove all thought from her mind.

SEASWEPT ABANDON (1905, $3.95)
by Jo Goodman

When green-eyed Rae McClellan agreed to be a courier for the Colonies, she never dreamed that on her very first mission she'd coldly kill one man — and hotly love another. Aboard the private schooner of a British sympathizer she was carried away with SEASWEPT ABANDON.

Available wherever paperbacks are sold, or order direct from the Publisher. Send cover price plus 50¢ per copy for mailing and handling to Zebra Books, Dept. 1891, 475 Park Avenue South, New York, N.Y. 10016. Residents of New York, New Jersey and Pennsylvania must include sales tax. DO NOT SEND CASH.

Passionate Romance in the Old West
SAVAGE DESTINY
by F. Rosanne Bittner